TEN PENNIES

SANDRA FROST

For Aurora

Thank you for teaching me what dedication truly means

Cover design by Sandra Frost

Cover model: Parker Magstadt

PROLOGUE

There was something compelling in the morning mist. It was cool as it moved past her, brushing against Maeve's porcelain skin. Not a clammy death-like coolness, but a soothing balm that beckoned her to stay and allow it to swirl around her. It was soft, renewing, and fresh. The five-year-old was caught up in the invitation as she lost all perception of time and distance. Her eyes followed it, winding ghost-like through the forest, and it caused her to breathe a little deeper. The haunting strains of her mother's voice singing Maeve's favorite lullaby echoed softly through her mind as she continued on. The lush green forest was Heaven, it had to be, and she didn't care if being there meant she had died and left her want-filled life behind. But as she wandered deeper into the emerald beauty the air grew colder and less welcoming. The discomfort was unsettling and the peace she had embraced was fading, replaced by something more familiar. Hunger. The aching in her belly caused its usual restlessness, misfortune caused her to shiver, and the shiver awakened her from her dream.

CHAPTER ONE

New York City 1859

The fire in the stove had gone out hours before, and the February wind was sneaking in through the cracks and crevices of the Delaney's tenement flat. The icy breeze cared not that there were children sleeping there. It felt no remorse for their shivering, no responsibility for their runny noses nor the fitful sleep its chill had caused them.

"Da?" Maeve called quietly. "Da, the fire's gone out." She waited for her father to answer but heard no reply. There was no movement about. Maeve hated to wake her father, but she surely could not get a fire going on her own. She arose from the thin homemade mattress that she rolled out each night on the cold wooden floor. Her three brothers were still settled upon their own, lined up cold and pale like the sad little bodies laid out in the street during the last cholera epidemic. She carefully stepped around Sean, Eamon, and Sorley and tiptoed to her parents' bedroom which was nothing more than a section of the apartment raised up one step and covered with a drawn curtain.

"Da?" she whispered.

"He's down at the docks, Maeve," Sean grumbled, awake now, cold and angry. His dark hair fell across his eyes and had he brushed it back Maeve would have seen the equally dark eyes smoldering beneath. The twelve-year-old's demeanor was typically unpleasant as he waged a daily battle with resentment. He was bitter that he was left in charge of his three younger siblings far too often, and he was angry that with each passing day the Delaneys were sinking deeper into the mire.

"Where's Mam?" Maeve asked.

"Where do ya think she is? She left before Da. She's over doin' chores for that jackeen, Andy Bingham." Sean's voice drifted off. He hated their pathetic life, their dependence on the belittling kindness of others, and the ragged existence that his parents provided despite their willingness to work, often at the most thankless and lowly jobs imaginable. Their mother worked for firewood which she reminded them was a blessing, but in Sean's way of thinking there was a healthy dose of shame attached to her groveling. It was an opinion he kept to himself, but it was apparent in his dark mood.

"Ah, good then," Maeve responded with her eternal optimism, "we'll be warm soon enough." Sean shook his head, brushed back his hair with his hand, and rolled his eyes. He wandered to the kitchen area in the corner of the apartment in search of something to feed his brothers and sister. The icebox, devoid of ice, had a smidgeon of milk and what remained of the bean soup Mam had made three nights before. The ham bone was still in the pot, a cold misshapen lump of discolored calcium that nearly turned Sean's stomach. The poor and hungry could not afford the luxury of vomiting and he turned away to settle his belly. The miniscule slivers of ham that had boiled off the bone had been the only source of meat they had eaten in five days, and it had only come their way from a well-meaning neighbor.

Maeve was aware of her brother's state of mind. The anger, the embarrassment, and the bitterness surfaced all too often. Mam said that Sean had the disposition of an angry old codger and that he had long forgotten how to be a child. Maeve felt sorry for her brother, and she hoped that growing up didn't mean she would become sullen and unpleasant like him. She knew better than to try and soothe his foul mood this morning or any other time for that matter. She walked past Sean to the loaf of bread on the table. It was covered with a small cotton cloth dotted with holes, too threadbare to keep the bread fresh and away from the vermin that had no regard for the Delaneys' hungry bellies. There was not enough butter to cover four slices, barely enough for three if it was spread thin enough, so Maeve sliced and buttered a piece for each of her brothers and ate hers dry. She was keenly aware of her mother's selflessness and how she always put her family's needs before her own, and Maeve emulated her mother's example at every opportunity. The tea in the pot was still warm from Mam's breakfast which was likely nothing more than tea and a piece of the same dry bread, and the four children shared what was left in the pot between them.

"I'm still hungry," Sorley complained. His freckled face was uncharacteristically darkened with a frown. Eamon mumbled in agreement, quietly, so as not to anger his older brother. Maeve reached out to touch Sorley's arm. He was three years older than his sister but often took comfort from her calm and pleasant disposition. She was a wee version of Mam, and it gave Sorley reassurance to have her near when they were left alone. Sean intimidated Sorley. Eamon, at ten, was less afraid but knew better than to cross him. So much had changed in the past year. Sean's innocent acceptance of life's challenges had been replaced by a dark countenance that the other three did not fully understand.

"There, there, Sorley," Maeve said in a low soft tone much like Mam would have done.

Sean bolted up from his chair startling his siblings. They sat wide-eyed as he let a tirade of anger and frustration unload from the dark void in his spirit. Though they knew it was not directed at them, the fury of his words felt like a physical assault. Sorley covered his ears and Maeve sat immobilized, fixed to her wobbly wooden chair.

"Doesn't it eat at your pride to sit there and nibble at crumbs no different than the rats we chase outta here every day? Don't ya know what people say about us? About the dirty micks that foul their city? Ya sit there in shame and ya eat your stale bread while Mam scrubs floors on her hands and knees for a couple sticks of wood! While your da stands at the back of the group every mornin' down at the docks hopin' there's enough offloadin' to do so the micks can work too! And what's wrong with *them*, anyway? Mam and Da, they have no shame! They would crawl on their bellies for a scrap of food not fit for any of us to be eatin'!" Sean's anger boiled over, and he swept his teacup off the table with the back of his hand. It crashed against the wall and shattered like the fragments of his parents' lofty dreams, their desperate hope that the poverty they had known in County Cork would stay behind in Ireland and not follow them to America.

"What on earth are ya doin' in there, Sean Delaney?" came a voice outside their door. The noise inside the Delaney's apartment had irritated Mrs. Callahan so early in the morning, and she marched her matronly self next door to get to the bottom of it. Maeve found the courage to rise from her chair and respond to the woman's question.

"I'm terrible sorry, Mrs. Callahan," she called through the closed door. "We've broken one of Mam's pretty cups. We'll be cleanin' it up now."

"Well, see that you do and hold down the noise! Mr. Callahan had a late night!" The sound of her heavy footsteps retreated back to her own door, and Maeve let her shoulders relax. She turned back intending to help Sean clean up the mess he had made, but instead of getting the broom he was pulling on his jacket, his dark features made darker by his mood. Sean, like his father, was often called Black Irish, trusted less than their fair-haired counterparts, making it even more difficult to assimilate into an unwelcoming society.

"You better clean that up before Mam gets home," he called out over his shoulder, his guilt adding weight to his words. He opened the door and left before Maeve could ask him where he was going. She would not have gotten an answer even if she had asked. Her head dropped, crowned in auburn waves. Her sadness was intense.

Maeve found the straw broom in the corner of the kitchen and began sweeping up the little slivers of the broken cup. She noticed how they shimmered when the light from the windows landed upon them just so, and she thought it odd how something shattered and broken could still be so lovely. She knew Mam would be terribly disappointed to know that one of her few remaining treasures from Ireland was now gone. She knew, too, that as much as Sean deserved to be reprimanded she would not tell Mam how it happened. Despite Sean's foul temper Maeve loved her brother dearly. He was a smaller version of her father, and Thomas Delaney was the foundation of their home, Maeve's rock and comfort, the center of her wretched universe.

Sorley and Eamon sat on their mattresses and watched their sister sweep up the tiny shards of the broken cup. A woman's work was not for a man to do no matter how young the man or how small the woman. Maeve swept the broken pieces onto a dirty piece of paperboard and dumped the shards of fine china into the trash, watching them filter down between yesterday's newspaper and the leathery orange peel from days before.

It had been a rare treat when Da arrived home from the docks with two fresh ripe oranges, one in each jacket pocket. He hadn't elaborated on where he had gotten them, and Mam didn't want to know whether they had been purchased, pilfered, or gifted. The Delaneys had gathered around the table as Da carefully peeled the sweetly pungent covering from each orange. Little droplets of fragrant juice burst forth each time he pulled away the peel, and Maeve had wished that the droplets would fall upon her head so that she, too, could smell as lovely as the orange. Da had divided the two oranges into nineteen segments and shared them equally, three for each, plus one extra that he had given to Maeve. She had responded with humility insisting that Mam have it or that Da be rewarded for the delicious surprise, but Da would hear nothing of it. His beautiful green-eyed angel would have it. Rather guiltily, Maeve savored the cool sweet juice of her extra piece. She would remember the sweetness of the fruit and the time gathered peacefully around the table, and she would store it safely away for when times were not so special. New York had not been kind to the Delaneys, and the promise of better times was nothing more than a dusty dream washed away by the rain of disappointment.

"Eamon, won't ya read to us?" she asked after returning the broom to its corner. Eamon and Sean both read well having attended primary school for four years, but school soon became an inconvenience and they were forced to stay home and learn from their parents instead. Sorley and Maeve had not yet learned to read though Maeve desperately wanted to. She dreamed of picking up a book like a fine educated lady and deciphering the strange markings that lined up so straight and perfect across the pages. Maybe one day when life was easier their reward would be an education. She desperately hoped so. She reached for her favorite book from the nearby shelf and handed it to Eamon as they settled down on the floor.

"Och, Maeve, not again!" Eamon grumbled. He was quite certain he had read *The Swiss Family Robinson* a hundred times and could likely recite it front to back without opening the cover. He set his brown eyes firmly on Maeve's lovely little face and gave her his best unrelenting scowl. The rigid lines of his expression melted away as soon as she spoke.

"Please, Eamon," Maeve asked in her soft, lilting voice. A smile, a slight tilt of her head, her green eyes sparkling like lake water on a sunny afternoon; how could he refuse her? And so he began, reciting the opening line from memory—*For many days we had been tempest-tossed.* Maeve closed her eyes and let the beautiful familiar words sink in, a welcome solace from Sean's violent outburst. Eamon's soft brown eyes left the page often as the words came from memory. Maeve watched him with rapt appreciation, his storytelling skills mirroring that of his father. She leaned back against the tattered, old couch and envisioned the adventure unfolding.

The morning remained cold, and the children huddled close with a blanket over them as Eamon continued to read. It was past noon when Mam returned home, pulling her wooden cart filled with firewood and smiling mischievously. The children jumped up and ran to greet her, begging her to light a fire in the stove and asking if she had any treats in the oversized pockets of her brown wool coat. Occasionally Mr. Bingham would give Mam a coin along with the firewood, most likely to add some polish to his tarnished reputation as a tight-fisted miser. It was never much but it allowed Kathleen to afford a lovely pastry or a piece of chocolate cake. She would stop in at Josef's Bakery on the way home and purchase something small. The German baker took pity on the pretty lady with the auburn hair and the emerald green eyes and would wrap her purchase nicely in a piece of printed paper tied with string. On those days in particular Mam could not wait to return home and share the treat with her family.

"Children, children," Kathleen said, "give your mam half a minute to settle in, will ya?" They offered their apologies but did not wander far. Mam parked her cart next to the stove, took off her scarf and coat, and hung them on a hook near the door. Sorley's eyes were fixed on Mam's coat pockets. They looked full of promise, not sad and empty as they did most days.

"'Tis colder than a kelpie's arse in here!" Kathleen's immediate contrition brought delighted laughter from the children as she crossed herself and offered a quick but repentant prayer to the Holy Father. She knelt down in front of the stove and set upon the task of getting a fire going, and she apologized more than once for leaving the children there to freeze. The flickering light of the flame inside the stove danced across her face, causing her green eyes to sparkle and her pale skin and copper-brown hair to glow warm. Even now, at thirty-two years of age and in the throes of poverty, Kathleen Delaney was a beauty. She closed the little door on the front of the stove, stood up, and turned to face the children. As she did she caught a glimpse of Sorley sneaking over to her coat.

"Young man," she said, "I don't believe that'd be your coat or your pockets. Would I be correct?" Her children did not fear the sternness in her voice as it was almost always tempered with love. It took more than a curious little redheaded boy to get her feathers ruffled. Da was another story. When something riled him his anger was genuine, and his foul mood was not to be taken lightly. It didn't surface often, but it gave life to the storied Irish temper that was often the brunt of many a joke and barroom slur. Thomas's hair was not red, but his anger could burn that way. His anger, however, would never compel him to lay a finger on his wife or children. He would die protecting them. He would throw himself in the path of impending harm to keep them safe. He would stand in abject humiliation day after day hoping to earn a few coins after the more-deserving laborers had been hired on. His family was his life, his very soul, and the heart inside that drove him to never surrender to the grievous conditions that might otherwise destroy them.

"Sorry, Mam," Sorley offered as he made his way back to the mattress where he had been sitting. Kathleen stepped near, bent down, and tousled Sorley's wild mass of red curls. He was the sunshine in her heart of hearts.

"I will make a pot of tea and later we shall see if a wee birdie dropped somethin' into my pocket, yes?"

"Sean broke your cup with the roses on it," Eamon blurted out. Maeve's heart lurched, and she intervened before Eamon told Mam the whole story.

"I'm sure it was an accident, Mam. Sean knows how much that cup meant to ya."

"Of course it was an accident. And where is Sean?" Kathleen thought it silly that she hadn't noticed his absence when she walked into the apartment.

"He went out," Eamon replied, now sorry that he had tattled on Sean. He wished he felt the same fierce desire to protect Sean as his sister did, but the brotherly bond was not standing the test of Sean's foul moods.

"Out where, Eamon?" Kathleen's voice took on a serious tone. She and Thomas had been worried about their oldest son. His mood had grown increasingly dark, and the amount of time he was spending away from home had both of his parents concerned. Callum O'Cleary, Mrs. Callahan's brother, had reported seeing Sean milling around at Chatham Square near the Five Points District. That report had led to a nasty argument between Sean and his father, and Thomas had forbidden him to return.

A knock on the door startled Kathleen from her thoughts. She opened the door cautiously, always afraid that bad news might be standing on the other side. It was Mrs. Callahan, there to make sure Kathleen knew about Sean's outburst. The children knew the truth would now be out, for their neighbor was a notorious gossip.

"Mornin', Katie," she said, using the shortened version of Kathleen's name like an older woman might do. She tucked a loose strand of gray hair behind her ear, put her hands inside the bodice of her ragged apron and folded them, resting them on her ample bosom as she always did.

"Mornin', Mrs. Callahan," Kathleen responded, addressing the older woman more properly.

"Your boy Sean threw quite a tantrum in here this mornin'. I heard somethin' about dirty micks and someone crawlin' on their bellies for a scrap of food. That was just before I heard the sound of somethin' shatterin' against the wall." Maeve was taken aback by Mrs. Callahan repeating the content of Sean's outburst, though she should have known that the paper-thin walls would not prevent the neighbors from hearing his every word.

"I'm sorry, Mrs. Callahan," Kathleen apologized. Her spirit was nearly broken by Sean's change in character. "I will speak to his father tonight, and we'll see that he doesn't disturb you again."

"It's not me I'm worryin' about, Katie, although Mr. Callahan's got a head like a bag o' hammers this mornin' and was none too happy about the noise. No, it's your wee ones here left alone with Sean that I worry over." There was a gentle warning in Mrs. Callahan's voice that Kathleen did not miss. The guilt she bore now became a larger fire to extinguish, and she was without the tools to do so. She dropped her head in surrender. Mrs. Callahan reached out and placed a hand on Kathleen's shoulder causing Kathleen's emotions to get the best of her and the unchecked tears to flow.

"There now, lass," Mrs. Callahan said, her tone softening with compassion. "We're all doin' the best we can, aren't we? It'll be fine, just wait and see." She smiled at the younger woman, sorry now that she had been the bearer of troubling news. Heaven knew the Delaneys had enough to worry over.

"Thank you, Mrs. Callahan," Kathleen whispered, nodding in agreement but finding it impossible to believe the older woman's words of encouragement. Mrs. Callahan left, closing the door behind her, and Maeve rushed to Mam's side. She wrapped her little arms around her mother's legs and held her tightly. So much empathy in a child so young was rare, and Maeve's tender compassionate heart often took Kathleen by surprise. Thomas always reminded his wife that Maeve was a special child, and Kathleen knew it to be true. She reached down, picked up her daughter, and held her close. She wished Maeve could have the life she deserved, filled with warmth and plenty, but she knew in her heart there was little chance of it. Kathleen set Maeve back down and softly ran the back of her hand over Maeve's cheek. She asked the children to return to the book Eamon had been reading when she arrived back home.

"Da should be home sooner than later. We'll heat up our soup," the groans of her disappointed children escaped in unison, "and then after dinner we may share a special treat."

"Is it in your coat pocket, Mam?" Sorley asked, knowing.

"'Tis for you to find out!"

Kathleen regained her composure and set about cleaning up the undamaged teacups from the children's breakfast. She hoped there was enough soup for one more meal. She prayed Tommy had found work on the docks this morning even if it were only enough to provide another meal for the following day.

She could hear Eamon's rhythmic reading of the story they all knew so well, it being one of the six books they possessed. The small shelf near the window held more what-nots than books. The small painting of Kathleen's mother framed in mother-of-pearl was the most prized. The Great Hunger took Mary Kearney before Thomas and Kathleen could bless her with a grandchild, and the sadness of her loss still weighed heavy in Kathleen's heart. The stack of well-worn books that lived on the shelf next to Mary Kearney's picture were *The Holy Bible*, *The Swiss Family Robinson*, *Gulliver's Travels*, *Rob Roy*, *The Count of Monte Cristo*, and the *Tain bo Cuailnge*, the epic Irish tale of the hero, Cuchulainn. It was the favorite book of Maeve's brothers, but it was written in Irish and Da was the only one of them who could read it. Occasionally, on a dreary winter's night they would gather close and listen to Da read

14

them the exciting tale of Cuchulainn and his battle with the warriors of Connacht, translating page by page as the story came to life. They all knew that Da embellished the story, for each time he read it there were slight variations in the battles, the heroic feats, and the details of the classic tale making it fresh and new with each reading. From time to time, Maeve would ask Da to read it to them in Irish so she could hear the lovely lilting sound of his native tongue.

Eamon passed much of the afternoon reading the adventures of the Robinson family to his younger siblings. The story was nearing one of their favorite parts where Mr. Robinson sets gunpowder to the wreckage of their ship, and *in a flash! a mighty roar—a grand burst of smoke* the gunpowder exploded in the ship. Just as Eamon read the description of the explosion, the door of their apartment flew open. Da walked in with a large sack over his back and a look on his face that told them it was time to put the book down and find a quiet corner to play in.

CHAPTER TWO

Thomas Delaney was in a dark mood when he left the Catharine Ferry Dock. He had stood for hours at the back of the group of hungry men, back where he belonged with the rest of the Irish waiting for the hiring man's finger to point at him. The February wind was bone-chilling and even colder coming in across the water of the East River. By early afternoon all the work had been doled out and Thomas stood, still hungry, with the group of other still-hungry Irish immigrants hoping to earn some coin that day. They were used to being passed over. They knew that most of the residents of New York considered them to be subhuman and viewed them as an unwelcome nuisance responsible for the unsightly problem of the overflowing immigrant neighborhoods. They had heard the scathing remarks, the ethnic slurs, the papist insults, and the merciless condemnations from all segments of society. They had spent countless hours and endless days waiting for work on the docks along the river, and they hated feeling grateful when they were chosen only as a last resort. Today was just another in a long line of wasted days and not a penny to show for it. Thomas would once again return home with empty pockets, an empty belly, and a hollow soul where self-worth once resided.

As Thomas left the dock and approached the Catharine Street Market, he considered stealing just enough food for a meal, just enough to sustain his family one more day. It was a fleeting thought, and he knew that their situation would have to be more desperate than it was now for him to risk being arrested and taken from Kathleen and the children. He shoved his hands deep into his empty pockets and hoped that tomorrow would be a better day.

The market was bustling with vendors preparing for the weekly Saturday night festivities. Though the market and the nearby shops were open every day, Saturday nights had evolved into a grand hooley, as Thomas called it. Vendors came by ferry across the river to peddle their wares, and revelers arrived to enjoy the music, the food, and the raucous celebrations. Most would stay the night and continue the festivities into the following morning. They would stay until midday on Sunday when they would take the ferry back to Long Island and return to their workaday lives. Thomas wondered what it must be like to stroll through the market and purchase whatever struck his fancy. He doubted he would ever know. He was burdened with a heavy sadness as he questioned again why he had come to America. The promise of a better life was left empty and unfulfilled. It lay trampled beneath the feet of thousands of other Irish families who had left poverty and starvation behind only to find it waiting for them again, there in the land of limited opportunity.

Thomas paused and leaned against a nearby lamppost watching the way life should be. He tried to escape the dread of having to return home once again without a penny in his pocket. He could smell the aroma of oysters cooking in butter and garlic from a nearby pushcart. His stomach tightened and rumbled with the deep hunger that comes from feeding your children first. He knew he had to try something, anything, and he headed to a nearby butcher shop. With a long history of humiliation behind him, he would allow the destruction of his pride to be waged against him one more time as he approached the shop to beg for a scrap.

"Off with ya, Mick!" the butcher called out as Thomas approached. It was what he had expected, for he rarely garnered anything but an insult from old man Caselli. He gave him a wave and a smile anyway. *Be the better man, Tommy,* he recalled his mother saying on more than one occasion. He tried, always.

Thomas walked across the street to a familiar produce cart. Oftentimes the kind woman who tended the cart for her husband would find a little something for him. She never gave him the best of their offerings, for she knew she would face an angry lecture from her husband should he discover her generosity. An apple or two with small rotten spots, a few potatoes that had wrinkled and started to sprout, or an onion just past its prime might make their way into Thomas's pockets and for even that Thomas was grateful. The woman smiled and waved as she saw him approaching.

"It's gone fierce cold, hasn't it, Mrs. Zimmer?" He found the Germans to be less hostile to the Irish, and Mrs. Zimmer was no exception. In spite of the wrinkles, her round face had a softness to it that spoke of her kindness and good character.

"Ja, for certain, Mr. Delaney! I was hoping you would come along today," she said with a genuine smile. Thomas admired the way Mrs. Zimmer always presented herself in a strangely elegant manner despite being part of the working class of New York City. Her hair was always perfectly styled and her clothes, though well-worn, were clean and tidy. "Mr. Zimmer and I are going over to Morristown to see his dear brother who has fallen ill with scarlet fever. His heart is weak, and his doctor isn't sure if he will survive it, poor soul."

"I'm sorry for his troubles, Mrs. Zimmer," Thomas offered sincerely. He knew too well the pain of losing a loved one to disease and suffering. Most of his village in County Cork had succumbed to the Great Hunger including his parents and his sister, Margaret. "'Tis a terrible thing to lose those we love."

"Indeed, it is. We can only ask God to spare him, so that is what we shall do. Now here, can you help me with this sack I have for you and your family?" Mrs. Zimmer reached beneath the cart and pulled out a large burlap sack. The strings had not yet been drawn and tightened, and the sack appeared to be full of produce. Thomas stood slack-jawed, frozen in disbelief for a few seconds before rushing ahead to take the sack from her hands. The weight of it told him it was, indeed, packed full of the Zimmers' produce.

"Mrs. Zimmer, I don't feel right takin' all this from ya, and ya know I can't be payin' ya for it," Thomas said. His guilt and his gratitude were at war, and he fully expected his guilt to be overruled. He shifted from one foot to the other. He wanted desperately to take the sack of fruits and vegetables but was at the same time fully aware that he would be taking advantage of Mrs. Zimmer's kind heart.

"Nonsense, now, you're doing us a favor by taking it home to your family. We'll be leaving in the morning for Jersey and won't sell all of this today," she said as she swept her hand over the cart. Thomas knew it was true, but he still felt the emotional turmoil raging inside. He was grateful that Providence had steered him to the route along Catharine

Street to Division rather than the frontage road along the docks. His reply came only in the nodding of his head, as he feared he could not speak past the lump forming deep in his throat. Mrs. Zimmer knew, and she leaned in closer and lowered her voice.

"Just between us, I traded some apples, onions, and carrots for a fine chicken from Mr. Caselli across the way. It'd be long bad by the time we return home, so you'll have to make use of it, too." Mrs. Zimmer winked at Thomas. He leaned forward and gave the kind lady a quick kiss on her soft cheek. She flushed at the gesture, and Thomas also felt the color rising on his face.

"Have yourself a safe journey, Mrs. Zimmer. My wife, myself, and all my dear children are in your debt," he said quietly, humbly. Mrs. Zimmer patted his arm and reassured him again that it was Thomas doing her the favor and not the other way around. She understood pride and the relentless poverty that was prevalent in many of New York's immigrant families. She and Mr. Zimmer had experienced it too until they had arranged to have their vegetable cart at the market. It gained them a livelihood and enough respectability that they could hold their heads up and not feel the oppression of unwelcoming stares.

Thomas walked along Catharine Street to where it intersected with Division, Bowery, and Chatham. Chatham Square was just to his left. The Bowery entrance to Chatham Square was a congested gathering place of unruly miscreants and an area that Thomas avoided. He wanted no trouble, today of all days, and God help any of them who might think to relieve him of the sack he carried. He approached the square without giving it much attention, keeping to himself and staying safe on the other side of the street. He heard some insults directed his way, and he told himself that nothing they called him would dampen his spirits. Thomas had food for his family that would last several days if they used it wisely, and he was walking on the clouds. As he rounded the corner onto Division Street, he noticed a group of boys huddled close under the awning of a tattoo parlor. They were in deep conversation, and Thomas would not have given them a second glance but for the familiar red cap he saw on the shortest member of the group. He slowed his pace as he peered across the way trying to determine in the fading afternoon light if his suspicions were correct. Thomas paused a moment and when he did the boy in the red cap looked up, saw him, and darted away through the crowded street. Sean. Thomas's blood began to boil. He had warned Sean to stay away from the square and away from the sort of trouble that gathered there. Thomas considered chasing after his son but only for a moment. Nothing would be worth risking the loss of the sack of food slung over his shoulder. He would deal with Sean when the boy returned home.

Thomas focused his thoughts on the evening ahead, a warm meal, and a full belly. He continued down Division Street to Montgomery where he made two right turns and arrived at their tenement building located at the corner of Montgomery and East Broadway. It was removed enough from the notorious Five Points District that they did not live in constant fear, but they were still close enough to trouble for it to be ever on their minds. A place fit for the dregs of the lower east side. A place reserved for the unwanted. And that's what they and thousands of other Irish immigrants were considered.

Now that he had arrived at the back door of their building, his parcel safe and sound, Thomas could not quiet the turmoil that brewed in his mind. His anger grew with each step as he stomped down the long hallway to their ground-floor apartment. Sean's irresponsible behavior and

SANDRA FROST

defiance of his parents' wishes had stolen the joy and the celebratory mood that Thomas had enjoyed earlier, and his anger increased as he thought about arriving home with Mrs. Zimmer's bountiful blessing in such a foul temper. He opened the door with a bit more force than he had intended, and the room fell silent. The children had been reading—he had heard the familiar lines from *The Swiss Family Robinson* from the hallway—but that stopped in an instant when the door flew open. The guilt hit him hard and fast as he watched the children scramble to the corner of the room. He knew it was unfair to let his family bear the burden of his dark mood, for they already suffered so much in quiet humility. He stood for a moment in the doorway. He glanced over at Kathleen and saw her worried expression, a sorrowful look that spoke the words *I know* to him without uttering a sound. He looked at his youngest three now sitting in the corner of the room pretending to play with the small wooden cars a kindly neighbor had whittled for them. The apprehension was thick in the air, and it quickly brought Thomas to his senses. He resolved to let his business with Sean be between the two of them. His family deserved more. So much more. He looked at Kathleen again and his heart melted as it always did when he saw the sparkle of her green eyes. His shoulders relaxed and he smiled. He could see the tension leave her immediately, and she smiled back. Thomas slid the cap from his head and hung his worn woolen jacket on a hook next to the one Kathleen had used earlier. He took a deep breath before turning around to undo what he'd done.

"And who's gotten such a fire goin' in a home without money or means?" he teased. The children, relief overtaking them, jumped up and all pointed to Kathleen.

"Mam did it with her very own firewood, she did!" Maeve replied. Her sweet voice was the panacea that, for Thomas, made everything better.

"She did not," Da responded. "How could such a poor, penniless woman buy firewood and strike such a fine fire?"

"I'll have ya know I worked my fingers to the bone for this fire, Thomas Delaney!" Kathleen strutted around the kitchen acting quite proud of herself. She tossed her hair back with the flip of her hand as Thomas watched her with more love than a heart should hold. The children laughed at their mother's antics, relieved that the tension had left their flat as quickly as it had entered. Kathleen turned to Thomas, curious about the sack he had carried in with him. "And how much money did they pay ya today, Tommy? 'Tis a large sack of somethin' you've brought home with ya!"

The children all turned their attention to the burlap sack Da had set down just inside the door. Sorley, always the inquisitive one, inched closer to the mysterious sack. Mam cleared her throat loudly, and he returned to the couch where Eamon and Maeve were sitting. Da walked past and winked at his red-headed son. He sat down at the table and beckoned for his family to sit there with him. Sean's absence was felt by everyone, and each one knew not to breach that subject. Kathleen sat close to Thomas. He was still handsome after years of nothing but hardship and pain. The weathering had refined him, given him character lines on his face and around the dark pools of his eyes. They were lines of worry, and lines of laughter despite having no reason to laugh, and they spoke of endurance and tenacity. They were beautiful to his wife, and she smiled at him as if this moment were theirs alone.

"I have a story to tell if ya would like to hear it," Thomas said. Storytelling was a long-held tradition in the Delaney family as it was in many Irish families, and Thomas had become quite masterful in the telling. As the children all chimed in, begging their father to tell his story, Kathleen got up and gathered two cups and the pot of tea she had made earlier. It was no longer steaming hot but warm enough not to waste. She brought it to the table and settled back in next to her husband. Thomas smiled at her and then again at the tiny likeness of her sitting on his other side.

"What story is it, Da?" Maeve asked. "Is it the *Tain*, or maybe the sad, sad tale of your journey to America?"

"Och, no, Maeve! There'll be no sad stories today," her father replied.

"Do tell, Tommy," Kathleen said, as curious as the children were about the contents of his sack. She glanced over at it, hopeful that it was filled with food and ashamed to be wanting so much. She poured the tea and waited patiently for Thomas to begin.

"It was a cold, cold mornin' when I left home with nothin' more than my tattered jacket 'round me. Poor miserable me, so cold and shiverin', I was." He was baiting Kathleen, hoping for a salty response for she too had braved the cold morning. She rolled her eyes at him but said nothing that might slow the telling of his story.

"When I arrived at the Catharine Street Dock there were already a hundred fellas waitin' for work. I took my place at the back of the group as I always do, back behind the Germans and the Italians, and I waited with the other Irish for a chance to work. Long hours passed and my belly growled. I took a piece of bread out of my pocket—a small piece I had taken with me this mornin'—and I started to eat it slowly, knowin' a belly fills quicker when the food is eaten slowly. About halfway through I noticed Kip O'Malley watchin' me good. That boy looks like he hasn't had more than a crumb and a morsel in forever and a day. I gave what was left of my bread to him and hoped I'd get to earn a few coins today so I could put some food in my own belly. There were so many ships in the harbor that I was certain today would be Tommy Delaney's lucky day."

"Which of the ships did ya work on, Da?" Sorley asked. "Was it a big one with twenty sails and *valbule* cargo?"

"Val-u-able," Eamon corrected his younger brother. Sorley flushed at the mispronunciation, but no one laughed at his error.

"Sadly, it wasn't a fine ship such as that," Thomas responded to Sorley's question. "In fact, believe me when I tell ya, it wasn't any ship at all. The hiring man left the Irish standin' with empty pockets and no hope for a penny to put in them."

"Poor dear Da." Maeve's compassion was sincere and as always far exceeded her five years. "But ya promised no sad stories today."

"And there shall be none, Stóirín!" Da used his pet name for Maeve—his little treasure—and it worked as it always did to comfort her. Whenever she saw her father happy, Maeve knew everything would be all right even when hard times were nipping at their heels like a hungry wolf. She stood up and leaned in close to her father; he held her tight against him for a moment. Tears formed in his eyes as he yearned for a life that would chase away all the want and fear. Thomas took a deep breath before his emotions got the best of him, and he sat up straight in the old wooden chair as Maeve returned to her own.

"When all the work was doled out and I was no more the richer than I was when I arrived, I turned to leave the docks. Just another penniless Irishman, my head hung low as I strolled along Catharine Street." Da's dramatic flair was in full swing, his voice full of pain and shame, and not all feigned as he continued.

"I passed by all the lovely people buyin' baskets of food and fine wares for their families, and I was stricken with grief. How ever could I return home with nothin' but my handsome face and a few breadcrumbs in my pocket?"

"Tommy, dear, your handsome face will always be enough for me, but it surely won't feed these hungry children," Kathleen said. There was enough levity in her voice to hold any intruding sadness at bay.

"Aye, Katie, beauty doesn't boil the kettle," Thomas continued. "So, I tucked my tail and wandered over to Caselli's Butcher Shop thinkin' the man might have mercy on me, but he chased me away before my feet hit the doorstep. I was about to lose all hope when I remembered Mrs. Zimmer, the kind woman who gave me the oranges. Remember, children?" Three heads nodded as they recalled that most delectable treat. "I crossed the street and Mrs. Zimmer saw me approachin'. She greeted me with some enthusiasm and then told me a sad account of her dear brother-in-law who's dyin' of the scarlet fever over in Jersey. The man's heart is givin' up the ghost, and he's not long for this earth." Kathleen crossed herself and ushered a silent prayer to heaven for the poor man suffering the fever.

"Da, the sad stories again?" Eamon was now as impatient as the rest of them.

"Sad, but then again not, Eamon, as you are soon to find out! I gave Mrs. Zimmer my condolences and that is when she asked me to help her with somethin' important."

"It was she who put you to work then?" Kathleen asked.

"No, not exactly. You see, she and Mr. Zimmer are to leave in the mornin' for Jersey and cannot sell their wares in time. She needed my help to make use of them!"

"What do ya mean, Da?" Maeve was struggling to follow her father's convoluted story.

"I mean that she and Mr. Zimmer would have come home to a pile of rotten vegetables if they hadn't found a kind soul to take some of them off their hands. And there ya be, along I came and helped the kind lady out of her predicament!"

"But, Tommy, ya had no coin to buy such a large sack!"

"There's the thing, ya see, she asked me to help her by takin' the sack and puttin' it to use. Just handed it to me as if it were Thomas Michael Delaney's birthday!"

"Who are we to receive such good fortune?" Kathleen whispered, her voice breaking as she looked over at the sack by the door. "What's inside it, Tommy?"

"I don't know! Well, I know there is a chicken ready to be cooked, so we'll need to get a pot goin' for it soon enough."

"A chicken! Thank you, dear Mrs. Zimmer!" Kathleen stood and found a large pot from the open shelf below the wooden planks that served as their countertop. She had two pots, and the other was still in the icebox with what remained of the bean soup inside it. The soup would not be wasted, but tonight there would be a feast. Kathleen lifted the water bucket she had filled earlier at the pump out back and poured water into the pot. She set the pot on the woodstove and stoked the fire inside it, then returned quickly to the table, afraid Thomas would reveal the contents of his sack before she was ready to see it. She turned to Thomas and waited. He leaned back in his chair and began picking at his fingernails, barely able to keep the smile from his face. Maeve could stand it no longer.

"Da! No more waitin', please! Can we see what's inside the sack?"

"Yes, yes," he laughed, "let's get it up here on the table and see what's inside. Now don't be gettin' your hopes up. It's the damaged fruit she usually gives me."

"Thomas Delaney, we will always be grateful for every kindness shown to us, isn't that right?" Kathleen made a point of looking directly at each of her children to drive home the point. Thomas agreed and lifted the burlap sack onto the table. He untied and loosened the drawstring at the top and laid the sack down on its side. As he shimmied the sack from side to side and the contents spilled out onto the table there were gasps of delight from the children and from Kathleen too. The produce that emerged from the sack was fresh and undamaged. More than a dozen potatoes, two large bunches of carrots, four onions, seven large apples, four rutabagas, and five turnips had all come from a farmer's root cellar to the Zimmer's vegetable stand and now were spread across the Delaney's table. Mrs. Zimmer had also included three small cloth pouches, one filled with salt, another with pepper, and a smaller one with a large spoonful of cinnamon inside. At the bottom of the sack, wrapped in two layers of brown paper, was a hefty chicken plucked and ready to cook. Kathleen put her hand to her mouth as the abundance of their blessing overwhelmed her.

"Tommy, it's so much," she whispered.

"'Tis neither too much nor too little, Katie, but rather it's just right. It is exactly what Mrs. Zimmer wanted to give, and we will leave it at that. When they return from Jersey, we'll do somethin' nice for them, yes?"

"Yes, dear, we surely will," Kathleen agreed, though she wondered what they could possibly give. She stood and carried the chicken to the cutting board. It had been readied nicely by Mr. Caselli. Kathleen pulled a few remaining downy feathers and set it to boil. She cut up half an onion and two carrots from the sack and put them in the pot with a sprinkling of salt and pepper. After emptying the bean soup from her other pot into a bowl and placing it back in the icebox, Kathleen picked up her water bucket and stepped out into the hallway to wash the empty soup pot so she could use it to cook potatoes. The long metal basin outside their door was shared by several families. The water was pumped out back and carried inside to facilitate cleanup, laundry, and dishes. Kathleen hummed a tune as she washed the pot. What a fine meal there would be on the Delaney's table that night! For a brief and wonderful moment, she remembered how joy felt. She carried the pot back into the flat, filled it with water, and cut the potatoes into it. She put the children to work, asking Eamon to refill the water bucket as Sorley and Maeve picked up the book and toys from the floor and rolled up the mattresses still laying where they were placed the night before.

Thomas settled himself on the couch that was given to them by their friend, John O'Riley. It had one of Kathleen's quilts thrown over it to cover the rips and stains, but it allowed for seating apart from the wooden chairs around their table. Thomas recalled John O'Riley giving his things away and moving out west last summer. The couch had been John's, and someone else's before him, and he insisted that Thomas have it.

"There's a better life out west, Thomas," the burly Irishman had insisted. "There's more work, more pay, more space, more of everything, and fewer people to share it with. They're still findin' gold, and folks are still gettin' rich. I'm headin' to the mountain they call Pike's Peak. You should come along."

"Sure and there was a better life to be had here too, John. I'm done believin' the dream of somethin' better somewhere else. I'll find it sure enough when I pass through the pearly gates, but not a day before."

"You were a miner in Cork, were ya not?" John asked, smoothing his wiry red beard with his hand.

"Aye, for a time I worked the copper mines until the blight took the potatoes and death took us all."

29

"Well, Tom, they're minin' ore all over the west. Endless amounts of it—gold, silver, copper, zinc, and lead. If you don't want to go now, I'll write when I get there and let ya know what I find."

That was eight months ago, and Thomas had not heard from John. He imagined his friend living much as he had in New York, scratching out a meager existence and going hungry most days. It seemed the way of the world, the new world, the changed world after the famine and the spoiled promises of America's bounty. Sitting now on John's couch, Thomas felt his sadness return, and then his anger at what he had seen at Chatham Square. Maeve watched the thoughts and emotions cast shadows across her father's face, and she felt the need to console him. She settled in beside him and snuggled close.

"Da, it'll be all right, ya know. We've a fine meal here and more to come. Don't be sad, Da."

"Och, Maeve, if only I could see the world as you do." He pulled her closer and felt a surge of regret. He was sorry he had ever left Ireland. It would have been better to starve to death with the rest of his village than to come here with dreams of a better life, only to live in rancid squalor and abject poverty every day after day with no end in sight. In Ireland, they were not hated and scorned. There were no signs in shop windows proclaiming *Irish Need Not Apply*. Despite the poverty they may have experienced in the old country, there was open space and fresh air. A man could tend a garden and have a few chickens. Neighbors were neighborly, and before the Great Hunger no one went hungry. Thomas felt like he had removed his family from the encroaching Hunger and planted them firmly in the throes of starvation. He laid his head back and closed his eyes. Maeve nestled in against him and enjoyed the nearness of her father, the smile on Mam's face as she prepared their meal, and the smell of the chicken in the pot. In that moment, for however long it lasted, life was good and there was a sense of contentment inside the four crumbling walls of their tenement flat.

Half an hour of peace and quiet came to a quick end when the Delaney's door opened, and the dark cloud returned to rain grief down upon them. Sean was startled by the quiet, by the lack of movement and noise, and by the enticing aroma coming from inside the flat. He almost took a step back to check the number on the door, but the dark expression on his father's face chased away any uncertainty. He kicked off his shoes and hung his jacket on a hook. His father noticed immediately that his head was bare, the telltale red cap discarded. Sean turned back to face his father. He was expecting a verbal confrontation and was prepared for his own defense. Maeve detached herself from Da's side and sat down on the little stool in the corner of the kitchen out of the way of the inevitable outburst.

"Where have ya been?" Thomas asked as calmly as his temper would allow, his voice flat and emotionless, his mind hearing the lies before they were spoken.

"Out lookin' for work," Sean said unconvincingly.

"Ah, and did ya find it there in the square with the rowdies?"

"Don't know what you're talkin' about, Da," Sean replied with enough guilt in his voice to convict him.

"You'll not lie to me, Sean Michael Delaney!" Thomas raised his voice, and his use of first, middle, and last name told Sean that his father would likely not hold his temper long. Sean had entertained a few scenarios, and concocted several explanations, all to cover the truth of what Thomas had seen when passing by Chatham Square on his way home. He needed to decide which story to present and stick to it like it was the holy gospel. He paused only a moment before looking his father straight in the face.

"Da, Will Connelly told me about a man in the square who pays ten pennies to muck out his stable. See, Da?" Sean reached into his pocket and pulled out ten pennies. He held them out toward his father as if those pennies were judge and jury and had proven him innocent. "It was a good day's work and I earned enough to buy a bottle of milk. I'm sure of it!" Sean's enthusiasm told his father that he was lying, for Sean was not an enthusiastic child. He was born serious and contemplative and had remained that way for the past twelve years, always to a degree that far surpassed his years.

"You tell me now where ya got those coins, and it had better be the truth!" Thomas was yelling now, and Kathleen's spirits were crushed. Their fine day was falling away before her, and she could not bear it to happen.

"Sean, tell your father the truth and let's be done with this," she intervened.

"Mam, 'tis true! I earned these ten pennies and brought them home to give you for food!" Sean raised his voice in response to his father's, but mostly out of desperation. If he could get Mam on his side, the victory might be his.

"Sean Delaney," Thomas interrupted, his voice low and heavy with warning, "do not play your mother against me."

"Please stop!" Maeve's small voice from the corner of the kitchen sounded fragile against the intensity of the exchange going on between Thomas and Sean. "Please, Da. Please, Sean." Maeve's hands were over her ears, and her eyes filled to the brim with tears.

Thomas stopped. There would be another time and another place to reprimand his son for defying their wishes and returning to Chatham Square. There would be a better opportunity to punish him for the lies he was telling. Here and now was not the time. Their flat had been filled with a lovely quiet contentment, now nearly spoiled, and he was as much at fault as the boy standing near the door with ten dirty pennies in his hand. There was a moment of great hesitation, of surrender, of regret and guilt and repentance. It came from both father and son, and it was thick in the air. Kathleen broke the silent uncertainties by walking over and removing the coins from Sean's hand. Whether they were earned or stolen she did not want to know, and in the grander scheme of things ten dirty pennies could mean the difference between sustenance and starvation. It was the sad truth of their pathetic existence.

"We will use it when things are runnin' low again, and I thank ya kindly, Sean, for your contribution." She dropped the coins in a glass jar on top of the icebox and turned back to the stove. "All right now, let's see if we can find a way to get some butter for our potatoes before this chicken is ready to devour! Does anyone have an idea? We're far too close to supper bein' ready to walk to the market, but maybe we could barter somethin' for a healthy portion of butter. Perhaps we could offer a couple of Sean's pennies."

"Chicken! Where did we get a chicken?" Sean's senses returned to the delicious aroma that had greeted him when he entered the apartment.

"Had you been here you would have heard the story," Thomas said, reluctant to surrender the battle but willing to do so for Kathleen's sake.

"Sorry, Da." There was a believable humility in Sean's voice, and it was enough for his father, at least for now. Thomas fought hard to let go. His anger and his disappointment were raw and unresolved, but he refused to let them or his wayward son steal the joy and the blessing that had come their way unexpectedly.

"Perhaps we could trade the rutabagas and turnips. I'm not fond of them myself," Thomas suggested, unwilling to use the coins in the jar. "I can take them out and knock on a few doors if ya like, Katie."

"That would be grand, Tommy. And while you're out, the children and I will set a fine table, won't we now?" They all nodded, even Sean, and a fragile peace was back in the air. Thomas gathered up the turnips and rutabagas, and took an apple, as well. Kathleen gave him a sad look.

"Katie, we've enough with what is left and our potatoes will taste that much better with a bit of butter melting over them, yes?"

"Yes, you're right, love."

Thomas left with the items to barter and hoped he could find a willing neighbor. The area was mostly poor, mostly Irish, but always willing to help when they could. That they had little to share would not stop them from doing so. Bartering, however, was a far better proposition. It saved one from feeling the beggar, and the other from feeling the guilt of hesitancy.

The Delaney flat was busy with chores. The children set about helping Mam find enough plates and flatware to set a proper table. Four matching plates, chipped and worn, were set for the children and two mismatched plates for Mam and Da. An assortment of knives, spoons, and forks were placed around the table. Not every place setting had every piece, but they would share as they always did. Maeve set a teacup for each of her parents. She glanced up at Sean as she did, and he looked away. Maeve felt bad that she had fueled his remorse, but maybe he had learned his lesson and would be less angry in the days to come. She looked up at him again, hoping to catch his eye and smile at him, but he had turned his attention to the pots Kathleen was tending.

"I hope your da gets back soon. Our potatoes are nearly done and so is this fine bird," Mam said as she poked the chicken with a fork. She lifted the chicken from the pot and placed it on the only large platter they owned. She paused a moment to admire the beauty and the savory aroma of the unexpected blessing before returning to the last of the dinner preparations. The cooking liquid from the chicken pot was divided into two portions, one to make a thin gravy and the other to use in mashing the potatoes. Kathleen laid a small towel over the top of the potato pot to keep it warm and turned her attention to carving the chicken. Her belly growled in anticipation as the savory juices flowed out onto the platter, tempting her to take a bite of it before setting it on the table. To do so would be to have more than her children, an unthinkable transgression Kathleen would never entertain. She finished cutting the chicken and was arranging it on the platter when Thomas returned with his head hung low.

"Och, Tommy, what is it now?"

"I did my best, Katie, to trade our vegetables and that one fine apple for just a smidgeon of butter. Sure and wouldn't you know that butter is as scare as a fat man in County Mayo." The children giggled at the sad analogy, having no knowledge of that region of Ireland being one of the hardest hit by the Great Hunger, but understanding their father's meaning.

"'Tis fine, Tommy, we'll be dinin' like royals tonight in spite of it," Kathleen assured her husband. "But where are the turnips, and the apple, and ..."

"Well, you see, poor Mrs. Leary has those five children, and her lazy man hasn't even looked for work in weeks. I walked past her flat and could go no further. I knocked and she came to the door lookin' thin and weary. I asked if she had a smidgeon of butter she'd like to trade for those fine vegetables and the apple. She eyed those things with a sinful envy, and I could not but give them to her."

"Da, you did the right thing," Eamon said. He often played with Jimmy Leary and knew that the Learys had even less than his own family.

"Aye, Son, and thanks for understandin'. I left the Leary's door and made my way down the hall thinkin' I'd step outside and figure out how to tell ya that I had no butter, nor did I have the goods I'd left home with. I was nearly at the end of the hallway when a large, sour-lookin' woman stopped me in my tracks. Standing there takin' up her entire doorway, she was. I swear to ya, she had the hint of a beard, and her eyes were small and cruel. I felt the urge to run, but I stood my ground!"

Even in their impatience the children couldn't help but laugh. Da's stories always entertained them, whether they were grand adventures or daily accounts of the most mundane things. He had a flair for the dramatic and he loved nothing more than to make his children laugh. And Katie. To see her eyes twinkle like the evening stars, and her radiant smile, was to gaze upon Heaven itself, and Thomas wondered if he would ever tire of it.

"What did she say, Da?" Sorley asked.

"She says to me, 'I saw what you did,' and I stuttered quietly, 'I'm sorry, Ma'am.' I took a step further hopin' to take my leave when she asked, 'What did you want from that poor woman?' to which I replied, 'Just a smidgeon of butter so my dear children can eat their potatoes properly.'"

"Did she hit ya, Da?" Sorley asked. Kathleen could not hold back the laugh that escaped at Sorley's question. Thomas laughed, too, but continued with his story so that Sorley would not feel embarrassed.

"No, son, she didn't hit me, but she did tell me she had what I was lookin' for. I hoped beyond hope that she might have a tiny bit of butter to bring home to you, but she did not."

There was a collective murmur as the dream of melting butter on their mashed potatoes was not to be, but they made certain not to give Da cause to suffer over it for he had done a noble thing.

"Not a tiny bit of butter to spare for the Delaneys, but she did have this!" Da lifted his hand from his jacket pocket to reveal a parcel of brown paper the size of a large potato. The family gathered in closer as he pulled back the paper to reveal a mound of butter much bigger than the width of his hand.

"Tommy!" Kathleen shouted. "You trickster! She had not a smidgeon of butter, but a king's portion!"

"The lady said I did a fine thing and she wanted our potatoes to be swimmin' in butter. I believe we shall fulfill her request." He bowed in grand fashion and presented the royal portion to his queen.

The table that night was a merry place. The chicken was eaten down to every joint and bone. Every plate was piled high with creamy mashed potatoes surrounded by a pool of melted butter. No one said a word. The only sounds coming from the Delaney kitchen were the clinking of utensils and crockery and the occasional delighted moaning of sated hunger.

Kathleen reflected on how differently food tastes when a person is truly hungry. Hunger becomes the normal way to feel when life places you in the throes of poverty, and unfortunately that is where the Delaneys resided. She was overwhelmed with gratitude for the kindness of Mrs. Zimmer, and the large scary woman who lived at the end of the hallway. She was grateful, too, for the opportunity to work for firewood. As miserable as it might sound to others, it kept her family warm and allowed them to cook a meal like the one they were enjoying. This morning when she finished the scrubbing and cleaning, Mr. Bingham had tipped her five cents but had reminded her not to expect it. His small gratuities were appreciated too, for it was more than Kathleen had in her pocket when she left home.

"Oh, my stars and garters!" Kathleen blurted out, startling everyone around the table. Sorley and Maeve laughed at Mam's funny expression as Kathleen made her way to the hook where her coat was hanging.

"The treat in your pocket, Mam! We forgot all about it with the excitement of our fine chicken dinner," Maeve said.

"What's goin' on now?" Da asked.

"Mr. Andy Bingham handed me five pennies this mornin' along with the cart full of firewood. I stopped in at Josef's Bakery on my way home and spent them on a treat. Sure and I thought it would be the biggest excitement of the day. Now 'tis nothin' more than a wee morsel after such a grand meal."

"Sorry to have ruined your surprise, Katie dear." Thomas was truly sorry, for he knew how much Kathleen loved to bring home a sweet treat when she had the means to do so. He gave her his best display of contrition, sad eyes and droopy mouth, his hands folded under his chin.

"Ah, hush yourself, Tommy. This little bit of nothin' pales in comparison to sittin' around our table eating like Albert and Victoria themselves!"

Eamon stood and paraded around the flat in royal fashion huffing and puffing in his best English accent. His siblings were in stitches, and Da considered that he might have some competition for his role as the storyteller of the family. Thomas was more than willing to relinquish his title in time, in the true Irish fashion of long revered lines of storytellers. Eamon would do him proud when his time arrived.

Kathleen returned to the table with two small packages wrapped in printed paper and tied with string.

"What is it, Mam?" Sorley asked.

Kathleen pulled the string on each package and opened the paper to reveal two sugar-coated apple turnovers, so delicate there on the rough wooden table, postcard perfect amidst the chicken bones and bits of gravy that dotted the dirty plates.

"I had worried over how we would all get enough of these lovely pastries divided between us, but now that our bellies are so wonderfully full I think a bite or two will suffice." Sean reached for the knife on the counter, wiped it clean on his sleeve and handed it to Kathleen. She cut each turnover into three pieces and invited everyone to enjoy it. It was the perfect small, sweet bite to end a perfect meal. Each of them felt a deep sense of gratitude for the kindness of others, both Mrs. Zimmer for the meal and, yes, even Andrew Bingham for the pastries he allowed Kathleen to purchase. Sean let go of his darkness long enough to enjoy the evening with his family. He knew Da was not finished with him, and he wavered between offering more lies to cover the ones he'd already told, or honesty that would get him into no less trouble but might restore some favor with his father. He would sleep on it.

Thomas stood and picked up the water bucket Eamon had refilled before dinner. He and Kathleen carried the dirty dishes into the hallway and together they washed them in the basin. Their mood was celebratory, and they sang together as they shared the mundane business of washing dishes. The noise of silverware hitting the metal basin and the cacophony of the Delaney's serenade drew Mr. Callahan from his flat next door. The sight of Thomas washing dishes like a doting housemaid garnered an exaggerated eye roll from the neighbor.

"Takin' on women's work are ya now, Tom?"

"Gladly, I am, Callahan!"

Mr. Callahan retreated back inside his flat, shaking his head as he closed the door behind him. Thomas and Kathleen picked up their song where they left off and sang louder than before.

CHAPTER THREE

The four weeks that followed the fine chicken dinner were not as decadent. Kathleen's cleaning job for the barrister at 281 East Broadway continued to supply them with firewood, but it did not put food in their bellies. Thomas was tiring of long waits on the dock for a pittance of coins that provided little for his family. He heard talk of others heading over to the Lehigh Valley in Pennsylvania to work in the coal mines. It was risky work and with the recent drop in the price of coal the wages dropped as well. Coal mining had with it an inherent danger, and Thomas was not comfortable with the risk. Coal mine explosions had killed over 150 miners in the past twenty years including fifty-five poor souls at the Midlothian coal mine in Virginia four years ago. March 19, 1855, shook Thomas to the core, for he had nearly signed on with a crew of men heading to that mine. When news came back that the very mine where he would have been working had exploded into a raging fireball killing fifty-five men, most of whom were Irish, Thomas knew he had avoided the call of the grim reaper by a hair's breadth.

Now, four years later, with the prospect of gainful employment for the Irish of New York fading quickly, Thomas was feeling a grievous sense of panic. The danger of working in the mines would not worry him if all he had to think about was himself, but the prospect of leaving his family penniless without him and destined to starve to death on the streets of the city was a risk he could not take. If there were any life left in him he would not allow his family to suffer such a fate. There was no easy answer. He understood the temptation to join the criminal elements in the city, sinful as it was, for it put coin in the pocket and food on the table. It was a cruel irony they were living, and he was becoming more embittered by the day.

The month of March passed quickly and ushered in a warm spring giving heat to the fetid rubbish lining the streets. Spring, a time of hope and renewal, offered neither to the poverty-stricken residents of the inner city. As the days warmed, the Delaney's need for firewood was now limited to cooking. Since Mr. Bingham continued to compensate Kathleen with nothing more she was able to sell half of what she brought home each week. It provided a few cents to their empty pot and was enough to put a minimal amount of food on their table. It kept them alive, but not much more. The boys often complained of being hungry which pierced the very heart of their mother. Maeve held tight to her eternal optimism and kept silent about the ache in her belly so as not to add more sadness to their lives. Eamon spent much of his time with Maeve and Sorley, concocting new stories to tell so they would not ask him to read about the Robinson family again for a very long time. Maeve's interest in learning to read never wavered, but Eamon had no desire to be a teacher and so she waited. Sorley had no interest. He loved to listen to stories, both told and read, and his curiosity was ever present as the tale unfolded, but he was far too lazy to do the work it would take to learn to read for himself.

"Katie, come sit with me here," Thomas called to his wife on a too-warm afternoon. She had been cutting up onions for soup. The noxious fumes of the overripe onions, the heat intruding through the filmy windows, and the sadness over the coming meal that would be nothing more than onions, carrots, and one potato in a large pot of water had put her in a dark mood. She took a deep breath to expel her irritation before putting her knife down and walking over to the couch. Kathleen was annoyed that Tommy had called her away from her dinner preparations, but his mood of late was dark as well and not worth testing. She sat beside him and looked at him directly. Her green eyes smoldered a darker shade of emerald which told her husband that he may have picked an inopportune time to have the ensuing conversation.

"What is it, Tommy?" Her voice was flat, and Thomas proceeded carefully.

"I've been thinkin', Katie," he started in his familiar way that told Katie there were likely changes to come. She braced herself, readying her shoulders for another burden to bear, and she wondered as she did how much more she could carry.

"Maybe we should be thinkin' about leavin' New York." Thomas felt her stiffen beside him. They had battled over this subject more than once. Every time Thomas brought up the idea of relocating to work in the mines, Kathleen reminded him of Midlothian and how close he had come to being taken from their lives forever.

"And what would you do, Tommy, work in the mines?"

"I know what you're thinkin', Katie, but listen now, I've somethin' to tell ya." Thomas paused and pulled a folded piece of paper from his shirt pocket. "Ya remember John

O'Riley whose couch we're sittin' on?" Katie nodded. "And ya remember he headed west to find a better life?" Again, Katie nodded. She could see where the conversation was heading and didn't wait for Thomas to plead his case. She reached for the letter he had pulled from his pocket and held it a moment, readying herself for the conversation that would follow. When she calmed herself, she read it.

Greetings Tom,

It was a long journey here, but there's a grand reward to be had. A man can get himself a pan, or a rocker box, and pull gold from the streams with little effort. I stayed at Pike's Peak through one of the worst winters God ever created, but I've moved on to the western Utah territory where more gold has been discovered. A nice little settlement they call Chinatown near Carson City. Katie and the children would like it here, and for a man willing to work there is money to be made. I've been pulling gold from the stream since I arrived. On occasion, a larger nugget will bring a sizeable payout. I'm not rich but it's more money than I've ever made, and if I tire of standing in the water and panning for my fortune there are mining companies set up all over the countryside where a man can sign on to work. They're a far cry safer than the coal mines back east, or so I'm being told, and I think I would be comfortable working there. It's a good life, Tom. No more standing with empty pockets on the docks along the river. Clean air and room to move. I'm here waiting and can help you get started when you're ready.

Your friend,
Johnathon P. O'Riley

Kathleen was grateful that the children had gone out to play for there was likely going to be an argument. The yard that connected their tenement with the one behind it was nothing but dirt and weeds littered with trash and broken glass, but the importance of fresh air, such as it was, compelled Kathleen to allow the children to play there from time to time. She gave Sean the responsibility of watching over his younger siblings, and his resentment grew. Nursemaid and nanny. His acquaintances at Chatham Square would bust a rib laughing at the demeaning position he was put in.

"Tommy, just how do ya think we could make it out west with no money in our pockets and four children taggin' along with us?"

"I don't know yet, Katie, but I know somethin' has to change. Livin' here gets more dangerous by the day, and I don't know how we'll survive another winter without me findin' a proper job. I'm afraid to let you walk these streets any longer, and I'm not trustin' Sean and his yearnin' to linger down at Chatham Square. Word has it the Daybreak Boys are startin' up a new gang and are recruitin' young lads like Sean lookin' for easy money and the rewards that come along with it."

"Thomas Delaney! Surely you're not thinkin' our son would join up with a gang like that!" Kathleen was appalled that her husband would even imply such a thing. Thomas, however, was well aware of the reality on the streets. The gangs lured young men who wanted all the things the city had stolen from them. They promised them money, respect, and a way to get even with every jackeen who ever looked down his nose at the Irish.

"Katie, they know how to draw them in, they know what these young men lack, and they make promises ..."

"Thomas, those boys are murderers!" Kathleen interrupted. "I heard Mr. Callahan tellin' another man that the Daybreak Boys killed countless innocent people these past two years. Sean is goin' through somethin' and he may be flirtin' with trouble, but he's not a murderer! And besides, the other man said the Daybreak Gang was taken down in a gunfight with the police and that most of them were killed."

"'Tis true, which is why they're lookin' to regroup. I hate to speak it, Katie, but Sean is ripe for the pickin'. He's frustrated. He's angry and bitter and hates the life we're livin'. He's embarrassed by me, and by you, grovelin' at the feet of anyone willin' to throw a scrap our way. If I'm honest, Katie, I am too. I'm tired of beggin'. I'm tired of bein' humiliated day after day watchin' the work doled out to everyone but the Irish. I'm tired of those hirin' men at the docks leavin' me standin' there while they smirk and shrug and get a fine sense of pleasure at seein' me and mine go hungry!"

"Tommy," Kathleen whispered in defeat, "it's too much. We haven't the means to leave here and go west. We've nothin' but a few trinkets and our name."

"And we could have so much more somewhere else." Thomas put his arm around his wife and pulled her near to him. He had no answer. She was right in saying they had no way to get themselves from here to there, to start anew and go in search of a better life. It truly was an impossible dream but one he was not willing to let fall by the wayside. He would start asking questions. He would talk to neighbors and dockworkers and shop owners and anyone he could engage in conversation. Something would work in their favor. He felt it deep in his desperate soul, and that spark of hope would keep him looking for answers.

The quiet comfort they shared was heavy with the unspoken, their mutual understanding of the pain and fear that plagued them, and the disappointment they had known since coming to America. Kathleen forgot about the soup waiting to be finished as she sat with Thomas and dreamed another dream, a far-fetched fantasy that she locked away in her hopeless heart. She would leave it there, refusing to give it even the smallest hint of possibility. She could not bear another failure like the one they were living now.

***

Their peaceful respite, each deep in their own thoughts, was short-lived, pierced by the shrill and unmistakable cries of Sorley. They were cries of pain, and both Kathleen and Thomas shot up off the couch and ran down the hallway to the back door of their building. Thomas flung the door open and was met by Eamon, his face pale with terror.

"Mam! Sorley tripped and fell on a broken bottle. There's glass," Eamon paused, visibly upset and struggling to relay what had happened. "It's stuck in his knee."

Thomas ran ahead and saw the blood soaking through Sorley's pant leg. He saw the rip near the boy's knee and a large piece of glass, as big as the boy's hand, sticking out. Thomas scooped Sorley up in his arms and ran back toward the building.

"Sorley!" Kathleen cried out as Thomas approached her with their son in his arms. Eamon and Maeve followed behind their father, both in tears and fearing for their gentle, freckle-faced brother. Sorley's cries were filled with pain and Kathleen's heart was shattering like the glass that littered the empty lot. Faces appeared in the windows that looked out over the yard, some curious and some angry at the noise, but they disappeared quickly, vanishing ghost-like into the familiarity of violence and anguished screams.

Thomas stopped at the back of the building and turned to Kathleen. "Go inside and get your cart, Katie. Put a blanket inside and come back as fast as you can." Thomas's words were calm and measured, masking the fear and panic he felt inside. He knew he needed to be the quiet in the storm for both Sorley and Kathleen. While they waited, he shushed Sorley and comforted him with words of endearment. Maeve and Eamon stood nearby feeling helpless and afraid, and it was then that Thomas realized Sean was nowhere in sight. He peered out across the open yard to see only a stray three-legged dog sniffing through the trash and a young woman drinking from a small brown bottle, aged before her time by the ravages of poor decisions. Thomas felt his anger surface. An internal battle began, and though he wanted nothing more than to scream out in anger and rage at the irresponsibility of his oldest son, the calming voice in his head won out. He would not throw lamp oil onto this fire.

"Come here, Eamon," he said quietly. He nodded at the boy and Eamon approached slowly. "Maeve, you too, Stóirín." The children walked closer, fearful of seeing the blood on Sorley's leg. "'Tis all right, yes?" They nodded with great uncertainty. "Children, can ya tend to yourselves while Mam and I take Sorley over to the doctor on Houston Street?"

"Aye, Da." Maeve's voice quivered. She could scarce bring herself to look at Sorley's face, twisted with pain and as pale as his porcelain skin could possibly be. Maeve put her tiny hand in Eamon's. They entered the building and made their way down the hallway, longer and darker than they knew it to be. Halfway to their flat they met their mother running with her cart, fighting the sobs that wanted to escape.

"Where are ya goin', children?"

"Da said you were to take Sorley over to the doctor on Houston Street, and we're to stay here on our own," Eamon uttered bravely. It was then that the absence of Sean hit Kathleen, just as it had Thomas a few minutes before. She knew there was trouble to come but, like Thomas, could not concern herself with it now.

"Be smart, be safe, my loves. If ya need anything, you'll go see Mrs. Callahan, yes?" The children nodded and turned to walk the rest of the way to their flat alone, the harsh reality of their pitiful existence demanding more of them than was fair, for poverty does not lend itself to innocence.

Kathleen pulled her cart through the open doorway and stepped outside where Thomas was waiting, still holding Sorley in his arms. She stared into her husband's eyes in silent agreement that Sean's absence would be dealt with later. She tucked the blanket inside the cart to afford the boy some comfort, but when Thomas laid him inside the cart Sorley's leg moved and he screamed in agony.

"Oh, dear Mary and Joseph," Kathleen cried out. She made the sign of the cross as they hurried across Division and onto Ridge Street. They walked the five blocks down Ridge Street until it intersected Houston and continued two blocks left on Houston to the doctor's house. The streets were a convoluted mishmash of dirt and oyster shell, gravel, and Belgian block cobblestones, none of which were suited for smooth travel for a cart or wagon. Sorley cried out in pain at every bump in the road, and Kathleen was certain she would die from the breaking of her heart. She remembered watching her mother leave this earth in a peaceful, sleep-filled death from the Great Hunger. Her heart broke at her mother's passing, but the agony her youngest son was suffering, the blood-soaked pant leg, and his helpless cries were more than she could bear.

It was late in the afternoon when the Delaneys arrived at Dr. Bermann's home on Houston Street. Two oversized windows were flanked by wooden shutters, and there was a spattering of red tulips just beginning to blossom in the window boxes beneath each window. The deep red petals reminded Kathleen of the blood coming from Sorley's leg and she looked away.

Dr. Bermann's small clinic was in a room near the back of the house. During business hours Mrs. Bermann would seat people in her living room and offer them tea and pastry on a doilied tray. There was no business shingle hanging above the door, and word on the street was that Dr. Bermann was not licensed to practice medicine in America and was operating outside of the law. Nonetheless, he seemed skilled and knowledgeable and was willing to barter services for goods for any of his patients, like the Delaneys, who had no money to pay.

The lights in the Bermann's living room were out, and Thomas knew it meant they had closed up shop for the day. It was Saturday, and he correctly assumed they were getting ready to head down to Catharine Street for the market festivities.

Thomas felt a twinge of guilt bothering the Bermanns when they had obviously finished their workday, but his son needed care and there was no alternative. The knowledge that they had no money to pay for services, and nothing of value to barter, intensified his regret. He hoped the doctor would be willing to work something out. He stepped forward and knocked on the door twice. There was no sound and no movement inside. Kathleen's hand went to her heart as she wondered if the Bermann's had already left for the market leaving no one to help her son. Thomas rapped on the door again, louder this time, and as he peered through the window in the door he could see the recognizable figure of Mrs. Bermann heading toward them, her perfectly coiffed hair and her belted blue dress in her usual fashion. She had a hand up, one finger raised, shaking it side to side as if to say, *Sorry, we're closed.* Thomas was sorting through the pleas, the arguments, the shameless begging he would employ to convince the doctor to see them, but when the doctor's wife opened the door and saw the child in the cart her demeanor changed. His leg was covered in blood, his cries were now hoarse and airy, his skin pallid.

"Merciful God," she whispered, then turned back and yelled for her husband. As Dr. Bermann neared the gathering at the door he had the same look of irritation. His also changed upon seeing Sorley. Dr. Bermann knew Thomas; he had treated him for an infection in his hand caused by unsanitary working conditions on the dock. The doctor had also cared for Kathleen two years ago when she contracted a case of influenza. He was well aware that the Delaneys were poorer than the proverbial church mouse and that Thomas struggled to find gainful employment, but a child did not deserve to be punished for the sins of the father. The aging doctor with the kind heart hurried them in and led them to his examining room at the back of the house. Carefully, Thomas and the doctor lifted Sorley onto the raised table, waist-high to the doctor and covered with a soft cotton mattress. Kathleen made her way closer, but Dr. Bermann shook his head and asked them both to wait in the waiting room.

Mrs. Bermann put the kettle on the stove and returned shortly with a teapot on a tray and two pretty china cups that had likely come with them from Germany. There were two shortbread biscuits on a matching saucer and a small crystal bowl filled with berry preserves. Weak and ashamed, Kathleen could not resist the desire to have some shortbread, and she spread the preserves generously over her biscuit with the tiny silver spoon Mrs. Bermann had provided. Even as she enjoyed the lovely treat, the sight of the teacups brought Sean's face to mind and her grief intensified. She raised the teacup to her mouth, and the doctor's wife did not miss the way her hand trembled. Mrs. Bermann was about to engage in conversation with the Delaneys, employing the useful tactic of distraction, but before she could utter a word she heard her husband calling for her. She instructed the Delaneys to stay put before rushing back to the examining room.

Dr. Bermann had administered a surgical dose of ether to a thick cotton cloth and held it just above Sorley's nose and mouth, speaking softly to the boy and asking him to breathe in and out slowly. It had taken only three or four minutes for his patient to be fully anesthetized allowing the doctor to inspect the wound without causing the boy any more pain. The doctor had carefully removed the shard of glass from Sorley's knee. It was lodged deep and though it did not sever the ligament it inflicted a serious laceration to it. The doctor had carefully stitched the ligament as best he could but was untrained in advanced surgical procedure. The healing would be slow, and the prognosis was difficult to predict.

When Mrs. Bermann arrived, her husband asked her to close up the wound. She had worked alongside the doctor for many years and was adept with a needle and thread, with cleaning wounds, and applying bandages and compresses. Though many doctors reached for the whiskey bottle when cleaning a wound, Mrs. Bermann still used honey as a natural antiseptic. Her grandmother had taught her about the healing properties of honey, and she and the doctor continued to use it to reduce scarring, minimize inflammation, and help reduce the chance of infection. As she carefully began stitching the laceration closed, Dr. Bermann went out to have a word with Kathleen and Thomas. When he walked into the room both of the worried parents stood, hands wringing with fear and worry, their uncertainty clearly read by the doctor.

"The boy is resting," he began in his thick German accent. He tucked a hand in the pocket of his blue suit jacket and continued. "I have removed the glass from his knee and inspected the wound. The ligament was lacerated, and I stitched it together the best I could. To be safe, I'd like to put his leg in a plaster cast to keep it immobilized for a few weeks. There is no way to know how it will heal, but this will give it the best chance to recover. The damage may be minimal, it may be worse, and be aware that there could be lasting effects from the injury."

"Damage?" Thomas asked, his mind in a fog. He felt like a child. He knew the doctor had just explained the situation but nothing he said had made any sense. It was as if the words had reached his ears and fallen to the floor, empty and meaningless.

"Mr. Delaney," Dr. Bermann began again, slowly, "the glass cut into the ligament in your son's knee. It is hard to predict how these things will heal. He may have a fairly successful recovery, or he may have permanent damage. There is no way to know for sure until we check it again after the cast is removed."

"How bad might it be?" Kathleen asked, barely able to speak the words.

"Worst case would be an inability to walk on the leg or use it for any practical purpose." Kathleen drew in her breath quickly, shocked by Dr. Bermann's response. "Best case would be a complete recovery," he continued, "and there is every level of possibility in between. My opinion at this point and I'm not a surgeon, mind you, is that he may have a limp, that the knee will always be frail, and that he will need to be cautious with it. He could find the use of a crutch, and later a cane, to be very helpful."

Kathleen turned to Thomas and cried on his shoulder. He held her close and stroked her auburn hair as he looked over her shoulder at Dr. Bermann. "Do whatever will give him the best chance, doctor." Dr. Bermann nodded and went back to join his wife, and to prepare the boy's leg for the plaster cast.

"That looks good, my dear," Dr. Bermann said when he returned to the back room and inspected his wife's handiwork. "Now let's prepare to set that leg in a cast."

Mrs. Bermann applied honey to the stitched wound and started to prepare Sorley's leg for casting. She cleaned the leg from end to end with antiseptic and put a soft cotton stocking on the leg that went from ankle to hip. The doctor removed a box of cloth strips from a cabinet. He mixed plaster powder and water in a large basin, and when it was the correct consistency he immersed the cloth strips into the liquid. He let them soak a few minutes before applying the strips to Sorley's cotton-covered leg. With the improved method developed by Dutch military surgeon Anthonius Mathijsen, plaster casts were now drying within minutes instead of hours. Dr. Bermann had read about the process in an 1852 edition of the medical magazine *Repertorium* before leaving Germany. He had adopted this more modernized application and found it much easier on the patient and less tedious for the doctor or nurse applying the cast. He wrapped the strips round and round the boy's leg until the cast was thick enough to immobilize it but not overly cumbersome. As the doctor and his wife waited for the last few strips to dry, Sorley began to stir. He was groggy and confused, and he whimpered in pain and fear. Dr. Bermann nodded to his wife, and she went out to get the Delaneys. She advised them to avoid letting Sorley see their grief and to be calm and comforting even if it was a façade. She gave them a moment to compose themselves and then led them back to their son.

When Thomas and Kathleen entered the examination room, they saw the blood-soaked cloths and detected the distinctive sweet smell of ether. They both remembered Mrs. Bermann's advice, and they put on their best brave faces. Kathleen moved to the bedside and took Sorley's hand, leaned in closer, and whispered words of comfort. Thomas stood back a couple of feet to let Kathleen soothe her suffering child, and more so because he was overcome with a boiling pot of emotions. A profound sadness for his youngest son's pain was foremost in his heart and mind, but the simmering anger over Sean's defiance and his poor decision in leaving the children to play alone in the yard could not be quelled.

"Da," Sorley whispered through the fog of ether that still clouded his mind. Kathleen turned and reached for Thomas's hand to pull him in closer. "Da, I'm sorry." The apology destroyed any resolve Thomas had left. He could no longer control his emotions as leaned over the boy and wept. Kathleen placed her hand on her husband's back to comfort him, and Sorley raised his little hand to place it on his father's head. The Bermann's left the room to give the Delaneys time to grieve, and then to find the strength to be the support their son would need. It was the natural order of things, and Dr. Bermann had seen it countless times before. Often the situation was far worse than the child's lacerated knee, but he would not discount the pain and sadness they were all feeling.

After a few minutes, Dr. Bermann returned to address the Delaneys. He reiterated what he had seen and done and the uncertainty that would be resolved with time and healing.

The Delaneys nodded. Thomas shuffled nervously, and the doctor knew why.

"Thomas," the doctor said before Thomas could begin his painful admission of poverty, "my wife and I have a small garden in the back. It needs tilling before Greta can plant her vegetables. Would you be willing to come back in a couple of weeks and take care of it for us? I think that should cover your bill today."

Thomas was moved by the doctor's sensitivity, his understanding of the situation, and his willingness to offer to barter for services without Thomas having to humble himself and admit to being penniless.

"I'm beholdin' to ya, Doctor," Thomas said in a low voice, broken by emotion. He swallowed hard to get past the lump in his throat. "My wife and I can never repay you for what you have done."

"Your help with the garden is payment enough," Dr. Bermann replied. "Now, I am sending you home with a small bottle of ether and another of laudanum." He removed two small brown bottles, clearly labeled, from a nearby cabinet and turned to instruct Kathleen as she would likely be Sorley's caretaker during his recovery. "The boy will be in some pain when he is fully awake, and it will be a week or more before he feels like trying to walk, with the help of a crutch, of course. I would caution against using the ether unless he finds it impossible to sleep. A small amount only, and only until you see him drift off to sleep. Pour a small amount of ether on a clean cloth and hold it just above his nose and mouth as he breathes the fumes. Do not touch the cloth to his face as it will render that area numb. Use the laudanum sparingly, as well, just three or four drops in a spoonful of water. It will be for pain management if he appears to need it. If he seems able to cope without the medication, I would refrain from giving it to him. And here," he turned and reached behind the door, "is a crutch an associate of mine made from a tree branch when his daughter broke her leg. It's not very refined, but it will do the trick."

"Sure and we'll be grateful for the use of it," Kathleen said. Thomas lifted Sorley off the table and carried him to the waiting area where Kathleen's cart had been left. Kathleen fluffed the blanket, and when Thomas laid his son in the cart Kathleen did her best to make Sorley as comfortable as she could, thankful that he was still groggy enough from the ether that it might lessen the discomfort of the rough ride ahead. The Delaneys thanked the doctor and Mrs. Bermann profusely before heading out the door for the walk home. The cast helped as it prevented the leg from moving when they rolled the cart over the countless bumps and the relentless jarring of the cobblestone. It was twilight, and the soft evening light took the edge off the harsh reality of the lower east side. The gas streetlamps flickered and scattered a warm golden glow around them as they walked. In another place, far away from the rancid streets of New York, it would have resembled a painted scene from a master's hand. For the Delaneys, it was more like *puttin' cologne on a cow*, as Kathleen's father used to say.

By the time they arrived back at their tenement building on East Broadway darkness had settled in for the night. It mirrored the darkness in Thomas's heart, for he knew there was more pain to come. If Sean were already home, he had likely heard the entire story from his two siblings who were waiting there alone. If not, his trouble deepened for being out after dark. The events of the day strengthened Thomas's resolve to find a way out of New York.

Thomas lifted Sorley from the cart and carried him into their flat, Kathleen followed behind him pulling the cart with the blood-stained quilt inside it. Sorley was asleep but moaned occasionally when a wave of pain would overtake him. A quick glance around as they entered the room revealed Sean's absence. Thomas struggled to focus on the task at hand as he worked with Kathleen to get Sorley settled comfortably. Thomas would sleep on the couch and let Sorley share the bed with Kathleen, something they did from time to time for one child who had earned favor by doing something special. The couch was not quite large enough to accommodate Thomas comfortably, but it was the very least he could do for his son. Sorley stirred when his father laid him down on the bed and cried out in pain when he tried to move on his own. Sorley looked up at Kathleen and two large tears escaped. He cried softly, trying to hide his pain, knowing how deeply his misery affected his parents.

"What's that on Sorley's leg, Mam?" Maeve asked as she and Eamon moved in closer.

"Never you mind for now," Kathleen replied. She turned to Thomas with a worried look. "Tommy, shall we give him a wee bit of the medicine from Dr. Bermann? Just enough to ease his pain, for his tears are breakin' my heart."

"Aye, Katie, just a bit," Thomas replied. Kathleen got a spoon from the cupboard and took the laudanum bottle from her coat pocket. She used her mother's hat pin, always on her lapel, to dip into the bottle and allow four drops of the medicine to drip into the spoon. She added enough water from the pitcher nearby to fill the spoon just as Dr. Bermann had instructed. Thomas put his arm under Sorley's back and lifted the boy forward so he could take the bitter liquid. Sorley's face twisted in disgust.

"It's terrible," he whined.

"I know, Son," Thomas agreed, his voice filled with empathy. "I've had it also and could barely bring myself to take it, but it'll ease the pain, Sorley, so ya need to be brave and take it when we ask ya to." Sorley nodded and Thomas laid him back down. Kathleen covered him with two blankets despite the warm April evening. It was an act of reassurance, of Mam's tender care, of love and nurturing, and it was all she had to offer besides the bitter liquid in the little glass jar.

Thomas stood and pulled his father's pocket watch from his coat pocket. It was nearly nine o'clock. He put the watch back in his pocket and began to pace. Kathleen busied herself rather than think about what lay ahead. She took the other bottle from her pocket and put it on the highest shelf in the kitchen. With nothing left to do, and the impending confrontation between Sean and Thomas looming large in the room, she returned to making the soup she had started hours ago. She realized none of them had eaten all day, and though exhausted from the stress and the long walk to and from Dr. Bermann's office, she felt compelled to get something cooking. There was enough bread for a small piece for everyone, but the soup wouldn't be ready for another hour. The bread would have to sustain them until the soup was done.

"Katie, I'm goin' over to Chatham Square to see if I can find Sean."

Katie knew by his tone there was no point in trying to change his mind. She wasn't sure how much more emotional turmoil she could handle, but not having Sean safe at home was also a worry. She nodded and a tear ran out of the corner of her eye, traveling down her cheek and falling to the floor, a tiny raindrop of pain and defeat.

"Onions," she said to cover her weakness.

Thomas left it at that. He knew she was fragile, worn thin, threadbare. He knew that a heated confrontation might be the end of her resolve, which was precisely why he refused to sit there and wait for Sean to arrive home and bring it inside the sad little flat.

CHAPTER FOUR

Sean had ignored the quiet voice of his conscience as he left the children playing in the yard. It was a voice without conviction, and it was easy to disregard. His inner battle raged, a war between his burgeoning independence and a familial tie that was still strong despite his aversion to being asked to play nanny to his younger siblings. As he left he had called out over his shoulder for Eamon to watch the little ones. Eamon was a bright ten-year-old and more responsible than his older brother, but the task was given to Sean and there would be a price to pay for his disobedience if discovered. He knew it, but he convinced himself he didn't care. The young men he had been meeting up with understood his turmoil, his anger and frustration, his refusal to accept that he was just another piece of Irish trash as worthless as the reeking garbage that lined the streets where they lived. Those boys understood it, had lived it, had risen above it, and they offered grand promises of the same way out for Sean Delaney.

Sean arrived at Chatham Square and spotted Reddy McCann. Reddy was leaning against the backside of a nearby flophouse smoking a cigar. At seventeen, he seemed far older than his years, wiser to the world, and he possessed more street savvy than many men twice his age. He had a shock of red hair that gained him his nickname, and his face reminded Sean of the bulldog that came around their tenement hoping for a scrap. Reddy was rough around the edges and not known to be friendly to outsiders, but he had offered a measure of congeniality to Sean after Cow-Legged Sam McCarthy had instructed Reddy to recruit new members into their association. No one Sean had spoken with had ever mentioned the word *gang*, but rather had presented themselves as an association where members could find respect and profit. Because of this, Sean could justify his interest in their invitation knowing full well what sort of association it really was. Reddy had been talking with Sean for a few weeks and was pushing for a decision.

"Sean Delaney," Reddy called out as Sean approached.

Sean waved and then immediately felt like a pathetic culchie. He shoved his hands down into his pockets and put on his best swagger as he approached the older boy. Sean tipped his head upward—a sort of backward nod—in the common greeting used by Reddy and the other fellas. He made a mental note to stop waving at people like an overeager schoolboy, for this was not a place where a child belonged. He had seen every sort of shameful behavior playing out in the dark shadowed alleys, doorways, and back entries of the tattoo parlors, saloons, tobacco shops, and flophouses in the district, and his mother and father would be mortified to know of the assault on his innocence.

"And what are you doing on this fine day wanderin' down here to such an unsavory part of town?" Reddy asked, his question loaded with sarcasm. He had been with Sean the night the younger boy had run off through the square after being spotted by his father. He blew a big puff of smoke at Sean's face. Sean coughed and immediately hated himself for it. Reddy laughed and shook his head.

"We'll make you a man, little Delaney, you can count on that."

"Ya told me to meet ya here today. Somethin' important to tell me, ya said," Sean reminded him. Reddy put out his cigar, grinding it into the dirt and blowing off the excess. He felt the tip to ensure it was no longer hot before putting it in his vest pocket for later.

"Ah, yes, so I did. Well, ya see, it's like this. Cow-Legged Sam has informed the members of our association that we're in need of a few more. Now, keep in mind we ain't just taking any ol' mick. Our members will be involved in certain kinds of, shall we say, activities. These activities are good for the association and good for the members. We all have money in our pockets, Delaney, how about you?"

Sean shook his head in embarrassment. His pockets carried nothing but holes.

"As I expected," Reddy continued. "We can remedy that, sure enough. What we need from you is a sworn oath of allegiance to the association. You've been thinkin' on it for a few days now, Delaney, so we'll be needin' your answer before long. Keep in mind that your life may depend on that allegiance. Once in, you're in for life. Got it?"

Sean nodded and tried to act older than his twelve years. He knew what he wanted. He wanted respect. He wanted enough money so that his family didn't have to eat the scraps from other people's tables. He wanted people to look at him with admiration rather than disgust. And yet, there were things Reddy had mentioned that made Sean uncomfortable. There was an unspoken understanding that the association was indeed a gang. It was a reality in this part of the city. The Five Points District was notorious for gangs, violence, and crime. Sean cleared his throat and took a deep breath before asking the question he wasn't supposed to ask."You're talkin' about a gang, right? That's what your association is?"

"Quiet, little man!" Reddy hissed. Sean had crossed a line. "There are certain things you don't speak of in the light of day! Sure and you're a ripe culchie, aren't ya, now?"

Sean dropped his head a bit. He had felt like a culchie from the moment he had approached Reddy this morning, like an ignorant country farm boy who knew nothing of the life he was pursuing. Mam and Da had done a diligent duty in sheltering their children from the world they lived in, shielding them as much as was possible from the ugly side of the city. Reddy's reaction to his question told Sean everything he needed to know and much of what he didn't want to know. There had been a great battle raging in Sean's heart these past weeks. As badly as he wanted to do more for his family, much more than Mam or Da seemed able to do, he didn't want to wander too far past the line that divided right from very wrong. He didn't want to do anything that would hurt or shame his parents. As ferocious as his anger and bitterness were most of the time, he still loved his family passionately, protectively. It was that deep devotion and concern that drove him to Chatham Square, engaging in conversation with the likes of Reddy McCann, seeking a way to provide even the smallest measure of safety and security for his family.

"You want a taste of somethin' better? You wanna come along on an assignment tonight and see the life you could have?" Reddy's voice was low, serious, and compelling. Sean felt powerless to resist it.

"Aye, but what must I do?" he questioned quieter than before.

"You just come along for the ride, Delaney. It's part of the trainin', so to speak. You'll get a cut and walk away with more than you had when you arrived. Now, when did you last eat?" It had not escaped Reddy's attention that Sean was thinner than he had been a week ago. Reddy McCann remembered being hungry, and he remembered the pain in his belly driving him to accept Bill Lowrie's invitation to be a member of the Daybreak Boys. At the time, upon giving an oath of allegiance, a new member was required to kill someone to show their loyalty. Reddy's hunger was a weightier burden than his conscience, and he killed a dockworker late one night to secure his spot in the gang. Everything changed a year ago when Bill Lowrie was found guilty of robbery and was sentenced to fifteen years at The Tombs. It was then that Cow-Legged Sam McCarthy took over. Reddy had known Sam for two years and did not hesitate to shift his allegiance over to the new leader of the Daybreak Boys, renamed the Wharf Kings by Sam to separate themselves from the previous affiliation.

"I had a piece of bread and some tea last night," Sean admitted in shame. He waited for the belittling and the condescending remarks that were sure to follow. Instead, there was just a hint of compassion in Reddy's response. Sean felt attached, invested, and now part of something that could fill the emptiness in his belly and his spirit.

"Let me show you what your life can be like, Delaney. Follow me," Reddy said. He turned and headed down Chatham to Pearl Street where they turned and walked a long block to the corner of Pearl and Park Street. Sean grew increasingly nervous as they wandered deeper into an ugly world where he had never ventured. The filth and garbage that lined the streets emitted a foul stench that nearly choked him. He caught a glimpse of a bloated carcass of a horse, lying where it had died, too large to carry out and dump elsewhere. There were unsavory characters of all sorts milling about. The men, women and children all had a different look about them, more callous, leering, and intimidating. Sean tried to keep his eyes averted, but it was difficult to avoid the harrowing scenes in every direction. Reddy talked the entire way, telling Sean how most of the Daybreak Boys had been gunned down in a shootout with the police a year ago, and how Sam had regrouped and recruited new members Beeny Cohen from the Marginals gang and Mickey Dillon from the Forty Little Thieves. Together with Reddy and a handful of other surviving members, Sam had formed the Wharf Kings a few months ago. Now they were seeking new members to beef up their ranks and better equip them to work the docks along the East River where the Daybreak Boys had always operated.

"Delaney! Are you hearin' a word I'm sayin'?" Reddy hissed. Sean nodded, his throat too dry to respond with words.

Reddy stopped in front of Muldoon's and beckoned Sean to follow him in. Sean breathed a sigh of relief upon arriving at their destination, thankful to be off the street and unaware that Muldoon's was where the Wharf Kings' headquarters was located. They entered and Sean followed Reddy to the bar and sat down. Muldoon's was dark and unsavory. The windows were coated with a thick film of grease and dirt giving the people outside the appearance of shapeless apparitions floating past. The dark wood of the bar had a sticky grime on it and there were chairs overturned here and there, left where they had fallen like dead soldiers lost in battle. It was not the sort of place where Sean would normally feel safe, but compared to the streets outside it felt like a welcoming haven and Sean was happy to be inside.

"Here, Mona, dish us up somethin' to eat!" Reddy called out. The ruddy-faced woman behind the bar all but ignored Reddy. She mumbled something under her breath about a wee boy in a big man's boots and disappeared into a room behind the bar. Sean's stomach wrenched tight from the smell of food coming from the kitchen, and it nearly doubled him over in pain. Mona returned after a few minutes, her portly frame filling the doorway as she maneuvered through it holding two metal plates piled high with the most wonderful mound of slop Sean had ever laid eyes upon. The woman noticed that the younger boy was nearly drooling, and she did not mistake the drawn look of his face. Like him or not, Reddy had done a good thing by bringing the boy in for some sustenance. Sean fought hard to suppress his emotions before the abundance of food caused him to break.

"Here ya are, lad," Mona said in a stout Scottish accent, setting the plate before Sean with a smile. "Eat slow now, your belly canna handle that much food too quickly." Sean nodded and picked up the spoon she had planted in the middle of a glorious mound of mashed potatoes. He took an enormous bite and nearly wept at the taste of it. There were sausages as well and a great deal of pan sauce poured over it all.

"Slow, Delaney, Mona's right. You'll retch up that pile of food if you eat it too fast and then what good would it do ya?" Reddy cautioned. He started in on his own plate and left Sean to his. There was no conversation between them, the weighty silence of the last supper filled the filthy saloon. Partway through the meal Sean was hit with a powerful wave of guilt. He saw Maeve's thinning face and her big green eyes, he saw Mam pulling her heavy cart filled with firewood just to put a pittance of food on their table, and he thought about the angry cries of Eamon's empty belly in the night as sleep offered some respite from the pain, but despite his guilt he was unwilling to stop eating or to even consider taking any home to share.

Sean was jarred into reality by a shrill scream outside on the street and the sounds of a violent encounter. He could not imagine what might be happening, but he knew it wasn't good. He looked nervously toward the door and then at Reddy who just shook his head and rolled his eyes, long ago having forgotten how fearful he was in the beginning. Sean took a deep breath and wondered if he could finish the last couple of bites on his plate. He sat a moment to rest but before he could decide Mona swept past and scooped up the plate. Sean wasn't sure what bothered him more, that Mona didn't ask if he was done, or the thought of leaving perfectly good food on a plate that someone else was paying for. Probably Reddy.

"Sorry I didn't finish," he said. "I was just takin' a rest."

"It's nothin' to worry over," Reddy replied, "there's plenty more where that came from."

"I feel bad about your payin' for it and me not finishin' it."

"Me? Payin'?" Reddy laughed. This lad was as green as the hills in springtime, and Reddy knew it was going to be easy to recruit him into the gang. "We don't pay, Delaney. This is Molly Muldoon's place and the headquarters for our...association. Molly is Sam's girl, so we eat what we want, when we want. It's part of the package, so to speak."

"It's free?" Sean wondered if his brain was clouded by his overindulgence, for he could not have heard Reddy correctly.

"Free? Well, not exactly, but as I said it's part of the package. We all work for Sam, and he takes care of us. We acquire certain items for him, we bring 'em back here," Reddy paused for a moment as he nodded his head toward a door to the left of the bar, "and then he makes sure we have what we need. We never go hungry, we have coin in our pockets, and we've got protection." Reddy lowered his voice as he spoke of protection. He realized he was talking too loudly and telling too much to a new recruit who hadn't actually agreed to join up.

Sean noticed Reddy's quieting tone and his quick glances around the nearly empty bar, and he followed suit.

"Do I have to hurt anyone?" he whispered.

"Can't make you any promises, Delaney. Count yourself lucky that you came along when you did. When I joined up I had to kill a man to prove my allegiance," he said quietly. He noticed Sean's eyes widening and his jaw dropping slightly, but he continued without defending his past sins. "We lost twelve of our good men in the past year. Sam needs workers now so he's not askin' for recruits to prove themselves the same way I had to. Your word will be enough, but you'll be held to it."

"You killed someone?" Sean's voice was barely above a whisper. "How could you?"

"Look, Delaney, no one brought me into a bar and fed me. No one looked after me. I lived on the streets after my dad got killed. Ma had six other kids younger than me, you get the picture?" Sean nodded. "When your belly is so hungry it hurts," Reddy continued, "it'll drive you to do things you might not otherwise do. I think you can understand that."

"Aye, Reddy, and I'm feelin' sorry for askin'."

"Don't be. Just remember that all the fellas have stories, and all of them came here to work for Sam because they wanted somethin' better. Are you ready for the same, Delaney?"

Sean sat quietly, caught up in a raging whirlwind of thoughts and emotions. He knew undeniably that what he was considering was wrong and that, if discovered, it would be a grave disappointment to Mam. He also knew it would set his father off into a fit of rage that Sean feared to even imagine. He was well aware, especially after coming into this part of the city, that it was a dangerous proposition that could get him hurt or worse. If he was being honest with himself, he was terrified. And yet, he and his family were slowly starving to death. They lived in a world with no respect, no hope, no light at the end of any tunnel, nothing good or encouraging. He was angry at Mam and Da for not being able to take better care of the family, and yet he knew it was not for lack of trying. Sean remembered two nights ago when Sorley had cried for want of just one more piece of bread and there was none to give and how Maeve selflessly gave her brother her own piece. Sean was angry at first that Sorley would take it from her and devour it like he had, but he was well acquainted with the pain that lives in the belly of the poor. Sean had heard Maeve's stomach crying out for a morsel of food all through the night, and it drove him to tears. He could not face a world where their only fate was to sit hopelessly in their rundown flat wasting away until death finally offered its quiet relief.

"I'm ready," Sean replied with more resolve than he felt. There was a detectable note of resignation in Sean's voice, but it was not Reddy's concern to worry over what kind of ethical battle Sean was fighting. If Sean joined up, Reddy would get an extra coin each time they completed a job for Sam. Ethics and morality did not reside in the Five Points District.

Reddy got up from the barstool and beckoned Sean to follow him. They walked toward the door to the left of the bar weaving in and out between the tables, most of which were vacant. Reddy knocked one time on the door, waited a few seconds, and rapped one time again. The door opened and a scraggly character blocked their entrance, leering at Sean with his beady eyes. Sean had a fleeting vision of a scrawny battle-worn stray dog. The man wore a long black overcoat, beneath it a green checkered shirt and blue suspenders. He had a black bowler hat sitting cock-eyed on his head, and his long black hair hung in greasy strands all the way to his shoulders. What teeth he had left were rotten, and his eyes were glazed. Sean assumed the man had been drinking some of Molly Muldoon's whiskey. Sean also assumed that this was their leader, Cow-Legged Sam, for he had the look of someone to be feared, though Sean acknowledged to himself that he did not know what the leader of a gang should look like.

"Why ya bringin' that scrawny pup in here, Reddy McCann?" the man asked. His speech was slurred, and his eyes narrowed further as he questioned Reddy.

"He's got a burnin' hole in his belly and a desire to change that," Reddy replied, showing no fear despite the other man's pointed question. "Sean Delaney, Sow Madden," Reddy offered the quick introduction as he squeezed past the man in the doorway.

"Delaney, huh?" Sow Madden questioned. "You belong to that no-good backstabber James Delaney over on Bayard Street? Ran like a headless chicken and joined up with the Bowery Boys after the shootout. He kin o' yers?" Sow Madden crowed like a rooster and leaned in close. Sean's nose was assaulted with a sickening sweet smell he could not identify. It wasn't whiskey, of that he was certain. He had smelled that more than once when Mr. Callahan had shared a glass of his with Da.

"No, sir, don't know such a person," Sean replied as peals of laughter rang out from inside the room.

"Sir! Oh, Sir Madden, or should I say Sir Sow?" another man called from a table in the corner. More laughter ensued, and Sean hated himself for failing once again to act the part of man. He'd been the brunt of enough scorn and did not want to team up with the Wharf Kings just to be their resident patsy. Reddy had promised him respect, and he hoped to find it there.

Sow Madden turned to yell out an idle threat to the heckler, and Sean slipped past him and caught up with Reddy. He made a mental note to act tougher than he felt. If he were going to survive this he would have to change his demeanor and feign a courage he did not possess. Reddy approached the larger table at the back of the room and directed his attention to the man sitting there behind a tall glass of ale. Sam McCarthy wore a fine suit and a top hat. He had gold chains around his neck and a gold cap over the eyetooth on the right side. It caught the light when he talked, and Sean was enthralled with the idea that someone might have enough money to put gold in their mouth. That tooth could likely feed his family for a month, maybe more. He stared at it, mesmerized, until Reddy broke the spell.

"Hey, Sam," Reddy said, less bold than he had been with Mona or Sow Madden. "I've found us a recruit. He's young and hungry just like I was when Bill gave me a chance."

"How old are you, boy?" Sam demanded, though not aggressively.

"Nearly thirteen."

"You understand what we do here?"

"Yes, I think so."

"You understand what happens to snitches?"

"I imagine I do."

"Make *sure* that you do. You go out with the boys tonight. They'll show you the ropes. You're in, and from here on out you'll be one of us, from now until whenever we decide you can go. The best thing you can do for yourself is watch your step and keep your mouth shut. Wharf Kings business belongs to no one but Wharf Kings. Understood?"

Sean nodded. His mouth was dry as stale breadcrumbs, and he feared his voice would summon nothing more than a raspy croak.

"You got a name?"

Sean swallowed hard, praying he would have a voice when he replied.

"Sean Delaney." It came out right. Sean noticed Sam stiffen at the name, and he reassured him just as he had done with Sow Madden that he was not kin to a James Delaney on Bayard Street.

"It would not bode well for you to be lyin' to me, Delaney," Sam warned.

Sean nodded. He was not so foolish as to set himself up for any trouble with the likes of Sam McCarthy. He followed Reddy out the door and back into the bar. Dusk was settling over the streets outside as Sean and Reddy stood awhile silently watching the comings and goings through the grimy windows. The ghostly figures of peddlers selling their wares, the street children and hungry vagrants who pilfered those wares, the men with ill intent standing in small groups, and the filthy workings of daily life in the streets surrounding the open confluence that formed the Five Points District were, collectively, a clattering opera of the disadvantaged. Sean was mesmerized with, and at the same time horrified by, the unsightly ebb and flow of the dark heart of the city.

"McCann!" A loud voice startled Sean back to the fearful reality of what lay ahead. Someone had hollered at Reddy, and Sean turned to see who it was.

"Red Kelly, where've ya been?" Reddy approached the other man, the two redheads both fittingly nicknamed.

"Bah! I tried makin' my way up to Philly to make an honest living in the mines, but my poor heart was yearnin' for the sight of your ugly mug," Red Kelly offered. The truth of the matter was that an honest day's work did not appeal to a veteran criminal accustomed to taking what he wanted. "I let Sam know I was back and he was glad to have me."

"Aye, it'll be good for the group. Sam's been carryin' on about losin' too many fellas. We've been recruitin', and I've got Sean here givin' his pledge and comin' along tonight." Reddy nodded in Sean's direction and Sean nodded back.

"Fresh meat, eh?" Red Kelly laughed at his own quip. "That's good, we'll need it. I met up with Chick McFee and Kid Coffey over on Mulberry. They're in tonight. Anyone else?"

"Spanish Marley should be here, too," Reddy added. "That'll make six of us, countin' Sean. Sam got a tip yesterday that *The Wanderer* would be dockin' today at the James Slip. Word is she's carryin' a good deal of silver items for the holy joes across town. We can go out in one skiff, be quick about it, and get back in good time to get our cut."

"Aye, and I like the way you think, McCann," Red Kelly replied.

Sean listened with both ears, his mind swimming with odd names and unsettling questions. There was little left to the imagination but enough to give cause to some worrisome thoughts. What if they were discovered trying to steal the valuables from *The Wanderer*? What if a guard or crewman had to be injured, or worse, in order for them to finish the job? What if the skiff overturned? Sean could not swim, though he would not let the others know it. He knew that his survival would depend on him creating a tough persona, an unyielding façade that would look hardened to outsiders. Sean knew that façade would crumble under duress, but he resolved to maintain it as long as he could.

Reddy McCann and Red Kelly could barely contain their excitement over what lay ahead. They gathered up several burlap sacks from a closet near the back of the bar. Reddy handed a few to Sean and led the way out of the bar and down Pearl Street, crossing over on Cherry to James and down James to the slip. Sean remembered being told he was just going along to observe but now with sacks in hand he was certain it would be more than that. The skiff was stored in Sam McCarthy's shack at the harbor. When the trio arrived, they were met by Kid Coffey, Chick McFee, Spanish Marley and another man, Danny Hurley. Sean was immediately wary of Hurley. He was the largest man Sean had ever seen. It was said that he was seven feet tall and could break a man's leg with his bare hands. His height was an exaggeration, his strength was not. Sean was unaware of his infamous reputation, but he didn't like the look of him. His eyes were too small for his head and set far apart. Reddy could tell that Sean was growing hesitant. He stood next to the recruit and clarified the plan in a quiet voice.

"Hurley isn't comin' along for the boat ride, Delaney, he'd sink the bloody skiff!" Reddy whispered. Sean responded with a nervous laugh. "He's our distraction," Reddy continued. "He wanders down to the dock where the ship is moored and causes a ruckus. While any of the crewmen left on board attend to the Irish giant, we make quick work aboard ship."

Sean felt himself relax. Not only would Hurley not be in the skiff, but he would also be lessening their chances of a run-in with a crew member. The sky was dark now, but the nearby streetlamp stole some of their cover. Sean looked on nervously as Chick McFee unlocked the padlock on the boat shack door and employed the help of Marley and Kid Coffey to remove the skiff and the oars. Sean could not prevent himself from glancing around, hoping to see no one but afraid that he would. The boys left the open lock hanging on the hasp so that when they returned they could get the skiff back inside quickly and disappear onto the streets under the cover of a starless night.

They lowered the skiff into the East River, and the six members of the Wharf Kings, including Sean Delaney, climbed down the dock ladder and loaded into the rowboat. Sean was impressed with the rowing skills of Red Kelly, his oars barely causing a ripple on the surface of the water as they floated along, silently skimming the calm shoreline of the river. They were at the James Slip in a matter of minutes. The area seemed deserted, which was normally the case as crewmembers went ashore for a much-needed break from life at sea. It was Saturday evening and most of the men from most of the ships were enjoying the festivities on Catharine Street. The noise from the marketplace could be heard from the slip, offering another welcome element of distraction. The weekly festivities just two blocks to the east made Saturday night the best time to board a ship and steal its valuable contents. Music, singing, shouting, barking dogs, and all forms of revelry filled the air.

Danny Hurley's job was easier on a Saturday night. He smiled as he approached the dock where *The Wanderer* was moored. Her sails were down and secured to the masts. Danny made his way from the wharf up the gangplank on the port side and onto the deck of the schooner. He stood a moment and listened. If there were any life on board there was no sign of it, no movement, and no sound but the lapping of the water against the ship's hull. Danny wandered to the bow and around to the starboard side of the boat. He listened again but heard nothing. He gave a low whistle much like the mournful cooing of a dove. The skiff was already tied to a piling near the wooden ladder that led up to the dock, and the Wharf Kings sat quietly awaiting Danny's signal that it was safe to board. When Reddy heard the whistle he grabbed a few burlap sacks and silently beckoned for his mates to do the same. One by one they climbed up and made their way to the port side of *The Wanderer* where the gangplanks allowed passage onto the ship.

To ensure the safety of the mission, Danny began to sing a rather boisterous version of an Irish folk tune. He inflected a slur into his words so that he sounded intoxicated, a ruse he often used to divert the attention of any watchmen stationed on board. As the gang members crossed the deck and descended the ladder into the cargo hold, two of the ship's crewmembers wandered onto the deck to see what the wailing was about. Their attention stayed focused on the starboard side as the hold below was being ransacked.

"You, there! What are doing on board this ship?" Danny's singing and the crewman's yelling awakened the other two men on board. They quickly made their way to the deck, and the four of them approached the obviously drunken man who had likely wandered there from Catharine Street. They kept a safe distance until they could assess the situation.

> "Says my auld one to your auld one
> We've got no beef nor mutton
> But if we go down to Monto town
> We might get drunk for nuttin'
> Here's a piece of good advice
> I got from an auld fishmonger
> When food is scare, and you see the hearse
> You'll know you've died of hungerrrrr..."

Danny's booming baritone rang out over the water as he sang all the verses of *Waxie's Dargle* without pause. The ship's crewmen looked at each other with empty expressions and no good thought on how to deal with the serenading giant. He wasn't hurting anything, but there would be swift retribution from the captain if he returned early and found them being entertained by an uninvited and intoxicated guest. On the other hand, the Irishman was a formidable sight and did not look like he would be easy to take down. While the four crewmen worried over how to deal with the intruder, Danny was happy to see that there were only four sailors to contend with, an easy task for the big man.

"Here, now!" the bigger of the crewmen yelled, "you need to get on out of here and back to where you came from!" Danny sang through the command with a wide grin across his face.

"What are we going to do with him, Razo?" his shipmate asked.

"He can't stand against the four of us, boys," Razo called out over Danny's serenade.

"I'm not so sure," argued a younger and more frightened crewman, "he's huge!"

While the crewmen continued to search for a solution to their musical dilemma, hollering empty threats while Danny sang, the boys below deck filled their sacks with silver platters and pitchers, tableware, and jewelry. Sean was hesitant and slightly annoyed that the promise of simply going along for the ride may have been a ruse to gain an extra pair of hands. There was nothing to do now but watch and learn and follow the lead of the other fellas. They worked swiftly and quietly, and when their sacks were full they climbed back up the ladder to the upper deck. Reddy was first up. He saw no one about and waved the others up. The prospect of such an easy heist was almost too good to be true. As Sean emerged—the last of the thieves to do so—he heard Crewman Razo yell from the other side of the ship.

"Let's get him!" There was the sound of shuffling feet. Danny's serenade stopped, and the obvious sounds of a confrontation followed.

Reddy and the others walked quickly and quietly across deck and down the gangplanks. They arrived at the ladder and climbed back down to their waiting skiff as the sound of something hitting the water garnered their attention. There was no time to stop and investigate. Once they were all safely in, Red Kelly rowed away from the wharf. As they departed, they could see the large form of Danny Hurley still on board and two reluctant swimmers in the water below. Danny waved his massive arms in the air and let loose with a holler that compelled the other two crewmen to run. His work was done for the night. He would collect payment from Cow-Legged Sam tomorrow. For now, he would wander over to Catharine Street and have himself some fun. A fight or two, a pretty girl, and a healthy portion of Irish whiskey would be a fitting end to a good night's work.

The Wharf Kings returned to the James Street harbor and unloaded the skiff. Spanish Marley and Chick McFee got the skiff back into the shack and locked up in a matter of minutes. The group split up, taking different routes back to headquarters so as not to draw attention to themselves. A single man carrying a sack on his back would not be an unusual sight, but a group of six would likely raise suspicion. Reddy allowed Sean to walk back with him along Cherry to Pearl Street and back to Muldoon's the way they had come. Sean was not yet familiar with the streets in the district, and Reddy did not want to risk having him wander and get lost. Alone and confused, Sean would be an open invitation to be followed, waylaid, and robbed of Sam's goods. They walked without talking, and Sean's mind became clouded with the dark reality of what he had just done. The terror he felt during the robbery had kept his feet and hands moving, following the lead of the others and pilfering whatever looked valuable. His normalcy was likely gone forever, lost now in a world of deception, denial, and secrecy. He thought about what he had done and how, in a few minutes aboard *The Wanderer*, his life was irreversibly changed. He felt detached from himself. He surely must be moving about in a dream, a wild fantastical dream created in his still-boyish imagination. His feet kept moving him forward, quickly and purposefully, and the sack he carried over his shoulder felt as heavy as his faltering conscience. They hurried on through the dark neighborhood, Sean thankful he could not see what unknown dangers surrounded them. He could hear Reddy's breath coming hard in the damp darkness, his own as well. He was grateful that the streetlamps that lined the harbors and the shoreline were not as well-maintained in and around the Five Points District. The darkness was a welcome refuge.

The six members reunited at Muldoon's, and there was an unspoken excitement surrounding the contents of the sacks they carried with them. Sam McCarthy was waiting, standing at the back of the room with his back against the wall, his fingers tapping against it behind him. His pock-marked face was serious, and the flickering lantern light caused a harsh shadow to dance across it. Sean glanced sideways at Sam, only for a moment, and thought now that his polish had been replaced by a sinister countenance. Each member had a sack—Kid Coffey had two—and they were all put on the floor in the middle of the room. With everyone accounted for, Sow Madden arose from his chair and locked the door. The only outsider in the room was Frank Grimmel, the junkman that Sam regularly conducted business with after a heist. Grimmel, a long-time criminal fence, never asked where the stolen items came from. The less he knew, the better. He was in the business of buying, selling, and trading items of value. Upon hearing the clinking of the silver items in the burlap sacks, Grimmel had risen from his chair and approached the sacks with great interest.

Sean watched as Sam made his way toward the pile of loot and for the first time Sean saw why Sam was known as Cow-Legged Sam. For all his finery and put-on airs, Sam McCarthy had a severe clubfoot which caused his body to stand crooked, affecting his gait with a profound limp. Sean immediately drew his eyes away so that Sam would not see his wide-eyed stare. McCarthy stopped in front of Reddy.

"How did the frightened pup do tonight?"

"He did good, Sam. He followed directions, paid attention, and went to work as soon as we were aboard ship."

"That true, Delaney? You're willing to work for a place around our table?"

Sean nodded and glanced up at Sam's face. There were scars not noticeable from across the room and his eyes were bloodshot and slightly cloudy. Sam's response to Sean's acceptance of his invitation was a hearty slap to the shoulder that nearly sent the boy across the room. Sow Madden laughed aloud at the boy, and Sean determined at that moment that he did not like anything about Sam's trusty henchman. He was certain there was a black heart beneath the checkered shirt and blue suspenders.

As Sam and Frank Grimmel began the lengthy process of sorting through the goods and bartering a price for it all, Mona was summoned for food to be served. Sean ate again, even after the enormous meal earlier that afternoon, and as he did he wondered what time it was. His eyelids felt heavy, and his body was exhausted. He would do his best to hide it from the men in the room, but he was eager to get home. The prospect of what lay ahead lit a new flame of fear in his heart. Da would go off like the Chinese fireworks that lit up the river last July fourth. Mam would cry at his rebellious behavior and the growing distance between Sean and the rest of the family. And the boys and Maeve would huddle in the corner and pretend to play while hearing every word of the argument that would ensue. Suddenly the food had no flavor, and Sean felt like he would retch if he took another bite. He would think carefully about coming back here and doing something like this again, though something told him he would have little choice in the matter. He had already given his allegiance, and any attempt to back out now would not be taken favorably.

"Delaney!" Cow-Legged Sam yelled a second time, shaking Sean from his musings. He had returned to his table and was gathering the boys around it. "Are ya with us, or are ya already fast asleep and dreamin'?" Again, the mocking laughter of Sow Madden pierced the room.

"Sure and I'm with ya Sam. Just thinkin'," Sean replied.

"Thinking about your cut, were ya? Wondering how much you'd be taking out of here tonight?" Sam was taunting, but not in the searing manner that came from Sow Madden. "Come here, boy."

Sean stood up and walked to Sam's table. Approaching the throne, he thought to himself. He was in the presence of the king, alone and unprotected. He suddenly wished Da were nearby. He felt small and powerless. It was not the place or time to tuck tail and run, and he stepped up to Sam's table as instructed. There was a large pile of coin and paper money on the table, so much so that Sean's fear rose again and rattled his resolve. This was serious business, and he had willingly signed on to be a partner in it. His brain was losing the ability to focus as the terrifying realization of who and what he was came flooding in.

"Reddy tells me you did everything the rest of the boys did, that you were an equal partner in the execution of our mission tonight. We need men like you," Sam said in a serious tone, baiting Sean with the proven tactic of referring to young recruits as men. "The cops murdered twelve good men from the Daybreak Boys. We're down to a mighty small crew—a good one, mind you—but we're in need of some beefing up. You understand?"

"I do, Sam." What else could he say? One night's participation was the sealing wax on the envelope, and he knew it. There would be no walking away.

"You earned your place here tonight, Delaney. You'll have another chance to prove that you're worth your salt in a few days. McCann will let you know where and when, you just need to be around and be close enough to find when we need you. Got it?"

Sean nodded. Of course he agreed. He was standing before the almighty ruler of the Wharf Kings, and the Daybreak Boys before that, backed up and protected by the leering parasite, Sow Madden.

"All right. Grimmel has paid a handsome sum for our merchandise. Move in closer, boys," Sam beckoned with a slight jerk of his head. Everyone moved in close to collect their cut, even Sow Madden who did nothing but sit in his chair and watch the door. Sean liked him even less now knowing he would get paid for the risk the other fellas had taken. He wondered about the immunity Sam gave so freely to someone like Sow Madden and decided there had to be a history there. Maybe Sow had saved Sam's life somewhere along the line. Maybe he was family. Sean's mind wandered again, and he was drawn deep into his thoughts until his ears heard the counting. Sam was doling out the cuts. He chided himself for letting his mind wander so easily and forced himself to pay attention to what was happening in front of him.

Sam was counting out each man's share, all equal except for the cut he kept for himself which was removed before the counting began. Though he fought hard to act like a seasoned ruffian, Sean knew he was wide-eyed with wonder at the sight of the small fortune Sam pushed toward him. Sean came from a home where the man of the house had never earned more than a dollar or two in a week, on a rare and profitable week, where the man's wife was paid in firewood, and where money usually came in the form of pennies and dimes and half dimes. Sean composed himself and wisely decided to delay the count until he was home. From what he could see there were several silver dollar coins—maybe six or seven of them—and a small handful of gold dollar coins numbering about the same as the silver. He noticed one larger gold coin, too, and had no idea what it was. Where, when, and how to safely count his earnings were questions racing through his mind as his feet remained planted beside Sam's table.

"Delaney, you got a problem with the cut?" Sam asked. Sean realized he had been standing there lost in his thoughts while the other fellas had walked away, and that he had not retrieved the cut Sam placed in front of him.

"No, Sam." Sean's answer was firm but subdued as he forced himself to put the childish excitement to rest. "More than satisfied."

"You're in, then?"

"I'm in." With his fortune before him, glinting in the light of the nearby lantern like the riches of Solomon, Sean was all the way in. His mam had read to them many times the proverb warning that the love of money is the root of all evil. It made sense to him now, for the first time in his young life, but the dire warning would not change his mind.

The other fellas had pocketed their payment and the group disbanded. Reddy beckoned for Sean to come along. Sean gathered his cut, placed it in his pocket, and followed Reddy out of the back room and across the saloon to the door. Once outside Sean stammered, embarrassed again by his boyish innocence.

"I ... I'm not sure how ..."

"I got ya," Reddy answered back, knowing Sean would never find his way back out to Chatham Square alone in the dark. "C'mon."

Sean followed Reddy in silence. He wondered where Reddy lived, where he would go to count his money and lay his head down to sleep. He wondered if Reddy lived alone, and if he lived in a rundown tenement or a nice home with food in the cupboards and comforts around him. He wanted to ask but didn't. They neared the more familiar surroundings of Chatham Square and continued another block or two before Reddy spoke.

"Where you livin', Delaney?"

"On down Division a ways," Sean answered vaguely. For the most part he trusted Reddy but giving out the exact location of his apartment would risk more than he was willing.

"I'll be with ya another couple blocks. I'm stayin' at a place over on Forsyth."

Sean nodded and again they walked in silence along Division Street until it was time for Reddy to turn towards home.

"You can make it from here," Reddy said matter-of-factly. It was the best he could do to sound encouraging, and he refused to show a soft spot for the boy who reminded him of a younger version of himself. If he remained tough he would show the boy how to do the same. It might save his life one day.

"I can. I know where I am now." Sean sounded confident even to his own ears. Though he knew where he was, he had never been out this late by himself and the darkness felt oppressive.

"Be around," the older boy called out over his shoulder as he turned up Forsyth and slowly disappeared into the darkness.

The air was thick with mist floating in off the river, and it felt cooler than it really was. Sean pulled his thin jacket tighter around him and felt the weight of the coins in his jacket pocket. They felt heavy, like a burden. *Dirty money is heavier than clean,* he reflected, and what he now carried with him was far heavier than the first ten pennies he had stolen a month ago in Chatham Square. Da was furious over the likelihood that they were stolen, dirty and dishonest. Sean thought about the battle he would walk into at home arriving after dark and without an acceptable explanation. He told himself that no matter what Da said, and no matter how many tears escaped from Mam's eyes, this night had been worth the risks he had taken. Another just like it would be as well.

The weight of the coins caused Sean to stop and consider how easily Da could discover them. If things got physical between father and son, if Da grabbed him or shook him the jingling of the coins would be heard. The loot would be confiscated, and the retribution for having obtained money in a disreputable manner would be swift and unpleasant. Sean remembered the cotton handkerchief in his other pocket. He pulled it out and was grateful that it was as threadbare as every other bit of fabric the Delaney's owned. It was easy to tear a thin strip off the edge. Sean placed the coins in the middle of the cotton square, drew in the opposite corners, and tied them together to form a little purse. He lifted his pant leg and used the strip of cloth to tie the coin purse to his calf just below the knee, the strip easily encompassing his thin leg. The baggy pant leg would not reveal it there, and it would be safe until he could find some time alone to tally his earnings.

Two blocks from home, at the corner of Division and Jefferson, a sudden movement in the dark caused Sean to jump back, his heart pounding for fear he would be robbed or beaten.

"Where've ya been?" The voice of his father, void of life and seething with anger, turned his fear to terror.

"Da?"

"Aye, your da. The very one ya shame by runnin' around all night while your family fears the worst and your brother lays in pain with the hope of not losin' his leg."

"What happened?" Sean's mind was reeling, trying to piece together the strange and sudden rush of information. Why was Da here in the dark, lurking and likely waiting for him? What brother? What pain? Losing a leg? Nothing made sense.

"You answer my question, boy. Where have ya been?"

"Just wanderin' around with some friends, but what happened? Is it Eamon or Sorley? What's wrong, Da?"

"You defied your mother and your father, and you left the children alone while ya wandered off to be a big man. Sorley fell hard on a shard of glass which lodged in his knee, and he may never use that leg again."

"Oh, no!" Sean's voice was full of concern, sadness, and guilt. "Da, I'm s ..."

"Do NOT apologize to me. We're beyond that now. You have defied us more than once and this will end now. I will not engage in a battle with ya here on the street, and I will not bring this home and into the presence of your sufferin' brother, Sorley. But it is not over. Do ya understand me, Sean Michael Delaney?"

"Aye, Da," Sean whispered. He turned and followed his father back to their flat. His heart was heavy with grief now, plagued with guilt over the pain Sorley was experiencing, and the sadness he had brought to Mam and Eamon and Maeve. The defiant voice in his head, now somewhat subdued, argued that the coins tied to his leg were worth it all, and that if he chose to share them with his family they would all benefit from his unscrupulous behavior. But the child that still lived in some small part of his soul wanted to cry out, to beg forgiveness, to weep in the arms of his mam until she soothed his guilt away.

The night was tense and quiet and accompanied by the moans and whimpering from Sorley who lay in the bed next to Kathleen. Thomas spent most of the night awake wishing he could take away all the pain his family had suffered. The pain of Sorley's injury, the pain of starving bellies, the pain of hatred and shame. All were tangible, aggressive, and unfairly cast upon them, thrust their way without care or concern by people who judged without cause, and Thomas was tiring of the battle. Sleep evaded Kathleen as well, dozing off intermittently when exhaustion defeated her resolve to be awake should Sorley need her. In the darkness they worried over their sons—the one lying beside his mam, and the one sleeping on the floor next to his siblings, slipping away into an existence they feared would take him from them forever.

CHAPTER FIVE

Sunday morning brought uncertainty to the breakfast table. The usual fare was set before each chair, minus one where Sorley usually sat. He remained in his parents' bed, groggy from the laudanum and grateful for the rescue it gave him. Thomas stared at the food on the table with a grave sense of regret. Tea and bread. Weak tea and drying bread with no butter to spread upon it. Sean glanced over at the bookcase. He had waited for one small window of time during the night when he could hear his father's gentle snoring. When he was certain Thomas was sleeping soundly, he had quietly crawled over and stashed his handkerchief purse beneath the little bookcase far back against the wall and out of sight. What a grand feast he could provide his family if only he took a couple of those coins and went to Catharine Street.

"Ya lookin' for somethin'?" The tone of Da's voice from across the breakfast table told Sean that he was still angry.

"No, Da."

"If you're wishin' your brother was here at the table with us, well, that would be your own fault. When he wakes up and isn't under the spell of that laudanum, you need to find yourself grovelin' at his bedside. Understand?"

"Aye."

Maeve looked down at her crumbling bread and wrestled with her sorrow. Her heart was breaking for Sorley and the uncertainties he faced, but also for her oldest brother and the burden of guilt he must be carrying. He had been wrong to leave them unattended, but his guilt alone should be punishment enough. She looked up, her green eyes sparkling from the water that threatened to spill over in tiny rivers of pain. She swallowed hard.

"Are ya still hungry, Sean?" She asked so quietly that he almost didn't hear her.

"No, Maeve, you eat." If Sean's heart wasn't breaking over Sorley's accident, it was surely breaking now. Maeve was thin, and her lovely green eyes looked far too big for her face. The familiar features of hunger had become more prevalent over the past few weeks, and she looked much like the endless sea of starving immigrants who inhabited the city. Sean had enough money to feed his family, probably for several weeks, but until he devised a believable lie it would stay hidden. Like Thomas and Kathleen, Sean's sleep had been fitful and tortured. He had lain awake most of the night rationalizing his behavior and justifying his thievery. He had stolen items of value from those who had more than their share so that those without a means to survive could eat. Any way he mulled it over and dissected it, it didn't look like a sin to him.

Da stood abruptly, knocking his chair backward and onto the floor. He was obviously angry, though it was difficult to tell if his anger was still directed at Sean or something else. Everyone waited, including Kathleen. The children averted their eyes, but Kathleen looked him square in the face. The emotional turmoil was wearing her nerves raw, her heart was tender and bruised, and there was little more she could endure.

"Tommy?" She said his name firmly, disguising the weakened condition of her spirit. If he began to rail at Sean, or anyone else for that matter, it would be her breaking point.

"I'm headin' down to Catharine Street. Times there were on a Sunday mornin' when a merchant would pay a coin or two to help with some extra clean up after the Saturday night hooley. Maybe they still do. This family needs somethin' on the table besides a loaf of stale bread." Thomas turned toward the door, paused a moment with his hand on the knob, and looked back over his shoulder to fix his dark eyes on Sean's face. "No one goes out. Anywhere." Sean nodded and his siblings followed suit.

Mam stood and walked to the door, following Thomas out into the hallway and pulling the door half closed behind her. She lightly kissed his cheek and whispered in his ear so the children would not hear.

"Take care, Tommy, and try to let go of some anger. It'll do nothin' to change our fate, and the weight of it will wear on ya night and day." Thomas leaned back and looked into Kathleen's deep green eyes, so full of pain and sympathy that it caused his own to well up. She was right and he knew it, but anger seemed his constant companion of late. He brushed a tendril of auburn hair off her cheek and put his arms around her. He held her tight to him, trying hard to absolve his guilt. When Thomas took a step back, she saw the tears on his cheeks.

"What is it, my love?" she asked softly, fully closing the door to hide their conversation.

"I can't sit here any longer and watch our children wither away and die, no better off than if we'd stayed in Ireland. Hunger is a relentless beast and it's got us one step from the grave. I could scarce control my sadness and my ragin' guilt when Maeve offered her bread to Sean. It's rippin' me to pieces, Katie."

"Tis not your fault, Tommy. We came here with a dream, full of promise, but the fates have not allowed us to realize that dream."

"Have ya seen her face, Katie, so thin and pale? I should never have brought us here. I should never have believed a dream that seemed too good to be possible, for now I know that it was naught but an empty promise. And still we suffered the journey, and we brought two more babies into this life of sufferin'. Now as I watch our precious Maeve fade into a shadow of herself it is a pain I cannot bear. 'Tis a pain *she* should not have to bear. She should not have to suffer for the dreams of her father." Thomas's last words were weak and defeated.

"Tommy," she said in a whisper, caressing his cheek with her hand, "ya know Maeve would never lay the blame for our sufferin' on you."

"And that's what makes it so difficult to bear," he replied, broken.

Kathleen's resolve was crumbling, and she turned away. She knew that nothing she could say at that moment would soothe her husband's pain or guilt. Thomas dropped his head and turned to walk the long hallway, carrying his heavy burden of grief like a millstone around his neck. For the children's sake, Kathleen put on a fresh face as she re-entered the flat. She would be strong for them, attend her maternal duties, keep light the mood, and cover over the fearful reality of what their future held if something didn't change.

"All right, everyone, time to roll up our bedding and tidy up."

Thomas reflected on Kathleen's words of comfort as he walked toward Catharine Street. Though his grief and anger had not left him, his anger was tempered by the great love he had for his family. He was determined to put that anger to action and to find a way to save them from the relentless grip of hunger and hopelessness. Thomas knew that his anger at Sean was driven by a greater fear that something sinister would happen to him. He resolved himself to find out what Sean had been doing and to do so in a way that did not drive him further from them. He breathed deep and relaxed his shoulders. The morning sun was already hot as he walked to the ferry slips. April's typically mild temperatures had grown unseasonably warm lending unwanted heat to the unpleasant temperament of the overcrowded city. He passed an alley where two men were fighting, likely still intoxicated from last night's revelry. Three stray dogs were tangled in their own fight just up the street, and Thomas crossed over to the other side to avoid ending up in the middle of it. Fighting. Everywhere he looked, there was conflict of one sort or another. The city was turning on itself, and intolerance grew more heated as the chill of the cooler seasons evaporated.

He made good time and arrived at the market before all the vendors were open. Thomas headed directly for Mrs. Zimmer's vegetable stand and greeted the kind woman with a grand, sweeping bow. He inquired after her brother-in-law who had taken ill a few weeks before.

"Ah, Mr. Delaney, thank you for asking. He is doing better, and it appears he'll be good as new in due time. He was two steps from the grave there for a while, but the good Lord has chosen to let him stay a while longer."

"Good news, indeed," Thomas responded sincerely.

"What can I do for you today, Mr. Delaney?"

"I was wonderin' if you might know if any of the shopkeepers need some extra cleanup, Mrs. Zimmer," Thomas replied. "I'm lookin' to earn a coin or two. Seems as though the regular crew has been slackin' on their duties lately and now that I think about it I haven't seen the normal fella around in a while."

"Oh, yes, poor Mr. Petri," she said. She shook her head slightly, indicating bad news.

"What was it, Mrs. Zimmer, the typhoid?"

"No, dear me, they slit his neck from ear to ear. It was a gang, or so they say, and no one has the courage to ask any more about it. He was leaving an establishment in the Five Points when it happened, and that is all I know."

The reality of the danger Sean might be entertaining hit Thomas to the core. He stood quietly, his face slightly pale as the fear for his son's well-being won out over his anger. He would work on showing some compassion to his son when he continued their conversation.

"I'm sorry, Mr. Delaney. I can see the sadness on your face. I didn't know you were friends with poor Mr. Petri."

"Ah, no," answered Thomas. "Just a sad thing and sure enough this city is more dangerous by the day."

"True, true. I'd not want to be raising a family here and now, begging your pardon."

"'Tis how I'm feelin' myself, Mrs. Zimmer."

Mrs. Zimmer looked past Thomas to someone crossing the street behind him. She waved and called out to a man named Henry. The man was in a policeman's uniform and Thomas could not help but feel a soup pot of boiling emotions as he came nearer. He had a broad chest and a square face suggesting a stern countenance, but he smiled as he approached and greeted Mrs. Zimmer kindly. She introduced Henry Engel to Thomas.

"Forgive me, Henry, for not introducing you as *Sergeant* Engel for you have worked hard to earn that title," Mrs. Zimmer apologized. She turned back to Thomas, "Henry's parents, God rest their souls, came to America when we did. Henry was a brave boy on the journey across the ocean, weren't you, Henry?"

"If you say so, Mrs. Zimmer. It all felt like a grand adventure to a ten-year-old boy. Fifteen years later I can see what a hardship it was for my parents and for the rest of those immigrating over from Europe." He turned to Thomas. "I'm sure you know what I mean, Mr. Delaney, if you and your family came over on such a voyage."

"Indeed, I do. It's been a tough row to hoe, as they say."

"Henry," Mrs. Zimmer interjected, "Mr. Delaney is looking for a bit of work. He's willing to help with the cleanup from last night's festivities. Do you have something for him?"

"Are you willing to push a broom, Mr. Delaney?" Sergeant Engel asked. The police department was in charge of enforcing and supervising sanitation measures in the city, as much as was possible. Certain areas like the Five Points District were rarely serviced as it would take much more than a man and a broom to clean up the stench, rubbish and filth that littered that area of the city. That, combined with the danger that lurked at every corner and alleyway, compelled the city government to turn their eyes away and let the district wallow in its own filth. The streets near the docks, however, were frequented by merchants and visitors alike, and the city made more of an effort to keep them presentable.

"Aye! Show me the way!" Thomas said with a sincere enthusiasm that Sergeant Engel did not miss. He also didn't miss the lean look, the receding fullness of a face ravaged by hunger, and the bony look of hands willing to work but denied the opportunity. Henry was determined to give

Thomas a fighting chance. A few coins in his pocket could save the man and his family from fading into the vaporous abyss where starving souls disappear to find eternal relief from the pain in their bellies.

Thomas followed the sergeant after offering a wink and a gentlemanly bow to Mrs. Zimmer. At the end of the street near the dock was a small shed. Henry unlocked the lock on the door and retrieved a large cart, a shovel, and a wide flat broom from inside.

"Here you are, Mr. Delaney. The department authorizes me to hire street sweepers to keep this area as safe and as clean as possible. We get a lot of visitors from across the river to the market, and they bring in revenue for the city. We don't have the workforce or the money to keep the entire city clean, though heaven knows it needs it. There's talk of a new department forming just to oversee sanitation. I'm hoping that happens," Henry said, realizing he had been rambling. "Unfortunately, we recently hired a new man to replace our previous sweeper but seeing as how you're a friend of Mrs. Zimmer I can hire you on as an assistant to Leo. It would only be part time, I'm afraid. Leo is new, and not overly fast. The vendors here on Catharine Street expect a certain level of cleanliness in order to maintain their businesses. I could use you Fridays to prepare for the Saturday night event, and then again on Sunday afternoons to help clean it all up. It normally pays a dollar and a half a day, but the merchants have set up a fund to share the burden of keeping the area clean. I pay Leo two dollars a day, and I can pay you the same. You'll get the full pay for your shorter afternoon shift on Sunday because there will be twice the work in half the time. Are you willing?"

"Aye! 'Tis been forever and a day since I had regular work." Thomas tried to hide the emotion in his voice, but his sense of gratitude and relief nearly got the best of him.

"Well, it'll be just two days a week unless Leo doesn't work out. I can let you know. For now, we'll need you to clean the rubbish from both sides of the street, from the dock to Chatham Square." Thomas bristled at the mention of Chatham Square but gave Henry his full attention. "I'll let you get started since you'll need to learn the ropes, but next Sunday I won't need you until noon. The market still has a lot of visitors and a lot of things going on until midday. Your cleaning duties include storefronts, the alleys behind the establishments, and the area surrounding the loading dock behind us, which usually gets done last. The rubbish is deposited there," Henry pointed to a large mound of garbage confined by wooden slats on three sides near the loading dock, "where it is picked up by a barge once a week."

"Got it, Sergeant. And I'll be thankin' ya for myself and my family when we've got more than a dry loaf of bread on our table."

"Happy to help, Mr. Delaney. Leo started on this side of the street an hour ago. Why don't you start across the street and work your way along until the two of you meet up. If he has any questions, send him to me. You'll find me in the dockmaster's office over there," Henry pointed again, "at the end of your shift. I can pay you then."

Thomas nodded, more encourated than he'd been in a long time. He placed the flat-edged shovel and the broom in the cart and headed across the street to begin his new job. It wasn't much, but even two days a week would put food on their table and keep the proverbial wolves at bay. Cleaning and sweeping would likely invite some derogatory remarks from passersby, but he cared not. He would allow nothing to take this opportunity from him. He would ignore the insults and stay focused, grateful to earn enough to save his family from starvation.

Thomas busied himself with the tasks he had been given—sweeping, shoveling the rubbish left behind by careless Saturday night crowds, and the numerous trips back to the garbage pile to empty the cart. He spoke with people along the way, most of them shopkeepers, and most were relatively friendly. Some of them thanked him for cleaning up and those, he determined, were the ones he would take extra care of in the future. Caselli the butcher was opening shop when Thomas arrived in front of his establishment. The hulking Italian opened his front door and stepped out onto the landing wearing yesterday's dirty apron, the blood of dead animals staining the once-white canvas. Thomas was ready for the insults, and they came sure enough.

"Well, well, look at the mick pushing a broom like a lady's maid!" Thomas went about his work without acknowledging the man. "About time you stopped begging for crumbs and went to work like a real man, although I'm not sure sweeping is a real man's work." The swarthy butcher laughed all the way back inside his shop, and Thomas cursed under his breath. Antonio Caselli could laugh all he wanted. Thomas was desperate to save his family no matter the heartless insults from men with no souls and no conscience.

When he arrived at the next block Thomas stopped what he was doing, rolled up his shirt sleeves, and wiped his brow with his forearm. Though the bright morning sun was growing uncomfortable, it reflected his newly optimistic frame of mind. He hoped Kathleen wouldn't worry about where he was, or how long he was gone. He would be delayed further by stopping on the way home to purchase a few items for his family, but what a grand surprise it would be. There was a small market a block over, at the corner of Monroe and Market Street, where he often stopped when he had a coin or two to spare. It was owned by an Irish man who had come to New York several years before the Delaneys. He had watched the decline of the city as more and more immigrants landed in America, and it saddened him to see their struggles. Seamus Carnahan did his best to add something extra to the sack when customers like Thomas came by. Thomas enjoyed contributing to the Irishman's success, though his contribution was miniscule. He looked forward to stopping there before heading home at the end of his workday.

***

For Kathleen and the children, the morning passed like molasses in February. The day was warm and the flat was stuffy and uncomfortable, but no one dared to leave and go outside for a bit of air. Da's dire warning still hung heavy in the room, a lingering presence, a dark cloud unseen but detectable. Sorley drifted in and out of sleep, crying when he was awake and moaning when he slept, which was a constant heartache for his mother and an endless ration of guilt for Sean. As the morning passed and Thomas had not returned, Kathleen decided to medicate Sorley again. She surrendered to his cries and gave him another dose of laudanum. She hoped that Thomas had found work of some kind, for even a coin or two would give them enough vegetables for a pot of soup. Eamon and Maeve busied themselves in the corner, playing quietly so as not to disturb Sorley. Sean was restless, desperately wanting to count his money, and pacing the flat as he concocted one lie after another to explain where the money had come from. He knew they all sounded like lies, and he knew Da would never believe any of them. He considered telling the truth, but when he imagined Mam's sweet sad face and Da's seething anger, truth quickly reverted back to deceit.

"Sean," Mam called from the doorway, startling him from his thoughts. "Sorry, son, I didn't mean to startle ya. I'm takin' some clothes out to the basin to wash and will be hangin' them out back when I'm done. I'll be a few minutes. You'll be all right here?" Kathleen felt bad for mentioning the yard where Sorley was injured, where Sean's selfishness had led him to abandon his responsibilities, but he seemed preoccupied and not bothered by the reminder.

"We'll be fine, Mam. I'll be here watchin' over Sorley like Da said," Sean responded. His heart leaped as he realized he was going to have the opportunity to retrieve his parcel of coins and count his earnings.

Kathleen nodded, slightly curious about Sean's sudden change in demeanor. She hoped it was nothing but his father's warning and a sense of responsibility for Sorley's pain that had humbled him, but the change seemed too sudden to have resulted from any self-reflection. She shook off her suspicions and headed out to the hallway to make use of the communal wash basins. They had little soap left so Kathleen used half as much as she needed and instead gave each garment more scrubbing time than she would have liked. It was tiring work and as she scrubbed each garment with the laundry brush, she wished for one of the washtubs she had heard about that were operated with a crank and had rollers to squeeze the water out of the clothes. *If wishes were horses, beggars would ride, Kathleen Delaney*, she whispered to herself.

Sean waited a few minutes until he heard the familiar sound of the stiff bristles rubbing life from the thinning cloth, and he took it as a sign that he was safe to proceed. He reached beneath the bookcase and pulled out his coin purse. He glanced over at Eamon and Maeve, immersed in their game and spinning tall tales of jungle adventures with their little wooden animals Da had recently carved from some of Mam's firewood. A quick look at the bed where Sorley was sleeping told Sean it was the opportune time to count his coins. He sat on the floor in front of the couch partially hidden from curious siblings. He untied the knots and opened the purse, carefully removing one coin at a time as quietly as he could. He was good with figures and could easily keep a running count in his head as he inspected each coin for the value it held. There were coins he was familiar with—pennies, dimes, and half-dimes—and a few Liberty Dollars. Sean summoned every ounce of caution he possessed to not gasp at the dollar coins. He had seen one or two when Da, on a rare occasion, would find work at the docks. Those days were all but gone and it had been a sad long time since he'd seen more than a few pennies, or a dime on a more profitable day.

The heavier coins had shifted to the bottom of the pouch as he walked home last night and that is where he found the dollar coins. Sean had counted ninety-five cents in small coin before he removed the dollars. He took them out one at a time, his heart pounding so hard in his chest he was certain Maeve and Eamon could hear it. Sean glanced back in their direction again and found them quite oblivious to the treasure located across the room in their brother's lap. He counted the dollars slowly... four, five, six, seven, eight Liberty dollars. Nearly nine dollars in total. His hands were shaking as he stacked the dollar coins in a neat pile. A darker coin, about the same size as the dollar coins, had shifted to the very bottom of his makeshift purse. It did not look familiar to Sean, and he wondered for a moment if Sam, or the junkman, had hoodwinked the new recruit. There was little he could do if that were the case. He would never confront them about it and risk retribution for his suspicion. He reminded himself that the coins he had already counted were a small fortune to a family who had survived on pennies and the generosity of their neighbors.

Sean reached down into the cloth, still slightly folded over, to remove the dark metal coin from the cloth so that he could return his money and tie it back together. He would return the pouch to its spot under the bookcase until he decided how and when to share his good fortune with Mam and Da. He was disappointed to find another one of the unfamiliar metal trinkets in the fold of the makeshift purse. He set them both down on the floor beside him while he placed his money back into the center of the cloth. As he was tying the corners together, he thought about giving the extra trinkets to Maeve and Eamon. They would be delighted to have some play money to add to the adventures they created. Perhaps it would be part of a long-lost buried treasure they would discover buried in the sand on a deserted island. He could tell them he found the coins in the alley, and they would have no reason to doubt him.

Sean slid the coin purse back under the bookcase and picked up the two dark coins from the floor. As he stood and turned toward the windows the glint of the metal coin he held between his thumb and forefinger caught his eye. He paused and looked down, more carefully now in the window light, and he saw the Liberty head, the date stamp 1858, and the thirteen stars surrounding the head of Miss Liberty. He slowly, almost fearfully, turned the coin over and saw the inscription at the bottom beneath the eagle. *Twenty D.* A muffled sound that resembled a cry escaped from Sean's throat and he slowly wrapped his hand tightly around the twenty-dollar gold coin. He tightened his grip on the other one safely concealed in his left hand, his breath coming quicker.

"What is it, Sean? Are ya all right?" Maeve paused her game with Eamon upon hearing Sean's muffled cry. "Are ya hurt?"

"No, Maeve, I'm fine. I hit my toe on the leg of the couch is all," Sean lied. His heart was pounding so hard that he was certain it would burst from his chest. Maeve nodded, content with his explanation, and returned to her imaginary adventure. Sean walked slowly back to where he had been sitting. His legs felt heavy, like a dead weight that he did not have the strength to move, and his hands shook as he sat down and looked at the coins, one in each hand. Two twenty-dollar coins. Forty dollars here, and just short of nine in the pouch, gave him nearly fifty dollars. Tears welled up in Sean's eyes. They were tears of fear and dread, tears of joy for the good it could do, and tears of a boy who felt lost and overwhelmed in a man's world. He moved cautiously back to the bookcase and when it was safe to do so he retrieved the handkerchief again. He untied the strip of cloth holding the purse together and placed the gold coins in with the others. Sean felt a great hesitation about putting the money back under the bookcase, for it would be easily discovered if Mam moved the small shelf to sweep beneath it. He remembered the loose floorboard that Eamon had found near the baseboard close to the wall. Sean wandered slowly, the purse tucked in between his belly and the waistband of his pants. He gazed out the window with feigned interest. Eamon looked up momentarily and followed Sean's gaze out the window but saw nothing that interested him. Sean watched out of the corner of his eye as the two younger children were devising a plan to capture a ferocious tiger. He hoped they would not notice what he was doing.

He placed a knee on the floor and quickly untied his shoe. If the children looked his way, he would have a reason for kneeling and could tie his shoe to appease their curiosity. One quick look back over his shoulder, and he knew it was his only opportunity. He pulled slowly but firmly on the end of the floorboard, and it came up just enough to slip the cloth parcel beneath it. He would invent the perfect lie and formulate a plan for the money after he had some time to think on it. For now, it was safe and out of sight. He thought about the potential of earning much more considering this had just been his initiation into the Wharf Kings. Sean knew that his ability to get out from under the watchful eyes of his mother and father would be far more difficult than it had been, but it would not deter him. He would find a way.

"Mam?" Sorley's weak voice startled Sean as the boy called out from his parents' bed. The afternoon light, the soft voices of his siblings playing together, and his desire to be part of it kept Sorley from resting well. Sean tied the shoelace he had loosened and rose up off the floor. He walked over to the bedside and sat down next to his brother.

"Mam's out doin' laundry, Sorley," Sean said softly. He felt his emotions rise as he looked down at Sorley's pallid face, made all the paler by the shock of red hair that fell in loose curls around it. "Och, you're so pale I can scarce see your freckles." Sorley tried to move and moaned in pain. "I'm sorry, Sorley," was all Sean could muster. His voice broke at the mention of his brother's name. He stood and walked to the door, peeking out into the hallway to see if Mam was still there. She was not, and Sean feared she would be too long hanging the clothes and he would not know how to properly care for his brother. He considered going out to look for her but the weighted words and icy glare from his father earlier that morning prevented him from leaving the children even for a couple minutes.

"There now, Sorley." Sean heard Maeve's voice behind him. Maeve was six months shy of her sixth birthday and possessed a level of compassion that her brothers would probably never have. It was no wonder she was Da's favorite. Though he denied it when accused, everyone was aware of the soft spot he had for his only daughter. Sean returned to the bedside and smiled at Maeve. She reached over and put her hand on her brother's arm as if to say she understood his battle with guilt, and shame, and life's relentless disappointments.

"Would ya like a story?" Sean offered. Sorely nodded and gave a brave smile. There was no animosity or blame in Sorley. It was not his nature to be anything but gentle and happy. He was much like Maeve in his character, and Eamon was more like Sean, though Eamon had not yet reached the age where cynicism and frustration would threaten to overshadow his still-innocent heart. Eamon left the wooden figures he'd been playing with and walked over to the bedside to be closer for the story. Sean could weave a tale much like Da, and the younger children missed the days when Sean was more present and more engaged with them and with their parents. Eamon and Maeve sat on the floor next to the bed as Sean began a great tale of an evil serpent named Sowmadden who swam up the East River in search of children to devour. He was amused with himself for naming the evil beast after the drunken henchman guarding the door to Sam's back room.

Kathleen hurried herself through the hanging of the laundry. It was unusual to see the Delaney laundry hanging haphazardly along the lines in the yard. Her family and the neighbors who knew her could always identify the Delaney's clothesline, for Kathleen took great care in hanging it all just so, small to large, straight and tidy. She endured the good-natured teasing with a knowing smile.

She knew there was more to it than just the washing of their tattered garments. The story of her life was unfolding in a direction she would never have imagined, and the makings of that story were beyond her control, unchangeable it seemed, penned by a maleficent hand with little regard for the lives it damaged. But laundry was something she could control. It offered a tiny glimmer of respite, a moment or two when her world was at her command, orderly and put together exactly as she wanted it. So silly and so meaningless, but it gave Kathleen an opportunity to abandon the role of the victim, if only for a few minutes, and play the victor instead.

Today, however, she pulled the clothes from her basket and draped them quickly over the line. She could not afford to linger in her imaginary world of an orderly life. Kathleen was nervous about Sorley's condition and about leaving him under Sean's supervision. She was concerned about Sean and his questionable behavior of late. She worried that her children and the close-knit relationship they had always shared was changing, slipping away, transforming into something less intimate, something driven by a base struggle for survival that might be their undoing. Kathleen draped the last of the garments over the line and picked up her fraying wicker basket. She met Mrs. Callahan in the hallway and the well-meaning neighbor delayed her for a quick chat and a few questions, as she always did. Mrs. Callahan had heard the crying and the frenzied voices yesterday, and she wanted to know if everything was all right. Kathleen quickly recounted Sorley's accident, omitting Sean's absence and Tommy's angry pursuit of his son, and she reassured Mrs. Callahan that all was well and that Sorley was resting comfortably. She hoped. She tried to edge her way past her neighbor, feeling guilty as she did, but she did not want to be further delayed. Mrs.

Callahan unintentionally heaped on an extra serving of guilt by asking if they had enough to eat.

"I've noticed Maeve lookin' quite drawn, Katie. Is there food enough for the six of ya?" Mrs. Callahan's hands were tucked in the bodice of her apron, as they always were, and her graying curls were neatly pinned in place. Though she often crossed the line between concern and nosiness, she always meant well.

"Yes, and thank you, Mrs. Callahan. We're makin' do."

"You'll let me know if ya need a loaf of bread?"

"Of course. Tommy's been gone since early this mornin'. I'm hopin' he found some work down on Catharine Street." Kathleen continued to inch her way around Mrs. Callahan, wondering how she could detach herself from the conversation.

"That place is not fit for a God-fearin' person anymore, Katie. The Saturday night revelry is overrun with hooligans now, comin' down from the Five Points, they are. Not to mention all sorts of humanity that come over on the ferry from Brooklyn. The worst of humanity, I'll say." Mrs. Callahan shook her head in disapproval.

"Aye, Mrs. Callahan. We stay away and don't go out at night. Thanks to you for your kindness and I'll be gettin' along to check on Sorley now," Kathleen added as she and her wicker basket made it around to the other side of Mrs. Callahan's stout figure in the narrow hallway.

As she neared the door to their flat, Kathleen heard a squeal and mistook it for a cry of pain. She ran the last few steps and opened the door more forcefully than she had intended. She was startled to find her four children gathered close, smiles of delight on their faces. All four heads turned in surprise to Mam's sudden entrance.

"What ..."

Before she could ask, Maeve began to recount the tale of Sowmadden, the evil child-gobbling serpent who lived in the East River. Kathleen glanced at Sorley, pale but content, the hint of a smile on his face. And Sean. Her dear firstborn, her dark and brooding child, sitting there at the edge of the bed where he assumed the role of storyteller in his father's absence. She felt a splitting pain in her chest and throat as she stood strong against her maternal weakness. Kathleen dropped the basket by the door, removed her shoes, and settled down on the floor with Maeve and Eamon to be party to the grand adventure. She looked at Sean with so great a love that he felt it from her gaze. She nodded to encourage him to continue, and he did. The afternoon sun brightened the flat, adding a gauzy glow of warm color to the drab surroundings. The mood was light and there was a feeling, even if only for that one rare morning, that there was nothing between them but love.

***

A few blocks away on Catharine Street, Thomas whistled a happy tune that matched his countenance and his immense gratitude. Two days of work each week, a pittance to some, would make a sizable difference in his family's struggle to survive. It would not get them out of the tenement, nor would it clothe them in finery or allow them to feast on the delicacies that adorned many a table in other parts of the city. It would, however, put food on their table to a greater degree than they had experienced these past months, and it would give Thomas back a small portion of his self-worth. He smiled as he whistled, wondering at his lightened mood when so much had gone so terribly wrong lately. Maybe Fate was smiling on them for a change.

"You, there!" a voice called out from the open doorway of a shop a few doors down the street. Thomas looked in the direction of the voice and saw a middle-aged man, small in stature, wearing a brown derby hat and a spotless black leather apron. He was contrary in every way to the temperamental butcher and his filthy apron. He was tidy and neat with a kind voice and a genuine smile. He was standing in the doorway beneath a sign that said, "Charles Conner, Shoemaker." He waved at Thomas, beckoning him to come nearer. Thomas was hesitant to leave his work but obliged the man's invitation and walked over to the front of the shop.

"Could you give me a hand, sir?" the man asked. Thomas did not miss the man's respectful address. He couldn't remember the last time someone had called him *sir*.

"I'd be likely to, yes, but I'm on the clock on my first day and wouldn't want to be losin' the job already," Thomas answered. The other man nodded. He glanced up and down the street and nodded again.

"I saw another fella on the other side of the street earlier this morning. If you're working together, I would think you're nearly done," he observed.

"Aye, close to it, I imagine. I'm thinkin' I'll likely meet up with Leo the next block up, somewhere near Henry Street. He started an hour before me and should have already rounded Catharine near Chatham Square. This end of the street shouldn't take long."

"Yes, the street is long, though not as long as some in the city," the shoemaker replied, obviously not hearing Thomas's remarks correctly.

"Aye, as I was saying," Thomas said in a louder voice, "this end of the street shouldn't take long."

"I see, I see," the shoemaker replied thoughtfully. He rubbed his chin a moment, clearly planning something, and then continued, "if you're nearly done, could you come by here at the end of your shift? I'm in a bind and need a strong fella to help me out."

"What's your trouble, shoemaker?"

"The man who delivers my leather drops it out back in the alley every Sunday afternoon. My nephew, Marley, usually comes by to get the heavy bundles into my shop. I've got myself a dodgy leg and have a hard time hauling in anything heavy like that." He paused and patted his right thigh as if to validate his condition. "Unfortunately, my nephew has become unreliable at best. I have reason to believe he's running with a new gang. Remnants of those Daybreak Boys, or so I've heard. Since he has stopped coming by here to give me a hand, I've had to scramble to find someone to help with the delivery. If I leave it out overnight, it'll be gone in the morning, sure as my name is Charlie Conner, and it is, by the way," the shoemaker added, pointing to the sign above his head.

"Thomas Delaney. So, Charlie, be you offerin' me a job, or are ya lookin' for some neighborly assistance? Either would be fine with me."

"Would you be willing to barter, Mr. Delaney? Do you have yourself a family and are they in need of shoes?"

Thomas let out a short, cynical laugh. "Does the pope need holy water?"

"I'm assuming that means yes, then, for I know that he does. If you could come by here every Sunday afternoon after you're done with your sweeping and get my delivery into my back room, I could provide your family with new shoes. Is that agreeable to you, Mr. Delaney?"

"Aye, 'tis most agreeable, Charlie. My lovely wife and I have four children, and they're walking around on more foot than shoe, if you know what I mean."

"We have a deal then. If I see my nephew, I will tell him I've hired a man. He'll be glad to be off the hook. He's my sister's only son, God rest her soul, and he's taken a bad turn, I'm afraid." The man's voice held a familiar sadness much like the struggle Thomas was having with Sean's behavior these past weeks. The two men shook hands and Thomas returned to his cart to finish up his first day of good fortune. As he neared Henry Street, just as he predicted, he saw another man pushing a cart and sweeping as he went. Leo was a small man, not much bigger than Sean, olive-skinned with black curly hair. He stopped when he saw Thomas working his way toward him. He stood where he was until Thomas drew near enough to hear him.

"And who might you be?" Leo asked with a noticeable Italian accent.

"I'd be Thomas Delaney, and I'm guessin' you'd be Leo," Thomas offered.

"And how do you know my name?" Before Thomas could answer, Leo fired off another question. "And why are you doing my job?" The man was suspicious, defensive, and obviously worried about his own new employment. Thomas could appreciate that.

"Sergeant Engel hired me on, just for Fridays and Sunday afternoons, mind ya, to help with the coming and going of the Saturday night market. I needed the work, and he thought ya might be able to use the help."

"So, he doesn't think I can do the job, is that it?" Leo questioned.

"Not at all, my good man, it's just a lot for one man to clean up after those hooligans come over and mess up the street with their rubbish." Thomas hoped Leo would relax and appreciate the help. He watched Leo consider his explanation, and he waited for a response. The little man tipped his cap back and wiped his sweaty brow with the back of his hand.

"It is a lot," Leo agreed. "Just don't be setting your sights on my job, Delaney. I was just hired, and I need this job. I've got six children at home and not enough of anything between them. Understand?"

"More than ya know, Leo," Thomas replied. "I'm just grateful for the couple days I'll be gettin'. I've no desire to rob a man of his livelihood."

Leo nodded, sensing Thomas was probably drowning in the throes of poverty just like he was. Thomas turned his cart around and let Leo take the lead back to the dock. They reached the rubbish bin for the last time, and Thomas turned to look back at their handiwork. The street was neat and tidy, swept and cleaned, devoid of any trash left in the aftermath of the market festivities the night before. There were small groups of people gathered here and there, some left from the night before and some just now starting their day. Cart vendors were opening shop, and shops were opening doors. It had a quaint feeling that disappeared when the sun set and a different crowd gathered on Catharine Street. Thomas felt a great sense of accomplishment in a good day's work. He placed the shovel and broom into the cart and followed Leo to the dockmaster's office to find Sergeant Engel. The office was up a short flight of stairs. Thomas waited below to keep an eye on the equipment while Leo went up to report the day's work completed. Henry Engel had seen the two men approaching and met Leo at the door. He stepped out onto the landing, put a hand above his eyes to shade them from the sun, and looked down the street as far as he could see. He went back into the office before coming out and walking ahead of Leo down to the street. Thomas watched them descend the stairs and was amused in the size difference between Henry and Leo, looking more like father and son than two full-grown men. He was smiling as Henry approached.

"Looks like the two of you did a good job, Delaney," he said as he walked past Thomas. He motioned to the two men to follow him with their equipment to the shed where he locked it safe inside. "It's nice to see a little polish and shine on this fine city of ours," Henry added. Thomas wasn't sure which city he was talking about, for there was little to call *fine* in any part of the city Thomas had ever visited, but he was happy to receive the validation of a job well done.

"I'm indebted to ya, Sergeant," he replied, "and happy to be workin' with Leo." Thomas hoped a kind word for Leo might secure his good standing with both Leo and the sergeant.

"I think you'll make a good team." Henry reached into the inside pocket of his jacket and took out a flat leather pouch. It had a large, black button on one side with a loop around it, which Henry unfastened to access the contents. Thomas could see several bank notes and could hear coins jingling as Henry shuffled through the money. Leo had been paid on Friday, so he turned to leave. He waved as he walked away, feeling somewhat relieved that Sergeant Engel had hired him some help on the two busiest days of the week. Leo felt confident that he could take Delaney at his word, and that his own position as head street sweeper was secure. He felt a little surge of pride as he thought about the self-proclaimed title, and the fact that he had another fella working under him. Leo would tell Stefania and the children about it when he got home.

"Do you prefer bank notes or coins?" Sergeant Engel asked Thomas.

"Coins, if it's all the same," Thomas answered. He knew that bank notes were as vast and varied as the stars above, and that a note issued by a particular bank was valid at their location and other local businesses, but many shop owners preferred government-issued coins.

Henry removed two one-dollar coins from his pouch and placed them in Thomas's waiting hand. He reached back into the pouch and drew out three dimes, handing them to Thomas as an afterthought. He knew the man was hungry, and his children were hungry, too.

"Here's something extra for your efforts. I appreciate your getting along with Leo. He can be a bit ... surly, shall we say? Reminds me of an angry little bulldog," Henry said with a laugh. Thomas accepted the extra coins and smiled at the sergeant.

"'Tis a fine thing you've done for me today, sir. I'll be on my way if we're done here. I promised the shoemaker I would help him with his delivery and then I'll be stoppin' at the market for a few things before I head home."

"Ah, yes, Charlie's nephew has taken a bad turn, I'm afraid. Left his crippled uncle high and dry with no way to get his delivery safely inside the shop. I hear young Marley has joined up with a gang working out of the Five Points. That's never a good thing."

"There's truth in that, Sergeant," Thomas answered, thinking again of Sean and fearing he could end up like Charlie's nephew. He was lost in his thoughts for a moment or two, standing with his coins in his hand and a worried look on his face.

"Off with you then, and we'll see you Friday morning. Leo starts at eight o'clock so I would recommend the same for your Friday shift," Henry said, bringing Thomas back from his musings. He tipped his head as if to offer his respects. Thomas was quite incredulous at the opportunities that had come along so unexpectedly. He would have to remember to thank Mrs. Zimmer next time he saw her. That kind lady was an angel sent by Heaven itself, and Thomas counted himself blessed to know her.

CHAPTER SIX

"I come bearing gifts!" The loud proclamation as Thomas burst through the doorway startled everyone inside. "Gather one and all!" Thomas bowed in an exaggerated manner that spoke of a rare and welcome frivolity.

Kathleen had just finished making tea, giving the last small spoonful of sugar to Sorley. She tried not to think about dinner and had resolved herself to begging Mrs. Callahan for another loaf of bread if Thomas returned empty-handed. Now, as she turned to see what the ruckus was about, she quickly noted a cloth sack containing unknown treasures. It wasn't as big as the sack Thomas had brought home from Mrs. Zimmer a couple of months ago but was still large enough to get everyone's heart racing.

"Thomas Michael Delaney, what have ya done now?" Kathleen said in her best scolding voice, though they all knew she was as hopeful and excited as they were.

"You, my lovely woman, are lookin' at one of New York City's finest street sweepers, workin' Fridays and Sunday afternoons on Catharine Street from now 'til the end of time!" The children laughed and Mam put her hand to her chest. A steady job, even two days a week, was a dream they had long ago abandoned.

"Tommy, really?" she whispered.

"Indeed, madam, and here I have the fruits of my labor to prove it!" Thomas waved his hand toward his sack, smiling broadly in obvious delight. His joy and the smile on his face took Kathleen's breath away. His dark features, deep brown eyes, and beautiful smile never failed to stir her heart. He stood waiting, smiling, soaking in the happy smiles on the beautiful faces around him. He was offering them a sackful of proof that this wasn't just another one of his wild stories. The children cheered, and Kathleen stepped forward and held her husband tightly. The children moved in close, all except for Sorley who, despite his inability to join the family, was as happy as the rest of them.

"Sure and now we've forgotten poor Sorley," Mam said as she hurried over to her son's side.

"It's okay, Mam," Sorley said quietly. "'Tis cause to celebrate."

Sorley smiled at Kathleen, wanting desperately to see a bit of joy back in their household. Despite his knowing that the accident was not his fault, he couldn't help but feel guilty for the sadness it had invited into an already sad existence. He looked around and saw the smiling faces. The joy was contagious, and the throbbing in his knee was easier to ignore because of it. His curiosity got the best of him as he fixed his gaze on the cloth sack Da had set down on the floor next to him.

"Da, what's there in your sack? Can we see?" Sorely asked.

All heads turned back to Thomas who was looking quite smug. It was getting near dinnertime and his stomach let go with a loud growl. He looked down at his belly with a feigned look of shock and embarrassment. The children laughed and Kathleen hoped against hope that Thomas had brought some food home to his hungry family. He picked up the sack, carried it to the table, and called everyone to gather round. He made them stand to either side so that Sorley could see from the bed a few feet away. Slowly, deliberately, he removed the items and placed them on the table one at a time. First out was a basket with a lid containing two dozen fresh eggs. Mr. Carnahan had loaned him the basket so that the eggs would survive the trip home in Thomas's sack, and Thomas assured him he would return it the following weekend. The eggs were followed by a pound of sugar, three pounds of flour, and two one-quart bottles of milk that were located on either side of the sack separated by a large beef roast wrapped in butcher paper. There was a gasp from his audience when the roast was laid on the table. The presentation continued as he removed more food from the sack—a paper parcel containing three pounds of sliced ham, a dozen potatoes, ten carrots, eight apples, and half pound of Mam's favorite tea. The sight of the tea was the spilling point for Mam's tears, and she surrendered to them. Thomas had spent all but two cents of his first day's income, and Mr. Carnahan had gifted him with one last item.

"Och, Katie, there's more, Mo Chroí," Thomas said lovingly. He reached into his pants pocket to retrieve a small square of printed paper tied with a piece of ribbon. He handed it to her with a look that spoke volumes of apology, love, and regret.

"For you," he said softly, love spilling out and filling up her heart.

Kathleen smiled and untied the ribbon. Inside the paper packet were a dozen sugar-coated lemon drops.

"Lemon drops!" she said, her voice breaking.

"Mam, your favorite!" Sorley called out from the bed.

"Aye, darling boy, 'tis my favorite," she replied. She turned to Thomas who was himself overwhelmed with the provision before them. "Tommy, my love, thank you," she said softly.

"Ah, but there's one more thing here for our other fine lady," Da said as he picked up the sack and handed it to Maeve. She was confused. She couldn't imagine why there would be something from Da's trip to the market just for her. She would share it whatever it was.

"What is it, Da?"

"Well, now, I'm thinkin' if ya open the sack and reach inside it we'll have the answer to that!"

Maeve reached down inside the sack and felt something rather unrecognizable, stiff and unyielding, but again, the shape of it, of them, was beginning to feel familiar. And yet, how could it be shoes? There wasn't money for food on most days, and shoes were a luxury. They were rarely replaced, and often patched with pieces of wool or burlap or even thin slats of wood until they became so tattered and uncomfortable that many children ran about barefoot all year round. The shoes on Maeve's feet were ready for the rubbish bin. Sorley had worn them until they were too small and then they were handed down to her. As Maeve pulled the shoes from the sack, the silence of astonishment fell upon the room. The blue stamped leather boots, ankle-high and laced up the front with black shoelaces, may as well have been crafted for Queen Victoria herself.

"Da," Maeve breathed, barely above a whisper, as she stared at the boots.

"Tommy, how?" Kathleen was equally astonished.

"I've another job! Each Sunday after I finish cleanin' the streets, I'll be bringin' the shoemaker's leather parcels into his shop for him. Seems he's got himself a bad leg, and a bad nephew who used to help but is now a fine, big man runnin' with a Five Points gang." Thomas paused to make a point but knew better than to ruin this good day with tension. He refrained from glancing in Sean's direction and the discretion did not go unnoticed by Sean or Kathleen. "The shoemaker, Mr. Charlie Conner, will swap me a pair of new shoes for every third Sunday that I help him. When I told him how badly this family needed shoes, and how our sweet Maeve was wearin' Sorley's tattered brogues, he insisted I bring these boots home for her. Apparently, a lady from The Heights across the river ordered them for her wee lass and then changed her mind after Mr. Connor worked hard to make them. Seems a bit rude in my way of thinkin' but maybe 'tis such a thing that they're now where they should be. Try them on, Stóirín!"

Maeve slipped her feet, covered in mended wool socks, inside the boots. Thomas bent down on a knee and laced them up, feeling for where Maeve's big toe was inside the boot. They were a size too big, but that only meant she'd be wearing them longer. On this warm day in April her face was aglow with the joy of a Christmas morning they had never known, and she danced around the flat like a princess at the royal ball. Thomas thought his heart would burst, and Kathleen's overflowed with gratitude as she watched her beautiful daughter so elated to have something as simple as a pair of new shoes upon her feet. Never would Kathleen have dreamed of such a day as this, and she leaned into her husband to share the rare and beautiful moment.

Maeve stopped dancing and rushed at her father nearly knocking him down. She squeezed him as tightly as her little arms possibly could, and she thanked him countless times for the most beautiful boots she had ever seen. Her brothers were smiling, happy for her, no bitterness about their own tattered shoes by the door. Their day would come, Da promised. Mam declared a topsy-turvy day, a day of nothing expected and everything hoped for, and announced they would have breakfast for supper. The children laughed at such a concept, but their mouths were already watering in anticipation of crisp pan-fried ham, scrambled eggs, and fried potatoes. Mam would use half of the eggs and some of the milk for this one meal, but the beef roast she would cook tomorrow would sustain them for several days. She wished for bread but could not bring herself to ask for a loaf from Mrs. Callahan, not with all this luxurious food spread out before them.

"I've two good pennies left in my pocket, Katie, if you're needin' anything else. You've that look about ya." Thomas knew it well enough and if he could, he would always oblige. He would tip the earth off its axis or fashion a crown of stars from the night sky just to see her smile.

"Just thinkin' a nice loaf of bread would go well with our breakfast supper, but I'll not be beggin' another loaf from Mrs. Callahan, and I haven't time to bake one of my own. The children are salivatin', and I'm fierce hungry myself."

"I'll be back," Thomas said as he headed for the door. Through the thin wall Kathleen could hear the knock upon their neighbors' door and voices engaged in conversation. She heard Mrs. Callahan's hearty laugh, and she smiled and shook her head knowing how charming Thomas Delaney could be. Kathleen was dicing potatoes when Thomas returned with a loaf of bread.

"You shouldn't have asked, Tommy. We've enough here for a fortnight if we use it wisely," Kathleen gently chided, though she was happy to have the bread. The meal would be a hearty one. They would all have full bellies and a restful night's sleep uninterrupted by the pains of hunger that often went to bed with them.

"The lady was grinnin' ear to ear when I handed her two pennies for her troubles," Thomas answered. "Asked me if I robbed Mr. Fulton's Bank!"

"I hope you assured her that you did not! And that was kind of you to pay her, Tommy. Too often we eat the bread of kindness from her kitchen."

"Aye, Katie, how many times has Mrs. Callahan helped us out?"

"More times than we could ever pay for, I'm afraid," Kathleen answered quietly, grateful for their neighbor's generosity.

"Sure and she'd not expect it, for that's the kind of neighbor she is."

Kathleen went about fixing supper. Potatoes were diced and cooking, and she put some lard in another pan to heat the ham slices. The eggs were beaten together with milk and were ready to cook when the ham was nicely browned. While dinner cooked, Kathleen placed the meat and milk in the icebox, thankful that there was still some ice inside to keep the perishables cool. She had bartered some firewood for a block of ice from the Levy family who lived next door to the Callahans. They were quiet and kind, and she was grateful for their willingness to trade with her. She sliced the bread into thick, even slices and hated herself for wishing for butter. The bread was fresh and soft and that was more than enough. Maeve set the table while Eamon and Sean tried to calm the wrenching emptiness in their bellies. When Kathleen turned to put the plate of bread on the table, she noticed Maeve had set six places around it.

"Maeve, darling, I don't think Sorley will be joining us here at the table," she whispered.

"I want to, Mam, if someone could help me over," Sorley called quietly from the bed, his voice raspy from the aftereffects of the surgery and the doses of laudanum to keep him comfortable. Thomas hurried to Sorley and smiled down at his son. His eyes looked lucid, and Thomas wondered how long it had been since he'd received a dose of the pain medication. He reached down and stroked the wild mess of red hair.

"Are ya needin' more medicine, son?"

"No, Da, I don't like the way it makes me feel. I miss bein' part of the family." Sorley pushed up with his arms and tried to sit up. Thomas quickly reached behind him to support his efforts and got him into a sitting position.

"The pain, Sorley, is it fierce?" Maeve's voice came from behind her father. Thomas moved slightly so Maeve could speak to her brother.

"Aye, it hurts, but I'll do all right. I don't want to miss out on the fun."

Kathleen wiped her hands on her apron and moved the hair that had fallen out of place with the back of her hand. She walked halfway to the bed and stopped.

"What shall we do, dear ones? Shall we let our brave Sorley attempt to sit and dine with us, then?" She knew the answer before she asked it, and everyone agreed Sorley should join them.

Da stood and lifted his son up, cradling him like a baby. Eamon ran ahead and pulled a chair out from the table so that Thomas could seat Sorley there. Mam turned her empty soup pot upside down and placed it under the table so that her son could rest his injured leg upon it. The boy winced slightly when his father lifted his injured leg just enough to set it on the pot, but that was the only indication of pain he gave. Maeve pulled the quilt from her parents' bed, folded it into a large square, and brought it over to the table. Da carefully lifted Sorley's leg up from the pot and Maeve slid the quilt under. Sorley nodded and smiled at his sister. Everyone else sat down, except for Mam who was finishing up the egg scramble. Sorley reached for a piece of bread. Another day would have seen him scolded for not waiting, but he was likely hungrier than the rest of them. He'd had next to nothing to eat these past two days. Sean directed a sideways glance at his father, waiting for the retribution, but Thomas just smiled and nodded.

"Here it comes! Make way and be ready for a bellyful!" Kathleen carried the food she had prepared to the table, and one by one the Delaneys helped themselves to the potatoes and ham, the soft fluffy eggs made heavenly with milk instead of water, and the thick slices of Mrs. Callahan's fresh soft bread, a familiar and welcome addition to their meal.

"There now, go easy, Sorley," Mam cautioned. "You've not had much food in your belly these past two days and more laudanum than a child should have. We don't want this fine meal to end up in a slop bucket." Sorley nodded and slowed down. A moment of grief and regret passed over Sean as he recalled the same advice given to him in a less respectable setting than this one. There was little conversation at the table after Mam's advice to Sorley. The food was too good to sacrifice the tasting of it to meaningless chatter. They savored every bite. Sorley found himself full long before he wanted to be, and he could not stop the disappointed whimper that escaped his lips.

"What is it, son?" Kathleen asked. "Are ya not feelin' well? Do ya want to lay back down?"

"My belly is full already," he whined. "I can usually eat more than Eamon, but now he's had more than me. I'm missin' out on my share." The base self-preservation of the hungry caused Sorley to mourn his loss of an equal share, and none of them thought less of him for it. He meant no ill will upon any of his family, and he didn't have a selfish bone in his body, but hunger blinds a soul to anything but the will to survive.

"No missin' out, and no shares here to be accountin' for, Son," Da responded. "Did ya hear me say I've found myself a regular job now?" Sorley nodded. "We'll have food on the table again, Son. As long as I'm workin', not a one of us should go hungry. Mam can put the rest of your plate aside and you can have it later, or tomorrow if it suits ya. Now, shall I carry ya back to the bed, or do ya want to sit out here with us for a spell?"

"I wanna stay." There was relief in Sorley's voice. He believed Da, and he trusted there would be more. If Mam would set his plate aside, he was sure he could finish it after his full belly had to time to settle.

"Tell us a story, Da," Eamon said. "Sean was tellin' us a fine tale before you came home, weren't ya, Sean?" Sean smiled a nervous smile and nodded slightly. He shrugged then, as if to discount his storytelling prowess which could in no way match his father's.

"Were ya then? And what was this fine tale about?"

Before Sean could answer, Maeve and Eamon once again recounted the drama of the river dragon, Sowmadden, this time to their father, and Thomas listened intently. He felt some pride in the storytelling skills that Sean was developing, and though Eamon seemed the likely heir to the family title, maybe it would be such a thing that two Delaneys would carry on the tradition. He was curious, however, how Sean had come up with such an interesting name for the serpent. It was not a name, or a character from lore, that Thomas was familiar with. He was about to question Sean when Sorley interrupted his thoughts and brought him back to Eamon's request for a story. He would ask Sean about the strange character in his story another time.

"Please, Da, a new story?" Sorley loved all his father's tales, but on such a grand night as this a new story might be the perfect end to it. Kathleen, too, was thinking the day was coming to a wonderful end. She retrieved her pouch of lemon drops and handed one to each of the children, a small but sweet dessert to top off a lovely evening. Thomas declined her offer, for it would have been too difficult to spin a tale fit for a Delaney with a lump of hard candy in his mouth. Besides, the candy belonged to Kathleen and though Thomas knew she would share with the children, he wanted her to enjoy the rest of her special treat. They moved from the table to the couch with everyone gathered around, sitting on the floor in front of it. Da and Sorley sat on the tattered, hand-me-down couch for Sorley's comfort and Da's need of a platform. All eyes were fixed on Thomas.

"I've a story about just how crafty a wee leprechaun can be. They're not to be trusted, full of trickery and mischief, they are. My own da told me this story many times when I was a wee lad in County Cork. 'Tis the story of Tom Fitzpatrick and the field of flowers."

"Tom, like you, Da," Maeve added. Though the name was true to the story, it added a personal touch that drew the children immediately into the fable.

"Aye, like me, but not near as smart as I." The children all laughed as Thomas continued. "Tom Fitzpatrick was wanderin' home after spendin' his last coin on a cold, dark ale to wet his whistle. He knew his missus would be more than a wee bit angry if he returned home with no money and nothin' for their table, but the ale was callin' his name loud and clear, and poor Tom could not refuse it. As I said, he was not nearly as smart as your da, for I provided a table full of food, now, didn't I?" Everyone agreed that he had provided most generously.

126

"So, Tom Fitzpatrick wandered around the outskirts of town, delayin' his return home and doin' his best to think of a story he could tell his wife about where their last coin had gone. Stopped by a band of hooligans? Robbed of his coin and left penniless by the side of the road? Yes, that would do! As he walked on, now feelin' rather full of himself for the grand tale he had invented, he heard a slight hiccup from the hedgerow alongside the road. He paused and listened, and sure enough he heard it once more. Tom approached the hedgerow and moved the bushes aside. To his great surprise he discovered a wily little leprechaun settled in nicely and drinkin' down a cold dark ale just as Tom had done an hour before. Tom thought it was an odd coincidence. 'Say, what are you doin' there, little man?' he scolded. The leprechaun didn't acknowledge Tom or his question and went about his drinkin'. Tom grew annoyed at the leprechaun's insolent behavior. He leaned down and pulled the wee fella out of the hedgerow with greater force than he intended, causing the leprechaun to drop his tankard and spill its contents on the ground."

"Oh, dear," Kathleen interrupted, every bit as enthralled as the children were with the story Thomas was telling. "One should never anger a leprechaun! They can be quite nasty, you know." The children looked at one another in great anticipation of the misery and despair Tom Fitzpatrick was bringing upon himself.

"Aye, 'tis never a good idea, but Tom Fitzpatrick was in a mood and not thinkin' with a clear mind. He stood the leprechaun directly in front of him. The little man turned and looked behind him at his drink seepin' slowly into the ground, which, of course, is a profound waste of perfectly good ale." Thomas paused and winked at the children, and they all giggled. "'I'm in need of some coin and I want ya to take me to your pot of gold,' Tom said to the leprechaun.

127

'I've heard tell of it for many a year but was never able to find it for myself.' The little fella agreed. They walked a long way down the road until they came to a grand field alive with the color of sunlight itself. Thousands of buttercups were in full bloom and stretched as far as the eye could see. 'Sure and this better not be your gold!' Tom threatened. The leprechaun shook his head and walked over to one particular plant, no different, no more brightly colored, no taller or shorter than the rest. 'Tis under this flower', the leprechaun said. 'Six feet down.'"

Thomas paused his story again, leaned back, and drew in a deep breath. He exhaled slowly. His wife and children all stared at him, waiting to hear how Tom Fitzpatrick would retrieve the pot of gold from deep in the ground. Thomas rubbed his full belly and closed his eyes, sighing in contentment. Delaying the climax was an integral part of the storytelling. Keeping your audience enraptured was an art, and Thomas was an artist.

"Da!" Sorley, sitting next to his father, could not stand the suspense. "What happened to Tom Fitzpatrick?"

"Ah, yes, you'd like to know, wouldn't ya? Well, poor Tom knew he couldn't dig six feet down with his bare hands, and he hadn't a spade with him, so he knew he'd have to run all the way home and fetch the spade from his shed. The sun was high in the sky, somewhere between dinner and supper. He would have to be quick about it. He would retrieve the gold before dark and return home to Mrs. Fitzpatrick, rich as Midas and avoidin' the trouble he'd otherwise be in. To ensure he would not lose sight of the one particular buttercup that the leprechaun had shown him, Tom tore a strip of cloth from the edge of his red handkerchief and tied it to the plant. He turned to the little man who stood nearby, looking unconcerned about old Tom diggin' up his treasure. Tom leaned forward and threatened the leprechaun. 'If you dare remove my marker from this plant, I will put *you* six feet in the ground just like your pot of gold, and there'll be no one comin' to dig you up!' The leprechaun assured him he would not remove the marker, on his honor."

"I don't trust him!" Eamon shouted, startling everyone.

"And well you should not, for ya know how the wee folk can be," Thomas agreed. "Tom Fitzpatrick ran all the way home, a full Irish mile and then some, and managed to get into his shed and grab his spade without his wife noticin'. He ran all the way back to the field with the afternoon sun hot upon his back, and when he arrived, what is it that ya think he found there?"

"The leprechaun took the marker!" Maeve called out the obvious answer, the one everyone was expecting, knowing how the wee folk can be.

"You'd be expectin' that, now wouldn't ya? But quite to the contrary, the leprechaun did not take the red marker from the plant!" There were murmurs of amazement that the one honorable leprechaun in all of Ireland might have been found by Tom Fitzpatrick. "In fact, the little fella was nowhere in sight when Tom returned, but what he saw in the field brought him to his knees. There before him was not one marker on one buttercup plant, no indeed, there were a thousand markers on a thousand plants! The field was a sea of yellow and red, and Tom had no possible way to find the one plant that grew above the spot where the gold was buried."

"Oh, no!" Kathleen laughed. "What a bright little fella! He kept his word and left the marker where Tom had tied it and still kept his treasure safe and sound!"

"Bright indeed. Crafty and mean-spirited, too, but I'll give him credit for keepin' his word and protectin' whatever honor a leprechaun has," Thomas said.

"What happened to Tom, Da?" Sorley asked.

"Well, poor ol' Tom dug up half that field lookin' for the gold and of course he never found it, and it was dark by the time he arrived back home, tired and hungry and covered in dirt. He returned the spade to the shed and went inside hopin' his wife had found a few scraps for a pot of soup. Mrs. Fitzpatrick took one look at him, dirty and forlorn, and gave him the boot. 'Out to the hogs with ya!' she hollered, and Tom spent the night sleepin' in a pile of manky hay next to Bessie the pig and her six wee piglets."

"Poor man," Maeve said.

"Aye, 'tis sad, but old Tom made that bed for himself, Stóirín. He had to pay the piper, so to speak, and that is a moral lesson for us all to learn. He spent his last coin on ale instead of food, and he mistreated the leprechaun and intended to steal his gold. 'Tis always better to earn an honest dollar." Thomas realized that even though it was not his intention to offer a pointed lesson to Sean, it would sound that way to his son's ears. He refrained from looking at Sean, hoping that he would hear the moral of the fable without feeling as though his indiscretions were being held up as an example. Thomas still did not have the details about what Sean had done. He was unaware of the thievery carried out by the Wharf Kings, but he knew that any involvement with a gang would lead to a life of crime. He hoped with all his soul that Sean was not aligning himself with a gang and the trouble they would bring to his doorstep.

"And that's a new tale, Sorley, my boy!" Thomas tried to lighten the mood after such a fine meal and a very prosperous day.

"It was a good one, Da," Sorley replied, "and I learned a good lesson about never tryin' to trick a trickster."

"Aye, those wee folk can be a nasty lot," Kathleen added. She smiled at Thomas, the regret in his eyes obvious to her. "Is everyone's belly good and full?"

"Och, I couldn't eat a crumb from the table," Eamon lamented, putting his hands on his belly as Thomas had done earlier. The others all chimed in, including Sean, and Thomas was feeling grateful for what he was able to do for his family that day. He hoped it would continue for a good, long time.

"Well, then, I'm thinkin' it's time to be gettin' some sleep. 'Tis no matter if a man be rich or poor, for it's a full belly that tells his worth," Kathleen recounted the old saying she'd heard from her grandfather, and her father after. She turned to her youngest son, concerned about how much time he had spent out of bed, and out from under the influence of the pain medication. "Sorley, dear, how is your knee feeling?"

"It's not so bad, Mam. Aye, sore, but this bit of stone wrapped 'round it helps me not to move it much. I think I can sleep without more of that medicine, if it's all the same to you and Da." Everyone smiled at Sorley's description of the cast.

"Are you sure, son?" Thomas asked. He was both worried for and proud of his young son for how bravely he had handled the trauma.

"I'm sure. I don't like layin' in your bed all day with my brain full of fog."

"Here, there's a brave boy," Kathleen said as she stroked Sorley's curly red hair. "Maybe just half a dose to help you sleep, then?" Sorley nodded, and it was agreed. The other children rolled out their thin mattresses on the floor, and Da carried Sorley back to the bed where he would sleep again, his mother beside him, safe and sound.

CHAPTER SEVEN

The waning days of spring welcomed a time of plenty for the Delaneys. It wasn't an abundance when compared to the people in the brick and brownstone houses across the river in Brooklyn Heights, but by the Delaney's standards it was indeed a time of plenty. Thomas arrived at the Catharine Street dock early each Friday morning and promptly at noon on Sundays. He didn't mind cleaning a week's worth of litter from the streets to prepare for the Saturday market or restoring order and cleanliness to the market area on Sunday afternoons. Sunday was hustle day as there was more to clean after the festivities, but Leo often started very early, and they rarely had trouble finishing by five o'clock. Thomas and Leo developed an agreeable working relationship once Leo saw that Thomas did not have his sights set on Leo's position as the head sweeper.

Sunday afternoons always ended with a stop at Charlie Connor's shoe shop to carry his delivery into the storeroom in the back. Charlie was a kind man who always asked about Thomas's family, and true to his word, rewarded Thomas with a new pair of shoes for one lucky Delaney every three weeks. Sundays were also Thomas's market day, stopping in at Carnahan's on his way home to purchase enough food for the week ahead. Mr. Carnahan was always happy to see Thomas, and they usually enjoyed some friendly conversation while Thomas shopped. The storekeeper was happy that Thomas could finally put food on his table, and still Mr. Carnahan never failed to add a little something for Kathleen or the children.

Thomas had kept his promise to Dr. Bermann and had spent a couple of afternoons tilling Mrs. Bermann's small garden plot. There was something very rewarding about pushing the wooden frame of the tiller up and down the straight rows, watching the blade furrow into the soil and turn it up on either side. It was a basic connection to the earth, to life, and to the things of nature that Thomas had left behind in County Cork. The doctor told Thomas that the garden was not overly productive, but Mrs. Bermann enjoyed seeing a bit of life springing up from the soil. Life in the city was oppressive for many of its residents, and Thomas understood the correlation between living things and hope.

The doctor advised Thomas that it would soon be time to remove Sorley's cast and recommended bringing the boy back to his office before the heat of summer made the cast unbearable. The doctor was sure to mention that the removal of the cast was included in their barter, though Thomas had already thought about the coins that were usually left in his pocket after the weekly shopping, and he felt certain he could pay the doctor for services rendered. He decided he would save up and set aside a dollar as a small token of their gratitude for what Dr. Bermann had done for them. The doctor would likely decline it, but Thomas would find a way to compensate Dr. Bermann.

The tension between Sean and his father lessened in the weeks that followed Sorley's accident. Thomas realized that Sean carried with him a significant burden of guilt, and to cause that guilt to fester would create lasting problems for the boy. He reminded himself, too, that Kathleen had been right in saying that Sorley's accident could have happened just as easily with Sean right there watching. As far as Thomas knew, Sean was staying close to home, though on Fridays and Sundays he was likely unsupervised while Thomas worked, and Kathleen tended to her chores.

Assigned laundry days were generally agreed upon by the residents of the tenement in order to avoid confrontations at the communal basins, though there were always times when the need to sneak in an extra day at the basin arose. Depending on the temperament of a person's neighbor, this could lead to some unpleasant encounters. The designated Delaney washday was Sunday, along with two other families on their floor. Kathleen tried to be the first one at the basin to avoid any bickering with the other wives who laundered the same day. The basin was just outside their door and Kathleen had heard many unpleasant arguments sounding to her ears like the hens in her mother's yard, cackling and squawking and fighting to get to the feed tray first. She wanted no part of it.

The month of May seemed to end as soon as it began. The end of the month signaled the appointed time for Sorley's release from *the bit of stone around his leg*, and they planned a visit to Dr. Bermann's office. The boy was understandably nervous about having the stabilizing cast removed from his leg even though he had been active and moving about with no pain for weeks. Thomas and Kathleen were hopeful as they watched him playing with his siblings, but they knew that the prospect of Sorley's full recovery was yet to be determined. It was a sunny Thursday morning when

Thomas removed the ten dimes he had tucked away under his mattress and loaded Sorley into Mam's cart.

"Och, Da, I can walk!" Sorley protested.

"Aye, ya can walk, but you've not walked as far as the doctor's house since gettin' that cast on your leg. You'll likely be tired before we arrive," Thomas replied. "If ya want to walk 'til you're tired, Mam can pull the cart 'til ya need to use it." Sorley nodded and Thomas knew it would not be long before the boy would surrender. He also knew that it would embarrass Sorley to be seen riding in his mam's cart like a wee baby, at least around their own neighborhood, and so they set out walking, Sorley hobbling along with the crutch he still used and Kathleen pulling the empty cart. Three and a half blocks down Ridge Street, Sorley admitted defeat and climbed into the cart. His parents did not remind him that they had told him so, but rather praised him for his gallant effort.

When they arrived at the Bermann's, there was a man in the waiting room holding his cap in his hands, fidgeting nervously, turning the cap around and around, his eyes fixed on the floor. Mrs. Bermann seated the Delaneys and brought out a small apple tart for Sorley to eat while they waited. The boy's eyes grew large as she neared him with the porcelain plate and silver fork, and Mrs. Bermann laughed at his excitement.

"You look like you're feeling much better than the last time we saw you, young man," she commented. Sorley nodded but refrained from answering, as he had already stuffed a large bite of the tart into his mouth. Kathleen thanked Mrs. Bermann for her kindness and declined the offer of something for herself or Thomas. They were told it would only be a few more minutes while the doctor finished up with another patient.

"Sorry to be keepin' ya from seein' the doctor," the man across from them apologized as Mrs. Bermann left the room. He was so visibly agitated that Thomas was concerned for him, or for the patient he had brought in to see the doctor.

"'Tis no bother," Thomas assured him. "Everything all right?"

"I'm hopin' so," the man answered. "My boy was bein' courted by a gang near the Bowery. He told them he wasn't interested in their offer and one of them jumped him with a knife. Lucky he wasn't stabbed, but he's got a nasty cut on his arm, and right deep it is. The doc and the missus said they can fix him up good as new. I'm hopin' so."

"We're sorry for your boy, but we can assure ya that Dr. and Mrs. Bermann are top-notch. They helped us when our boy here had a terrible accident." Sorley looked up and smiled at the man, his cheeks stuffed with the last large bite of Mrs. Bermann's delicious dessert. The man couldn't help but smile back at the freckle-faced boy.

"I'll take your word on it then," the man said. He was about to say more, to go on about the gangs in the city and what a threat they were to everyone's safety, but Mrs. Bermann appeared with the man's son beside her. The boy was about Sean's age, and Thomas was uneasy with the knowledge that this could be his own son here needing medical attention to keep him from bleeding to death. This boy's injury resulted from his refusing to join up with the gang, or so he had told his father. Sean's might be from his association with them, or a change of heart that would not be looked upon kindly. It was difficult to look at the boy, and Thomas swallowed a lump in his throat before speaking.

"Good luck to ya, now," was all he could say.

Dr. Bermann appeared in the waiting room as the man and his son were leaving. He called out a reminder about caring for the wound before turning to Sorley.

"Well, young man, you look a fine deal better than the last time we saw you."

"Aye, much better. If I'm bein' honest, though, I don't remember bein' here, but I'm guessin' that's because of that awful medicine you gave me. It tastes terrible, and it makes my brain soft."

Dr. Bermann laughed, knowing the bitter taste of laudanum was offensive to most folks, and it had made him question for many years how someone could become addicted and willingly ingest it day and night. He turned toward Thomas and Kathleen and asked them about Sorley's progress, about how long since he'd used the pain medication, and he was happy that the boy refused it after two days. He explained what the removal process would entail and asked them to wait while he and Mrs. Bermann took Sorley back to the examination room to begin. Sorley glanced at his parents as he followed the Bermanns, and Kathleen gave him a nod and a smile of reassurance.

While the doctor asked Sorley a series of questions about his injured leg, Mrs. Bermann filled the elevated washtub in the corner of the room with large buckets of water that were placed near the tub. There were two large iron kettles on the woodstove, always heating and ready to use when needed. She dumped those in, along with a jar of vinegar.

"Whose takin' a bath?" Sorley asked, fearful of stripping down in front of strangers though heaven knew he needed a bath in the worst way.

"Just your leg, son," Dr. Bermann answered. "We'll sit you on this tall chair," he continued as he moved a chair from the other side of the room next to the washtub, "and you'll just dangle that leg in the water with a good measure of vinegar in it. It will dissolve your cast so we can take it off your leg."

"Can I watch?" Sorley's constant curiosity was piqued, and he looked forward to watching the process from start to finish.

"Not much else for you to do but watch," Dr. Bermann replied kindly. The doctor would have liked to immerse the boy into the water and give him a good scrubbing, but he reminded himself to be merciful knowing the miserable conditions the Delaneys lived in. He had noticed when he greeted them in the waiting room that the boy's pant leg had been roughly cut off about five or six inches below the crotch to allow for the girth of the cast. Dr. Bermann hoped the boy had another pair at home with both legs intact.

"We're ready here," Mrs. Bermann advised. She swirled her hand around in the warm vinegar water to make sure there were no hot spots from the near-boiling water she had added from the stovetop.

Sorley made his way over to the washtub tentatively, but the Bermanns were kind and he trusted them. Mrs. Bermann pushed the chair up next to the edge of the washtub and Dr. Bermann lifted Sorley up onto it. He thought, as he did so, that a boy of eight should be much heavier than Sorley was, and he felt the same sadness for the Delaney family as he did for many of his patients. He instructed the boy to put his cast into the water as he sat him down on the chair. It was mildly uncomfortable sitting as he did, legs spread apart and one leg over the edge of the tub and in the water, but the warmth of the clean water was a wonderful treat even with the smell of cider vinegar wafting up in the steam.

It took about ten minutes before the cast started to soften. Sorley watched with great interest as his weighty companion changed, and he noticed small pieces of it coming off into the water. Dr. Bermann waited until the leg had been soaking for nearly half an hour. Mrs. Bermann stood nearby with a towel and when her husband lifted the boy from the water, she wrapped the towel around his leg. The doctor laid Sorley on the examination table and began cutting the cast away.

"That smells bad," Sorley whined. "Is that my own leg smellin' like that?"

"It's nothing unusual, Sorley. Don't you worry." Mrs. Bermann put her hand on the boy's arm to comfort him. Having no children of her own to coddle, she welcomed every opportunity to give an extra measure of love to the ones who came to their clinic.

The doctor removed the last of the plaster and pulled off the cloth stocking that was beneath the cast. Mrs. Bermann instructed Sorley to lie still while the doctor removed the stitches, which he did so carefully that the boy barely felt a thing. When the doctor was done, he helped Sorley sit up on the table.

"What's wrong with my leg? Why is it so white and wrinkled and smaller than the other?" Sorley was visibly upset to see his once-healthy leg looking like it belonged on a pale old man two steps from the grave.

"That's perfectly normal, too, don't you worry. It will catch back up to the other one in no time." Dr. Bermann did his best to reassure the boy, but he still looked anxious. "You will need to use your leg now, but remember it's going to be weak at first. Be sure to get enough exercise, take a walk every day if you can." Sorley gave a hesitant nod of his head, and Dr. Bermann regretted his advice as soon as the words left his mouth. It was doubtful that the children in Sorley's family, or any of the families living in the tenements, got adequate exercise and fresh air. He would give Thomas and Kathleen some helpful advice about things the boy could do to build up some strength in the leg.

"Here now, let's help you down off this table and see how it feels," the doctor said. He helped Sorley down to the floor. Dr. Bermann took the boy's right arm, Mrs. Bermann took the left, and Sorley attempted his first steps without the cast. He faltered, taken aback by how weak the leg was and disheartened as some pain returned to the knee as it bore his weight without the support of the cast.

"It will take time, and you must be patient. You should continue using the crutch to help support you as you build back some strength," the doctor advised. Mrs. Bermann retrieved the crutch from beside the examining table and returned it to the boy. He relaxed noticeably when he had the familiar crutch to help him move about, and the Bermanns encouraged him to walk around the examining room a couple of times to get the feel for it. Sorley complied and felt some of his confidence return, though he now felt the fool for the ridiculous pair of pants he was wearing. This time, he would gladly ride in the cart through their neighborhood. To be seen in a one-legged pair of pants, and the exposed leg a pale, puny excuse of a limb, would be more humiliation that he cared to deal with.

The Bermanns walked Sorley back out to his waiting parents. Kathleen drew in her breath, shocked and unsettled by the appearance of Sorley's leg. Thomas was near to crying for his son's weakened condition. Dr. Bermann expected their responses and spoke with them at length about the normalcy of the leg's appearance and the work ahead to restore the strength in it. The doctor assured them they were welcome to keep the crutch, for he no longer needed it. Sorley would need it in the weeks ahead, and there was a possibility he would need it far longer if the knee did not regain its strength and mobility. The Delaneys thanked the Bermanns profusely.

"Does he have another pair of pants at home?" Mrs. Bermann couldn't help but ask.

"Aye, he does. A bit tattered they are, but still enough thread to cover him," Kathleen answered. "And I will sew the other leg back onto this pair as best I can." It saddened her to think about her son wearing pants with a sewn-on leg, visible as it would be to those who cared to look but it was the burden of life they bore, and she would not lower her head in embarrassment. She would not bring shame to Thomas for he was doing all he could to provide for them.

"All right, then," Dr. Bermann said, "Unless something doesn't feel right, we should be done with the knee. The path ahead depends on how hard you are willing to work, young man, and the grace of God. We've done what we can do, and you've been a brave and admirable patient." The doctor patted Sorley's head, and the Delaneys expressed their gratitude again, taking their leave and getting Sorley settled into the cart at his request. Thomas was aware of his son's embarrassment and his wanting to avoid being seen by onlookers as they walked home.

After the Delaney's left, Mrs. Bermann helped the doctor empty the washtub and clean up the examination room before heading back to the waiting area to gather up the plate and fork from Sorley's pastry. She lifted the plate from the small side table and found ten dimes beneath it. She swallowed hard and her eyes filled with tears. The Delaneys were good people who were proud even in the face of abject poverty, their hope depleted by years of insurmountable struggles. She hoped Providence had something better for them, that the winds of change would carry them to a place where life would show them some mercy.

The Delaney's walk home was a silent one, heavy with uncertainty, as Thomas and Kathleen wondered how much progress Sorley would make and how much use he would regain in his weakened leg. Sorley was only concerned about being seen in a one-legged pair of pants and was fearful that his injured leg would always look as it did now. He resolved to keep it covered forever if it never again looked like the other.

Thomas was relieved to see all three of his other children in the flat when they arrived home, happy that Sean had resisted the temptation to wander off while unsupervised. The children gathered around Sorley as Thomas helped him up out of the cart. Maeve could not hold back the gasp when she saw Sorley's bare white leg, so pale and no bigger than her own. Kathleen put her hand on Maeve's shoulder to reassure her. She quickly realized that she may have been insensitive to Sorley's insecurity by reacting the way she did, and she mumbled an apology filled with guilt and sorrow.

"Tis no bother, Maeve," Sorley reassured her. "The doctor said that's how they all look after the cast is removed. He said it'll be much as it was after a time." Maeve smiled at her brother and nodded, hopeful that the doctor was right.

While the Delaneys gathered around Sorley, reassuring him and making light of the sad-looking leg, no one noticed that Sean had drawn back and turned away. He was shocked by the ugly scar, the stitch marks, and the weakened condition of Sorley's leg. His guilt left a sour taste in his mouth. It weighed him down with a grief so heavy that he wasn't sure he could bear it. He quietly headed for the door, his exit undetected until Thomas and Kathleen heard the door close behind him. Thomas started toward it, meaning to follow Sean and find out where he was going, but Kathleen's hand on his arm stopped him. She looked at her husband with unspoken words that were immediately understood. She didn't need to remind him of their oldest son's grief and guilt, the shock of seeing the damage done under his failed watch, and the embarrassment he would suffer if the family watched him weep. Thomas stopped, nodded almost imperceptibly to his wife, and let the boy go. He hoped Sean would make the right choice about where he was headed, both now and in the days to come.

No more than an hour had passed when Sean returned, sadness written on his face and his spirit crumbling. Thomas felt a surge of compassion for his troubled son and knew it would be a difficult afternoon and evening if he didn't do something to lift the mood.

"Shall I tell us the tale of Cuchulainn?" Thomas asked, reaching for his worn copy of *The Tain*.

"Please, Da," Sorley replied and that was enough. Their brave boy wanted to hear the beloved tale, and so it would be. Thomas hoped it would draw Sean from his dark place and help him engage with his family, and so the telling began. Thomas recounted the familiar tale of the Cattle Raid of Cooley with his usual flair, mostly from memory. The lines and descriptions were deeply imbedded in his heart and mind from a time in Cork when he was Sorley's age listening to his granddad tell the story. It was the ancient tale of Queen Mebh and King Ailill from Connacht waging a war against Ulster to steal their great brown bull. All the warriors of Ulster had been cursed with a lingering illness cast upon them by the goddess Macha, leaving only seventeen-year-old Cuchulainn to stand against the raiders. He defeated countless champions of Ulster in a months-long battle. As always, Thomas embellished the tale with different champions, more creative battles, interesting twists and turns, but never veered from the final outcome.

"In a desperate effort to defeat the magnificent Cuchulainn, Mebh offered the warrior Ferdiad, a friend of Cuchulainn, everything a soul could hope for," Thomas continued, reading now from the book, "Warrior, Mighty, Famous, All the treasures of the earth shall to thee be given."

"I imagine it was a dream too big, and that the want of it consumed poor Ferdiad," Kathleen said, offering a sympathetic assessment of how Ferdiad could turn against his friend.

"Aye, and it was the death of him," Thomas replied. They all knew the outcome, and that Cuchulainn, magnificent hero of folklore, would be victorious once again, and his friend Ferdiad would die in the battle against him.

"I feel bad for Ferdiad," Eamon commented when the story had ended. "Is it so very wrong to want for riches or to have the treasures of a king?"

"If the want of it leads us to unforgiveable behavior, aye, 'tis wrong, Son," Thomas responded. "And yet, I understand how hard it is to keep our want at bay. If it were in my power, I would grant you all exactly what Mebh promised Ferdiad. I'd give you all the treasures of the earth so that you'd never want for anything ever again."

"And we could share the treasures with everyone like us. Their bellies would all be full, and they'd have fine new shoes from Charlie Connor. What a grand dream it is, Da!" Maeve said.

"'Tis a lovely thing to dream of," Kathleen said, "but let's not forget to be grateful for what we have, yes?"

Everyone agreed, and the storytelling came to a close. Sean felt some relief from his sadness. Eamon, Maeve and Kathleen were happy Sorley had chosen their favorite tale for it had brought all hearts together after a difficult time. And Thomas kept the knowledge to himself that he recounted Mebh's words a hundred times daily, his mantra, his deepest desire, his unreachable prize, to give all the treasures of the earth to his brave and beautiful family.

CHAPTER EIGHT

By late June the heat of the inner city began to take its toll on the residents who lived there. There was little relief from the hot heavy air that laid low between the rows of brick tenements, the walls rising up and enclosing them all inside the crumbling ovens of the lower east side of the city. Moods grew intolerant and the streets became more dangerous because of it. Fights broke out nearly every day between differing factions, be they gangs or nationalities or neighbors who were no longer feeling very neighborly. Kathleen and the children stayed close to home, though she allowed Sean some time away, occasionally, on a Sunday afternoon. She knew he was feeling constrained, penned, and frustrated, and she made the maternally soft decision to give him some freedom when Thomas was at work and his relentless scrutiny was not a constant source of tension.

Unbeknownst to Thomas and Kathleen, Sean had mastered the art of living a double life. He quickly realized that the only way to keep peace in the Delaney home, not break his mother's heart, and continue to add to his growing stash of money, was to operate with the Wharf Kings on a part-time basis. Cow-Legged Sam had balked at the idea when Sean and Reddy McCann first approached him with it. He didn't know the boy well enough to trust him completely, but in the end he decided he would give him a chance. If Sean betrayed him, he would suffer the consequences of that betrayal. Besides, Sam liked the proposition the boy had presented to him.

After Thomas was hired to clean up the Catharine Street Market, and after hearing the stories Thomas told them about the aftermath of the Saturday night festivities, Sean realized Sundays were ripe for the picking. Over-indulgent revelers were often sleeping late and suffering the lingering effects of too much alcohol. Many others who had awakened to a throbbing head had left their room seeking food and coffee to ease the painful drumming between their temples. Sean quickly learned how easy it was to enter an unlocked ground-floor window of a hotel, and how if one were very quiet it was a simple task to empty pockets and gather anything of value from the room. Over the weeks he had developed a route. He never robbed the same hotel two weeks in a row to lessen his chances of being caught. It wasn't long before he knew where the more profitable establishments were located, and he divided his time among them. The Sweeney Hotel, the Moss Hotel, and Crook's Hotel—aptly named, he thought—were all located near Chatham Square and were easy targets. There were numerous other establishments within a twenty-minute walk from Muldoon's. The trick was to be in the area without being close enough to be seen from Catharine Street where Thomas was working.

With more money than he knew what to do with, Sean made use of the horse-drawn omnibus to get to some of the outlying hotels. He used the public transportation every two or three weeks when pilfering the Sinclair House at 8th and Broadway, a mile and a half from the Five Points. On one particular Sunday, outside the back entrance in the alley behind the Sinclair House, Sean heard a conversation about the St. Nicholas Hotel. The St. Nicholas was in a part of town where the Delaneys never ventured and didn't belong. On Broadway, between Broome and Spring Streets, the St. Nicholas was constructed six years ago and was the premier hotel in New York City. As Sean listened to the deliverymen carrying boxes of produce from the alley into the Sinclair House kitchen, he was intrigued by the prospect of patrons with deep pockets. According to the men in the alley, The St. Nicholas was the most expensive hotel ever built in the city, costing one million dollars to build and nearly three-quarters of a million dollars to furnish. Sean had no way to comprehend how much money that was. He watched the men working, the easy and seemingly unnoticed coming and going through the back entrance, and he formulated a plan to visit the St. Nicholas Hotel the following weekend.

The week between inched along, slowed by heat and monotony. Sorley was moving about better, and Sean regularly encouraged him to walk up and down the hallway several times a day to keep the leg moving and to strengthen the atrophied muscles. Kathleen was pleased with Sean's interactions with Sorley and was content with the way things were going. Their existence remained meager at best, but they were able to keep the wolves at bay and their hunger sated. Kathleen knew it was more than they would have had if they had stayed in Ireland, for death surely would have taken them all. That fatal dark cloud had driven them to leave their home and board a ship bound for a better life. That life, promised, had not materialized and their struggle in America had been nearly as difficult.

The tragic similarities between starvation in Ireland and in New York were all founded in prejudice and hate. Though Ireland's devastated potato crop was a natural disaster caused by disease, English hatred led that government to initiate an attempt at genocide, exacerbating the blight into a famine. The starvation the Irish suffered in New York was due to the same level of hatred and the withholding of a viable income from the poverty-stricken immigrants. The promise of refuge, hope, and a better life was as tarnished as the pennies that barely sustained them.

Sunday morning arrived too warm and with little promise of a cooling breeze. Thomas left the apartment whistling, looking forward to his steady routine, the money it would put in his pocket, and the weekly visit to Mr. Carnahan's market to buy food at the end of his workday. Sean listened to the sound of his father's footsteps fading down the hallway and out the back entrance. He reflected momentarily on the great chasm of difference between their own East Broadway and Broadway Avenue where the St. Nicholas stood like a white marble beacon to a class of people far removed from the rows of tenements where the Delaneys resided. Mam had drawn water from the pump in the yard and was scrubbing the laundry in the basin in the hallway. Sean checked to see that the children were occupied before retrieving enough coin from his stash beneath the floorboard to pay for the omnibus. He would walk to Houston Street, away from the prying eyes of well-meaning neighbors and would catch a ride up to Broadway and Bleecker to Pfaff's Beer Cellar, a popular drop-off location for the omnibus. Pfaff's was the preferred meeting place for writers, artists, and intellectuals, and was frequented by local characters and out-of-towners alike. Most of them had money and most of them enjoyed the frivolities of the beer garden late into the evening.

Sean arrived at Pfaff's around noon, peeked inside, and saw the place was already active with patrons. He rightly assumed that these would be the visitors to New York, newly arrived, and the teetotalers who would not have overindulged into the wee hours of the morning. Just hours before, in the typically overcrowded beer cellar, two ardent gamblers had engaged in a serious marathon of poker, made less skillful and more heated by the influence of a bottle or two of whiskey.

Samuel Clemens had been celebrating his licensure as a riverboat pilot, and Mr. Whitman was lamenting the refusal of society to embrace his book of poetry. Mr. Whitman was in a foul mood, distracted enough by his self-pitying to fail at any semblance of strategy, and had lost a great deal of money to the celebratory riverboat pilot from Hannibal, Missouri. Mr. Clemens had gathered his winnings, downed a final shot of the imported Irish whiskey, and had bid the sulking Mr. Whitman a fond farewell. He promised to return the following evening and give Mr. Whitman a fair chance to win back some of his losses. Clemens walked the three blocks to his lodging, the opulent St. Nicholas Hotel, desperately hoping he would not be robbed of the night's earnings on his way there. Even in the better parts of the city hooligans and thieves were a constant concern. Clemens had picked up his pace, impaired as it was by the whiskey, and arrived at his room on the first floor in good time. Sleep consumed him the moment his body settled into the soft cotton mattress.

Sean stood in front of Pfaff's for a few minutes, checking in every direction for the police. Seeing none, he turned and followed the same short walk Mr. Clemens had made the night before. He hoped that some of the hotel's patrons were still sleeping off their Saturday night excesses. Around the back of the hotel was an alley bustling with deliverymen and cleaning crews. Sean wandered into the gathering unnoticed. He watched for a while, fascinated by the intricate workings of the men and women who weaved in and out through the crowd of tradesmen and vendors. He made his way to a spot near the door where a careless maintenance man had left his wooden toolbox. It was an easy move for Sean to walk over and pick it up. He was struck by how heavy it was, filled with chisels and wood planes, hammers and wrenches, and other assorted tools. He tightened his grip on the wooden dowel that served as a handle, looked around to make sure an angry carpenter wasn't watching him pilfer the tools of his trade, and turned to walk through the storeroom with purpose. No one even glanced his way. He hoped he would find his way inside to the hotel rooms as he crossed the storeroom and exited through a wide double door.

A man in a suit walked toward Sean, a large metal ring of assorted keys jingling in his right hand. He greeted Sean as he passed by, obviously assuming the boy was there to repair something. Sean nodded in return and continued down the hallway, relief sweeping over him as he focused his thoughts on the opportunity ahead. He looked behind him to make sure no one was there as he walked down the hallway and began to test the doorknobs of the rooms he passed. He worked quickly and carefully, silently, watching this way and that for prying eyes. He knew it was just a matter of time before one doorknob would turn and allow him access. It was common for an intoxicated patron to stumble into their room and into bed without remembering to lock the door behind them. The first one Sean tried was locked, the second and third as well, but the fourth turned easily and allowed him to enter. His plausible explanation, that he was there to fix the window frame, was well-rehearsed and ready to offer if his presence in the room was discovered and questioned. A quick apology for having entered the wrong room should placate an angry patron.

Sean entered the room and closed the door quietly behind him. He heard heavy snoring from the massive four-poster bed and stopped for a moment to take in the ornate furnishings. He was slack-jawed and envious, and more determined than ever to find a way out of the poverty that had his family firmly in its grip. Reminding himself of the task at hand, Sean noticed a small table near the window covered with an impressive stack of banknotes and coins. He set the toolbox down on the imported carpet just to the right of the door and moved closer, making not a sound. He moved across the room silently, the carpet padding the floor with a layer of prevention. When he reached the table he began stuffing the bank notes into his pockets as quickly and quietly as he could. Coins were always risky, as their telltale jingle would alert his victim far too easily. He took only the twenty-dollar gold coins now familiar to him, picking them up one at a time and slipping them carefully into his pockets between the bank notes. It was one of the larger amounts of cash that Sean had pilfered, and he hoped to impress Sam with his solo effort. As he stuffed the last of the money into his pockets he noticed a certificate he had uncovered declaring Mr. Samuel Clemens a licensed riverboat pilot.

Sean paused for a moment, thinking what a wonderful life it would be to spend your days aboard a riverboat far away from the oppressive walls and filthy streets of the city. On the table beside the remaining coins was a gold pocket watch. The crystal glinted in the sun that was peeking through the slit in the curtains, and Sean decided for the first time that he would not disclose the entirety of his spoils to Sam McCarthy. He removed his flat cap—a hand-me-down from Da and the same cap worn by nearly every Irishman in the city—and stuffed Mr. Clemens' gold watch in between the lining and the wool cap. The cotton lining had been torn for months and he had been meaning to ask Mam to mend it but now he was happy for it. He pushed the watch to the back of the cap and hoped it would not be detectable there. He took one last look at the red-haired man in the massive bed before turning and exiting the room as quietly as he had entered it.

Halfway back to the storeroom Sean realized he had left the toolbox in the hotel room. He paused for a moment and thought about going back for it but with so few people in the hallways and so many people bustling about in back, he rightly imagined he could walk to the storeroom and out to the alley without a word from anyone. Mr. Samuel Clemens would likely report to the hotel manager that he had been robbed. The culprit was a carpenter or a maintenance fellow if the toolbox were any sort of clue at all. Pleased with his Sunday morning take, Sean made use of the omnibus to get him a good distance from the St. Nicholas and then continued on foot to the seedier side of town, the place that welcomed desperate souls and undesirables such as himself.

There was a ruckus going on in the back room of Molly Muldoon's when Sean arrived at the bar. He was startled by the loud voices, loud enough to be heard from the bar. He hesitated for a moment, wondering if he should wait to go in and turn over his loot to Sam. He took a quick look around the bar and noticed three men in the corner, their heads close together, discussing some nefarious plans in loaded whispers. Sean decided it would be a better idea to get inside the gang's headquarters where it was relatively safe. He gave the familiar one knock, followed by another a few seconds later, and was surprised that the door was opened by Chick McFee, not Sow Madden.

"He's a lyin' backstabber!" Sow Madden was yelling as Sean entered the room. "He's been dippin' his fingers in the pot, sweet-talkin' Mona and helpin' himself to what's in the till!" Sow Madden's speech was heavily slurred. Sean didn't want to get in the middle of anything especially if Sow Madden's temper was at the boiling point. He spotted an empty chair in the corner of the room and got past Sow as quickly as he could.

"He's lyin', Sam," Spanish Marley countered. Dishonesty was a serious accusation leveled against someone of Sow's long-time affiliation with Sam. Sean was shocked to see that it was Marley who was being accused by Sow Madden and was fearful for his friend.

"You better watch yourself, boy." Sow Madden's voice was low and threatening, and there was a deadly undertone that made Sean's blood run cold. He had never trusted Sow Madden, never liked him, and would never cross the line that would put him on the bad side of someone so evil. It surprised Sean that Marley had placed himself in that position, which told Sean that Marley might be guilty of the things he was being accused of. Why else would he risk his life with such weighty accusations?

"Quiet!" Sam's voice was loud and impatient. "I've heard enough from both of you! You, boy," Sam looked directly at Spanish Marley, "will pay with your life if you've been stealing from me. And know this; the truth will come out. It always does. And you," he turned to Sow Madden, "get back to your chair and let me take care of my own business. And lay off that damn laudanum! You haven't had a clear thought in months and I'm tired of it. If you're not sharp, you're no good to me. You understand?" Sam's words were crystal clear. No one in the room breathed and all eyes were averted away from the disgraced henchman. No one had ever heard Sam utter a cross word to Sow Madden, and it punctuated his demand with deadly seriousness.

The tension in the room was thick and suffocating. Sean did not move a muscle. He barely allowed himself to breathe as the drama unfolded. He had always liked Spanish Marley, and he hoped the things Sow had accused him of were not true, for Sean knew what Marley's fate would be if he were guilty. The East River was deep and dark and took many a man without a trace. Sean thought about the gold watch inside his cap, resting against the back of his head. The realization of what he was doing—the very thing that Spanish Marley was being accused of—caused the weight of the watch to feel like a cannonball tucked inside the lining of his cap.

"Delaney!" Sam's voice jarred Sean into cognizance, unaware that Sam had called him twice before. "You do a lot of daydreaming, boy! Come over here." There was no sneering laughter this time from Sow Madden. His mood was sullen, and he knew better than to further annoy Sam.

Sean nodded and walked to Sam's table. He stopped in front of it directly across from the angry leader of the Wharf Kings and emptied his pockets. They were stuffed full of banknotes and though he had not had the time to pay attention when he pilfered it from Mr. Clemens' room, he noticed now that many of them were hundred-dollar notes issued by the Bank of New York. Sean grew uneasy, taken aback by the large haul he had brought to Sam, and he worried that it might be perceived as fishing for favor in the gang's hierarchy. He did not want Sow Madden to level his anger in his direction. Sean started explaining where he had gotten the money now piled on Sam's table, but Sam cut him off. He didn't care where the money came from, he never did. His biggest concern was that it was a clean heist, and he required the same guarantee each time—that no one saw, and no one followed.

"I went in quiet as a mouse. The only one in the room was sleepin' it off from last night and not a person looked my way as I left," Sean offered.

"That's good. You know there would be a terrible price to pay for leading someone here, don't you, boy?"

"Aye, Sam."

"All right then, shall we see what you've got here?"

Sean nodded as he reached deep into his pockets to remove that last of the stolen money. He removed six twenty-dollar gold coins and added them to the pile of banknotes. Sam looked pleased. He had noticed immediately that the paper currency was from the Bank of New York. The local notes were worth more than those from other states and there was an impressive amount of them in the pile Sean had placed on the table.

"That's a good haul, Delaney. You've got a good trick going, and it appears to be getting better. How do you think we should divvy this up, then?"

"Whatever you say, Sam," Sean offered weakly. He would never presume to know what share he should receive. Asking too little would show weakness and insecurity. Asking too much would draw anger and suspicions of power-hungry self-promotion from the other members. He shifted nervously, uncomfortable with the dangerous question.

"What'll the cut be, Delaney?" Sam repeated impatiently. He was in a dark mood after the confrontation with Sow Madden and Spanish Marley. Sean hoped he would not be thrown into the fire of Sam's furious temper for what he was about to say.

"Seventy-thirty?" Sean tried his best to sound like a man, basing his answer on previous payouts and splits. Thirty percent was slightly more than he typically received, but up until today he had not been given the opportunity to set his own terms.

"Seventy-thirty?" Sam's voice was flat and emotionless, his expression impossible to read. It set Sean's fragile nerves at the precipice, in danger of shattering altogether.

"Seems fair," was all he could muster.

"Then seventy-thirty it is." Sam set about counting Mr. Clemens' winnings which amounted to a grand sum of one thousand four hundred and eighty dollars. "By my calculation, your thirty percent would be around four hundred and forty dollars. Does that suit your fancy, Delaney?"

Sean's heart was racing, his breath coming quickly. He had known there was an impressive sum of money sitting on the table, but he never dreamed he would take home a cut that large. He nodded his approval to Sam. His mouth was so dry he feared he would not be able to speak. Sam counted out four of the hundred-dollar banknotes and four ten-dollar notes and handed them to Sean. He noted the boy's hand shaking, and he reminded himself to go easy on Sean. He was young and green and still had the innocence of one not yet jaded by the dark life that Sam had lived for a very long time.

"You keep doing what you're doing, Delaney. You keep your nose clean and don't step out of line and you might find yourself a better position in this organization." Sam's meaning did not escape Sow Madden, seething with anger from his chair by the door. Sean swallowed hard but the lump in his throat was lodged in place. He was both excited and terrified, and he dreaded the walk past Sow Madden to exit through the only door in the room.

"Thanks, Sam," he said in a strained response. He needed water. He left the backroom and stopped at the bar to ask

Mona for some water before he headed home. Mona could see the pallid color on Sean's face and the sweat on his forehead. She noticed his hands shaking as he reached for the metal tumbler.

"Everything okay, Sean?" Mona rarely asked about what happened on the other side of the backroom door, but her heart was soft where Sean was concerned. He was so young, and he had a still-innocent demeanor that the others had lost long ago.

Sean nodded. After the first initial sip to chase the dryness down his throat he guzzled the entire contents. He set the tumbler down and thanked Mona, still too agitated for conversation. He looked around and saw that the bar was empty but for one old man sitting in the corner, his head dropped down with his chin on his chest. Asleep, Sean thought, or dead. He had not the time nor the interest to find out. He sat down at a table in the opposite corner and removed one of his sturdy new shoes, compliments of Charlie Conner. Sean carefully folded the banknotes and laid them inside his shoe before putting it back on. Mona witnessed the entire thing and knew that the boy had more money tucked in that shoe than he had ever seen in his short life. She prayed he would make it home safely. The daytime hours offered a better chance of that than the dark of night. Sean knew Mona had watched him, and he knew he could trust her. He waved back to her as he left the bar and caught of glimpse of Mona's chubby hands making the sign of the cross. Sean was happy to have the blessing to accompany him home. He needed all the help he could get even if he didn't deserve it.

Sean returned home much earlier than normal on that Sunday afternoon, having made a small fortune from his visit to the St. Nicholas. There was no need to pursue other possibilities, and Sam had seemed more than pleased with the one heist. Sean walked carefully so as not to cause any damage to the notes in his shoe. The heavy cotton paper the notes were printed on was strong enough to survive the walking motion, but he took extra caution with each step of his left foot just in case. It was far too much money to be careless with. He rounded the corner from East Broadway into the alley that ran between the tenement they called home and the one too close to it. He spotted Mam hanging clothes on one of the lines tied between the two buildings. She saw him approaching and paused.

"Are ya all right, son?"

"Aye, Mam, why do ya ask?" Sean immediately felt the guilt rearing its ugly head.

"I swear I saw ya walkin' like ya had a gimpy leg. Did ya hurt yourself?"

"'Tis nothin', Mam. I twisted my ankle when I stepped over the wheel of a cart someone left beside the road," Sean lied. Again. The guilt felt like poison in his belly.

"Do ya want me to take a look?" Kathleen asked with genuine concern.

"Naw, I'm fine, Mam!" Sean sounded slightly annoyed, hoping his tone of voice would remind her he was nearly thirteen and didn't need his mam to be coddling him like a baby. She nodded and continued with hanging her laundry. Sean hoped he hadn't hurt her feelings for it was not his intention. At the same time, he needed to be off and away to the flat to stash his earnings before Mam got done and came back inside.

Maeve and Eamon were acting out Sean's story of the river dragon, Sowmadden, when Sean entered the flat. Normally he would have been pleased to have given them a new story and a new creature to fantasize about, but the deadly glare on Sow's face earlier that morning still burned in his memory. His siblings called out their greetings and invited him to come and sit by Mam's bed and play along, but he feigned a sore ankle and encouraged them to continue. When they were once again fully engaged in the story Sean sat himself down on the floor next to the loose board. He untied his shoes slowly and carefully, taking his time in case one of the children turned to see what he was doing, though he had conveniently placed himself slightly out of sight behind the end of the couch. He slowly worked the loose board up and slipped the bank notes inside the cloth bag that Sam had given him, now storing his riches safely beneath the floor. Sean removed his cap and retrieved the watch from inside it, adding it to his stash before carefully and quietly replacing the floorboard. The couch was vacant, and he flopped down upon it hoping his pounding heart and shaking hands would recover before Mam and Da were home. Da had been quietly suspicious of Sean's every move recently, and Sean was aware of his suspicions. Thomas kept his thoughts to himself for the most part but questioned everything Sean said and did.

Mam returned shortly, singing and happy. Life had been better since Thomas had found steady work. Sean was home more often and never went out at night, and for that great relief Kathleen was more than thankful. Tension had subsided and her family seemed in a good place, or at least that was her perception of it. She was oblivious to Thomas's lingering suspicions, and she was completely unaware of Sean's criminal activities. Sorley's knee was healing nicely, and he had discarded the crutch, though he still experienced a weakness in the leg that might require the use of a walking stick if he were going very far. Thomas had found a vendor's broken tent pole while working one Sunday morning and had asked Henry's permission to take it home to carve a walking stick for his son. Henry agreed that it was a fine idea, and he asked after Sorley often since that day. He was a good man, and Thomas was grateful that folks like Henry and Mrs. Zimmer still existed in the unwelcoming city where he lived.

The savory aroma of lamb stock cooking on the stovetop filled the apartment and set everyone's mood a good notch higher. Lamb stew was a favorite of the Delaney family, made just the way Kathleen's mother had made it. Early that morning Kathleen had cut the lamb from the bones and placed the meat in the icebox for later. She placed the bones in the largest pot they owned, filled it with water, and added onions and carrots, celery and parsley, salt and pepper. The stock cooked most of the morning while Mam tended to the laundry, but now that she had finished that chore it was time to strain the stock into her other pot and start working on the rest of the ingredients. She dusted the large chunks of lamb in seasoned flour and browned them in the bottom of the stockpot. She added the stock back into the pot and cut up fresh pieces of potato, carrot, and onion to add in as well. A large pinch of parsley, a tablespoon of flour, and more salt and pepper were added to the pot before Kathleen put the lid back on the pot and left it to cook all afternoon.

"Mam! The smell of it's causin' my belly to roar!" Eamon complained. "When can we eat?"

"Eamon, dear, you know full well that this stew must cook all day, but I promise you the wait will be worth it."

"I know you're right, Mam. Your lamb stew first came to earth from the angels in Heaven. Da said it himself. I just hope I don't die of hunger before it's ready." Eamon put the backside of his hand to his forehead and fell to the floor in an impressive show of drama. Everyone laughed, and Maeve joined in the fainting spell. Sean realized his stomach was growling, too.

"Mam, is there anything left of yesterday's bread?"

"Aye, Sean, there is. Butter is runnin' low, but I'm hopin' your da will bring us some more after work today. I'll put the tea on to boil and we'll all have a slice of bread and butter while we wait for Da to come home."

The children gathered around, Sorley limping over from the couch and the others allowing him to take a seat first. Mam spread the butter thin so that everyone got some on their bread, and she treated the children to sugar in their tea. It was a lovely time together, and they played a favorite game called *If I Could, I Would*. Everyone took a turn, and again, they let Sorley go first.

"If I could, I would buy a fine house with a yard covered in grass where we could run and play and roll around like circus performers. The yard would have a fence 'round it so no one could get in, and we'd have a lovely garden where Mam could grow flowers and lots of vegetables so she could make lots of lamb stew."

"Ah, Sorley, 'tis a wonderful dream, is it not?" Mam reached over and ran her hand along her son's freckled cheek. He smiled at her, and her heart swelled.

"Eamon?" Mam asked, indicating it was his turn next.

"If I could, I would be a writer of grand adventures read by children all over the world."

"Ya know, Eamon, that's somethin' you could do. Ya read so well, and ya love a good story. Sure and maybe one day your dream will come true," Mam encouraged.

"Yes, Eamon, I believe it will!" Maeve added.

"What about you, Maeve?" Sean asked. He was happy to see her pretty face filling out and the thin, drawn look of hunger gone from her eyes.

"Hmm, well, if I could, I would find a way to make everyone happy forever."

"And how, sweet Maeve, would ya do such a thing?" Mam asked.

"I don't quite know, Mam, but I'm workin' on it!" Mam giggled at her daughter's optimism, touched by her undying belief that everything would always be all right. She desperately wanted Maeve's innocence and idealism to stay with her for years to come. She prayed that hope would protect her daughter's heart from the rigors of the city. Too often, hopeless surrender eroded the heart and soul of those living in squalor and took the naivete from the youngest far too early.

"If I could, I would do the same, Maeve," Mam agreed. "Let me know when ya discover the secret to doin' that, won't ya?" Maeve said she would and turned to her oldest brother.

"What about you, Sean?"

"If I could, I would be a riverboat captain with a fine white boat deliverin' folks from one place to another along a lazy green river. The shade of the trees along the riverbank, and the breeze that the boat stirred up, would keep us cool on a hot summer day. There would be a great dinin' hall on the boat where we would wear our finest clothes and dine on rich folks' food every night."

The room was silent as Mam and the children imagined the delightful scenario Sean had so aptly described. The three younger children listened intently to their brother's vision, each already planning a new playtime adventure. Sean sat staring down into his half-empty teacup. Mam sat staring at Sean. This transparency was new for him. He had hidden much of himself away from his family since the day he was old enough to figure out how. Mam had no idea that he had any aspirations at all, let alone a fanciful dream of operating a riverboat.

"Son, how is it that you've come by this dream?"

"Just kinda sounds nice. I'm sick of the heat in this city. I'm sick of the dirt and the garbage and the smell. I suppose the thought of bein' out in wide open spaces far from the city sounded like a grand dream to have."

"And would you truly want to be wearin' fine clothes and dinin' on fancy foods?"

"Naw, I'm thinkin' not," Sean admitted, then added, "but it might be nice to try." He smiled directly at Mam, the wide shining smile he possessed but rarely shared. Kathleen's heart caught in her chest, skipped a beat, and ached for the heavy burden of sadness Sean seemed to carry with him. She reached across the table and took his hand. He let her, and if he were uninhibited enough to admit it, it felt wonderfully warm and reassuring. Sean missed that, and he quietly mourned the hardening of his heart and the shedding of childlike emotions that came with growing up. He felt a lump forming in his throat and gently pulled his hand away. Kathleen understood.

"All right, then," she said. She took a deep breath to chase the trembling from her voice. "Da should be home in an hour or so. Who would like to help me bake a new loaf of bread to have with our stew?"

Maeve and Sorley both volunteered, and though their help would be questionable Mam loved having her children nearby as she worked in the kitchen. It took her back to a better time, a time when she would pull up a chair near her own mam and help with dinner. She slid two chairs over from the table and placed one on each side of her for the children to stand on. Laughter ensued and all three of the bakers were powdered with a dusting of flour when it was over. The children offered to help Mam clean up and together they restored order to the kitchen.

Sean sat on the couch and watched the kitchen activity for a few minutes before turning his attention to Eamon. His brother sat quietly in the corner with an open book, and Sean assumed he was re-reading one of their well-told tales. He watched his brother for a while and realized he was writing on the blank pages in the back of the book. Da had surprised Eamon with a pencil after returning home from work a couple of weeks ago. Discarded by someone the night before, Da quickly snatched it up and put it in his pocket. Pencils were a luxury that was rarely known in the Delaney household, and Thomas would not sweep it up into the trash pile. Eamon had been overjoyed by the gift. Now, sitting there in the corner, he seemed deep in thought. Sean wondered if Eamon was writing a story, for that was his dream. The next time he pilfered a fancy hotel room Sean would set a coin or two aside to purchase some paper and a box of pencils for his brother, and then he would figure out a way to explain the purchase.

***

Thomas left the market a happy man. He had stopped by Charlie's shop after completing his work and found Charlie had a very small delivery to bring in. Thomas politely asked if there was anything else he could do while he was there, and Charlie shuffled nervously. Thomas found his suspicions to be correct when Charlie told him he would no longer need his services.

"Thomas, I'm sorry to say I may not need your help for a while. I had a visit from my nephew yesterday. He told me he's fallen on hard times, that he needs a job and place to stay, to lie low, he called it. I think I told you, Thomas, that I believe he's been running with one of the gangs from the Five Points and if that's the case and he's wanting out, I feel a need to help him." Charlie's tone was apologetic, and it spoke clearly to Thomas about his valuation of family. It was something Thomas treasured above all else, carried over from Ireland, and a virtue he hoped he was instilling in his own children. He wasn't sure about Sean, but the younger three seemed to value the strong bond they shared.

"Charlie, my friend, there's no need to apologize. You're a good man and you'll be doin' a good thing by helpin' your Marley out of the gangs and into a better life." A quick moment of fear rattled Thomas as the suspicion about his own son cast a shadow over his heart. He wondered if he would be in a similar situation one day helping Sean leave a dangerous situation and find refuge at home. Thomas hoped not, for it could bring harm to the rest of his family and he would not have it. He dreaded the choice he might face, of choosing to help Sean or protecting his family from ruthless gang members. He didn't know where he would send Sean, or who he could trust to shelter him safely, but if it came to that he would make that choice. Charlie's voice drew Thomas back to the conversation.

"I suppose you're right, Thomas. I have my concerns if I'm honest with you. Marley's been here and back more than once and rarely keeps his word or honors his intentions. He came 'round yesterday and asked if he could move back into the room at the back of the shop. He offered to help out around the place in trade for a place to sleep. I'm expecting to see little of him, but time will tell."

"I wish ya both well, Charlie, and I thank ya for what you've done for me and my family. You've been a good friend and more than generous. When do you expect Marley, then?"

"He mentioned bringing his stuff around in the next couple of days. He's never very clear on what his intentions are, but I'm thinking he'll be around next weekend to help me with the delivery." Charlie gave a slight shrug. His nephew was unreliable, but Charlie continued to give him the benefit of the doubt hoping one day he would settle into a responsible life.

"Charlie, if ya like, I can come by next Sunday after I'm done just like I always do to make sure things have gone as planned. How's that sound?" Thomas offered.

"I wouldn't want to ask you to stop by if Marley ..."

"Charlie, it's right on my way home," Thomas interrupted. "It's no bother and the least I can do."

Charlie accepted Thomas's kind offer and the two men shook hands. It had been a comfortable and equitable relationship, and each of them was grateful for what they had gained from it. Thomas waved back over his shoulder as he headed for Carnahan's Market on his way home. Kathleen had promised her mother's stew this Sunday, and Thomas was distracted with the thought of it as he chatted with Mr. Carnahan and gathered up another week's worth of food from the market.

As he walked home, Thomas could not keep himself from scanning the side streets that led to Chatham Square. He worried he would see his son there against his wishes, and he could not shake the gnawing feeling in his belly that it would happen sooner or later. Thomas's mother had been gifted—or cursed, as she described it—with *an dara sealladh*, the second sight, and had often said that Tommy had a bit of it himself. He was never sure, and he held little belief in the old ways, but with this situation involving Sean, Thomas felt it might be true. Like his mam, he couldn't say for sure if it were a blessing or a curse, but he hoped that if the time came it would serve him well.

As with every other one of Thomas's Sunday afternoons, he saw no sign of Sean on the streets nearby. He would not wander nearer Chatham Square for that would mean he had surrendered every ounce of trust he had in the boy, and Thomas did not want that to be the case. He would remain watchful and always hope for the best. As he approached their tenement building his stomach growled loudly. He smiled and glanced down at the flat belly beneath the threadbare cotton shirt. "*Hang on, my good man, we're nearly there,*" he whispered to the empty rumbling.

Thomas opened the door to their apartment and was greeted by the intense aromas of Katie's stew and freshly baked bread. His knees felt weak, and he worried he would not have the strength to lift Maeve up into his arms as she ran toward him. His hunger, easily ignored while he was busy working was now intense, and the busy workday and long walk home had tired him. He placed the sack of food from Carnahan's Market on the floor near the door and leaned down to lift his daughter up into his arms.

"Och, Stóirín, you're gettin' too big for your tired old da to lift ya," he said. He noticed the sadness on her face and quickly reassured her he would always try, always welcome her into his arms, and that even if he was a feeble old fella of a hundred and ten he would sit first and hold her in his lap. She would always belong there. Maeve kissed his cheek, her green eyes sparkling with joy and curiosity.

"What did ya bring us, Da? Did ya get us more butter for the grand loaf of bread I made?"

"You made?" Kathleen questioned with a smile.

"Well, then, I helped to make!" Maeve responded.

"Aye, there is butter in the sack and also some vegetables, a chicken, a small ham, a few apples, and a wee little cake made with orange that we can share for dessert!"

"Oh my, what a treat!" Kathleen said, delighted that he understood the importance of a sweet surprise to keep their spirits up. What others counted as the normal way of things was considered an incredible blessing to those who went without.

Thomas sat down beside Sean on the couch and took off his shoes. He reflected on his conversation with Charlie as he removed the shoes Charlie had made for him. Charlie was a skilled shoemaker, and the Delaney family was now outfitted with strong footwear that should last them a good long time. Thomas wondered if their alliance was over, and whether Marley would finally keep his word and be a helper to his uncle. If so, Thomas would be glad for it and would still count Charlie Connor as a good friend.

"What goes on in the life of Sean Delaney?" Thomas asked as he pushed his shoes to the side.

"Nothin' much, Da."

"Well, we'll have to remedy that," Da responded.

"How?" Sean asked suspiciously.

"I'm thinkin' we need to find somethin' for ya to do. Idle hands, ya know. The devil gets ahold of those and bad things happen."

"I don't know what you're talkin' about," Sean shot back defensively.

"I'm not talkin' about anything, Son, other than the importance of havin' somethin' to do. It's not good for a soul to sit and ponder and think too much. I was rememberin' the doctor and Mrs. Bermann today. When your brother's knee was injured, we didn't have money to pay the doctor. He's a kind man and asked only that I come 'round and plow the little garden behind his house. I took care of that a few weeks ago and I'm thinkin' Mrs. Bermann's vegetables are comin' up nicely now along with a healthy crop of weeds. I think it might be a good idea for ya to wander on over there and weed her garden."

Thomas looked at Sean in a way that told him it was more than a suggestion. As much as Sean would have liked to protest, as much as he would like to reveal the fortune beneath the loose board in the floor, he felt a strong sense of obligation to the doctor for repairing Sorley's knee. The guilt still weighed him down at times and maybe this bit of service to the doctor and his wife would help ease some of it. He nodded to his father and agreed to visit the Bermanns the following day.

Mam cleared her throat softly, signaling the end of that conversation. Always the peacemaker, she often felt the burden of keeping things from escalating between Thomas and Sean. Her way was to change the subject, most times, and that was exactly what she did.

"Would anyone be hungry, then?" The three younger children raced to the table. Sorley arrived last but seemed unbothered by it as long as he had a place to sit. Thomas and Sean followed, any conflict between them diminished by the meal about to be served. Kathleen dished up generous helpings of stew and set a mismatched bowl in front of each chair around the table. It was times like this in the days following his employment with Sergeant Engel that Thomas wondered if they had all died and gone to Heaven, living there with the angels and eating at God's table, for this was a meal fit for saints and too many years had passed without them partaking. He'd heard stories told of folks who died but didn't know it, and he found himself wondering from time to time if cholera had taken them all and unbeknownst to them they were dwelling in the heavenly realm. How else could they be sitting down to a meal such as this? And then he would shake himself from his musings, for surely Heaven had better accommodations, and he would remind himself to send his gratitude heavenward for such delights here on earth. Thick slices of fresh warm bread were piled onto a large platter, and Kathleen placed the generous mound of butter from Thomas's sack in a bowl next to the bread.

"Mam, I'm about to drool down my chin like a teethin' baby!" Sorley agonized.

Kathleen giggled and sat down. Thomas said a brief blessing over the food before them. Following an enthusiastic chorus of amens, five pieces of bread quickly vanished from the plate, arms crisscrossing in the rush to grab one and sink it into the bowl of hearty goodness before them. Kathleen was at first startled by their lack of manners but couldn't keep from laughing at their show of appreciation.

"Sure and every one of ya looks like ya haven't had a crumb to eat in a fortnight!" No one answered. *A quiet table is a sign of good food and hungry bellies*, Kathleen thought to herself. It gave her immense pleasure to be part of this simple calling in life, to prepare a fine meal for those she most loved, to set it before them and watch a communion of sorts, a sharing of gratitude. It was a closeness that could rarely be duplicated. She dipped her own bread into the hearty stew and reminded herself to be just as grateful on the days ahead when a cup of tea and a piece of bread without butter would be all that would sustain them, for those days would surely return.

CHAPTER NINE

Samuel Clemens awoke with a beast of a headache. He sat up in the oversized bed and put both his hands on his head to stop the throbbing. He pressed hard against his temples, but the pounding persisted. At twenty-four years of age, he was too young to be entertaining a life of excess and carelessness, and he knew it. He was no saint, but a little temperance might allow him to enjoy a libation or two without waking up in his current condition. It was easy to rationalize last night's overindulgence when he remembered why he had come to New York City. The joy and relief of completing his two-year river trek along the Mississippi and his subsequent licensure as a riverboat pilot were accomplishments worth celebrating. And yet, his celebration was haunted by the memory of his younger brother Henry who had joined him on the river at Samuel's invitation. Shortly after Samuel resigned his position on the steamboat *Pennsylvania* the boiler had exploded, and the ship sank. Two hundred and fifty people lost their lives including Henry Clemens. Samuel carried the guilt of that horrible day with him, for if he had not invited Henry to join him he would not have met such a terrible end. Logically, he knew it was not his fault. Emotionally, his guilt was a relentless, prowling demon. Ethically, he knew the remedy did not lie at the bottom of a whiskey bottle. The pounding in Samuel's head eased enough to allow him to try to move, albeit slowly, from the bed where he still sat. He turned and let his legs hang over the side as he tried to sort through disjointed thoughts and memories, flashes of images too dim to discern, his clouded brain still struggling to find some clarity.

"What the devil," he muttered. Bizarre, disconnected tangents were swimming through his mind in a murky slough. Samuel was angry at himself, at his confusion and lack of coherence. He took a slow deep breath and tried to piece together the past forty-eight hours, his arrival in New York, checking in at the fabulous St. Nicholas, and the short walk to Pfaff's Beer Cellar. He was attracted to the reputation of the place, known to be the spot where the Bohemian movement had started and where creative types such as actress Ada Clare and poet Walt Whitman might be found on any given night.

Samuel focused hard on the previous night's timeline, and his memories became clearer. He recalled sitting at a table near the back of the establishment watching the engaging conversation around the room. He heard impassioned debates on such topics as a splintering Democratic party, the recent publication of Mr. Dickens' A *Tale of Two Cities*, and the groundbreaking trial of New York congressman Dan Sickles who was recently acquitted for the murder of his wife's lover, successfully using a plea of temporary insanity for the first time in a United States court of law. The fog in Clemens' head continued to clear, and he recalled the occupants of the table next to his engaged in a heated debate.

"It is not a question of whether his actions were appropriate or justified, Ada. Rather, we are supposing that this plea of temporary insanity might now be applied to any and all situations in a court of law," argued the man who sat directly across from the lady.

"Come now, Henry, how can we worry over such an indeterminate concept when the real issue here is that of the continuing suppression of women in our society, still, in the middle of the nineteenth century? Mr. Sickles cheated on his wife with a prostitute while Mrs. Sickles was pregnant with his child. He displayed a complete lack of decorum by taking his consort to England and presenting her to Queen Victoria! Apparently, the needs of a man far surpass those of a woman, and when Mrs. Sickles sought the attention of another man and engaged in a similar affair it was apparently considered grounds for murder. I suppose we should be thankful it was not her that Mr. Sickles shot and killed!"

Henry Clapp knew better than to argue with Ada Clare when she was incensed, and he backed down. He leaned back in his chair and looked around the room, finding all the usual faces and a few unfamiliar ones, which was the usual way of things with so many visitors wanting to experience the Bohemian atmosphere at Pfaff's. He turned around to look at the table directly behind him and saw the red-headed stranger listening intently.

"There's room for you here at our table, my good man," Henry invited. "Come join our lively conversation if you dare."

"I've listened to much of it but admit to being unfamiliar with the players in this drama. Also, I make it a habit to avoid conversation that pits man against woman. It never ends well," Samuel said with a charming smile that kept Ada's temper at bay. He stood and took the empty chair at their table, introduced himself, and answered their questions. They were curious what brought him to New York and when they heard of his two-year venture on the Mississippi they were enthralled. Samuel launched into a lengthy accounting of every small and sizeable adventure of interest that he had encountered along the mighty river, omitting the tragedy of his brother's untimely death. His audience listened silently, hanging on his every word, his rich and descriptive narrative, and his captivating delivery.

"Mr. Clemens, you would be well-advised to write about these adventures. Many a reader would draw to the telling and you might find success as a writer and an orator if that lifestyle appeals to you." Henry Clapp was the editor of the New York Saturday Press, and he knew a good story when he heard one.

"Writing seems a fanciful pastime for the bored and the aged," Samuel replied, his tone dismissing the idea. He leaned back in his chair and hydrated his dry throat with the whiskey in front of him. His glass was empty, and he felt the need for a refill.

A scoffing grunt escaped from a gentleman sitting at a nearby table. Samuel turned his head in the direction of the noise and saw a middle-aged man with a bushy graying beard, his icy blue eyes staring directly at the out-of-towner. The man did not look happy, and Samuel assumed that he had taken exception to his comment about writing. *Another overly sensitive author, no doubt*, he thought to himself as he turned back around to give his attention to the friendlier faces at his own table.

"Mr. Whitman is in a foul mood tonight," Ada said quietly. "Pay him no mind."

"Would you care to join us for some conversation, Mr. Whitman?" Henry asked.

"I'm more interested in whiskey and cards tonight, Henry. Is your adventurer skilled in the game of poker?" Samuel was an accomplished poker player but was not sure Mr. Whitman would be congenial company. All eyes turned to Samuel, and he nodded slightly. Mr. Whitman put out his hand to invite Samuel to take the chair directly across from him, and Samuel obliged. Whitman poured whiskey into two glasses, and the dealing and wagering began in earnest.

Two hours passed and the card players were into their second bottle of the golden liquor. Ada and Henry, still at their own table, stood to leave. Henry Clapp paused a moment to once again encourage Samuel to write about his adventures and offered to review and endorse his efforts if he did. It was a doubtful venture in Samuel's mind, but one never knew what the future would bring. He shifted his attention back to the cards and his growing pile of money. Walt Whitman had remained a sullen and uncommunicative opponent until the second bottle of whiskey loosened his lips. It was then that he lamented his firing from the Brooklyn Daily Times and the failure of his poetry collection to find the critical acclaim he sought. The more he talked the more he lost, though he didn't appear to notice until the last of the whiskey was emptied into his glass and the table in front of him was devoid of money. He looked up at Mr. Clemens with an expression of confusion and surrender.

"To lose it all is a fitting way to end this night," he said.

"I can return tomorrow night and give you the opportunity to turn the table on me," Samuel responded, hoping to soothe the man's bruised ego. There was no reply, only a great and dejected sigh that escaped from somewhere deep in the man's despondency.

Whitman downed his remaining whiskey in one large swallow and stood to leave. He was out of money and defeated at both cards and career. He wobbled slightly, grabbed the back of his chair until he got his bearings, and wandered out into the night. Samuel waited. He would not take the chance that a desperate, angry, and overly emotional poet stood waiting in the darkness to recover his losses. He gathered up his winnings and stuffed the banknotes and coins down into his pockets. Samuel lingered a few minutes longer thinking about what Henry Clapp had suggested. Could he be a successful writer? After his encounter tonight with the brooding Mr. Whitman he would only consider writing if he could find some measure of success in it. Dealing with a constant sense of rejection and failure was not something he was eager to invite into his life. He might be better served pursuing the path he had been on, from apprentice printer to traveling typesetter to licensed riverboat captain. Writing interested him—he had written a few articles for his brother Orion's newspaper in Missouri—but the thought of it being his main pursuit in life seemed doubtful.

Twenty minutes passed and Samuel felt it was safe to exit the beer cellar and walk back to the St. Nicholas. Thinking on it now, he remembered struggling to find his room, swearing in the hallway, and being told to quiet down by a sensitive patron. That was where his memories became clouded and difficult to discern. He did not remember finding his room, taking off his pants and shirt, and crawling into the big bed. He did not remember how long it took him to fall asleep, although he was certain that the abundance of whiskey propelled him quickly into the deep slumber of intoxication.

He sat on the edge of the bed now, fragments of a disjointed dream coming into focus and then fading, leaving him feeling witless and frustrated. *Damn whiskey*, he thought. The remnants of the dream remained constant, repeating the same account each time they reappeared in his troubled mind. A blurred vision of a carpenter entering his room, ignoring his presence and rifling through his belongings as Samuel laid there incapacitated by the liquor still running through his veins. He wished he knew what such an odd dream meant but there would be no reasoning through it until food and coffee cleared his head completely.

As he struggled for clarity, Samuel remembered his promise to return to Pfaff's for another round of poker with Mr. Whitman. If he kept his word and returned he would not indulge to the same degree, no matter Whitman's dark mood or the frivolities of the establishment. He nodded slightly as if to affirm to himself that moderation would be the better choice. He arose from the edge of the bed and noticed a peculiar sight near the door. A toolbox. His heart began to pound, and he fought the urge to panic. An encroaching sense of regret, of terrible realization came over him. He didn't remember locking the door after arriving back in his room last night, but then he remembered little of the previous evening. He stared at the toolbox. Some irrational part of his sobering brain told him it was only a figment of a whiskey-soaked imagination. He walked across the room and stopped in front of the toolbox. He stood motionless, staring at it, feeling a mindless fool for overanalyzing such a simple thing. It had to be real, for it was right there in front of him. He kicked it harder than he had intended and hollered in pain.

"Damnation!" He hobbled back to the bed and glanced around the room for a water pitcher and a cloth. It was then that he saw the table by the window. A sudden clear recollection of emptying his pockets on the table before falling into bed last night jarred him into sobriety. Samuel hobbled over to the table and stared down at it with a grave sense of regret. It was now painfully obvious that his dream had been reality. He had laid in bed, drunk and powerless, while someone had robbed him blind. They left a few coins and his pilot's license. He was grateful that the thief saw no value in the license, but they had left his room with pockets full of money and the gold watch that had belonged to Samuel's maternal grandfather, Benjamin Lampton. The money mattered not to him, but the watch was dear to his heart. Samuel was angrier with himself for allowing the opportunity than he was with the thief who seized the careless invitation.

Knowing now that he could not give Mr. Whitman the chance to win back his earnings in another game of poker, Samuel began packing his satchel. He would return to Missouri and put his pilot's license to practical use. There was good money to be made piloting steamships from port to port along the Mississippi River transporting people and freight. He gathered up the coins left on the table—enough to get him home—and left New York in as foul a mood as Mr. Whitman had entertained the night before.

CHAPTER TEN

Monday morning was clouded over, the air heavy and thick, but the promise of a summer storm initiated a sense of great anticipation from the tenants crammed into the maze of brick and decay. Rain had been scarce during the spring and early summer of 1859, and though rain usually brought about the unpleasantries of the poverty-ridden inner city, it also held a weak promise of renewal. A large rainstorm would turn the dirt streets into mud, making travel with a horse and carriage all but impossible. The streets that were brownstone would wash over with silt and garbage, disappearing beneath the unsightly veneer of mud and refuse. A sizeable storm would cause rain to pool along the edges of the streets and alleys creating a rushing stream of rubbish and animal feces into open areas and water sources. Contamination would cause disease to spread throughout the city, and lives would be lost because of it. Thomas and Kathleen had arrived in New York City near the end of the 1849 cholera outbreak and had witnessed the death of more than one acquaintance before the disease had run its course. Knowing all of this, however, could not take away a small glimmer of hope when the rain washed down upon their filthy surroundings. God was trying to do something beautiful, something that would look and feel like restoration, but the failings of mankind tarnished the hope of renewal.

"Looks like we might finally get some rain," Thomas observed out the hazy window. "Sean, are ya still plannin' a visit to the Bermann's?"

"Aye, Da, I'll be leavin' shortly." Sean never minded the rain. From the time he was five or six years old he would stand outside in a deluge, let it drench through his clothes, and wash over him. Even before he could put a name to it, he found it to be a cleansing balm to his soul, refreshing, revitalizing. And now, on the edge of manhood, it lifted the heaviness of life to a tolerable weight and restored hope in the process. All of that from the drippings of heaven, as Da called it. He had felt it early on and never questioned it. Never talked about it. It was his alone, and he doubted he would ever share that connection with another human being, for he could not bear to see it devalued by scorn or cynicism.

Kathleen walked to the kitchen to refill her teacup and lightly tousled Sean's hair as she passed by him. "You've always liked the rain, Son." Sean nodded. Mam was the only one who recognized his affinity for the rain, though he doubted she would ever know how deep his feelings ran. Sean followed Kathleen into the kitchen to have some of the tea still warm in the pot and a slice of bread with plenty of butter before venturing out into the coming storm. The tea and bread would be plenty to start his day. His belly was still full after the previous night's decadent meal and wonderful dessert. They had divided the little orange cake into six small portions, but it was more than enough after stuffing themselves with Mam's stew and warm bread.

Just a touch of sweetness to end a good day. Good and profitable. Sean smiled slightly as he thought about the small fortune lying beneath the floor.

"Somethin' got ya tickled?" Thomas asked from the couch. He saw the smile form on Sean's face for no apparent reason and as always he was immediately suspicious.

"Naw, just recallin' how we all dived into dinner last night, and the look on Mam's face as we did," Sean lied. Innocent enough, so there was little guilt to bear, though it occurred to him how quickly and easily the lies now came.

"Och, we gave her a fright, I'm thinkin'," Thomas agreed.

"Sure and ya did!" Kathleen agreed. "But there's nothin' that makes me happier!" She smiled at Sean, then Thomas, and prayed silently for an uneasy peace if that's all they could have, for it was better than the burdensome pain of constant conflict.

"I'm headin' out," Sean remarked as he downed the last bit of tea in his cup.

"Do you want to take your da's coat along with ya?" Kathleen asked.

"Mam, it's been blisterin' hot out there! If we're lucky enough to get rain, I'll be lucky enough to be out in it," Sean replied as he headed for the door. "I'm assumin' the Bermann's have what I need to care for the garden?" he asked his father.

"Aye, Sean, you'll find a small shed beyond the garden attached to the fence, and inside will be the things you'll need. If I recall it correctly there was a shovel, a hoe, and a cart to collect the weeds in. Be sure to have Mrs. Bermann show you which are weeds and which are vegetables so that you're not pullin' up her crop."

"Aye, Da, I'd already thought of that," Sean replied flatly. In a few weeks, he would be thirteen. He wished his father would treat him less like a child and more like a man. Sean turned and left. Thomas felt a twinge of guilt for being so hard on Sean, for showing little trust or confidence in him, but the boy had brought it on himself by the bad choices he had made. Thomas glanced at Katie and saw the sadness on her face.

Sean crossed Division Street and headed north on Ridge to where it intersected Houston. He walked beneath a heavy sky and the air smelled of rain, but none came as he made his way to the Bermann's. As Sean turned left on Houston Street, he could see the Bermann's place two blocks down. He was nervous. He didn't know if Mam and Da had shared the details of Sean's negligence when Sorley was rushed into their office for medical treatment, but as angry as Da had been it was likely that he told them everything. Sean expected a cold reception and a healthy dose of condemnation from Dr. Bermann. He swallowed a lump in his throat and knocked on the door. There was no immediate answer, and he wondered if they were not at home. He knocked again, louder this time, and the doctor opened the door. Sean remembered him from a visit there once when he had contracted bronchitis. The doctor, however, did not recognize Sean. Far too many patients had come through his door for him to remember them all, and children changed greatly as they grew and matured.

"Are you ill?" Dr. Bermann asked.

"No, sir, my name is Sean Delaney, son of Thomas and Kathleen. You rescued my young brother's knee a couple months ago. Sorley is his name."

"Oh yes, yes! I remember your family and brave young Sorley!" Dr. Bermann said. "Is he well? Is there a problem with the knee?"

"No sir, he is quite well. I'm here to weed Mrs. Bermann's garden. My father sent me. I'd be much obliged to do this for you and your wife considerin' all ya did for my brother."

"Well, then," Dr. Bermann responded, "let me show you around back and please be sure to thank your father for us." Sean followed Dr. Bermann around the side of the house to the backyard where the small vegetable patch was located. The doctor continued talking the entire time. "Mrs. Bermann is quite under the weather suffering from a long bout of the grippe. She's been bound to her bed for eight days now and frets constantly about the condition of her garden whenever she's awake. I expect this will be a great boon to her recovery, young man."

"Sorry to hear about Mrs. Bermann, sir," Sean responded.

"I think she's on the upside finally, and I think seeing her garden tidied up a bit will be good medicine." They stopped at the shed, and Dr. Bermann removed a hoe and a cart. "Are you familiar with vegetable plants and flowers? Can you recognize a weed if you see it?"

"I'm not completely sure, but I was thinkin' that whatever is planted in rows and looks the same as the other plants must be what belongs there."

Dr. Bermann let go with a hearty laugh leaving Sean in a state of uncertainty, for he was not sure if the doctor was laughing at him and his childish assumptions or was amused by his quick analysis of the task at hand.

"You've got yourself a logical mind there, young Delaney! I don't think you need any help from me," the doctor reassured him. Sean thanked the doctor and shrugged. It seemed obvious to him, but it was nice to have an adult give him some credit for being able to think rationally and make sound decisions.

"You go ahead and weed out what doesn't belong. I'm sure you'll do fine. Give a knock on the front door when you're finished up, will you?" Sean nodded and bent down to start his chore as Dr. Bermann wandered back to the front of the house.

The growing things that were sprouting up between the rows were the first to go. They were certain to have blown in on the wind and planted themselves there. Once that was done, Sean stood and looked carefully at each row of vegetable plants, seeing the similarities in size and shape, color and design. He began weeding out what did not belong, careful not to disrupt the thriving vegetable plants. He found the process strangely calming and lost track of time as he worked his way through each of the rows, and around the perimeter where Mrs. Bermann had planted a border of marigolds to attract butterflies and bees, and to ward off certain pests. Sean thought about Sorley's wish that they would have a grand house with a yard and a garden for Mam, and Sean thought now that it was a wish he shared with his brother. He knew Mam would enjoy cultivating beautiful flowers and also food for their table. He was rounding the last side of the garden when a large raindrop splashed down on the back of his head.

Sean wiped the back of his head with his shirtsleeve and hurried through the remaining section of flowers. He didn't mind the rain, but he didn't want to be stomping through his handiwork and make a muddy mess of it. He smiled as he thought about the rain coming at exactly the right time. The weeding was done and now it was time for the watering. He finished up and pushed the cart back into the shed after emptying the contents in a nearby pile of compost. He set the hoe inside the shed and shut the door and turned to face the garden for a final inspection. Sean felt a sense of pride in the job he had completed, and he was grateful that he could repay the doctor and his wife for their kindness. He walked back around to the front of the house and hesitated before knocking on the door with his dirty hands. He rapped on the door softly with one knuckle, and Dr. Bermann appeared almost instantly.

"You're all done, then?" Dr. Bermann asked.

"I am, Sir," Sean replied respectfully. "Would ya like to see?"

"I trust you, Son. Your father did a fine job getting the soil ready to plant and I'm sure you're as capable as he is. Do you need a ride home? I can arrange one as I see it's starting to rain."

"No thank you, sir. I rather like the rain. Wish your wife well for us, will ya?"

"I will do that. Here, wait, I have something for you," Dr. Bermann said as he leaned toward Sean with a couple coins in his hand.

"Thank you kindly, Sir, but we're fine," Sean replied as he walked away. He was happy to do the work for the Bermanns. Happy to repay one kindness with another. Happy that the doctor had not appeared to know the role Sean had played in Sorley's accident, for he had treated him with respect. Sean felt slightly amused at the difference the past few weeks had made in his life. There was a time when he would have snatched up those coins the moment they were extended in his direction. Now, no matter how much the doctor would have offered it would seem a pittance compared to what lay beneath the floorboard back home. He did not consider Dr. Bermann's gesture to be insufficient, for that would be unkind, but he felt a bit full of himself for the impressive amount of money he had accumulated on his own. What he would do with that money remained a mystery but for now it was his.

The rain fell hard, and the large drops pummeled against the thin cotton shirt Sean was wearing. He liked the feeling. He felt alive, his senses keen and aware, his skin tingling as it welcomed the cooling water against it. He noticed the smell of the dirt as the rain fell upon it, and he watched the people scurrying here and there to take cover from the downpour. He noticed how the rainwater pooled in the low places and the interesting patterns that formed on the surface as the drops fell hard upon the standing water. Sean could hear the beautiful sound of rain falling hard on tin roofs and the thin, wooden shacks where squatters had settled in vacant lots. And he did not miss the irony, the stark contrast of the cleansing rain and the filth it tried in vain to wash away.

Sean paused a few minutes to enjoy the deluge and to consider his walk home. He had walked to the Bermann's on Ridge Street, Da's approved route, the one he told Sean to take, and the one that would go directly back to Montgomery and East Broadway. Clinton Street would take Sean in the very same direction, though it would deliver him a couple of blocks west of home. Sean had been curious about Clinton Street since overhearing a recent conversation between Sam and Sow Madden. Sam was questioning the payouts he was getting from Frank Grimmel, the junkman he'd been using, and Sow Madden had offered to make a trip over to Clinton Street to talk with Marm Mandelbaum. Fredericka "Marm" Mandelbaum ran a haberdashery on Clinton Street, which was a front for her extensive criminal activity. She recruited gang members, financed the gangs, trained young street urchins to be pickpockets, fenced stolen goods, and engaged in a blackmail protection scheme extracting money from other business owners to protect them from the very gangs she controlled. Sow Madden told Sam it was common knowledge that Mandelbaum paid well for stolen goods.

Sean's curiosity got the best of him as he chose the forbidden route and wandered down Clinton Street. He felt a false sense of security and anonymity shrouded by the heavy storm clouds overhead and the uncharacteristic darkness of the day. His first impression was that Clinton

Street didn't look much different than any of the other streets in the city. There seemed to be fewer shady characters milling about but that was likely because of the storm. He shoved his hands down into his pockets and lowered his head as he walked past 79 Clinton Street. He had noted the sign above the door saying *Mandelbaum's Haberdashery* and had cowered so as not to be solicited by anyone inside. Refusing to join a gang did not always go well, and he had no desire for a confrontation. He hoped he would be unnoticed if anyone inside looked through the dirty, rain-streaked window as he passed by.

Sean could not resist the temptation to cast a subtle glance at the window as he walked past. There was an obvious deal being negotiated inside between a large unpleasant-looking woman and a slouched figure of a man. He was holding a strangely familiar silver chalice, and Sean narrowed his eyes slightly. The man's face was close to the woman's, staring her down, apparently insulted by her offer. Sean saw clearly the profile of Sow Madden. His breathing stopped, and the wave of fear that swept over him nearly caused him to wretch. If Sow Madden saw him passing by, saw him witnessing a shady deal with Sam's belongings, he would kill him. With every ounce of self-restraint he could summon, Sean slowly turned his face toward the street and continued to walk. His pace remained slow and steady to avoid attracting attention, though the grave prospect of death made him want to flee as fast as his feet could carry him. The violent beating of his heart caused his chest to ache and his hands, still in his pockets, were surely trembling. He walked another block to Delancy Street, cut over to Ridge and started running. He ran down Ridge until he arrived back at Division Street, just two blocks from home. It was there that he stopped and ducked under a canvas awning above the doorway of an abandoned bakery. The awning was tattered in places and the rain leaked through. Sean stood there a few minutes to calm himself before returning home. He took several deep breaths and waited for his heart rate to slow down.

"You okay, boy?" came a voice from beside the awning. He turned to see a police officer standing there, the rain running in rivulets off his tall, rounded hat.

"Aye, sir," Sean replied as contritely as he could. "I got caught in the rainstorm as I was comin' home from givin' a hand to the good Dr. Bermann and his sick wife over on Houston Street. I ran most of the way and just stopped here to catch my breath."

"And what's wrong with Mrs. Bermann?" the officer inquired. He knew the Bermanns, as most folks in the area did, and was suspicious of the boy's story.

"The doctor says she's had a case of the grippe for eight days now."

"Is that so? And if I visit Dr. Bermann will I get the same story from him?"

"Aye, sir, I imagine you will. He had no reason not to be truthful with me," Sean said. "I just live over there on Montgomery, sir, if it would be all right for me to continue on then."

"Go on ahead, bogtrotter. Get yourself a cup of hot tea like a good little mick before you catch a case of the grippe yourself."

Sean forced himself to nod, to remain humble and subservient, all the while wishing he could lash out against the officer, verbally and physically, in response to his intentionally offensive language. He caught the officer's gaze and they stared at each other for a few seconds, each one challenging, and each one knowing their mistrust of the other might well be unfounded. It made for an uneasy truce. Sean thanked the officer and walked back out into the pouring rain toward home. He was almost grateful for the officer's interrogation, as it gave his body some much-needed time to recover. His heartbeat had slowed substantially, and his hands felt steady again. By the time he reached home, he was drenched to the bone but otherwise calm and ready to face the maternal fussing he would receive from Mam. It started the moment he walked through the doorway.

"Oh, dear Lord in Heaven!" Kathleen called out. She bolted up from her chair at the table where she had been mending a sock. "Thomas, put the kettle on!"

"Mam, I'm fine," Sean lamented. There would be no stopping it.

"You're not fine! You're soaked clear through to the bone and beyond! Oh, Mary and Joseph, don't let him get sick." Kathleen made the sign of the cross and rushed over to pull a blanket off her bed to wrap around her son.

"Mam! 'Tis a warm summer rain. There's not a chill in the air and no chance of me catchin' the grippe like Mrs. Bermann."

"Oh, no!" Kathleen responded, crossing herself again.

Thomas had put the kettle on and seated himself at the table, watching the fussing and enjoying the rare opportunity for Kathleen to coddle her nearly grown son. Thomas continued whittling away at a piece of wood, hoping to craft a small wooden dog for Maeve to play with. It would likely be the closest thing to a pet she would ever have. Thomas continued carving as he battled the relentless regret that burdened in his soul.

"How was the doctor? Were you able to get the garden done before the storm moved in?" Thomas asked.

"I got it done just as the rain started to fall," Sean replied. He offered nothing else. He knew it would annoy his father, yet he couldn't find it in himself to care.

"And?"

"And what?"

"Dr. Bermann. How is he?"

"Fine, I'm thinkin'. We didn't talk much. He took me 'round back to show me what I needed and asked me to stop by the front door when I was done."

"And you did?"

"Aye, Da, I did." Sean's patience was running thin. He did not like the way Thomas always questioned him, the suspicion heavy in his father's voice. It always sounded to Sean like he was accusing him of something even though he had no reason beyond the one incident the night of Sorley's accident. In Sean's mind, his father had no evidence against him so his suspicions were unfounded.

"Well, son, can ya tell us about it then?" Thomas asked in a thin voice, trying his best to remain congenial. It was times like this, with suspicion and defensive responses engaged in battle, that Thomas would admit to the great sadness he felt at his deteriorating relationship with Sean. His firstborn had always been somewhat drawn into himself, introspective he had heard it called, but in times past he had been better, lighter, more carefree. Sadness gripped Thomas, and he surrendered to it. He put down his whittling and walked over to the small bedroom. He laid down on the bed and prayed for the sleep that had eluded him the night before, that it might come and rescue him now.

Kathleen dabbed at the corners of her eyes with the back of her hand before turning around to place the teapot on the table. She got two cups, one for her and one for Sean, and poured each one full. The two of them sat silently waiting for the right words to break the tension. Sean added sugar to his cup from the bowl on the table and stirred it into his tea, the spoon clinking on the edges of the porcelain cup. In the silence, it sounded like the clashing of cymbals, and he quickly stopped.

"Son, was Dr. Bermann well?" Kathleen asked softly.

"Aye, Mam. He asked after Sorley and said he remembered him bein' brave that day," Sean said. He watched Sorley playing quietly with the four small tin soldiers that Da had found in a Catharine Street alley one Sunday morning.

"He was that, Sean, and he's doin' quite well," she reassured, knowing the conversation would end now as it always did when the subject of Sorley's accident was mentioned.

"Aye," Sean whispered. And the conversation ended.

CHAPTER ELEVEN

The rain fell relentlessly for two days after Sean's visit to the Bermann's. The drippings from Heaven lost their allure as the inner city became a soup pot of mud and decay, feces, filth, and stench. The city government had initiated a campaign several years prior to clean up the city and rid the streets of thousands of roaming pigs, but it was a long and difficult process. What had started as a way for city dwellers to add low-cost protein to their diets had become a nuisance. The poverty-stricken residents argued that pigs, being scavengers by nature, would keep the streets free of the garbage that collected everywhere. The more financially secure citizens, developers, and government officials argued that pigs added more filth than they consumed, were a threat to children, spread disease, and caused accidents by running out in front of carriages and people. In an attempt to clean up the city the pigs were driven north of the city proper, and when the Central Park construction began in 1857, the government officials drove the pigs further north. The venture was somewhat successful, though it was impossible to rid the streets of all animals. It was not unusual to encounter pigs, chickens, geese, a goat or two, and countless packs of dogs on the streets of the city. Horses pulling wagons and carriages littered the streets with feces and careless drivers rarely took the time to clean up after them.

"Och, the city stinks to high heaven," Thomas said in disgust. "There's no escapin' it!"

"Aye, Tommy, 'tis always the way of it when the rains come." Kathleen grew quiet, introspective, reflecting on memories of a place and time that seemed a lifetime ago. Thomas watched the memories change her expression, soften her countenance, and he knew where her mind had wandered.

"Rememberin' the grand soft rains of Cork, are ya, Mo Ghrá?"

"There are times I miss it so, Tommy. Even with The Hunger, it was still a better place than this, don't ya think?" She cast him a longing glance through mist-filled eyes.

Thomas nodded, sadness filling his heart. His greatest burden would always be the guilt of bringing Kathleen here for what they imagined would be a better life. It had not come to pass. That promise was nothing more than a sad, empty dream. And unlike the famine they had left behind there seemed to be no hope that things would get better in time. America's version of poverty was relentless, like a rain-soaked muddy slope, keeping its victims slipping back down whenever they tried to climb out of the mire. It sapped the hope and optimism from the souls of those trapped in its grip. And the hatred that contributed to that poverty made the bearing of it even more difficult.

"I am so sorry, Katie," came a quiet whisper, Thomas's voice faltering like his resolve.

"Don't be. We agreed together. We've nothin' to do but the best we can," she reassured him. They sat at the table across from one another, two cups of cooling tea between them. The children busied themselves with what they could, for going outside for any reason would not happen until the rain stopped and the mud and muck began to dry. The chamber pots brought the stench of the outdoors inside as they waited to be emptied until after the storm had passed. No one living in the tenements was willing to walk to the outhouses in the alley between their building and the next, for the surrounding ground was an unhealthy mix of mud and excrement. The chamber pots, as foul as they were, would suffice until the earth dried.

By Thursday morning, the rain had subsided and the sun began its work. Just seeing the light in the sky improved everyone's mood, and Mam decided to make apple dumplings. Thomas made it a habit to purchase a few items from Mrs. Zimmer each week before finishing his shopping at Carnahan's. Last weekend, it had been a dozen beautiful apples from a local orchard. Kathleen now set about peeling and coring the apples to wrap in pastry dough with butter and sugar and cinnamon. Thomas sat as comfortably as one could on John O'Riley's ragged couch reading a days-old newspaper he had found in the hallway.

Sean was nearly climbing the walls by the time the clouds parted and the sun reappeared. He was used to getting outside even if it was just to walk around the block. Most times, though, he would wander down Montgomery Street to the riverside where he could watch the ships moving along the East River or the ferry running to Brooklyn and back. There was a great unrest in his spirit on that Thursday morning as he paced the flat.

"Mam, I'm walkin' down to the river for a bit," he said to Kathleen. Rarely did he ask permission, and rarely did he communicate his plans to his father. Thomas could hear

Sean even though he had lowered his voice to exclude his father from the conversation.

"I'm makin' apple dumplin's so be sure you're home soon enough to enjoy some," Kathleen advised.

"I won't be long, I just need some air."

"The air's still not smellin' right," Thomas said over the top of his newspaper. "I wouldn't want to be out in it."

"Aye, but that's you, and the air is always better down by the river," came Sean's reply. Thomas shook his head ever so slightly and raised the newspaper back up to hide his irritation.

Sean walked out into the morning air, still smelling dank and unpleasant in the hollows between the tenement buildings. He had been correct in saying that the air along the river was almost always better, and he headed down Montgomery toward the water. There were six short blocks between their tenement and the East River. It was a path Sean was familiar with, a path that felt like escape even though it wasn't. As he neared the river, the stench in the air began to clear. He smiled, silently telling his father, I told ya so. He walked four blocks on Front Street along the river to Pike Street intending to complete a circle by walking up Division and back home. As he rounded the corner at Pike, he noticed Reddy McCann and Spanish Marley standing between two shacks deep in conversation. He slowed enough that it caught their attention, and both looked his way. Sean dipped his head slightly to greet them, and Reddy waved him over.

"Looking for somethin', Delaney?" Reddy asked. His tone seemed edgy, and Sean wondered if he was bitter about Sean's burgeoning favor with Sam.

"Not a bit of anything, just gettin' some air," he replied.

Spanish Marley looked at Reddy and there was an uncomfortable silence. Marley looked down at the ground and shuffled his feet. Reddy took a deep breath and turned to Sean.

"Are ya with us, Delaney?" He offered no explanation but there was little need for it. Sean's loyalty was his guardian and the lack of it would be his undoing.

"Aye, of course I'm with ya. Why would ya doubt me?"

"There's trouble brewin'. You heard the ruckus between Sam and Sow Madden and the accusation against Marley here, did ya not?" Reddy nodded in Marley's direction and then peered straight into Sean's eyes. If there were even an inkling of deceit or hesitation in Sean's response, Reddy would sense it. They were at a pivotal point in Sean's alliance with the Wharf Kings, and after the ensuing conversation he would be all in or in grave danger for knowing too much and not showing the loyalty they demanded.

"I did. Last Sunday mornin', it was. Sow Madden accused Marley here of stealin' from Sam," Sean stated without flinching, relating exactly what he had seen and heard last weekend. The memory of what he had witnessed on Clinton Street crept back into his memory, and a sudden realization of what was going on came clear to him.

"You know, now that I am recallin' what I saw a few days ago I think I know what's goin' on under Sam's nose."

"What did you see, Delaney?" Reddy asked slowly.

"I was makin' my way home from Dr. Bermann's place where I went to lend a hand in payment of my Da's debt. I decided to walk down Clinton Street." Sean paused when he saw Reddy and Marley look at one another. "It was rainin' like Noah's storm, so I had my hands in my pockets and my head lowered as I passed by Marm Mandelbaum's place. I glanced in—just curious, I suppose—when I noticed a familiar figure at the counter barterin' with the woman inside. The man turned his head as I walked past. I saw who it was, and I recognized the silver chalice he was holdin'."

"The missing chalice!" Spanish Marley blurted out.

"Quiet yourself!" he snapped at Marley.

"So, he's the one stealin' from Sam," Sean affirmed quietly, knowing his days would be numbered if Sow Madden ever caught wind of who had ratted on him.

"Well, it sure isn't me! I'd like to live to see another day, thank you," Marley replied.

"Delaney, would you be willin' to tell Sam what you saw?" Reddy asked.

Sean expelled a long breath and ran his fingers into his hair, his hand sitting atop his head as he thought it through. He felt a nauseating fear rise inside of him, the same fear he had experienced when he had passed by Mandelbaum's and discovered Sow Madden's dirty secret. He had seen enough of Sam's temper to not want to be at the receiving end of it. Sean hated and feared Sow Madden. He sensed the evil that lurked in his dark heart, and he wanted no part of it. And yet, Marley's life could depend on Sean's testimony regarding what he had witnessed through the rain-soaked grime of Mandelbaum's window.

"I don't know, Reddy. I'm not sure I want to get caught up in a war between Sam and Sow Madden. Someone's gonna get hurt. Maybe killed."

"Well, here's the deal, Delaney. If we don't help Marley, he's the one that's gonna get killed." Reddy stared straight into Sean's troubled eyes. He understood the hesitation and the fear, but Delaney needed to learn the unspoken rules of this life he had chosen. "We stand together, Delaney," he reminded the boy.

Sean knew that everything Reddy had said was true. Sow Madden would do whatever was needed to maintain his good favor with Sam and implicate someone else in the thievery. The burden of risk grew tenfold in that moment, and as Sean thought about the possibilities he also knew that if he were walking in Spanish Marley's shoes he would hope they would do the same for him. Stand together. Honor among thieves. The fragile camaraderie born of crime and danger was about to be put to the test.

"What's the plan?" Sean asked Reddy. His fate was sealed.

"There's word on the street that there's gonna be another riot like the big one two years ago. A little history for ya, Delaney. After Bill the Butcher died it was Michael Walsh holdin' the Bowery Boys together. Since his passin' three months ago there's been a power struggle goin' on and no one's risen to the top just yet. I hear tell that the Dead Rabbits are plannin' to make a move into the Bowery again."

"Sam knows this?" Sean asked. He was unfamiliar with the gangs and the characters Reddy had mentioned, but he would not admit to being so young and green that none of Reddy's comments held any relevance.

"He's aware. He knows they might ask us to join up with the Rabbits and some of the other fellas from the Five Points if it comes to that."

Sean expelled a deep, troubled breath. This was more trouble and greater danger than he ever wanted to be a part of, and yet he knew he was a Wharf King now and that came with certain expectations. He would not be allowed to pick and choose how and when he would demonstrate his loyalty. They would just as soon kill him and get him out of the way if his allegiance ever fell into question.

"Sam is worried about the boys bein' able to defend themselves with nothing more than hayforks and clubs. Weapons are in short supply right now with Boss Tweed tryin' to clean up the city."

Sean knew nothing of politics. It was more than he cared to think about and most of it was well over his head. He heard names and he heard people talk about those names, but he rarely paid attention. Sean was aware, however, that Boss Tweed was a powerful, albeit unscrupulous, local politician and not someone to cross.

"Now here's the thing, Delaney. We got word that the *Swift Justice* sittin' over there at the slip," Reddy pointed to a large sailing ship, "is being loaded for a trip across the pond and there's several cases of Samuel Colt revolvers in the captain's quarters. My cousin James has worked these docks for years and told me about the guns last week. Says these ships have been takin' guns over to sell to the Brits after Colt closed their London factory a couple years ago. Me and Marley mean to get those guns and deliver them to Sam in a show of loyalty, and that's when you can tell Sam what you saw at Mandelbaum's."

Guns. The gravity of the situation grew more burdensome. Sean felt himself being drawn into a perilous situation that had little options and no way out. He knew too much to walk away safely. His heart was racing, and he wished he had stayed home in his overcrowded lifeless neighborhood where minding one's business was common, where a person could safely disappear into a sea of drawn faces and drab dilapidated tenements. The poor and downtrodden wore the cloth of anonymity, be it a burden or a boon, but it was no help to him now.

"Tomorrow night, Delaney. James told me that on Friday night the guns will be in the captain's quarters. and the crew will be in town havin' a bit of fun before setting out across the ocean. We're meetin' right here at nine o'clock. I'm warnin' you right now, Delaney, if there are any crew members left on board we could run into trouble. I would advise you to bring somethin' you can use as a weapon—a hammer, a club, a knife, you decide, just don't come unarmed."

"Right," Sean replied. His head was spinning. He wished with all his being that this was nothing more than a terrible dream, but he knew it was the inevitable reality of swearing his fealty to the Wharf Kings. It was now *his* reality, the life he had pursued and welcomed. He was seeing the ramifications of a long chain of poor decisions firmly attached to his scrawny ankle and dragging heavy behind him. For the want of money and respect and something better for his family, he was now being asked to cross a line. Once crossed, there would be no turning back, no undoing whatever fateful thing happened tomorrow night. He was moving past the petty crime of thievery to the potential for something unspeakable. He swallowed hard past the dry lump in his throat and nodded.

"See ya here, then."

Reddy remembered being at the pivotal place where Sean was now. He knew the regret, the self-admonition, the fear, the urge to flee and escape the unknown. Sean would prove himself tomorrow night as a loyal Wharf King or a turncoat whose future would likely lie in the dark murky waters of the East River. Reddy hoped Sean would make the right decision.

Sean's feet led him home. He remembered nothing of the walk. He was blind to the city and its ugly face as he wandered back to the place where he was safe, loved, and valued. It was then, nearly at his doorstep, that he conceded to a monumental admission. He had lost sight of what love and respect looked like. He had replaced the value of familial, all-encompassing love with an unsavory promise of respect and protection, and the exorbitant price it would cost him. The love he had devalued stretched so far past the boundaries of what he had found on the street that Sean wondered now how his mind could have confused the two. He had allowed frustration and bitterness to breed desperation. The darkest form of desperation had taken root. It had alienated him from his family and placed him, and possibly them, in grave danger. It had condoned his actions, holding out the ripe fruit of justification, and it had backed him into a corner, defenseless to leave, trapped and now a powerless victim to whatever fate it handed him.

Sean stood outside the back entrance of their tenement and leaned against the wall. He needed to let his heartbeat slow down and his shaking hands steady themselves before he could enter the building. The stench remained, and on any other day he would have been unable to force the deep, calming breaths he took, but he was preoccupied with what lay ahead, and he barely noticed it.

"Like that smell, do ya?" a wizened vagrant taunted as he passed by.

"Off with ya," Sean called out to him. He thought about the poor old codger and how easily it could be Da, or him, or the entire family scrounging for food along the garbage-lined streets. He had no animosity for the man, only pity and a hope that they would never end up that way.

One last breath and Sean turned and entered the building. He walked down the hall and opened their door, the room looking much like it had when he left. It was inconceivable how profoundly his life had changed in the last hour while time seemed to have stopped inside the walls of their flat. He stood there longer than he had intended, and Mam watched him carefully, trying to read the thoughts that shadowed his face. Thomas looked up from his whittling and missed the signs altogether.

"Had enough?"

"What's that?" Sean replied, confused by his father's question.

"Had enough of the perfumes of Manhattan?" Thomas laughed at his own joke.

"It's better down by the river. It always is."

"Son, are ya all right?" Kathleen questioned. "You seem out of sorts."

"Fine, Mam," he responded, "there was a fight broke out right in front of me as I was comin' home. I had to cross the street to avoid gettin' in the middle of it."

"And that's why I'm not fond of ya walkin' around alone like ya do," she answered.

"He's fine, Katie," Thomas interjected. His defense of Sean's desire to get out of the flat and have some time to himself took both Sean and Kathleen by surprise. Thomas just smiled and continued to whittle. Kathleen smiled at Sean, and he couldn't help but return the gesture. Maybe Da was starting to trust him again. If so, it would make his nefarious activity tomorrow night a little less difficult. He had already devised a plan, another lie to offer his parents. Though the lies weighed heavy in his heart, he knew it was what he had to do to survive.

CHAPTER TWELVE

Friday morning greeted the Delaneys with sunlight beaming through the grime and fog on their windows. The filmy surface cast a filtered light into the flat, giving it as much beauty as it would ever see. It was enough to send Thomas off to work in an optimistic frame of mind, and it set Kathleen to tidying up while she sang *Reilly's Daughter*, one of her father's favorite songs. The thought of him lost to The Hunger, sad as it was, was not enough to quell her cheerful mood and for that she was thankful. The children played with Thomas's newly finished wooden characters whittled from scrap wood. He had carved an entire family much like their own and a little wooden dog they had named Finn, and the children were having a grand time creating adventures with their new playthings. As Sean watched them, remembering a different time when he would have been on the floor playing alongside them, he thought about how much his life had changed in such a brief span of time. And that led him to his next lie.

"Mam, I forgot to mention it last weekend, but Dr. Bermann asked me to come around tonight after supper to help him with his door," Sean said, laying the groundwork for his upcoming absence. He knew he would be gone much later than he should be and that his lie would not cover the hours he would be away, but it was the best he could come up with.

"Oh?" Kathleen was mildly surprised. She fought hard not to assume the worst of their son as Thomas nearly always did, and as he would again tonight.

"Aye, last week when I was there tendin' to Mrs. Bermann's garden he showed me the back door where someone had tried to break in. The doctor surprised them and they ran off, but the door was damaged. He said he had a new one comin' this week and could I come and help him hang it."

"Well, that'd be a kindly thing for you to do, Son. We owe the Bermann's much, though they'd never admit to it," Kathleen said. She quickly changed the subject so as not to draw a shadow over the lovely morning. "Ya know, there's a birthday comin' for one of my wee ones," she said louder, hoping to draw in the other three. They stopped and listened, smiling, knowing their oldest brother was nearing his thirteenth birthday.

"That's Sean!" Maeve called out. "He's about to be a man!" Everyone laughed and Maeve blushed, thinking she'd made a silly mistake though she had heard Da say much the same thing lately.

"A young man, yes," replied Mam. "I'm thinkin' we should have ourselves a fine meal on Sunday after your da gets home. What would ya like for your birthday supper, Sean?"

Sean hesitated, thinking to himself that he would be fortunate to see his thirteenth birthday. He hoped nothing would go wrong tonight and that life could continue without tragedy knocking on their door. To be home with his family celebrating his birthday on Sunday might be the best gift he could hope for.

"Son?"

"Just thinkin,' Mam," he replied. "I'm not sure what I'd like for my birthday supper. Whatever you want to make will be fine." He gave her a smile and because of that she did not force him to make a decision.

"Lamb stew!" Sorley called out.

"Coddle!" Eamon pleaded.

"Oh, now, we've not had a fine Dublin Coddle for the longest time!" Kathleen agreed. "But then, 'tis not my day to be decidin' what we'll have." She turned and looked at Sean, hoping he might agree and the decision would be made.

"That sounds grand, Eamon," Sean replied with a noticeable enthusiasm in his voice. Everyone was pleased that Sean had chosen coddle for his birthday dinner.

"Coddle, it is! I shall see about takin' a special trip to the market or perhaps Da can. I think a warm loaf of my Aintín Riona's sweet bread with apple and raisins would go nicely!" Kathleen looked forward to the wonderful meal she would cook for her family and was grateful for Thomas's employment. Her aunt's bread was a favorite of hers as a child in County Cork, and she hadn't had it in years. She could almost taste it, warm from the oven with a bit of butter melting over a thick slice of it.

Once the plans were finalized the afternoon passed quietly. It was the calm before the storm. No one was aware of the coming tempest except Sean and even he did not know the severity of the darkness approaching. His stomach churned as he thought about the vast unknown of the night ahead and the countless ways it could unfold. The sun was lower in the sky as Sean peered through the windows, and he knew Thomas would be home soon. Though Sean had told Kathleen that he was going to the

Bermann's after supper, he realized that leaving the flat before Da arrived home would be well-advised. He would let Mam offer his lie to his father. It might not sound as suspicious coming from her.

"Might I have a piece of bread and some beans from last night's pot? I'm thinkin' of headin' over to the Bermann's now so that I can be done and home before it gets dark." Sean offered the premise to his mother who saw nothing but logic in it.

"Sure and there's plenty enough for ya, and then some," Kathleen offered. She was in the kitchen peeling potatoes for the night's supper. "But you'll miss out on the boxty I'm makin' for supper tonight."

"Not to worry, Mam. I'll have some later if there's any left when I get home."

"All right, then," she replied as she tore a piece of bread from the loaf and dished up a serving of beans from the pot that was already on the stove warming for tonight's supper. Beans and boxty would be hearty enough to tide them over until Sean's birthday meal on Sunday. Sean ate quickly and headed for the door. He stopped and looked back at Mam and his siblings and all that he held dear, and a lump formed in his throat.

"Sean?"

"Bye, Mam," was all he could mumble.

As he approached the back entrance of the building he recalled Reddy telling him not to show up unarmed. He had no weapon. Da had an old shillelagh given to him by John O'Riley before John had set out in search of his fortune. It was always propped in the corner next to Thomas and Kathleen's bedroom, and Thomas would surely notice its absence if Sean took it. He wandered across the yard, in no great hurry to begin the evening's activities. He walked beneath the makeshift clothesline and saw the makings of a weapon hanging there. Sean glanced around quickly and, seeing no one nearby, he pulled a woolen sock off the line and shoved it into his pocket. He would look for a rock he could slip into the sock, creating a crude but effective weapon if there was need for it. He left the yard and headed down to the river, knowing Da would arrive back in their neighborhood soon. It was not the time for Sean to be delayed by questions and suspicions.

Front Street was his familiar route along the river, and it was the one he would take to meet Marley and Reddy near Pike Street. It was early, far too early to head that way, so Sean turned left and walked a couple blocks until he was halfway between the Brooklyn Ferry dock and the Jackson Ferry dock. He noticed a pile of discarded wooden crates nearby, stacked by someone else who had likely stopped there to watch the ferries come and go across the river. He climbed up on them and watched as the Brooklyn Ferry was just departing, taking the passengers back across to the better side of New York. Sean imagined stowing away on the ferry and looking for something finer on the other side. His thoughts wandered to the amazing adventures the riverboat pilot at the St. Nicholas must have had. He longed for a life that didn't look like his, a city that didn't look like this one, and an existence void of want and danger and disappointment. Up until his meeting with Reddy and Marley yesterday, he thought he had found that life. His error in judgment would likely be his undoing.

Sean sat and watched the river traffic for a long time, dreading the night to come but knowing there was nothing for it. He would meet up with the boys and let fate deal whatever hand it decided they deserved. As the sun descended and dipped down low to meet the horizon, Sean climbed down off the crates and made his way to where he would meet Reddy and Marley. He watched the sides of the road as he walked and was thankful to have found a smooth round rock slightly bigger than his fist. He slipped it down into his other pocket and hoped that in the fading light no one would see the odd bump on his leg. When Sean reached the corner of Pike Street, he walked over to the shacks where he had encountered his accomplices the night before. As he turned into the alley between the two shacks he noticed three figures there, not two, and immediately felt a great uneasiness in the pit of his belly. He walked closer, slowly, and recognized the scarred face of Beeny Cohen. It was not a face he liked or trusted, and his resolve began to fragment into shards of doubt and fear. He looked at Reddy, and his question was evident on his face.

"We can use an extra hand, Delaney, don't you worry yourself," Reddy explained. "Beeny here was runnin' with the Marginals over on the Hudson before you grew out of your short pants."

Beeny and Marley both laughed at Reddy's joke, but Sean saw no humor in it. He stood back and said nothing, knowing the tension and trouble he would create by questioning Beeny's loyalty. Cohen was intimidating, and Sean would not dare to challenge him. He nodded and took half a step backward to await Reddy's instruction.

"Here it is, boys." Reddy spoke quietly and leaned in closer in case anyone who might pass by was within earshot. "James said the crew goes ashore by nightfall, and they usually stay until the wee hours of the mornin'. There will probably be two or three flunkies left on board to stand watch. He said that most times they're drinkin' and playin' cards, so we might get on and off the ship unnoticed."

"And if not?" Sean whispered. He knew the answer, so why hadn't he stopped himself from asking? He expected the belittlement that followed.

"Ya got yerself a weapon, little man?" Beeny Cohen asked. There was a sneer on his face that conjured images of Sow Madden, and Sean thought to himself that they were likely cut from the same cloth.

Sean pulled the sock out of his left pocket and the rock from his right and slipped the rock inside the wool sock. He heard Beeny snicker and his annoyance intensified, mostly because of Beeny's response, but also because Reddy and Marley had decided to include Beeny Cohen in the endeavor. There was little to recommend him to an alliance built on trust. He was rarely around Muldoon's and seemed to only show up when he was hungry, thirsty, or broke. Reddy saw the anger on Sean's face and knew he had to put an end to any bickering before they headed down to the dock. Personal issues aside, they had to work as a team, or they would invite a world of trouble aboard the *Swift Justice*.

"Cohen, you know as well as I do that a good knock from that rock can take down a man as big as Danny Hurley," he said with enough command and warning in his voice to convince Beeny to cooperate.

In response, Beeny Cohen tapped the right side of his long overcoat and then moved it slowly aside to reveal a pistol. Sean's belly wrenched, and Marley shifted uncomfortably. The two reactions were for entirely different reasons. Sean wanted no part of a murderous encounter, and Marley knew that a gunshot would likely bring unwanted attention to the docks.

"Gunfire is a last resort, Cohen," Reddy advised. "You fire that gun and it'll draw the kind of attention we don't want. Understand?"

"Yeah, yeah, McCann. I been doin' this awhile and don't need no instruction from the likes of you. Let's get on with it." It irritated Beeny that the younger and less experienced

Reddy McCann was berating him. However, he understood the hierarchy of the heist. He knew that whoever planned and put together an exploit was lord and master until it had been fully executed. He would yield to McCann this one time because this heist would bring favor and good standing with Sam. Beeny was tired of being at the low end of the ladder. His experience and knowledge should have been considered when Sam recruited him into the Wharf Kings, and this heist tonight just might get him the attention he deserved. He had given it much thought and had come up with a plan that would see him elevated to a higher position in the pecking order. He would have to play his cards right and maneuver through some well-planned fabrications, but he was more than capable of spinning a story his own way.

The *Swift Justice* was one of the newer medium clipper ships built in Massachusetts and used to transport cargo and passengers. Though not as fast as an extreme clipper ship, its ability to haul more cargo and still sail in good time proved to be a highly successful design. The ship stood ready, its sails affixed to the three masts, awaiting the departure date to England. All but two of the thirty-five crew members were ashore enjoying the pleasures that ports of call provide. The four Wharf Kings made their way to the dock and noted the absence of activity on the deck of the ship. Reddy led the way and beckoned for the other three to follow him up the gangplank.

Once on board the four thieves stood and listened. There were faint voices coming from below deck. Reddy estimated two, maybe three, remained on board. No other sound or movement was detected. They made their way quietly back to the stern, and Reddy opened one of the three doors that led to the area below the raised quarterdeck. He had boarded enough sailing vessels to know where to find the captain's quarters. They noticed a dim light coming from beneath the closed door and a moment of panic seized Sean though the others appeared unworried. Reddy opened the door slowly and peeked inside before giving his accomplices a slight jerk of his head, inviting them to follow him in.

There was a lantern on the captain's table casting a golden light around the quarters. It was rich in carved wood and impressive souvenirs from the captain's travels. Sean again entertained the thought of living and working aboard a ship but there was no time to be daydreaming, and he tucked the fond wish deep into the safekeeping of his heart.

"Delaney!" Reddy whispered loudly. Reddy's voice jarred Sean from his musings. He looked over to where the other three were standing, waiting for him to join them. They had located a stack of five medium-sized wooden crates in the corner of the captain's quarters. The top of each crate was branded with the information they were looking for. *Colt Patent Fire-Arms Manufacturing Company, Hartford, Connecticut, Case of 8.* Sean's heart was racing. This was it. Reddy whispered for each of them to grab a crate and make their way back to the door and onto the ship's deck. They complied and with Beeny Cohen in the lead, they stepped back into the open air. Reddy stayed behind until the other three were out. He noticed a small satchel on the stand beside the captain's bed. He grabbed it and stuffed it into his pocket before following the others out the door with the fourth crate. On the deck of the *Swift Justice*, the four thieves were greeted by two of the ship's crewmen, and all six of them knew there was going to be a brawl. The thieves hastily set down their spoils and got ready for the fight. Instinctively, Sean pulled the sock out of his pocket as his only means of defense. He hesitated a moment too long and

Beeny grabbed it from his hand and slammed it into the side of the closest crewman's head. The man crumbled into a heap on the wooden deck, blood flowing from his wound. Sean froze as the other crewman ran straight at him.

Before Reddy had the chance to pull his club from his belt, Beeny removed a large knife from a sheath on his own belt and ran it into the belly of the oncoming crewman. He fell to the deck, his blood mixing with that of his crewmate.

"Let's go!" Reddy said. His voice was still low in case there were more crewmen below deck who may have heard the scuffle. If that were the case, they would be on their way to investigate. Time was of the essence. The longer they remained on ship, the greater their chance of being discovered and apprehended. Sean hesitated a moment, his feet planted firmly on the polished wooden deck as he stared at the growing pool of blood surrounding the injured crewmen. He realized the others were hurrying away without him, and he picked up his crate and made his way to the gangplank. Onto the dock and away from the river's edge they ran without stopping to regroup. Sean was the youngest, smallest, and the least experienced. He lagged behind, unable to run as quickly as the others with the heavy load he was carrying. The fear of being grabbed from behind by an unseen pursuer kept his feet moving. They ran up Market Street and turned onto Monroe, just a block away from Charlie Connor's Shoe Shop. Sean knew they were closer to safety with each block they put between themselves and the harbor. He knew stopping for any reason was not a wise move, but the weight of the gun cases was becoming too much for all four of them. They would need to stop for a few minutes. The alley behind Charlie's shop was dark and relatively protected from suspicious individuals who might be out and about on a warm summer's night. They all followed Reddy's lead into the alley, grateful for a moment to rest and catch their breath.

"I think we're safe here, boys," Reddy said quietly as he set down his crate. He stood up and breathed deep, trying to get his pulse to calm and his breathing to return to normal. The others followed his lead. Reddy stood quietly for a minute or two, thinking carefully about their next move. "Marley, is your uncle awake, do ya think?"

"He's usually asleep by now," Marley said. "Why?"

"I'm thinkin' this would be a good place to store the crates until we have the right opportunity to walk them into Muldoon's. We just don't want your uncle wakin' up and asking dangerous questions."

"He's half-deaf, so he never hears me comin' and goin'." Marley walked over to the back door of the shop and opened it, peeking inside his uncle's storeroom and the small bedroom area where Charlie allowed him to stay. He could hear Charlie's loud snoring coming from his bedroom located down the short hallway. "It's safe," he whispered.

The thieves picked up their crates and carried them quietly into Charlie's back room. Marley's bedroom area was to the left, and they followed Marley there. They pushed the crates under Marley's bed, in deep and against the wall where they would not be noticed. They didn't linger there but went back out into the alley to discuss the next part of their plan. Reddy pulled the captain's satchel from his pocket and opened the drawstring. He walked back out onto Monroe Street to find some light from a nearby streetlamp. The others followed, curious what the pouch contained. Reddy emptied the contents into Beeny's waiting hands and surveyed the number of coins there. He smiled at the nice bonus they would receive for their troubles.

"I'm thinkin' we'll split this up between us, boys," Reddy suggested. Everyone nodded in agreement. "And what would be our fate if Sam got wind of it?"

"He'd surely slit our throats," Marley offered.

"There's that possibility. It wouldn't be a good end for us, and that's for certain. So, I don't need to tell any of you that this payout stays right here with us, and we'll never speak of it again to anyone, ever. Understood?" Reddy paused and looked at each of the other three directly. Again, they all nodded in agreement, knowing their lives depended on their silence. Beeny rolled his eyes, amused by the younger fellas' fear of skimming. Seasoned gang members always skimmed a bit off the top before turning over their loot. Just one more reason he belonged at the top. He knew the game. He knew the way to keep the boss man happy and still pad his own pockets with more than the share he'd be given.

Reddy did a quick count and divided the money between them. It wasn't a huge haul, but enough to make it worth their while. Sean put the money in his pocket as his mind devised another lie to cover his earlier one. He would put half the coins in his shoe and show the rest to Da when he questioned him, claiming it to be from Dr. Bermann in payment for his help with the door. It would give his alibi some credibility and hopefully allow him to escape his father's wrath when he arrived home much later than he should have.

"So, how are we gonna move this stuff out of my room to Muldoon's?" Marley asked.

"I think we need to get off the streets in case the river patrol starts lookin' for suspects," Reddy said. "Let's meet up at the Square tomorrow around noon and we'll make a plan. Now off with ya. Four lads, four different directions. Got it?" All agreed and headed out into the city. Sean watched the other three run off before turning and doing the same. He walked down Catharine one block to Cherry and ran the six blocks back to Montgomery. Once there, he paused before heading up to Broadway and home. He leaned against the side of a barber shop, long closed for the day, and removed his shoe. He retrieved the twelve coins from his pocket and placed most of them inside the shoe. In the dim light it looked like a dime and two half-dimes left in his hand which seemed fair payment for playing the part of a handyman, and he put them back into his pocket. Sean replaced his shoe and leaned there a few more minutes. The gravity of their actions on board the ship hit him hard there in the darkness. He recalled the sound of the rock hitting the crewman's head, and the sight of Beeny Cohen's knife blade sinking into the other man's belly. Tears formed in his eyes and spilled over. At that moment, he did not care if he was reacting like a culchie, like a silly child, for this was his first encounter with death, and he was complicit in it. The sailor who suffered the blade of Beeny's knife would surely die. The other might recover but there would be no way to know for sure. Sean wiped his face and took a deep breath. It would not benefit him nor the validity of his story to enter their flat with tears on his cheeks.

He walked a fast pace to their tenement. Once inside the hallway, he drew in one last deep breath before opening the door to whatever awaited him on the other side.

CHAPTER THIRTEEN

"Where the devil is he?" Thomas yelled. Darkness had fallen two hours ago. Thomas paced in fear and dread which fueled his anger. Things had been going well. Why now? Why would Sean throw it all to the gutter in this obvious act of defiance?

"Thomas, our wantin' him home won't make it happen," Kathleen offered.

"I know that, Katie, I do. I'm afraid for him bein' out this late, and angry that he has once again put us in this position especially after the progress we'd made. Now we're right back where we were. Nothin' about this is right. There's somethin' wrong, I can feel it."

Thomas's foreboding sense, his *an da sheallad*, cast a dark presence into the flat. The children were already fearful for Sean's safety and now were growing anxious wondering how Da would react when their brother arrived home. Thomas's angry outburst and the fear that something was amiss should have been kept inside him, and he knew it.

"Children, come," he beckoned them over as he sat down on the couch. "'Tis fine. Da is angry and ya know my temper, yes? I'm worried for Sean, and when he arrives home I'll not holler at him. If he and I need to talk we'll do it alone, man to man, now that he'll be thirteen in a couple days." Thomas smiled and his children relaxed. Da was always good to his word, and they trusted he would follow through with his promise to avoid an unpleasant scene.

Eamon and Sorley flopped down on the floor and began to wrestle, carefully if that were possible, according to Mam's instructions as she still worried over Sorley's weakened leg. His knee had healed well enough though it had yet to regain its full strength and could leave him unsteady at times. Maeve stayed on the couch next to Thomas, whispering a fine story as she played quietly with the little wooden family and their wee dog, Finn. He looked down at her. His love for her and all his children so overwhelmed him that he found it hard to breathe. He felt the water in his eyes threaten to spill over and wiped at them with the back of his hand before anyone could notice, though it was not missed by his wife. Kathleen walked over and stood behind the couch, placing her hands on his shoulders to affirm that she understood, and that she also felt a grave concern for Sean's safety. He reached up and placed his right hand on hers, and peace returned to the flat for a few minutes.

The door opened carefully in case the occupants were sleeping. Sean's heart sank to see that they were not, and he prepared himself for the fiery exchange that was sure to follow.

"Da, I'm sorry," he started. "The door was not havin' it. It didn't fit right, and the doctor had to file away at it over and over. It was dark when we finished, and then Mrs. Bermann pulled a fresh apple pie from the oven and twisted my arm to stay and have a slice of it. I know ..."

"Sean, we'll talk about it tomorrow. It's late and I'm thinkin' we all need some sleep," Thomas interrupted. Sean worked hard at keeping his jaw closed. It was not the response he had expected from his father.

"Aye, Da," was all he could say. He had been prepared to offer explanations, more lies, and more empty alibis to cover his criminal activities. He had thought it through carefully and felt certain he could convince his mother and father that the story he would tell them was true. The real truth of tonight's activity would only come to light if the Delaneys needed Dr. Bermann's services again, and Thomas or Kathleen thought to mention the time Sean helped hang the new door. Sean hoped it would be a very long time before any of them were ill or injured enough to seek the doctor's assistance.

"Sure and we're all ready for happy dreams to take us somewhere wonderful, are we not?" Kathleen asked. She was proud of Thomas for the way he had handled the situation and for keeping his promise to the children. She was grateful that none of them had to suffer the angry outburst that she too was expecting when Sean returned home. She helped the children get their mattresses rolled out and tickled her three youngest as they stripped down to their worn, torn, yellowed drawers. Kathleen looked past the sad state of their undergarments to the smiles on their faces. She cast a grateful look to Thomas who returned her smile. He would talk to Sean, it could not be swept beneath the carpet, but he would keep his word and do it in a civil manner. It would be easier in the morning when new light would give some clarity to a situation that the darkness would surely cloud.

Kathleen took off her dress and laid it across the foot of her bed. Her undergarment was as worn and tattered as the children's were. As she snuggled in beside Thomas she was oddly grateful that they were all clothed in garments of humility dealing with life's difficulties together, beside, and equal. Thomas reached over and pulled her close to him, safely encircled in his arms. *May it always be this way*, she thought as she counted the reasons they had to be grateful. Blessings look different to those who have little, and the scale by which they are measured is unknown to those without want. Thomas and Kathleen, despite their circumstances, recognized their blessings.

The night was restful for the Delaneys, each exhausted by their own worries, the tension that had invaded their home as they waited on Sean's return, and the relief of Da's promise to handle the situation peacefully and away from the family. For Sean, his exhaustion was every bit as deep as his family's, but his weariness came from a night rife with fear, guilt, panic, and regret. The entire fiasco had been a bungled mess, beyond what he would have imagined, and the burden of guilt for his complicity would weigh heavy on him for a long time to come. He drifted off to sleep with his shoes on but stirred a couple of hours later and quietly removed the coins still inside. He tucked them under the couch for the time being and did his best to fall back asleep, to find shelter, and to escape the darkness that, for him, would not disappear at sunrise.

The morning was clouded over, and Sean thought it matched his soul well enough. Mam put a pot on to boil, and the children stirred when they heard the noises from the kitchen. Saturday morning was typically a quiet one for the Delaneys. It was the day between Thomas's workdays, and they would typically enjoy a late breakfast of eggs and bread, and maybe a rasher or two to share if there were any left from Da's last visit to the market. Saturday afternoons might see Da storytelling, or a round of *If I Could, I Would*, or another activity the family could share together. Sean knew he would have to get away around noon to meet up with Reddy and the boys, and as Mam started preparing the eggs he carefully devised another lie. He would offer a half-truth, which he hoped would ease half his guilt, but he doubted it.

"The tea is nearly ready, dear ones," Kathleen said. "We've eggs and potatoes to fortify us against those dark, cloudy skies outside our windows."

"Katie, darlin', 'tis not cold but only dark. All the same, I'll not say no to eggs and potatoes or your sweet fussin' over us, Mo Chroí." Thomas teased.

"Och! That reminds me, Tommy! Do we have coin enough left for a large skillet of Dublin Coddle for Sean's birthday tomorrow?" Kathleen asked.

"Aye, I believe we do, and that sounds good. Been a time too long since we had us a coddle!"

"Can ya visit the market today then, so that I can have it ready when ya get home from work tomorrow?" Kathleen was hoping there was enough money for a sweet treat for Sean as well but was hesitant to ask.

"And would there be enough so that our young man might have somethin' sweet on his birthday?

"I don't know, Katie, but I will surely do my best."

"But look here, Mam!" Sean interjected into their conversation, grateful for the unexpected opportunity to work his lie into the day's plans. "Dr. Bermann paid me these coins for my troubles. I told him no, and that it was nothin' much for me to help, but he wouldn't take to my answer and insisted I have it." Sean reached into the pocket of his pants, still laying at the foot of his mattress, and pulled out the coins he had left there.

Thomas felt suspicion rearing its ugly head, and he calmly questioned his son about the money.

"He paid ya, then?"

"Aye, Da, he was feelin' bad for how long it took us. He wanted to hire me a horse and buggy, but I told him I'd be fine walkin' back home. That's when he paid me and thanked me for my help."

Thomas milled over the story quietly as Kathleen poured tea into cups and prayers into Heaven. With Sean's birthday so close, her heart ached for peace to prevail. Try as he might, Thomas could not find fault with the story Sean was telling. He accepted it for now but would visit Dr. Bermann soon and hear his telling of the door hanging.

"Sure and it was kind of him to pay ya for your troubles. It feels right to work hard and be paid in return, does it not?" Thomas addressed his suspicions indirectly, hoping to make a point without stirring up another argument. "Many in this city think the Irish are lazy and unwillin' to work for their keep. Truth be known, 'tis all we want to do. In my way of thinkin', it makes a man proud to have sweat on his brow and coin in his pocket."

"Aye, Da," Sean replied. "It does feel good. I was thinkin' that if you can get the things Mam needs for the coddle, I'd like to visit the bakery over there on Orchard Street and pick out somethin' sweet for my birthday. I like the idea of spendin' my own money on what catches my eye."

Thomas hesitated. He had trusted Sean enough to believe his explanation of the coins in his pocket, but now he had to decide if he trusted him to take those coins to the bakery and return home without being waylaid by ill intent. He wanted desperately to take the boy at his word. Lately, though, each time Sean offered an explanation to his whereabouts and his activities, it sounded thin and hollow. Thomas refused to believe that his suspicions were coming from the second sight. He was certain it was a visceral reaction to a child who had lied before and had not yet given them enough reason to trust him again. Kathleen saw Thomas's hesitation and stepped in to preserve the peace.

"Tommy, I think it would be fine for Sean to pick out his own birthday treat, yes? He'll be thirteen tomorrow; he's nearly a man now!" She smiled at Sean and then at Thomas hoping her tender arbitration would bridge the growing abyss between father and son. At least for today and for Sean's birthday tomorrow.

"Aye, I suppose it'd be fine. I'll be makin' a trip over to Carnahan's Market after breakfast. Son, when do ya think you'll be leavin'?"

"Not long after, Da," he replied. "I don't suppose I'll be too long unless I can't decide." Kathleen laughed. Thomas smiled, and Sean allowed himself to do the same. If he could make his plan work and could meet the boys at Chatham Square for a few minutes, he could be back home around the same time as Thomas. He would stop by the bakery before heading home and pick out anything that looked good.

Breakfast was heartily devoured, and Thomas got himself ready for the walk to Carnahan's. He grabbed his empty sack from a peg on the wall and kissed Kathleen before leaving. It was nearing eleven o'clock by the time he was ready to depart.

"I can almost taste that coddle now, my love," he said. He glanced at Sean and there was no condemnation on his face. There was, however, a serious enough expression to remind Sean that he still had doubts and suspicions that had not yet been laid to rest. "I'll see you Delaneys back here before ya can say Brian Boru," he declared.

"Brian Boru!" Maeve called out from her parents' bed where she was playing with her wooden figures. Eamon and Sorley laughed, as did Thomas. Sean grinned at Maeve and nodded to his father. He hoped the timing of it all would work in his favor.

Thomas left and Sean helped Kathleen clear the table. It was a rare display of kindness, and though she didn't know what prompted it, she gladly accepted the help. They worked in silence and once the table was cleared Sean finished getting dressed. He sat down near the couch to put on his shoes, and when no one was watching he slid his hand underneath and recovered the rest of his coins. He had no qualms about putting them into his pocket this time since Da was not around to question the jingle of dirty money. Sean laced up the sturdy leather shoes from Charlie Conner. They were the nicest article of clothing he owned, and though he hadn't yet had the opportunity to thank Charlie, he knew Da had done so repeatedly. Once the guns were removed from the back of Charlie's shop, Sean thought he might like to visit him and thank him in person.

"You take care now and find yourself a fine cake or some other lovely birthday treat. And if ya haven't enough to buy for us all, you get yourself what ya want, yes?"

"I'll get enough for us all," Sean responded.

"Can ya get one of those Charley Roosh cakes like Mrs. Levy shared with us last year?" Eamon suggested. He had not forgotten the moist spongy cake topped with a sinful amount of whipped cream. The edge of the round cake was lined with cookies that Mrs. Levy had called ladyfingers, but try as he might Eamon could not see the resemblance. It would have been one fat lady whose fingers looked like the wide, flat cookies on the cake. They were delicious, though, and his mouth watered now as he recalled it.

"I'll see what I can do, Eamon," Sean called back over his shoulder as he left. He had waited a good twenty minutes knowing that Da would be well out of the immediate area by then. Sean hoped that Thomas would walk directly down Monroe Street as it would put a good three blocks between their routes and give Sean a buffer zone, keeping him out of his father's field of vision.

Sean walked a fast pace down Division until he arrived at the Bayard Street split as it broke away from the main thoroughfare. He took Bayard to increase the distance between himself and Carnahan's and entered Chatham Square from a side street. He saw Reddy, Marley and Beeny Cohen milling around the corner near TJ *Wayne's Tobacco Shoppe*, the sign above proudly declaring *Havana Segars*. It seemed a safe place to meet, distanced somewhat from the seedy flophouses and brothels in the area. Sean walked up and greeted the other three with the usual backward nod of the head.

"About time," muttered Beeny. Sean looked at him with resentment. If he was late, it was only by a few minutes.

"All right!" Reddy interrupted. He was immediately annoyed by Beeny's incendiary remark and had regretted inviting him along as soon as the four of them had met up to board the *Swift Justice*. Reddy sensed a meanness in Beeny, and though that was not uncommon among thieves and criminals, it was a meanness that spoke of disloyalty. He hoped he would not pay dearly for the error in judgment.

"What's the plan, then?" Sean asked, anxious to hear the plan and get over to the bakery.

"I'm thinkin' we leave the items in question where they are for now," Reddy started, keeping his conversation vague so as not to divulge any incriminating information to passersby. "There's a lot of commotion down on Catharine Street on Saturdays and Sundays. Too many pryin' eyes and questionable folks that might want to relieve us of our goods. Mondays are quiet. Folks have gone home back over to Brooklyn, and the locals are carryin' on with their business."

Sean was relieved to hear they were willing to wait until Monday. If they had attempted to move the guns tomorrow, he would surely have been seen by Da during his workday on Catharine Street. He could stay close to home for his birthday, keep the peace with Mam and Da, and then concoct another falsehood to get him out of the flat on Monday.

"What time?" Marley asked. "My uncle gets up early on Mondays and takes his shoes to sell in some of the other shops in the market area. He's usually home by noon. He's got a couple carts that he uses for deliveries and usually takes the smaller of the two. If he does that on Monday, we can load the items into the bigger one and cover them up with a blanket. It'll make it easier to get them over to Muldoon's without lookin' suspicious."

"Eight o'clock, then?" Reddy asked.

"Eight o'clock," Marley repeated.

It was clear that the meeting was over, and each of the four accomplices left in a different direction. Sean backtracked through the square the way he had come and walked back down Bayard to Division. The *Part de Gâteau Patisserie* was located on Orchard Street three blocks off Division. The Frenchman who owned it had moved to New York two years ago, and his business had steadily increased as talk of his fine pastries circulated around the city. Sean's only experience with his delectable creations was limited to a small piece of the delicious cake shared with the Delaney family on Mr. Levy's fiftieth birthday. Such a fine thing would never have graced the Delaney's table any other way.

The bakery had a fancy pink-and-white striped awning above the door. Sean hesitated, realizing now that he would look painfully out of place in such a fine establishment. He tugged at his clothes hoping to tidy himself up a bit, but he knew it was futile. Poor was poor, and it looked just like him. A quick glance through the front window revealed just one customer inside. It was now or never, and to return home without a birthday treat was not an option. Sean reached out and opened the door. The baker and his customer both looked at him suspiciously.

"Merci, Madam Perrault," the baker said, handing his customer a fancy package that spoke of something exquisite inside. The lady nodded and scurried past Sean who stood to the left of the door perusing the three large baker's racks against the wall. The shelves were filled with pies and pastries, fancy breads, and cakes.

"Is there something you need?" the baker asked. His question was surly and uninviting, and he hoped that his lack of congeniality would turn the boy away.

"I had a bite of cake from your shop last year, and I've not forgotten how good it was," Sean said. "I'm havin' a bit of trouble readin' the names here on your shelves. 'Tis not the king's English, I'm afraid."

"Not English. French," the man said flatly, obviously insulted.

"Well, the nice lady who shared your cake with us called it a Charley Roosh, I believe."

"Beurk!" The baker was obviously disgusted with the boy's ignorant pronunciation. "You are speaking of a Charlotte Russe, no doubt!"

"I suppose," Sean replied. He was feeling small and worthless, and these days it wasn't a feeling he took kindly to. He felt his anger rising, but this would not be the time or the place for a scuffle.

"You want me to give you one, eh? From the look of you there will be little coin in your pocket!" The baker turned to walk away.

"I can pay," Sean responded with a serious tone that set the Frenchman back down a notch.

"There is a Charlotte there," he pointed to a large wooden case open at the top, "the one with the strawberries on top."

Sean walked over to the case and spotted the cake that the baker had referred to. The contents of the case were cooled by compartments below where large blocks of ice were placed. The coolness felt good, and Sean stood there for a moment. The cake was incredibly beautiful, and strawberries were a delicacy the Delaneys had only enjoyed a time or two. He stared at the deep red berries sitting pointed-end up atop a thick layer of whipped cream. If it took every bit of the money in his pocket, he would purchase that cake for his birthday. He couldn't wait to see the look on the children's faces when he walked in with such a magnificent treat. He suddenly felt like the man he nearly was.

"How much?" he asked matter-of-factly.

The baker paused. He did not want to sell one of his beautiful cakes to this dirty boy who would never appreciate the intricacies and nuances of flavors, nor the quality of ingredients he had used. He smiled slightly, and at that moment Sean decided he would have the cake no matter what price the man quoted him.

"The cake is one dollar and twenty-five cents."

Sean knew the baker had elevated the price to drive him away. There was, however, that much and more in Sean's pocket. He reached in and pulled out all the coins and threw them down on the counter. The baker stood motionless, a look of both shock and embarrassment on his face.

"You'll be puttin' it in one of those fancy boxes like you did for your lady customer, yes?" Sean said.

"Oui, I can do that. And I owe you some change back, I believe," the baker said, more contritely.

"You keep it." Sean's response was dead serious, and the baker knew better than to argue the point. He'd been one-upped by a schoolboy and he didn't like it, but he was smart enough to back down and finish the transaction. Boys as young as Sean could be hardened gang members, and the baker was alone in his shop. He removed the cake from the wooden case and selected a decorated paperboard box printed with a small floral design from beneath the counter. Sean had a fleeting moment of embarrassment about carrying such a girlish item home with him, but he had waged and won a battle for his dignity with the baker, and he was not about to back down now. The box was square and deep enough for the cake to sit inside. It was open on the top and the baker placed a piece of white butcher-block paper over it and tied it around the outside with a string. He handed it to Sean and waited, hoping there would be no more reprimanding to come.

"Thanks," was all the boy said as he turned and left the patisserie.

Once outside Sean breathed a deep sigh, letting go of the anger he had felt under the haughty Frenchman's scrutiny. He walked a quick pace toward home not wanting the whipped cream to melt in the midday heat. He felt older and more confident than he had this morning. Sean felt a lightness of being, and his steps were purposeful. He felt a glimmer of value and worth. It felt good but it was a small fleeting victory, and he knew it. Sean's bitterness had taken root, born in the dark heart of the city and nurtured by the shame he had felt in being part of the city's undesirables. It had driven him to join up with the Wharf Kings for better or worse. On the upside, his recent activities had placed a small fortune beneath the floor of their flat. Just now, inside the bakery, he had stood his ground with a much older and more influential man and had found victory in doing so. But the weeks ahead were uncertain. The consequences of Beeny Cohen's savage attack on the crewmen of the *Swift Justice* could still catch up to them. Sean assumed the authorities would be investigating, and although there were no witnesses the surviving crewman could certainly give a detailed description of the perpetrators. If he survived. The man who fell victim to Beeny's knife likely died within minutes of the Wharf Kings leaving the ship. The hovering fear that he could be implicated in the crime, wrenched from his home, and incarcerated at The Refuge House on Randalls Island was an oppressive weight, an ominous cloud that no amount of positivity could disperse.

The Refuge House was the country's first reformatory for juvenile delinquents. What had started with the best of intentions had, over time, become embroiled in rumors of abuse, neglect, and indentured servitude. The older boys were contracted out to builders, developers, sanitation crews, and other purveyors of physical labor, and all the income from their service went directly into the pockets of the administrators of the reformatory. The lack of educational programs and the policies of corporal punishment as a means of reforming the youth gave rise to The Refuge House becoming nothing more than a children's prison. Sean knew of the place, of its reputation, from conversations he had heard on the street and at Muldoon's, and it was a fate he knew he could not endure. Even if he could not be identified, he had no confidence in Beeny Cohen's trustworthiness. If questioned, Cohen would not hesitate to incriminate the others to save his own skin. Sean was certain of it.

***

Thomas had tarried a while at the market, talking with Mr. Carnahan about the big park being constructed north of the city. Many Irishmen were initially encouraged at the opportunity to be hired as laborers for the massive project. Their excitement was quickly replaced by anger at the starvation wages they were paid. Many times, they were not paid at all forcing them to scramble for a second job elsewhere to put food on their tables. It was no different from any other opportunity offered to the Irish, empty and meaningless.

"When will it all end, Thomas?" Mr. Carnahan had asked.

"'Tis a good question, Seamus, and one I'll not have an answer for," Thomas replied. "It seems we're destined to go hungry no matter where it is we call home."

By the time Thomas gathered up his items and bid farewell to Mr. Carnahan, nearly an hour had passed since he entered the market. He had meant to stop in and check on Charlie Connor since he lived close by, but the lengthy conversation had changed his plans. He decided he would stop in and say hello in the morning before work. Thomas was nearly home when he thought about Sean and wondered if he had kept his word and gone directly to the bakery and home again after. Thomas wished he could chase the suspicion from his mind and restore the bond that had been frayed by mistrust and deceit, but every time it felt like they were making progress something happened to render that bond unreliable.

"There shall be coddle!" Thomas proclaimed as he walked through the doorway with his sack. The children, minus Sean, squealed with delight and Kathleen giggled happily. Sean's absence was noted, but Thomas tucked it away so as not to spoil the lighthearted celebration of what was to come. Tomorrow's supper would be something to look forward to, and Thomas hoped Sean's continuing defiance would not spoil the anticipation or his birthday celebration.

Sean was just a block away from the tenement when he saw Da rounding the corner with his sack of food. *Perfect timing*, he said to himself, relieved that he would avoid another verbal assault from his father. He carried his cake down the hallway and held it carefully in one hand so that he could tap lightly on the door. He smiled as he heard the sound of happy voices inside. Mam opened the door and her smile increased when she saw the lovely box in Sean's hands.

"Delivery for the Delaneys," he said in a deep voice.

"Can I see?" Maeve called out, jumping up and down to see if she could catch a glimpse of what was inside the floral box. When she did jump high enough she was disappointed to find the box covered with paper.

"Calm yourself, Daughter," Kathleen chided gently. "Let's let the delivery man inside so we can all see what he has brought us."

Mam and Maeve moved aside, and Sean walked to the table. Everyone gathered around, and he removed the string and the paper that covered the box. There was a collective gasp as the exquisite cake covered in whipped cream and strawberries was revealed.

"Charley Roosh!" Eamon shouted.

"Sure and that name got me scolded by the baker!" Sean complained.

"Sorry, Sean," Eamon responded, "but I'm thinkin' that's what Mrs. Levy called it."

"Och, no worries, Eamon. I set that baker straight when he tried to treat me like a worthless mick." Thomas did not like Sean's tone of voice, and though he understood better than most the demeaning behavior of others, he did not want his son to be disrespectful or rude. There was too much joy in the room to spoil it with reproof and disapproval, and Thomas added it to the growing list of things he would speak to Sean about in the days to come. He told himself that as soon as Sean's birthday had passed it would be time to sit the boy down and have a serious conversation with him. Maybe they would take a walk down to the river and talk there, though he knew Sean well enough to know he would be annoyed by Thomas's intrusion into his place of refuge. Regardless, the reckoning would come, and Thomas hoped he could make it gentle enough to not further alienate his son.

"It's lovely, Son," Kathleen said, jarring Thomas from his thoughts. "I'm thinkin' there's enough left of our block of ice to keep it chilled until tomorrow." She walked over to the icebox, lifted the latch, and opened the door. There was room inside, always, and it felt cool enough to preserve the beautiful cake until the birthday celebration was underway tomorrow evening. Sean carefully set the cake down in the icebox, and Kathleen closed the door. She watched Sean seat himself at the table. He picked up the old newspaper Thomas had brought home, leaned back in his chair, and began to read it. He looked older, and Kathleen's eyes filled with tears. Her firstborn, her beautiful boy with the dark cloud above him, her child on the brink of manhood. She loved him softly, intensely, and unconditionally, and yet she knew that the city, and the times, and the hardships were changing him. She knew it was beyond her control and that he would become who he was going to be with or without her hand upon it. Kathleen could only hope and pray. She turned to the kitchen and crossed herself before sorting through the food Thomas had purchased. She would busy herself with chores and stay focused on the simple joy of having them all there with her, healthy, fed enough, and still loving one another through the difficulties.

CHAPTER FOURTEEN

Beeny Cohen paced in the alley behind Muldoon's. He had no problem double-crossing Reddy, Marley, and the Delaney boy. They were all novices compared to him, and he deserved a place above them in Sam's hierarchy. He didn't particularly like Sow Madden, but he saw him as a way into the inner circle. Going directly to Sam might seem traitorous, and everyone knew how Sam felt about that. The way Beeny saw it, he could ingratiate himself to Sow, maybe form an alliance of sorts, and then could turn on him once he was in. Sow's laudanum use was increasing, and he spent most of his time sitting glassy eyed by the door acting as an ineffective sentry who offered no real force of power or protection.

Beeny had watched from the alley as Sam left the bar. Sam spent most evenings with Molly Muldoon at her house on Beekman Street. The house and the bar were left to her when her husband died. The house was small but sufficient and far enough from the heart of the seedy district to give her some comfort and security. She and Sam were building a dream home across the river. It was nearly complete and would be ready to move into soon, but they would keep the little house where they could stay during the week.

Beeny stopped his pacing and stood still for a moment, recalling and rehearsing the plan he had formulated. He would bring Sow Madden into the heist, tell him where the guns were stashed, and encourage him to get them out of Charlie's back room before the boys showed up on Monday morning. His mind played and replayed the conversation, the coercion, the devious advantage he would level against Sow Madden's intoxicated brain. His scheme was impressive, and it was time to set things in motion.

There were a few regulars scattered around inside Muldoon's. Beeny paid them no mind and ignored Mona's nod from behind the bar. It further solidified her loathing of the little weasel, as she had determined him to be. Beeny hoped the Wharf Kings headquarters would be empty except for Sow Madden. He opened the door and stepped inside. The intoxicated sentry was asleep in his chair by the door. Two younger members, Mickey Dillon and Kid Coffey, were playing cards at one of the tables. Beeny would need to get rid of them. He sat down at a nearby table and stared at them. The boys sensed Cohen's heavy scrutiny but continued playing their round of poker and eating the plate of food Mona had brought them earlier. Beeny grew impatient for them to be done and gone. He removed his knife from the sheath on his belt and stabbed the tabletop repeatedly, continuing to stare at the younger, more easily intimidated gang members. The boys shuffled nervously, whispered something, gathered up their things and left.

Beeny looked over at Sow Madden who had hadn't even flinched at the opening and closing of the door. He would need Sow's full attention if his plans were to work as designed. He stepped out to the bar and told Mona to get him a pitcher of water. She walked away muttering but returned shortly with the requested item. Beeny Cohen stepped back inside the room, closed the door, and dumped the entire pitcher over Sow Madden's head.

"What the bloody hell!" Sow Madden screamed as he leaped from his chair. The sudden rise from his sitting position, and his impaired brain and balance, caused him to reel sideways and fall to the floor. Beeny Cohen laughed hard as Sow Madden lay on the floor groaning, trying to get his wits about him so that he could retaliate.

"You're damn pathetic!" Beeny scoffed. He walked away shaking his head, waiting for Sow to pull himself together. He sat down at a table a few feet away and drummed his fingers on the tabletop. The mocking gesture angered Sow Madden further. The adrenaline flowed, clearing the fog in his brain more quickly than normal. He stood, tugged at his clothes, and headed for Beeny Cohen.

"You know Sam's beginning to lose his patience with you, don't you?" Beeny asked before Sow reached the table where he was sitting.

"Shut up," Sow yelled. "What do you know about it?"

"Oh, just what I've heard, but if you think you're still in his good graces, that's fine. I can find someone else to let in on the opportunity."

"What opportunity?" Sow was instantly intrigued. He knew Beeny was right. Sam had threatened him more than once lately. He felt himself falling from Sam's favor which drove him to the laudanum even more than before.

"You want in? You want a surefire way to ensure your place with Sam?" Beeny stared hard at the pathetic man in front of him. He needed to plant fear and doubt in Sow's foggy mind, and he also needed to read him, analyze his words and intentions, and make sure that even in this dishonest venture he could trust Sow completely.

"Go on," Sow muttered.

"I took part in a heist last night with some of the lads. They're too young and too green for a heist of this value. The goods are stashed safely away for now, but I'm thinkin' we should deliver them to Sam instead of letting the wee boys take credit for it. Believe me when I say it would secure us a certain level of favor with him."

"What kind of goods are we talkin' about?" Sow asked.

"Four crates of Samuel Colt pistols, thirty-two guns in all." Beeny spoke slowly and deliberately, making sure that the value of what they could deliver to Sam would penetrate through any remaining fog in Sow Madden's brain.

Sow let out a low, slow whistle and tipped his hat back on his head. This was a serious heist. The talk of another city-wide riot was a daily occurrence, and the Wharf Kings were not sufficiently armed. Securing more weapons than some of the other gangs in the Five Points District would put them in an excellent position to gain members and territory, and it would allow Sam to regain some of the respect he had been seeking since the Daybreak Boys disbanded. Sow nodded now, seeing the implications. This was a weighty opportunity and was one that the younger boys did not deserve.

"Where are they?" he asked.

"In the backroom of the shoemaker's shop where Spanish Marley stays." Beeny smiled as he divulged the information. He knew Sow Madden hated Marley for casting suspicion on him during their recent argument.

"Oh, I'll get 'em," Sow assured him with a dead calm that caused Cohen some fleeting discomfort. Beeny made a mental note to proceed carefully with his future plan to discredit Sow. For now, he would need to cover his intentions at every turn. "It'll be my pleasure," Sow continued. "I'll head over there in a few hours, sometime after midnight. If I have a violent encounter with that little turncoat so much the better!"

"I noticed an open shed beside the shop and two carts inside it," Beeny said, recounting the information that Marley had given them after the heist. "You can load the crates in one of those carts and get them back over here easy enough. Stack 'em up in the corner over there," Beeny nodded toward the back corner of the room, "and throw somethin' over 'em. We can turn them over to Sam tomorrow."

"He and Molly are heading across the river to their new place in the Heights. Sounds like it's nearly done, and they'll have themselves a highfalutin place to retire. Nice for them. The rest of us will just wallow here in the filth." Sow's words were heavy with self-pity. Beeny thought about reminding Sow how much money he wasted on laudanum, whiskey, and women. He might not have to spend his nights sleeping in a chair, or on the cot in the storeroom behind the kitchen, if he were a little wiser with the overly generous cuts Sam paid him after every heist. Cohen kept his comments to himself since he needed Sow's help to bring his plan to fruition. Turning on him later would be a simple task.

"You need to lay off the happy juice for the rest of the night."

"Yeah, yeah, I got it," Sow shot back at Cohen. In the past he was convinced he performed better under the influence, but tonight nothing could go wrong. He couldn't afford to lose this opportunity to win back Sam's favor. He wiped at the corner of his mouth with the back of his hand.

"I'm gonna track down the wee lads and give them an earful," Beeny continued. "I'll educate them to how things work around here and that the spoils now belong to you and me, and I'll remind them what Sam thinks of traitors, troublemakers, and liars. I'll tell them that if they attempt to take the credit and tell Sam we're lying, he'll see it as stirrin' the pot. I'll make sure they understand how meaningless their lives are to him and that if they want to stay alive, they'll need to stay quiet. If you find Marley at the shoe shop tonight, give him the same message. I'll track down McCann and Delaney and deliver the unfortunate news."

"Delaney was in on it?" Sow Madden asked with a snide grin on his face.

"Yeah, he was so scared I thought he'd piss his britches," Beeny laughed.

"This is gettin' better all the time," Sow remarked. "I never liked that little bogtrotter."

"When will Sam be back?" Beeny asked.

"I think he said Tuesday," Sow answered, trying to recover the conversation from the mire of his wasted memory.

"Good enough," Beeny responded. "That'll give us time to get the guns here and keep an eye on the snot-nosed ruffians. I don't think they'll be any trouble after I put the fear of losin' life and limb into them."

With that part of the plan in motion Beeny Cohen hit the streets looking for Reddy McCann. He was confident he could put a healthy dose of fear into the younger man, and he would let him relay the turn of events to Sean Delaney. He realized that Sow was right. Sean had given them little reason to trust him. He shared nothing about himself with anyone. As far as Beeny knew, no one could account for who Delaney was, where he lived, and how loyal he would be if push came to shove. And then there was the matter of him working on his own, setting his own rules, and convincing Sam to let him do things his own way. Suspicion flared in Beeny's mind, and he decided then and there that Sean Delaney needed a physical reminder of how small and worthless he was. A sound beating and his first knife wound would do the trick. Beeny and Sow Madden had earned their standing—time and experience counted for something—and he would make sure young Delaney didn't get too full of himself before he had contributed his share of blood and sweat.

Sow Madden left Muldoon's to get some fresh air, clear his head, and find a meal and a cup of coffee. He was excited about the opportunity to prove himself to Sam, and to exact some revenge on Marley Briggs and the Delaney boy. He felt invigorated, more so than he had in a long time, and it stirred an evil component in him that had been lying dormant beneath a thick blanket of laudanum and whiskey. The anticipation of what lay ahead cleared his mind and sharpened his thoughts, enough so that he was able to plan out his visit to Charlie Connor's shop in detail. That same sharp edge also cautioned him against trusting Beeny Cohen completely. There was something about him that even Sow Madden didn't like.

CHAPTER FIFTEEN

Sunday morning was dark and overcast and not a fitting day for a birthday celebration according to Kathleen. Sean, however, thought it fit his mood perfectly. Since returning home last night with the cake he had been racked with guilt. There had been a different and reminiscent atmosphere in the Delaney household. Sean's siblings were nearly bursting with excitement at the thought of Mam's delicious Dublin Coddle to be followed by the mouth-watering cake waiting in the icebox. There was singing as Mam had prepared their Saturday night supper, and she and Da had danced together as he sang *Eileen Aroon* in Irish. The children were not fluent in their parents' native tongue, but they recognized a few of the words as Thomas sang them sweetly to his wife. It was a rare and lovely evening, and as Sean watched and listened he grew melancholy for the days when he was younger, and life was less disfigured by want and crime and suspicion.

Thomas left for work an hour earlier than normal. He planned to stop in and say hello to Charlie before meeting up with Leo to start their workday. Despite the dark skies, he felt happy. Last evening had been a lovely reminder of days gone by, and though it might only resurface on the rarest of occasions, he relished the love and the closeness of family. He had noticed Sean smiling, relaxed, himself again. There had been a respite from the weight of poverty and despair, and in those precious moments it was easy to ignore the realities of their wretched lives. Thomas smiled as he walked, his steps light and worry free, and he wondered if his good mood was due entirely to the lingering joy from last night or the supper that awaited him after work. *Probably a bit of both,* he said to himself.

Rolling thunder in the distance called out in ominous tones trying as it does to rob folks of their happiness. It would have from a lesser man, but Thomas Delaney had survived many a storm without surrender. There wasn't much that could set him back on his heels. The day before him held great promise and he scoffed at the ominous sky and its growling.

The last of the market festivities were wrapping up when Thomas neared Catharine Street. Most of the visiting vendors from across the river were packing up their tables and tents to head back home. Thomas stood and watched the hustle and bustle, thankful for the market and how fate had brought him here at the right time, on the right day, and had granted him steady employment. The part-time position had changed their lives and kept them from starving to death or losing the roof over their heads, such as it was. Dreams of a better life in a better place still filled his head day and night, but for now this blessing was enough. He nodded slightly as if to affirm his gratitude and looked down Catharine Street to the next block where Charlie's place was located. He walked the short distance to the shoemaker's shop. As he neared he thought it odd that Charlie had not flipped his *Closed* sign to *Open* and that the place looked devoid of any activity. It was not like Charlie Connor to sleep late or take a day off which led Thomas to think that maybe Charlie was under the weather. Once again he wondered if he had inherited his mother's second sight, for something had surely prompted him to call on Charlie before work.

Thomas made his way up the little walkway that led from the street to the shop, fighting back a feeling of dread that would not relent. He approached Charlie's front door slowly, peering through the windows to see if he could discern anyone moving about inside. There was only stillness. He stepped in front of the door and tried the handle, finding it securely locked. Thomas wondered if Charlie might have gone out of town to visit family, and he realized then that he had never taken the time to ask Charlie about his family. He knew from one of their first conversations that Marley was the child of his deceased sister, but beyond that Thomas knew very little of Charlie's life outside the shoe shop. He felt guilty for having not been more engaged with his friend and decided he would remedy that in the future.

"Maybe he's in the back room," Thomas said aloud, willing it to be so. He walked around to the back of the shop where he had on many occasions carried Charlie's deliveries into the storage room. There was a delivery waiting to be carried in, and it saddened Thomas to think that Marley had once again failed to uphold up his end of the bargain with his uncle. Thomas reached out to try the handle on the back door and noticed the door was slightly ajar. His heart raced as his feeling of dread intensified. He took a couple deep breaths and tried to calm his nerves before opening the door a few inches to look inside. He could see nothing from where he stood and knew he had to enter. He only hoped there was no danger waiting inside. Kathleen and the children would be turned out onto the street without his income ensuring food and a flat.

Thomas pushed on the door but it stopped halfway, blocked by something behind it. The opening was large enough for him to get through, and he entered the familiar back room to investigate. His heart hammered in his chest as he glanced across the storeroom in the direction of Charlie's small residence located between the storeroom and the shop. Thomas let out a cry of grief as he spotted Charlie laying in the hallway just beyond the back room. A pool of blood surrounded his body, his throat brutally slashed from one side to the other. Thomas took a couple steps toward Charlie's body but fought the urge to rush to him, to see if he was still alive, as his better judgment kept his feet planted where they were. There was no saving Charlie. He had likely died hours ago judging by the amount of blood he had lost. Thomas's mind raced with questions. Had Marley committed this heinous crime? Why would anyone do this to a kind soul like Charlie Connor? Thomas cut his musings short; he knew he had to leave immediately. To tarry would be far too risky, and as bad as he felt about leaving poor Charlie lying there he could not risk being implicated for the crime. There would be no fair and impartial judgment if a poverty-stricken Irish immigrant were found inside the home.

Thomas turned back toward the door and saw what had blocked it from opening. A young man that Thomas assumed to be Marley Briggs was slumped against the wall behind the door, blood coming from his mouth and left ear. He had bruises and lacerations on his face and head, indicative of a sound bludgeoning from a blunt object. Apparently, he too had been a victim of the intruder's rage. Marley's breath was coming quick and shallow the way it does when a soul is not long for the earth. Marley moaned and moved his mouth but no sound came out. Thomas moved closer to the young man and kneeled down beside him so that he could hear Marley if he needed to say something. Whether it was a confession or an apology, the lad had a right to be heard before death took him.

"Be you Charlie's nephew, Marley Briggs?" Thomas asked. Marley nodded slightly, too weak to do much else. Thomas leaned closer as it appeared Marley was trying to speak again. The weak and airy words escaped Marley's lips in a desperate last effort, and when those words fell on Thomas's ears an intense fear gripped him, no less terrifying than if the angel of death lingered there in the room waiting to take him as well.

"Sow ... Mad ... den," Marley quietly breathed the name of his murderer. "Mul ... doon's."

With his dying breath, Marley changed the fate of the Delaney family forever. Thomas fell back on his haunches, his head spinning with fear and confusion. His chest was tight, and he found it nearly impossible to breathe. In an instant, his mind reeled back to the children's story of the river monster first told to them by Sean, and the evil beast Sow Madden. Thomas now knew that it was no fanciful invented name but the name of a killer, and one that Sean apparently knew. With his dying breath Marley had also revealed where to find the killer. Thomas got back on his feet, his heart pounding like an Irish drum line. It was deafening and disorienting. He gasped for the deepest breath he could extract from his constricted chest, crossed himself, and sent a quick prayer heavenward on Marley's behalf. There was no time for last rites, and Thomas had no business carrying out that holy business anyway. He stuck his head out of the open doorway and quickly glanced in both directions. With the way clear, Thomas slipped outside and walked back to Monroe Street toward home.

He walked slowly to avoid drawing attention to himself, pleading with God to protect Sean from the madman who had murdered Charlie and his nephew. He begged God with every reverent fragment of his soul for an answer, for a way to get Sean out of the gang, and for the family to be safe after doing so. Thomas knew enough about how the gangs operated to know that leaving their ranks rarely ended well. As he walked, and prayed, and panicked, the name of John O'Riley came quietly into the tangled knot of his fears, and Thomas knew immediately what they must do. How to execute such a plan was a mystery with no solution, a question without a logical answer. He knew that the Harlem Railroad had train service out of the city and as far north as Albany before a connector could take a traveler west. Train fare for a family of six traveling over 150 miles would be prohibitive to a man who worked two days a week for just enough money to feed his family. He continued to walk, wandering slowly through the streets between Catharine and Montgomery. The plan was there, and he believed it had been given to him in a Divine response to his prayers. If the plan was given, the means to carry it out would be given too. He knew it, and he waited for the answer as he wandered.

Thomas knew of Muldoon's Tavern though he had never had cause to visit there. Leo had spoken of it often, of Friday night poker games where a skillful player could make a nice pocketful of coin. He had insisted it was a place where the undesirables were a bit less undesirable than those who lurked in the heart of the Five Points District. After the horrors he had just witnessed, Thomas wasn't so sure that was true. He recalled a conversation with Leo as they worked on Catharine Street one Sunday morning. Leo had arrived at work with a black eye and a split lip. He had brushed off Thomas's concern explaining that, though

247

innocent, he had been accused of cheating by another man playing at his table. Thinking on it now, Thomas was certain that Leo had called the man Madden, and though the name had been meaningless to him at the time, it now held a weighty connection. Thomas wondered if Muldoon's was simply a place Sow Madden frequented, or if it was the place where the gang was headquartered. Knowing little of what he might find at Muldoon's, Thomas decided to go there at nightfall in search of money and the revenge he would have in taking it. Thomas crossed himself and begged for God's mercy upon his soul. He turned and ran the rest of the way home.

Kathleen was humming a tune as she gathered the ingredients to make a loaf of bread to serve with supper. She was mildly concerned about Sean and his dark mood on his birthday of all days. She told herself it was nothing more than his usual shadowed countenance. Sean was a hard one to read, always had been. She allowed him some space and time to sort through his feelings, and when he told her he was going on a walk she nodded and smiled. The sadness that threatened to cast a cloud on her spirit was kept at bay by the lingering joy from the night before and the anticipation of the one to come. She thought to check the cake in the icebox to make sure it was staying cool enough. A melted mass of sugar and cream would do nothing to remedy Sean's melancholy. Kathleen walked to the icebox and peeked inside. The cake looked only the slightest bit droopy but was otherwise in fine shape. As she closed the icebox door and latched it, the door to their apartment flew open and Thomas burst in, out of breath and red in the face.

"My good Lord in Heaven, Thomas!" Kathleen cried out. "What is it?"

"Come with me a moment, Katie," he said in a voice calmer than he felt. He quickly surveyed the room and found one child missing. There was no time for anger, for this day would require calm minds and complete cooperation. As he took Kathleen's hand he saw the uncertainty on the faces of his three youngest, startled by his sudden entrance into the flat.

"Children," he said calmly, "Mam and I must have a chat. 'Tis a surprise I'll have for ya later but first for Mam, yes?" They all nodded, and he smiled. He moved through the doorway still holding Kathleen's hand, and she closed the door behind her. She walked beside him, fear stirring in her belly. She knew without Thomas saying it that whatever news awaited her was deadly serious. Thomas rarely excluded the children from anything. He let go of her hand as he exited the hallway into the yard. There were a few children about playing with little more than sticks and imaginations. Thomas found a spot away from them as he took Kathleen's hand again.

"Tommy, what is it?" she asked, her hand trembling in his.

"Katie, I've heard the wailin' of the Banshee and we need to flee now before she takes him." Thomas sounded strange even to himself. To Kathleen, his words were irrational, filled with fear, and completely unlike him. She wondered what had thrust him so suddenly into a fit of terror. He was overshadowed by ancient legends and fables and superstitions he had never believed in. The last time Kathleen had heard stories of the *bain sí* she was sitting in front of a peat fire in her grandmother's home in County Cork.

"Tommy, my love, what's gotten hold of ya?"

"Katie, 'tis real enough. Our Sean is part of a vicious gang, the handiwork of which I've seen with my own eyes this mornin'. They've killed Charlie Connor, Katie, and his nephew, too. There's no tellin' how long it'll be before they do the same to our son!"

Kathleen reeled at the news of Charlie's death and more so at the insinuation that her son would be part of something so evil. Her mind defied the words Thomas had spoken. Not her son. It could not be true.

"Thomas, no," she whispered, "this cannot be. This news of Charlie's death is surely tearin' at my heart, but Sean? Part of this? Part of this gang who murdered poor Charlie and his nephew?" She crossed herself and whispered a brief prayer for the souls of the departed. "How can you know of Sean's ties to these men? How can you be certain? I cannot conceive of it, Thomas!"

"I stopped in to check on Charlie this mornin' and found him lyin' in a pool of his own blood. His throat was slit clean across." Kathleen's hand flew to her mouth in shock before crossing herself again. "His nephew was at the threshold of death's door when I found him, but he told me the two things I needed to know before he crossed over."

"What did he say, Tommy?" Kathleen's words were hesitant, but she had to know.

"He said Sow Madden, and Muldoon's."

Kathleen put her hand over her heart, her mouth open with no words escaping. Just as Thomas had done, she immediately connected the name of the river beast Sean had included in his story to the reality of the beast's existence. She shook her head back and forth, and the tears spilled out and down her grief-stricken face. Thomas wanted desperately to comfort her, to tell her everything would be all right and that they would get through this together as they always had, but he had not the time nor the luxury to hand out empty promises. Saying it would be a lie unless they acted quickly.

"Katie, listen to me. We must leave tonight. We must stay two steps in front of the grim reaper or 'tis Sean's soul he'll take next. Our son is in real danger, and we will not be safe here any longer. Do ya understand, Mo Chuisle?" His endearing term was the best he could offer her right now. When Kathleen nodded, Thomas continued before she had the chance to question his decision, to ask how they would do something so preposterous, and if there might be a better way to protect Sean.

"I intend on goin' to Muldoon's tonight after I talk to Sean and make sure it's where the gang meets up. I'll get us the money we need to leave this city for good. I'll make sure I have enough to pay for our fares on the last train north to Albany tonight. If I recall the conversation I had with Callahan a few months back, the last runnin' of the Harlem Railroad is at ten o'clock. We can catch the horsecar at Houston and Bowery and connect to the steam train at Thirty-Second Street."

"Tommy," Kathleen said in a flat, emotionless voice, "just how will ya get us the money we need?" Her question was slow and pointed. One crime did not justify another. They both knew it, but Thomas's encounter with death and violence that morning had, in his mind, given him license to do what needed to be done.

"If Muldoon's is where they're headquartered, there'll be money there. Sean can confirm this for me. Where is he, Kathleen?"

"He was feelin' somethin', and now I know what it might have been. He went out to clear his head," Kathleen stated. She grieved for her son and for the monumental guilt Sean was likely burdened with these past few months. All of Thomas's fears had been realized. All her optimism destroyed. It was more than she could process, it was too much too quickly, and she felt her resolve crumbling.

"Tommy, I can't ..." she faded. She couldn't find the words.

"Katie, we must. We have to protect Sean, and we have to keep this family safe at all costs no matter the sacrifice it demands. We endured a miserable trip across the ocean to get here, my love, we can do this as well." Kathleen nodded, surrendering, too devastated to question any further.

"What must we do?"

"Begin packin', my love. Use your mother's small chest for the things you cannot part with and pack up some clothes in three or four of the cloth sacks ya made. We can each carry a sack, and I can carry an extra one for Maeve. There is little of value here so the sacks should be more than big enough to travel with. We'll be walkin' tonight to the station at Houston Street so we cannot be weighed down with too much, yes?"

Kathleen nodded. She was too defeated to protest leaving things behind. She was too fearful of what might happen if they stayed. The realization that Sean's birthday would be an unhappy occasion for him, and the rest of them, crept into her mind between the fear and uncertainty, and she couldn't help but address it.

"Tommy, 'tis Sean's birthday. Our fine Dublin Coddle and our lovely cake. Are they to go to waste then?"

"No, Katie, but can ya have it ready for an early supper? We can eat our fine meal and enjoy it well enough. There'll be no cleanin' up, no worryin' over anything but bein' ready to leave when I return from Muldoon's later this evenin'."

"I fear this will dampen our spirits, but the food will be good I can promise ya that if nothin' else." She managed a smile and Thomas's heart filled with love and respect and admiration for his wife's tenacity. She had endured much over the years without complaint or negativity. It was this, and the beautiful children she had blessed him with, and his strong will to keep them safe and secure that would carry him through the danger of the night ahead. He was certain that God Himself had whispered John O'Riley's name in his ear, and it would be God Himself who would lead them to safety.

"Aye, Katie, dinner will be a treat for us all and one I'm lookin' forward to. Can ya make up an extra loaf or two of bread and gather whatever we can eat while we're on the train? We'll pack it in our sacks along with our clothes so that we don't go hungry while we're makin' our way to Albany."

"Sure and it wouldn't be the first time we've gone hungry," Kathleen reminded him.

"I'm hearin' a better life callin' us, Katie. On the way home I was beggin' the Holy Father God to give me an answer, and he said to me *John O'Riley*, plain as day."

"We're goin' out west, then?"

"Aye, I believe we are," Thomas responded. He watched the doubt shadow Kathleen's expression. "God suggested it, He'll provide for it, yes?"

"Yes," Kathleen answered. "I'll get to cookin' and packin' up what we'll be takin' with us. The children, will they be told?"

"Aye, we'll go back there now and present it as a grand adventure. They can help you pack. After we talk to them I will go out and find Sean. I have some questions for him and will need his help to make this work."

"Be gentle, Tommy. He's hurtin' right now." Thomas nodded. He knew Sean was hurting, tortured, and guilt-ridden. Thomas would treat him like a man, ask for his help, and offer some unexpected mercy as well.

The walk back through the hallway to their flat was silent, heavy with the impending threat of danger and uncertainty. They arrived at their door and opened it to find Eamon in the middle of a new story, one he was inventing as he went along, and it had the younger two rapt with anticipation. Eamon's voice faded away as he noticed the somber expressions on his parents' faces.

"Children, come here," Thomas said as he seated himself at the table.

The three of them joined their father at the table. Maeve was the last to pull up a chair, and as she sat down next to Thomas she hoped their Dublin Coddle had not been canceled.

"Who's ready for an adventure?" Thomas asked. The children's excitement was immediate. "Who's ready for a grand adventure?" Thomas continued, louder than before. All three chimed in their enthusiasm for whatever Da was planning.

"And what if I told ya we're leavin' here on a train and travelin' to far-off places we've never been?" Thomas asked.

"Are we takin' a holiday, Da?" asked Sorley, incredulous that they could do such a thing.

"Better, Sorley, we're gettin' out of this dirty city for good." Thomas paused to watch the children's expressions, to try and read their reactions, and to be ready to reassure them if they seemed nervous about the prospect of leaving the only home they had known in America. They were hesitant, quiet, thinking it through in true Delaney fashion. Their father could brood over something for weeks, so the announcement of a hasty decision to leave town was both unexpected and quite unprecedented. Thomas gave them time. He understood.

"Will Sean be comin' along, too, Da?" Maeve asked.

"Of course he will!" Thomas laughed. "You three just got in on the secret before him!"

"Where will we go, Da?" Eamon asked.

"We're goin' out west, Son. There are wide open spaces there, room to move and run about, fresh air and a better life for us all," Thomas replied, hoping that all he had heard was true. He refused to believe that he would once again propel his family from one miserable existence to something even worse. Once in a lifetime was enough, and surely God could not have that in store for them. It had to be better where John was. Thomas trusted John's report of life out west, knowing he had a proper gauge to measure it by. He had done his time in the festering filth of New York.

"I'd like to run about," said Maeve.

"Aye, me too," added Sorley.

"When will we leave?" Eamon was still analyzing the information.

"Tonight," Da said.

"After Sean's birthday supper, children," Kathleen added. It was a sad commentary on the life they lived that a decision as monumental as moving away at a moment's notice was worked around a good meal, and that the food they had purchased should not go to waste. That would be a sin greater than most.

"All Delaneys agree?" Thomas asked. Everyone agreed. "Now I need ya to help your mam. We've just a wee bit of time to get ready and we'll not be takin' everything with us. You listen to your mam and ya do as she says, yes?"

Thomas stood and prepared to go look for Sean. He knew he'd find him somewhere along the river watching the ships come and go. It was where the boy always went when he needed time to think. Kathleen followed him to the door. Thomas kissed her and whispered, "Only what we need, Mo Chuisle. I'll be back here with Sean for his birthday supper and then gone for a short while after. When I return we need to be ready to go. We cannot tarry. I don't know what'll happen at Muldoon's but I'll be returnin' in a hurry with no time to help finish things up."

"Aye, Tommy," Kathleen whispered. She watched him walk down the hallway and breathed a silent prayer that this day would end with hope not grieving. She closed the door and pulled her mother's chest out from under a kitchen shelf. Kathleen dusted it off and lifted the lid open with the brass handle on top. The hinges were loose but intact. It was five hands by three, as her mother would have said. It would not hold much—necessities and a couple meaningful items—but it would be light enough to carry. Kathleen went to the bedroom, set the chest on the bed, and removed a large cloth sack from where she had tucked it between the bed and the wall. She pulled another large sack and three smaller ones from inside it and handed a small one to each of the children.

"Listen, children, you'll each have a sack to carry. In it, you'll put your other change of clothes and anything ya feel bound to. Remember, ya must leave room enough for some bread and an apple, and more importantly, ya must be able to carry it yourself, so don't fill it full of meaningless things." Kathleen wondered at her last piece of advice. She wasn't sure that any of them could fill a sack full of meaningless things, for together they had few things between them.

The children nodded and got to work. They seemed excited about the adventure, and Kathleen would leave it at that. There was no need for them to know the threat of danger that lurked so close to their door, nor the things that their brother might have done to his discredit. Kathleen left the two large sacks on her bed next to the chest. She would get to them soon but she needed to get the coddle started and the bread baking. Supper would come earlier than she had planned, and she needed to work quickly to get it ready on time.

An hour passed. The food was cooking, the bread was baking, and the children had packed their things and set their sacks by the door. There was an air of excited anticipation that the children, in their innocence, could not contain. The adventure was born of danger and violence, the threat of harm, and the impending trouble that Thomas faced, but for the little ones it was a storybook come to life. The perils of travel, the endless hours of discomfort, the resettling in a strange new place, and the uncertainty that once again awaited Thomas and Kathleen were unknown concerns for the children. Thomas and Kathleen, however, were painfully aware of what might lay ahead.

Once the coddle was simmering and the bread was in the oven, Kathleen started packing her own things. Her teacups had survived the trip from Queenstown, Ireland to New York, and she hoped that the few she had left would be safe on the trip ahead. She tore strips of cloth to wrap around them and hoped for the best. She packed the cups into the chest along with the framed picture of her mother and two of their six books. Their Bible would never be left behind nor their copy of the Táin bó Cúailnge which had belonged to Thomas's father. She debated a moment or two about the others but knew they could be replaced. She was certain Eamon could recite The Swiss Family Robinson cover to cover and thought it might be a way for him to refine his storytelling skills. Kathleen filled the empty spaces in the chest with small cloth pouches of spices from the kitchen, a sewing kit with needles and a few spools of thread, and a couple small keepsakes of little value save what meaning they held for Kathleen. She closed and latched the chest and set it near the children's sacks.

One of the two larger sacks was for Sean, and the other she packed with a change of clothes for her and for Thomas along with their ragged coats. She added two thin, worn quilts and a metal canteen for water that Thomas had brought home from the trash on Catharine Street. There was plenty of room for bread and any other food that might travel well. Thinking about food alerted Kathleen's senses to the smell of bread nearly done. She returned to the kitchen and checked inside the oven. The bread was nicely browned, and when she tapped it she heard the familiar hollow sound that told her it was perfectly done. She removed the two pans and while the bread cooled slightly she started another batch. If they had to survive the trip on bread and water she would make sure they were prepared. She checked the coddle and smiled despite the seriousness of her mood. The thick brown gravy was simmering, coating the hearty chunks of potato, onion, and pork sausage with layers of flavor that had married together as it cooked. Kathleen looked around the kitchen to see what else she might put to use. Everything not used today would be left behind for the scavengers, be they human or animal, and she struggled with the guilt of wastefulness. Kathleen remembered the bottle of German ale that Mrs. Zimmer had given to Thomas months ago, still waiting to be opened and enjoyed. The ale would give the coddle a robust depth of flavor that made her mouth water just thinking about it. It would be perfect. She opened the bottle and poured the contents into the coddle, the color of it growing darker and richer as it blended together. The aroma traveled the room with intent, causing stomachs to growl and groan as they all awaited their fine meal. It would be a delicious way to bid farewell to their life on Montgomery Street.

CHAPTER SIXTEEN

Sean wasn't sure how long he had been sitting on the stack of wooden crates. He had returned to the same spot between the Brooklyn and Jackson ferry docks on South Street where he had gone two days ago to await the heist aboard the *Swift Justice*. He was deep in his sullen mood and introspection, prisoner to more questions than answers, and heavily burdened with uncertainty and guilt. Sean was torn between two intense desires: the desire for respect, success and affluence, and the desire for the family dynamic that he had experienced the night before. The tug-of-war between them was intense and he feared the battle would destroy him. He realized that he needed to make a decision, to choose between the two and find peace with that decision. One could lead to physical harm and a heart that would be forever hardened by crime and cynicism. He knew if he chose that path he would never be the same again, but he would be able to provide the things that his family lacked. He also knew that if he walked away from that path to seek reconciliation with his father and a restored relationship with his family, he would risk retaliation from the gang. If he walked away, a penniless existence would be their reality. Hunger and want would be with them for the rest of their days, and he wasn't sure he could endure a lifetime of it. There was no easy answer. He wished he had someone to guide him, to help him decide what to do, and to reassure him that once he made his decision the turmoil would cease. More than that, he wished he had never pilfered those first ten pennies, never surrendered to temptation, and never turned a blind eye to the immense burden of dirty money. Sean thought about asking God for help but what would God want with a wretched sinner like him? He was certain that his prayers would fall on deaf ears even if he had the courage to offer them heavenward. He leaned back and rested his head against the crate behind him, closing his eyes as he searched his soul. The intense loneliness of one without connection, without solace, without hope, overtook him, and he knew he was on the verge of weeping like a child.

"Sean?" Thomas called out when he noticed Sean sitting on the crates a few feet from the corner of South and Gouverneur.

"Da?" When Sean opened his eyes he was startled to see his father there. It was Sunday afternoon well past one o'clock. Thomas should be down on Catharine Street working. The dreaded possibility that his father had lost his job gave Sean a moment of panic, as it would limit his options to one—stay with the Wharf Kings in order to provide for his family. He had almost decided to walk away and take his chances. He wanted peace. He wanted to see joy on the faces of the people he loved. Staying with the gang would never allow that to happen, but if Da were no longer employed he would have no other choice. He would not allow his family to go hungry again. Fleeting thoughts and a barrage of questions fired rapidly through Sean's mind as Thomas approached. Sean prepared himself for the reckoning he knew was coming. He could no longer avoid the inevitable. Da had postponed asking difficult questions and demanding truthful answers, but judgment day had arrived.

"Are ya all right, Son?" Thomas's voice was soft and filled with concern. It was genuine and comforting and it nearly took the breath from Sean.

"Aye, Da, but why are ya here? Did ya lose your job?"

"No, Son, but we need to talk," Thomas paused and looked around. There were a few dockhands half a block away and a small group of men across the road sharing a bottle of something.

"Will ya come with me?" he asked Sean. Sean nodded, hesitant about the conversation to come but willing. *Best to get it over with*, he thought. But today? On his birthday? And him with a hundred desperate questions swirling around in his head, unknown to his father but impossible for the boy to ignore.

Thomas beckoned for Sean to follow him as he made his way past the group of men. They walked up Scammel Street to the Friends' Meetinghouse where the Quakers gathered for their services, and Thomas led Sean into the alley behind the building where it would be safe to talk. Sean found it ironic that they were about to wage a verbal battle here at the gathering place of the most peaceful people in the city. Sunday services were going on inside, so no one was likely to see them and question their loitering in the alley.

"Sean, there is terrible trouble nippin' at our heels. I know what you've gotten yourself mixed up in, and I know why. Sure and I know the shame that bein' penniless brings to a man. I know the lure of the quick money, the dirty money. I know why you stole those first ten pennies months ago and how easily it leads to a life of thievery. I know that the easy way seems like a solution too temptin' to refuse, for I was also approached by those who offered a fast way to prosperity when first we arrived here. I couldn't risk leavin' your mam a widow strugglin' to care for you and Eamon if somethin' happened to me, and I chose the more difficult path. Poverty is a heavy burden to bear, and for that reason I will not take ya to task for what you've done."

Thomas watched Sean's face as he listened to his father's words. They were both unexpected and overwhelming. He saw Sean's tears welling up, and he saw the face of a child still young and needing his family, needing a safe place where love and worth were unconditional. He reached out and placed his hand on Sean's shoulder as the boy's tears flowed over and down his cheeks. Thomas did not stop his son's grieving for he needed to let go of the tremendous guilt he had been carrying, packed tightly inside and shared with no one.

"Da," Sean said, his voice wavering, "I only did it to try and help. Seein' Maeve's face growin' thinner by the day, hearin' Eamon's belly churnin' with hunger, I couldn't take it, Da." Sean leaned forward, and Thomas pulled him close. Sean wept into his father's chest until he felt the cleansing release of regret absolved by confession. He stood up straight, took a deep breath, and wiped his face with both hands.

"Da, I'm so sorry," he whispered. "I never meant to bring shame to you or Mam, and I never thought it would go so far. I'm in over my head and drownin'."

"All is forgiven, Son, but there is much to tell ya and time is not on our side." Thomas hated rushing his son from grief and confession to the horrific news he had to convey, but time was indeed their taskmaster. "Are ya able to hear what I need to tell ya? It's not an easy thing I have to say." Sean nodded slowly, afraid to hear but recognizing the urgency in his father's voice.

"I left earlier than usual this mornin' so that I could stop by and check in on Charlie Connor. It's been a while since I last saw him, and I wanted to know that he was well and to thank him again for the fine shoes we're all wearin'." Sean felt a great uneasiness in the pit of his belly when Thomas mentioned Charlie's name. The conversation did not bode well, and his heart started to pound hard in his chest.

"When I arrived at his shop the front door was locked, and I saw no one around. I went 'round to the back and found the door unlocked and open a couple inches. When I went inside I found a terrible sight," Thomas paused to cross himself, "for there on the floor was Charlie lyin' in a pool of his own blood, his throat cut and his soul havin' departed."

A mournful whimper escaped from Sean's throat, and he followed his father's lead in crossing himself. He didn't know how or why Charlie's death had come to pass, but it was not in the plans made yesterday at Chatham Square. Sean allowed himself to consider that Charlie might have been the victim of a random crime, though deep in his soul he knew it was not the case.

"I turned to leave, not wantin' to be found there and suspected of doin' the killin' myself. As I turned to the door I spotted Charlie's nephew slumped behind it."

"Marley?" Sean asked quietly. There was no longer reason to put on false pretenses. Everything was out in the light of day now, and for that small thing Sean was grateful. "Was he ... dead?"

"Not when I found him, though he was only a few breaths away. He whispered two things before his spirit left him: Sow Madden and Muldoon's. I connected the beast in your story to the name young Marley whispered, and that is how I knew of your alliance with the gang."

"He *is* a beast," Sean said, his voice full of hate. Obviously, Sow Madden had gotten wind of the heist and had gone to Charlie's to get the guns and claim the heist for himself. Sean correctly assumed that it would have been Beeny Cohen who involved Sow Madden. Beeny and Sow were two of a kind, evil to the core. The reality of Sean's situation sank deep to his very soul as he thought about how insignificant he was to Sam McCarthy. He came to terms with reality, that he was nothing more than one of Sam's toadies. He was a desperate child, and McCarthy was a master manipulator whose priority would always be himself and the depth of his pockets. He also knew that he held no favor with Sow or Beeny and that they wouldn't think twice about killing him. The vision of Charlie lying dead in a pool of blood, and of Marley left there to die, took control of Sean's mind and created a new, intense fear of the danger he and his family were in. He raised his hand up and placed it on top of his head, visibly trembling and completely panic-stricken.

"Ya understand how serious this has become, don't ya, Son? 'Tis there on your face," Thomas offered. He had watched the emotions darken his son's countenance, and he saw the threat of danger become reality as Sean considered his expendability. Sean nodded in agreement, no answer coming quick to his young mind. How he would escape violence and retribution was a question without an answer, and Sean allowed the child inside him to be frightened and to need his father.

"I'm scared, Da," he whispered. "There's no answer. Nothin' for it. I'm surely doomed to the same fate as Marley." Sean leaned back against the wall of the meetinghouse and hung his head.

"Sean, listen to me," Thomas said firmly, his voice slightly louder than before. He needed to have Sean coherent and cooperative. "Does anyone know where ya live?"

"No, Da, I never told anyone for fear they'd come around and my terrible lie would be out."

"Good, then, but I'm thinkin' they can find us if they want to. If my plan works out we'll not be there when they show up, but I'll need your help, yes?"

"What do ya mean we'll not be there? Do ya have a safe place for us to hide?"

"No, Sean, if my plan comes together we'll be leavin' this filthy city for good," Thomas said. "We've no time to linger here long. I have need of some information and that is where ya can help me." He stood and watched his son's face—the fear, then the hope, and then the doubt. Sean shook his head slightly, almost imperceptibly.

"Aye, Da, but how?" His mind was racing with possibilities, none of which seemed plausible. Thomas could see it but there was no time for Sean to ask countless questions or for Thomas to answer them.

"Later, Son. I'll be sharin' my plans while we enjoy your birthday supper in a short while. Mam is gettin' it ready as we speak."

"Da, we don't have to. I'm not feelin' very deservin' at the moment," Sean admitted. How could he sit before his family, the cherished ones he endangered with his wicked secret, and allow them to honor him? He would choose to hide here at the docks if it were up to him, but Thomas had made it clear that he needed his help and that a plan was in the making. Sean would do nothing to undermine their safety and their escape. He would do whatever Da needed him to do no matter how uncomfortable the burden of guilt would make it.

"Your mam has been workin' hard to make this special supper for us, and the little ones are near droolin' at the thought of it. If I'm honest, I am too. I think this supper will be just what we need to welcome ya back, Son." Thomas smiled and offered his reassurance with a softness in his voice that Sean had desperately missed and welcomed gratefully.

"What is it ya need from me?" Sean asked, willing to do whatever he could to end this shameful chapter of his life.

"Muldoon's. The tavern there on Pearl Street?" Thomas asked. Sean nodded. "Would that be where this gang meets up?"

"Aye, 'tis their headquarters. There's a room to the left side of the bar where all the business is done." With that smallest bit of information out, spoken, and confessed, Sean sealed his fate. Escape or die, there could be no other outcome.

"And Sow Madden, is he the leader of this gang?" Thomas asked. Sean scoffed and shook his head.

"No, Sam McCarthy is our ... their leader," Sean stopped himself from further aligning himself with the Wharf Kings, and it felt good in his soul. Release and freedom came suddenly and unexpectedly when he chose truth over deceit. "Sow is his henchman. Mostly he just nurses a bottle of laudanum and sits in a chair by the door. He's supposed to be guardin' the place, but when he's deep into the bottle I'm thinkin' Maeve could stand her ground against him."

"And how many members would I find inside on a normal evenin'?"

"Da, you're not goin' over there," Sean cautioned. "It's too dangerous, Da. If Sow is in his right mind or Beeny Cohen is about, it would not go well."

"And is there money to be found there?" Thomas continued, ignoring Sean's warning. The same words that

266

had haunted Sean moments earlier were seared into his father's brain as well. Escape or die. There could be no other outcome. He waited for Sean's reply.

"I ... suppose," Sean answered slowly, his father's plan now becoming apparent. He wouldn't live to see another day if he were caught stealing from Sam McCarthy. "Da, this is far too dangerous. I'll go with ya. They know me and might not suspect anything."

"No." Thomas's answer left no room for debate. "Is Sam usually about in the evenings?"

"Not usually, and I heard tell that he and Molly—that's Molly Muldoon who owns the place—would be over across the river till Tuesday."

"Even better," Thomas said, piecing together the details of his plan. "Here's what we'll be doin' then. We're headin' back home shortly, and we'll have our fine meal to celebrate your birthday. Happy Birthday, Son," Thomas said after a pause. He chided himself for having let anything come before acknowledging his son's special day. The weight of the worry was good reason, but he would not allow it to excuse his omission. Sean smiled, no sadness or bitterness present in his response. He understood the gravity of the situation and knew that it had to take precedence over anything else. Thomas reached out and put his hand on Sean's shoulder, a momentary gesture that spoke volumes about where they were, what had been recovered, and a newfound hope for the days to come. Thomas smiled and continued.

"Mam and the children know we're leavin'. I instructed them to start packin' up only what they need. We'll be carryin' whatever we take with us for a good long way and most of what we have is not worth the burden. When we're finished with our supper I'll need you to stay, pack up a sack of your own, and be watchin' over the preparations for me."

"Da, what are ya gonna do?" Sean could barely speak the words.

"I'm goin' over to Muldoon's, and I'm gonna get us enough money to get far away from here forever," Thomas stated without hesitation. "If Sow Madden is bedeviled by the laudanum and no one else of any consequence is nearby, I shouldn't have any trouble."

"If," Sean said quietly. He feared for Thomas. He could not bear to lose his father now when their reconciliation had just begun and a better life was so close.

"I'll be mindful, Sean. I'll be watchin' and payin' attention. I have a plan. Trust your da, yes?" Thomas reached out and put his hand behind Sean's neck, reassuring him by the gentle presence of his strong hand. Sean nodded, still afraid but willing to trust. It was then that he remembered his own stash of money.

"Da! I have money. I can help get us away from here!"

"Son, it's gonna take a lot of money," Thomas replied, touched by his son's wanting to help. How much could the boy have? A few dollars, maybe.

"Da, I have more than five hundred dollars stashed in the floorboard," Sean said cautiously, awaiting the reaction that was sure to follow.

"What?" The incredulous tone of his father's voice held no anger.

"Aye, I've been puttin' it in a safe place. I couldn't spend it or share it because I'd be givin' myself away. I don't really know what I was gonna do with it," Sean's voice faded. All the guilt, the fear, the lies and deception had given him a small fortune that was worthless, for it did not provide even a loaf of bread for his family. The full understanding of what a foolish decision he had made became clear. He had been a child in a man's world, out of place and used by the men who, unlike him, could enjoy the fruits of their labors.

"Well, Son, dependin' on what I'm able to find at Muldoon's we might need some of that dirty money of yours," Thomas said without casting blame or judgment. He was simply calling it what it was, and Sean understood. "If you're willin' to use that money to aid our cause and get us away from here you'll be a man of good character." Sean did not miss his father's changed attitude, his encouragement, and the camaraderie they had both desperately missed. Thomas seemed willing to look at the past with empathy and move forward with hope. Sean wanted nothing more in that moment than to please his father.

"Aye, 'tis what I want, Da," he replied. A man of good character. Words he had given up on. Words he never dreamed his father would say about him.

"Settled then," Thomas said. "Let's make our way back home and do our best to enjoy our last meal in that wretched place. We'll have a merry time, and I'm sure enough lookin' forward to it. When the merriment is over and the night falls, I'll go pay a visit to Muldoon's. We'll need to be prepared to leave as soon as I return. I need to know that you will make sure everyone's ready. Can I count on ya?"

"Aye, but there's a question I still have, Da."

"What is it, Sean?"

"Where is it that we're goin?"

Thomas chuckled. In the seriousness of the day and with danger lurking so close at their heels, he had omitted that one important detail.

"We're headin' out west, Sean. Out where there are open spaces, more land than people, and opportunities for a far better life than the one we'll be leavin' behind us."

Sean considered this for a moment. He had heard stories. He had read the letter from their friend John O'Riley. Sean had thought many times that living in a place where there was more land than people, as Da had put it, would be life changing. He was happy with Da's decision and looked forward to the adventure. Getting away from the stench, the crime, the danger, the hopelessness, and the abject poverty would change their lives in countless ways, and he was uncharacteristically optimistic about the days to come.

"Tis a good plan, Da," Sean said as he smiled at his father. His face was radiant with child-like excitement, and his dark eyes sparkled. Thomas felt the strong emotional tug at his heart just as Kathleen did whenever Sean smiled. It was in those rare moments that the beauty and wonder of their firstborn came flooding back, and the pain and disappointment of their world was washed away. Thomas reached out and pulled Sean to him. They hugged tightly and much was unspoken but understood—forgiveness, joy, love, resolution, and for the first time in a very long time, hope.

"Let's go eat," Thomas said with a smile.

They walked back down to South Street and on to Montgomery toward their flat. Sean thought about it being the last time he would walk those streets and that after tonight home would no longer be the downtrodden place where they lived. It felt good. He thought about what he needed to take with him, and except for his one change of clothes he had little that he cared enough about to pack for the trip. Leaving old things behind seemed the right thing to do when heading to a new life. There were few things that any of them would consider irreplaceable, and if all went well whatever they left behind could be replaced by finer things.

Kathleen was giving the coddle a final stir when the door to the flat opened. She looked up at the expressions on the faces of her husband and son, and it took the breath from her. They looked like different people. They looked renewed, redeemed, and transformed by something that could only be love. She tried to speak but her voice caught in her throat. She put her hand to her cheek and smiled at them both.

"There's the scent of somethin' divine in this place!" Thomas called out. "If we're not careful the queen herself might come knockin' on our door lookin' to have herself a plateful of that Dublin coddle! And a hefty servin' it would have to be to fill that belly, I might add."

The children laughed. Sean laughed, too, and Kathleen did not miss it. Something good had happened, something she had long prayed about, and she was overcome by it. She wiped the tears from the corners of her eyes. Sean walked forward and gave his mother a warm hug, bringing tears to his own eyes. Kathleen knew if she did not reign in her emotions she would be sobbing uncontrollably there in Sean's arms. She stepped back, wiped her eyes, and placed her hand gently on her son's cheek.

"What's there to cry over?" Eamon asked. "We're not sharin' this birthday meal with the queen, or anyone else for that matter!"

"Now, Eamon, that is not a very charitable attitude!" Kathleen scolded in jest as she smiled at Sean and wiped her eyes again.

"Truth be told," Thomas chimed in, "I'd not share it with the queen, the pope, nor President James Buchanan himself!" Sorley rose up off the couch and paraded around the flat with his walking stick, looking as portly and important as he could, and everyone laughed at his charade.

"Now, my dear wife," Thomas said, "when will we be able to enjoy that food that's makin' my belly growl like a bear?"

"Give me a few minutes to slice up some bread. Who would like to help me set the table?" Kathleen looked toward the children, but it was Sean who responded.

"I'll help, Mam," he said as he walked toward the table.

"But, Son, it's your birthday," she said.

"Aye, then I'm guessin' you'll have to let me if that's what I want." His response was playful and lighthearted. He followed her to the shelf where the mismatched plates and silverware were stacked, and he set six places around the rickety wooden table. The last time. It felt like a dream to be thinking that, and Sean relished it with every stop around the table.

Thomas noticed the four loaves Kathleen had made. They would eat two of them today with supper, and the other two would have to tide them over on the first part of their journey. He also noticed the sacks sitting near the door and was proud of his children for doing as he had asked. The journey ahead would be difficult for them, and he told himself now that he would need to exercise a great deal of patience with them. For all their struggles, all their wants and unmet needs, all their days lived in fear and hunger and misery, the Delaney children had always given their parents cause for gratitude. They were well-behaved and kind and they rarely complained, though they had reason to do so.

The table was set, and Kathleen proudly placed the coddle in the center. She sliced the bread and placed it in a large bowl next to the coddle. On a smaller plate was the entirety of butter purchased by Thomas at Leary's Market. Everyone was drawing near when Sorley noticed the mound of goodness on the saucer, golden and inviting. In the Delaney household Mam usually doled out the butter, spreading it thin on the slices of bread before serving it to them so it would go further and last longer.

"Mam, are ya not puttin' the butter on our bread for us today?" Sorley asked.

"Not today, Son. Tis your brother's birthday and our last meal here at this table," her voice broke. Thomas moved closer to her and put his arm around her. She took a deep breath and continued, "I'm not sad for leaving this place but only the memories we've made. Today we'll make another, for we can't be takin' the butter with us." She laughed and announced with a sweep of her hand, "Have all the butter ya want!"

Everyone sat down immediately, and the coddle was dished up onto the empty plates. Hands reached for bread until Thomas reminded everyone that it was Sean's day and he should go first. When Sean tried to protest, Maeve took a stern tone of voice with him that caused everyone to laugh. Within minutes the room fell silent except for the occasional groan of sated hunger.

"Katie, you've outdone yourself," Thomas raved. The children all agreed it was the best coddle they'd ever had. Kathleen smiled and her heart was full. It was a small thing, and it was everything. Thomas took the opportunity while the others finished their supper to share a brief explanation of his plan. He told his family that they would leave the city, going north by train, and would then head west to begin a new life in a better place. He skipped the details, and he was fearful of telling them the reality of traveling over fifteen hundred miles by coach from St. Louis to the Utah Territory. It would be an arduous journey, and he did not want to dampen their spirits just yet. Everyone agreed it was a good plan, and as the meal ended everyone also agreed that they couldn't eat another bite.

"Don't any of you Delaneys forget about that cake!" Sean reminded them as they complained about how full they were. Just like the butter, the cake could not travel with them.

"I'm so full my belly might burst," Thomas complained as he rubbed his hands over his flat stomach. He looked out through the dirty windows and saw daylight still present. He pulled his father's pocket watch out of his pocket and realized it would be an hour and a half, maybe two, before he would start making his way to Pearl Street. There would be time to let the meal settle in their bellies before enjoying Sean's cake.

"Mine, too," agreed Kathleen. The children all chimed in with the same complaint, though no one was really complaining. Even with Thomas working enough to put food on the table it wasn't often that they could eat until they were full to the top.

"Let's sit an hour or so and give our bellies time to make some room," Thomas suggested. Sean looked at him with concern and Thomas nodded slightly to reassure him he had time. Kathleen stepped out to the basin to clean the plates and spoons they had used for supper so they could use them again for the cake. She finished the quick task and sat down on the couch next to Thomas.

"Tell us a story, Da!" Maeve suggested.

"And what shall it be?" Thomas asked, hoping with all his heart that no one asked for the tale of the river beast Sowmadden.

"Oisín and Niamh!" Maeve requested. She adored the love story of Niamh, the beautiful woman from the otherworld, and her lover Oisín, the legendary son of Fionn Mac Cumhaill, though the story's ending was a sorrowful one. Da began to tell the story of the journey the lovers made on the back of Niamh's magical horse who could run across the surface of the water. They traveled to the island of Tír na nÓg where they would find everlasting youth, beauty, health, abundance, and joy. Though his family had heard the story countless times, they were glued to Thomas's every word as he related the cherished tale with his usual mastery, adding bits and changing things up. He knew the secret to keeping the same audience captivated. He knew that a good story is alive and changing and that it keeps the listener attentive, awaiting each untold nuance, every new twist and turn.

"Are we goin' to Tír na nÓg, Da?" Maeve interrupted. No one laughed. There was a heavy pause filled with hope and anticipation, not for finding Tír na nÓg but for finding a place that would feel like their own telling of it.

"Ah, Stóirín, 'tis but a story we tell, but I believe that the place we're goin' will seem much closer to it than where we're livin' now," Thomas answered. He continued with the tale of Oisín staying in Paradise with Niamh for three years before yearning to return home, and how Niamh had given him her magic horse and a warning not to touch the soil of his homeland. When Oisín returned home he discovered that it was not three years, but rather three hundred years since he had left, and his world had changed beyond recognition. In a state of shock, Oisín fell from the horse, landed on the ground, and immediately began to age three hundred years. Oisín, son of Fionn Mac Cumhaill, lover of Niamh the queen of Tír na nÓg, died of old age within minutes. Though the children knew how the story would end, they all expressed sadness at poor Oisín's tragic fate.

"Will we die if we return here one day?" Sorley asked. The prophetic musing of his young son struck Thomas hard. His heart missed a beat. He was certain that Sean's life would surely be cut short if they returned, and that none of them were safe from retaliation. Sean knew it, too.

Kathleen could barely breathe. Thomas reacted quickly to save the magic of the day.

"Remember, Son, 'tis just a story. I think, though, that we would not make the same mistake as poor Oisín. He was not content with his new home and the beautiful things he discovered there. I think we will find a better life and should want to spend the rest of our days enjoyin' it, yes?"

"Aye, Da," Sorley agreed.

"I think he just wanted Niamh's magic horse!" Maeve chimed in.

"You could be right, Maeve," Thomas said, "so maybe 'tis a lesson in appreciatin' what we have and not always be wantin' for more." Thomas was thankful that Sorley's question had been downplayed and so quickly dismissed even though it was only he and Kathleen and Sean who understood the weight of it.

The conversation shifted to the journey ahead. Thomas reiterated to his family that when he returned from his one last preparation everyone should be ready to leave. He told the children that he was leaving Sean in charge, and they all agreed to mind their brother and do as he asked. Thomas spoke of a long walk, a horsecar, and a steam engine pulling a long train behind it. He told the children that it would be a long night and that once they boarded the train they should all try to sleep. There were questions about what they would do once they reached Albany, a far-off place they had never heard of, and Thomas assured them there would be another train heading west. The children could barely contain their excitement. Thomas, Kathleen, and Sean silently worried about the evening ahead, about how easily their plans could change if things did not go well, and how profoundly their lives would change if Thomas didn't return. Kathleen could not entertain the thought of it. She prayed silently that God would grant them this chance at a better life.

"Let them eat cake!" Thomas announced. He noticed the fading light through the windows and when he checked the time on his watch he was surprised at how quickly an hour and a half had passed. The lengthy storytelling session, and the questions and answers that had followed it, had hurried the evening along. The sunlight was fading and he knew it was nearly time to leave. There was a welcome excitement as Kathleen got the cake out of the icebox and placed it on the table. Everyone gathered back around, and Kathleen cut the first large piece for Sean.

"Happy birthday, Son," she said. Everyone called out their birthday wishes to Sean, and his heart swelled with the love he had for his family. He desperately hoped Da's plan would be successful and that their journey would take them away from his sins to a new and better place.

Cake was dished and devoured, once again in silent appreciation. It was every bit as good as the small sampling the Levy's had shared with them—maybe better—and they savored the moist cake, the rich whipped cream, and the plump sweet strawberries that circled the top. They finished slowly, quietly. All but Thomas ate every bite of the piece on their plate. He knew he couldn't afford to be weighed down by an overfull belly, and his mind wandered from the beautiful delicacy before him. He rose from his chair and got ready to leave. Thomas reminded them again of the urgency and to be ready to go out the door when he arrived home. He put on his jacket though the July evening was plenty warm, and he retrieved the bottle of ether from the shelf in the kitchen. He stuffed the bottle and one of Kathleen's cleaning rags in his pocket, picked up his shillelagh from the spot where it always leaned, and turned back to the room. He paused just long enough to look at each face, studying the familiar details and searing each one into his heart and mind. He caught Sean's attention and gave a subtle nod of his head indicating Sean should follow him. Thomas looked directly at Kathleen, hoping to inject some calm into her as he and their son headed for the hallway.

"Give us a moment, Katie," he said as they passed by.

Thomas closed the door behind him and looked in both directions. There was no one about. He beckoned Sean to come closer and when the boy was standing right next to him, Thomas leaned in and lowered his voice to nearly a whisper.

"Son, if anything goes wrong tonight..."

"Da, don't even speak it," Sean interrupted, his fear apparent in his trembling response.

"There's no time, Sean. Just please listen and then I must go. If somethin' goes wrong and I don't return in good time, take your money and get your mam and the little ones out of here. Go as far as your money will take ya and find yourself some honest work. God will provide it if ya need it. Do ya understand me, Son?"

"Aye, but I'm not willin' to believe that's how this night will go. You'll be safe, Da. You'll find what you need and you'll get out safely. God will provide it if ya need it." He looked at Thomas and smiled ever so slightly. He hugged his father tightly, willing the night to go well and their hopes to be realized.

"I love ya, Son. Now send your mam out here for a quick minute." Sean nodded and went inside. Kathleen appeared in the hallway almost immediately, closing the door behind her, her face full of fear and doubt. She walked over to Thomas, standing close and pressing herself into him, wanting to feel the strength of his body and find some assurance that he could do what he was setting out to do. She wavered, faltered, and surrendered to her fear.

"Tommy," she whispered with a sob.

"Katie, trust me. Ya must trust me. I'll be careful, and I'll be back here in time for us to get to the station before the runnin' of the last train north." He kissed her forehead and walked down the hallway with purpose in his step. Kathleen stood for a long while outside their door. She prayed silently. She begged for God's protection over Thomas as he walked toward a place where death and danger lurked, where the devil himself would slit an innocent man's throat without a second thought. Her heart cried out for delivery from evil, for hope to be realized, and for their lives to be blessed by something better than the wretched existence they had experienced in the nine years since coming to America.

Inside the apartment, Sean packed his sack. He went to the kitchen and dumped out the flour that remained in a small three-pound sack he found on a shelf. There was little left inside it after Mam had baked four loaves of bread, and what was left would not be used. He turned it inside out and shook it hard, causing a small cloud of flour to swirl around him. *Like an angel*, he thought. He walked over to the floorboard where he had hidden his stash, pulled the board up, and gathered the money from the small cloth bag Sam had given him. He would take nothing associated with the Wharf Kings except the money, for they might need it to escape. He stuffed it inside the flour sack, twisted the top and tied a knot, and placed it in the bottom of his larger sack. It would be safely hidden by his change of clothes and anything else he packed inside it. He finished just before Kathleen returned from the hallway, and he was thankful that she didn't see what he had been doing. Sean knew his secrets were out, that Mam knew of his association with the Wharf Kings and his reprehensible activities. Even so, he did not want to shock her with the amount of money he had saved from his thievery. He knew she would be appalled, and rightly so. He would speak more about it later when they were safe and resettled and the danger he had invited into their lives was no longer a threat. Their restoration was tender, new, and fragile, and he would avoid anything that might cause it to crumble. He knew that restoring the fractured bond with his family was the only thing that would heal his wounded soul.

Kathleen wandered around the apartment looking carefully for anything of value that they might also take with them. She found nothing more, and she wondered why she had even bothered to look. She knew better. She took a quick mental inventory—their clothes were packed, some bread and fruit and water also, and the few things she had placed into her mother's chest were safely packed inside it. Everything waited by the door, the cloth sacks lined up like ragged watchmen desperately awaiting their captain's return. The three younger children huddled together on their parents' bed, fully dressed and shoes on, enjoying the momentary freedom to break the rules. Shoes on the bed were never allowed, but tonight they could grant themselves that privilege. Eamon had picked up his storytelling from earlier in the day, keeping the little ones occupied and helping to pass the time. Sean sat on the couch staring at the wall as his mind remained fixed on all the unwanted outcomes this night could bring. The waiting was tortuous. Kathleen sat down beside him and snuggled in close. Their shared concern, unspoken, was eased by their nearness. There was no conversation between them, for it would have been nothing but empty chatter. Their bodies were tense, their nerves on edge, as they silently waited to see Thomas walk back through their door.

CHAPTER SEVENTEEN

Thomas was gripping the shillelagh so tightly that his hand ached and his fingers went numb. He forced himself to loosen his grip and give his hand some relief. His steps continued forward, purposeful and swift. His heart was pounding, not from the walk for he was used to that, but from the adrenaline racing through his veins. He envisioned the encounter with Sow Madden over and over in his mind, all the while knowing there was no way to predict what he would find waiting for him at Muldoon's. He could hope that Sunday nights were quiet compared to Friday or Saturday. He could hope that by the time he arrived the place would be nearly empty. He could hope that Sow would be well into the laudanum bottle and all but incapacitated by then. He hoped it all but he recognized that anything could happen. Thomas knew he was walking blindly into a potentially lethal situation where all he could do was react. He was at a grave disadvantage and he knew it. He felt sinful praying to God for help in what he was about to do, but he prayed it anyway.

Night was descending upon him and it felt strangely comforting, embracing him in anonymity. Thomas walked down Cherry Street avoiding his normal route down Monroe to the Catharine Street Market. He could not bring himself to go anywhere near Charlie's shop. For all he knew, Charlie was still lying there. He crossed himself and moved along Cherry Street passing Catharine, Oliver, and James before turning right on Roosevelt. His plan was to come in behind Muldoon's unnoticed so he could check out the area surrounding the establishment. Thomas stood beneath a nearby streetlight and checked his pocket watch. Eight-thirty. The overcast skies caused the darkness to arrive earlier than usual. He reached down and felt for the ether bottle in his pocket. He ran through some potential scenarios again, all the while telling himself he was a fool for thinking he could plan for what was about to happen. Moving quickly down the alley, Thomas passed the back entrance and walked around to the far side of the building. He watched a while longer as a handful of patrons left Muldoon's, one by one, over the course of the twenty minutes he stood there. He was torn between wanting to make certain the place was empty and knowing he had little time to spare. If they were going to catch the last train north he would have to work quickly.

"I'll beat you next time!" came a slurred, familiar voice too near for comfort. Thomas pressed against the side of the building and watched as Leo staggered by on his way home from another loss at the poker table. He had probably gotten paid after a difficult workday and headed straight to the tavern. He was likely angry with Thomas for not showing up for work, and he would be angrier still that the workload would fall entirely on his shoulders after Thomas left. Leo had grown accustomed to Thomas hurrying through their shift, and in doing so, carrying the greater burden of their workday. He would lose his self-imposed title of head street sweeper now that he would no longer have an assistant. Leo would be bitterly disappointed, and though Thomas felt bad for abandoning Leo there was no alternative to their dire situation. He thought briefly about the good people who had been kind to his family—Henry Engel and Mrs. Zimmer, the Bermanns and Mr. Carnahan, and of course, Mrs. Connelly—and how they would wonder at the Delaney's sudden disappearance. He was sorry that he wouldn't have the chance to thank them all once more.

Distant thunder rumbling across the darkened skies gave Thomas a nudge. He needed to act. He walked around to the front of the tavern and peered in through the dirty windows as he slowly passed by. There was little movement inside. He could see a woman walking about, picking up items left on the tables and taking them into the kitchen. There didn't appear to be anyone else inside. The fates were on his side as Thomas entered the tavern and glanced to his left. He spotted the door Sean had told him about, but before going in and confronting whatever was on the other side of it he walked up to the bar.

"I'm thinkin' of closin' it up early, Mister, if it's all the same to you," Mona said. She was tired. The night had been slow, and the week had been long. She usually had Mondays off but due to Sam and Molly being over in Brooklyn until Tuesday she would have to work tomorrow. Sam and Molly usually paid her well for covering for them, but as the years passed the money meant less to her than being rested. Thomas sensed a goodness in her despite where she worked and who she worked for. She did not deserve to get caught up in anything dangerous.

"Who's inside?" Thomas asked, nodding his head toward the door. Mona instantly sensed trouble, for it had come through the door of Muldoon's on more than one occasion. She hesitated to say anything, but with no one about and the only one inside being one she despised more than any other, she answered the stranger's question.

"Only Sow Madden," she replied in a low voice. Thomas nodded.

"You need to get your things and go," he whispered. Mona acted immediately. She grabbed her things from the kitchen and waddled out into the tavern. She paused and walked over to the Wharf Kings' door. With some effort, Mona bent down and ran her finger along the underside of it, tripping the emergency latch and unlocking it so that Thomas could enter. She left and Thomas breathed a prayer of gratitude for her good heart. He took a deep breath, and did his best to prepare for whatever waited for him on the other side. He glanced around one more time just to be certain he was alone before turning the doorknob and slowly opening the door. Thomas heard someone snoring and was immediately grateful. Sow Madden's addiction would be a boon to Thomas's objective. The rumbling noise was coming from behind the partially open door. Thomas closed it quietly and took a good look at the unkempt character slumped in his chair. He appeared to be heavy under the influence. There was drool running down his chin, his senses numb to the fact that anyone else had entered the room. Thomas looked around to get his bearings before searching for the money he hoped would be there.

On a nearby table, a dim lantern illuminated some of the finery in the room. It seemed out of place in that bar, in that neighborhood. The gang was apparently quite successful in their endeavors, and it became apparent to Thomas how Sean had garnered such a sizable pile of money in just a few months. There were two beautiful armoires on the back wall, one on either side of a fancy table. Thomas guessed correctly that this would be Sam's table and furniture. Sow Madden stirred, snorted, and shifted in his chair. Thomas stood still and waited but Sow remained asleep. It was time to put his plan into action. He walked over, locked the door, and poked Sow Madden hard in the belly with the blunt end of his shillelagh.

"Wake up!" Thomas commanded. The physical assault and loud voice startled Sow awake and he fell from his chair. "Get up!" Thomas said more forcefully than the first time.

Sow Madden's confusion was obvious as he stood up. He had been rudely awakened, assaulted, and was now standing face to face with a man he didn't know inside Sam's domain, the very one he was given to protect. There was trouble written all over the situation, and he panicked and lunged at the man. Thomas saw him coming, drugged, clumsy and lethargic, and as Sow got closer Thomas slammed the shillelagh into the side of his head. Sow Madden was out cold immediately and hit the floor without resistance. Thomas reached into his pocket and drew out the bottle of ether and the cloth. He soaked the cloth in ether, rolled the unconscious man onto his back, and laid it across Sow Madden's face. He remembered Dr. Bermann cautioning Kathleen against holding the ether rag directly on Sorley's face for it would render it numb. All the better. With Sow already unconscious, the laudanum in his system and the ether-soaked cloth on his face would ensure he remained that way. Thomas could not take the chance that Sow would awaken while he was ransacking the place. Thomas stood and placed the bottle of ether on the table near the lantern so he could find it again in a hurry should Sow recover or an intruder show up unexpectedly.

He scanned the room once more, trying to determine where Sam McCarthy might stash his dirty money.

There were four other tables around the room, a pile of stuff in one corner covered with an old quilt, and some shelving against the wall to the right of Sam's table with a variety of items that were obviously stolen. And the armoires. Thomas was certain he would find what he was looking for inside the armoires. The first one had more stolen items—silver, jewelry, a few pieces of art, and other assorted valuables. Thomas glanced over at Sow before opening the second armoire. His body looked lifeless except for the slow rise and fall of his chest. Thomas opened the second armoire and found two small chests adorned with gold leaf, sitting side by side on a shelf. His heart was pounding as he opened the first chest. He found several strings of pearls and a small wooden box containing ammunition. Thomas thought it strange that Sam had placed the bullets with such items of value, but he quickly realized that in the world he had invaded tonight ammunition was likely as valuable a commodity as rubies or pearls. He set the ammunition box on Sam's table and turned back to the chest. He moved the jewelry aside for it would not pay their passage out of the city. He found what he was looking for beneath the necklaces, rings, and fancy gold watches.

Thomas reached into the chest, his hands shaking as he pulled out a large bundle of bank notes tied with string. He flipped through the loose ends and could see that most of them were hundred-dollar notes and twenty-dollar notes, and most were issued by The Bank of New York and the Chemical Bank of New York. Although local banknotes were more valuable locally, Thomas knew that the further west they traveled the more those notes would depreciate. He decided to take as much as he could find. The more cash in his pockets, the better their chances of a successful exodus out of the city. He slid the other chest forward and opened the lid. There were several cloth pouches inside, and when Thomas picked one up he could hear the jingle of coins. He opened the drawstring at the top and poured some of the coins out into his hand. Sam McCarthy obviously knew that coins held their value and were the one constant in a less-than-stable economy. Thomas shifted the coins around and saw that many of them were twenty-dollar gold coins. He didn't have the luxury of time on his side, so he did not try to calculate how much money the pouches held or how many pouches he would need. He reminded himself that stealing only what they needed would not absolve him of his sins. Thomas stuffed two bags of coins in each of his jacket pockets. He put the bundle of banknotes inside the back of his shirt and tucked the shirt into his pants. His jacket would hide any suspicions, especially in the darkness.

The urgency of the evening compelled Thomas to finish up and get ready to head back to Montgomery Street. He was confident he had enough money to get his family to safety far off in the Utah Territory. He picked up his shillelagh and walked over to the corner of the room, lifting the blanket off the contents beneath it with his stick. Thomas saw the wooden crates, the stenciled Colt trademark, and felt a cold rush of fear. This gang was planning something that would result in death and carnage, and had Thomas not decided to leave the city Sean would have been caught up in the middle of it. He placed one of the crates on the floor and pried the lid off with the narrow end of his shillelagh. Thomas removed a pistol and tucked it into the waistband of his pants, to the side and under the cover of his jacket. He walked back over to Sam's table and picked up the carton of ammunition. He wasn't sure if it was the right caliber but stuffed it into one of his pockets on top of the coin pouches just in case.

The doorknob rattled and Thomas froze. He glanced down at Sow Madden again and had no concern that he might awaken, but there was obviously someone on the other side of the door. Thomas gripped his shillelagh tightly and waited, moving back against the wall between the door and the shelves. A man's voice called out Sow's name once, and then again. The doorknob rattled once more before the door burst open from the impact of a heavy boot. Thomas stayed where he was, pressed against the wall and hoping the man wouldn't hear his heart pounding. He saw the man walk in cautiously, surveying the room for any intruders. Thomas saw the look of confusion on the man's face when he looked down and saw Sow Madden lying on the floor with his face covered. He kicked his foot against Sow's body but got no response. The man looked over and saw the open crate of pistols on the floor and Thomas knew there was likely going to be a violent confrontation.

Beeny Cohen leaned down to see if any of the pistols were missing. Thomas came up behind him quietly, but as he neared the man's hunched body a floorboard creaked beneath his foot. Cohen turned around and stood up to defend himself from the unknown assailant. Thomas leveled his shillelagh against the man's head causing him to stagger backward a step or two. Thomas turned to run, but the man recovered enough to lunge forward and grab the back of his coat. Thomas brought the shillelagh down on the back of the man's hand. He screamed out in pain and let loose of Thomas's coat. As he did, Thomas stumbled forward and into the table where he had left the ether. The bottle tipped and the nearby flame from the lantern ignited the fumes of the highly flammable liquid.

Thomas could not risk the man following him out of the tavern and back home. He rushed at the man and swung the shillelagh around, hitting the back of his head with the blunt end of his stick. Beeny Cohen fell forward, completely immobilized. The fire was spreading quickly, and Thomas had a momentary battle with his conscience. Leaving Sow and the other man lying there would surely result in their deaths in the worst possible manner. He quickly rationalized that Sow Madden deserved death for what he had done to Charlie and his nephew, and the other man was likely involved too. Thomas knew it was not his place to sit in judgment nor to decide the fate of either of these men, but he could not risk his own life and the safety of his family to stay behind and save them. He had to leave. He ran through the tavern and out into the dark of the night before the flames would become noticeable to anyone nearby. Thomas ran blindly, tears streaming down his face as he quietly pleaded for God's mercy upon him. The sins he had committed this night would die with him, unconfessed to anyone but the Almighty.

Thomas's feet carried him toward home without any conscious effort from him. His mind was filled with guilt and desperation, and the two engaged in a violent battle that threatened to destroy his resolve. He ran along Cherry Street without slowing until he reached the intersection of Clinton and Cherry. Though there was little time to spare, Thomas had to stop. He was exhausted from running with the extra weight of the money, the weapons, and the shame he carried with him. He noticed a wooden bench in front of a milliner's shop and sat down. He took several deep breaths and tried to compose himself, wiping his face with his sleeve, his hands shaking. It would not benefit the difficult night ahead if he returned home in a state of fear and grief, and he had little time to compose himself. Each minute that ticked by was one lost, one less they would have to make it to Houston Street in time to catch the last train north. With his heart still beating hard in his chest, Thomas knew he had to get up and get back to his family. He stood up, took one more deep breath, and walked the block between Clinton and Montgomery, rounding the corner toward their flat. He passed the stench of the outhouses and entered the back door of the decaying tenement they called home. *The last time*, he thought to himself, *dear God, deliver us from evil.*

CHAPTER EIGHTEEN

Kathleen paced nervously, praying silently, barely restraining the urge to let her fear and emotions surface. Sean watched, and he knew her turmoil for he was consumed with the same nervous fear that Thomas would not return. If that were the end to this day, Sean knew that their only hope was to take the money he had saved and flee. He had no concept of the cost of transportation and travel, no idea how far was far enough, and no capacity to plan and execute a daring escape from the danger they were in. He knew he would have to stand in Da's place and make it happen. He dare not dwell on the tragic outcome they would meet if he failed. He silently willed his father home.

"When are we startin' our grand adventure, Mam?" Maeve asked.

"When your father returns!" Kathleen replied with an edge to her voice that her children did not miss. "I'm sorry, Maeve, I did not mean to snap at ya," Kathleen responded with a forced smile. "I'm just hopin' it's soon, for I'm tired of waitin' just like you." Maeve walked over and wrapped her arms around Kathleen's legs. Kathleen stroked her daughter's hair and wished desperately for this unpleasant chapter of their lives to be over. All of it. The hunger, the living in squalor, the uncertainties they faced every day, the terrifying secret life that Sean had been living, and now, the intruding fear that Thomas would fall victim to harm, even death, and leave them completely destitute.

"Let's go!" Thomas barked out the command as he flung the door open.

"Oh, Sweet Lord Jesus, Tommy," Kathleen let out a sob and ran to him. He gave her a brief hug and stepped back to look at Sean.

"Everything ready?"

"Aye, Da, we're ready to go," Sean replied. He got the children's sacks, handed Eamon and Sorley theirs, and offered to carry Maeve's and his own. Thomas nodded and picked up their own sack. Kathleen grabbed Maeve's hand and her mother's chest with her other hand.

"Everyone out, no last looks," Thomas said sternly. "There is nothin' here we need that isn't already packed. Now we need to move, and move quickly." Kathleen and the children went out the door and down the hallway, Sean behind them, and Thomas at the back of the line. He left the apartment door open as if to confirm to himself that there was nothing left there for them but sad memories and worthless belongings, and that the sorry world they were leaving was welcome to it all.

Thomas moved to the front of the group and asked Sean to follow behind, making sure that the younger boys kept up and didn't get distracted. They had forty minutes to get to the station at Houston and Bowery. Without delays at a normal pace, it was a thirty-minute walk. Kathleen and the children followed Thomas up Montgomery to Grand. Thomas chose Essex to connect to Houston Street as it was not prone to the trouble often found on Clinton Street. As they walked up Essex, Sorley began to lag behind and Maeve was tiring. Thomas felt his patience being tested sooner than he anticipated, and he reminded himself of Sorley's lame knee and Maeve being just five years old. His children were not used to exercise, for they had lived secluded lives, unfortunate prisoners to the shackles of crime and danger. Guilt replaced his impatience. He paused briefly and waited for Sorley to catch up.

"Here, Son, let me carry ya on my back," he said to Sorley. "It's been a long while since ya walked this far." Thomas turned to Kathleen. "Can ya carry Maeve, Katie?"

"Aye," she replied. Kathleen had Sean give Maeve's sack to Eamon, and she gave the chest to Sean. She lifted Maeve up, and they walked at a faster pace. Maeve was small for a five-year-old due to the sparse existence she had been born into, and in that moment Kathleen was ashamed to be thankful for it.

They reached Houston and headed west to Bowery, moving along more quickly once the two youngest were not holding them back. The last horsecar was at the station, and Thomas was relieved to see it was only half full. He found a spot nearby where Kathleen and the children could wait while he purchased their fare. Before he approached the window, he carried their large sack into the shadows alongside the station and loosened the drawstring. He removed the four bags of coins, the ammunition, and the pistol from his pockets and his waistband and put them into the sack. It would be heavier now, but he could carry it. Thomas untucked the back of his shirt and pulled the parcel of bank notes from under his shirt. He untied the string, removed a small stack of the notes, and placed them in his pocket. He re-tied the rest of them back together and put them in the sack with the rest of the money.

"Six to Chatham Four Corners," Thomas said as he came around the corner and approached the ticket window. The very name of the small village north of the city, named for William Pitt, first Earl of Chatham, was difficult for Thomas to speak after the night's horrors which were all born at the Square of the same name near the Five Points.

"You've barely made it," the man said.

"Aye, but we did," Thomas replied. "How much?"

"Six adults?"

"Two adults, four children," Thomas answered.

"Oh my, you've got the patience of Job, I'm guessing," the ticket man said.

"Not really. How much?" Thomas asked with a little more urgency in his voice.

"All fares from here to Chatham Four Corners are $2.60. Size of the body doesn't matter; they all take up a seat. Six fares will be $15.60." The ticket man's voice was flat and held the familiar tone of one who despised the Irish for simply being Irish.

Thomas wondered why the man had bothered to ask if it were six adults boarding the train if the ticket prices were all the same, but he didn't have time to confront him about it. If the man didn't like the look of them and had overcharged them because of it, it would be on his own conscience. Thomas had enough on his. He pulled out a $20 bank note and handed it to the man behind the ticket window. There was a moment of suspicious hesitancy. Thomas sensed it and his heart began to race again. He did not take his eyes from the man's face. To drop his gaze would indicate he had something to hide and there was no time for more questions or delays. The ticket man finally relented. He handed Thomas his change and six tickets to the station at Chatham Four Corners. Thomas did not thank the man for his degrading scrutiny. He took the change and the tickets and walked back to his family, gathering them close and heading to the waiting horsecar.

Once seated, Maeve and Sorley were visibly excited. It was later than normal for them to be up and awake, and seeing the looks on their faces gave Kathleen little hope that they would sleep on the journey. After the thirty-minute ride in the horsecar they would transfer to the steam train at 32nd Street and take that to Chatham Four Corners, transferring again from there for the much shorter trip to Albany. There would be far too much excitement, too much boarding and departing, for the children to settle down and rest. For now, they watched out the windows of the horsecar as they passed the streetlights and buildings in the unfamiliar part of their city. They had never ridden in or on anything except their father's back when he gave them piggyback rides. Sean had traveled in an omnibus several times while on his crosstown early morning heists so he was less intrigued by the novelty, but the other three children were held captive. The grand adventure was starting in a magical way, but the magic was lost on Thomas, Kathleen, and Sean as they hoped their escape from danger would be successful. How far and how relentlessly Sam McCarthy would hunt for them was a question none of them could answer.

"What shall we do upon arriving in Albany in the middle of the night?" Kathleen whispered to Thomas.

"I've been thinkin' on that, Katie," he answered. "It'll depend on when the trains run west from there. If they travel at night we will as well. If not, we'll find ourselves some lodgin' and wait 'til mornin'."

"Tommy," she hesitated a moment before continuing, "do we have money enough to pay for a hotel and still make this journey you've planned?" She wanted to know, and then again she did not. Knowing would bring with it more questions than answers, and those questions were too terrifying to ask.

"Aye, Katie, we do." He smiled at her, and her heart warmed. Her mind was filled with conflicting emotions, but for now she was thankful that Thomas was beside her and that they were all together and safe. She would not allow herself to dwell on anything that would overshadow her gratitude. There was much behind them that should stay there, right where it belonged, for she refused to drag misfortune and illicit behavior into their future. The day might come when Thomas would share the events of his visit to Muldoon's but only when he was ready. And if he chose to keep it closed up and buried in his own heart for the rest of his days, she would respect his decision and trust there was a reason. For now, she would leave it at that.

"I worry for the children. They're so excited and I'm thinkin' they'll not sleep a wink unless we stop for the night." She spoke in a low voice so that the children, and anyone nearby who might be listening, could not hear their conversation. "And where will we go from there?"

"I spoke with Mr. Carnahan at the market a few months ago when I was nursin' a whim to leave the city," Thomas replied. "He told me there's a train from Albany to St. Louis. From there ya must hire a coach if ya want to travel further west. It'll be an uncomfortable journey, Katie, but I'm certain that takin' it will lead us to the life we're hopin' for."

"Oh dear, Tommy, can we not just stay in St. Louis? It seems far enough from our troubles."

"And what shall I do there, Mo Chuisle? Find us another rundown flat and spend my days tryin' to find work in a crowded city filled with men doin' the same? Bein' Irish in another city that likely doesn't want us? Watchin' the children go hungry because I can't find an honest job? 'Tis why we left the last city behind us, and I've got no intention of returnin' to the same life in a different one."

Kathleen was silent, reflecting on what Thomas had said and trying to convince herself that he was right. Fear of the unknown held sway over the validity of Thomas's concerns. Her mind knew that he was right. Her heart was doubtful and unconvinced that the promise they pursued would be realized, for none other in this supposed land of opportunity had been.

"Da's right." Sean had been listening intently to their conversation. He was as curious as Kathleen was about the plan, the destination, and the details of how it would all come together. He heard the doubt and hesitation from his mother, but louder than that he heard the truth from his father. Another crowded city, another place where immigrants were not welcome, another life no different from the last.

"What is it, Sean?" Kathleen asked.

"Mam, Da's right. If we move from one city to another we're just takin' our troubles along with us. I don't want that life anymore, Mam. I want somethin' better for us." He paused and looked at Thomas. "Da, we need to go out west, to those open spaces ya talked about where there's more work than men and a better life waitin'."

Thomas nodded. He looked at Kathleen who now forced a smile and nodded. Outnumbered by her two men, she would trust their judgment and prepare for the difficult journey ahead.

The horsecar came to a stop and a man opened the door and asked the passengers to step out. They had arrived at the 32nd Street Station where they would transfer to the steam train. Thomas showed their tickets to the conductor; he nodded and waved his arm toward the waiting train. He smiled and waved at Maeve. She giggled and waved back. She turned around and called out her goodbyes to the horses who had pulled the horsecar, and the conductor laughed out loud. He thought her a delightful child and hoped the future would be kind to her, but from the looks of the family there would likely be difficult days ahead. He'd seen more than one destitute family heading west in search of something better. He didn't know for sure if they found it or not, but with so many of them heading that direction one would expect the opportunities to diminish over time. The Delaneys boarded the train and found three double seats in a row that were unoccupied. Thomas got Maeve and Sean settled into one, Eamon and Sorley in the next, and he and Kathleen took the third. It would take the train three to four hours to reach their next destination, and it would give them an opportunity for a bit of rest if they were able. Kathleen leaned forward and encouraged her children to try to sleep on the trip to Albany, though she didn't expect their excitement to allow it.

The engineer fired up the steam engine, and the rumbling began. The slow churning start of the train's forward progress got all four children leaning toward their windows. Kathleen felt a twinge of excitement, too, for she had never traveled by train and it seemed a luxurious thing to be doing. Thomas reached down and took her hand, smiling at her and hoping she would remember this leg of their journey when they were traveling in a crowded coach rattling across the desolate rangelands of the west.

The train picked up momentum as it pulled away from the station. The children settled in and watched the windows from time to time, though the darkness took much of the interest away from the landscape. Kathleen could see Maeve's head just above the seatback where she and Sean were sitting. She was leaning into her brother and was likely drifting off to sleep. Sorley and Eamon were talking quietly about what they imagined they would find out west, speculating about far-fetched things like dragons and giant lizards, all sorts of wild animals, and the very real possibility of seeing the people they had heard called Indians who lived there. Eamon's voice, low and lyrical, caused Kathleen's eyes to grow heavy. She leaned into Thomas, and he put his arm behind her and cradled her to him. He breathed a long, deep sigh and felt the tension leave his body for the first time since that morning when he had discovered Charlie and his nephew at the shoe shop. *'Twas a year of a day*, he thought to himself, remembering one of his granddad's favorite sayings. Indeed, it had been. Minutes later his eyes were closed and he was breathing deeply, sleeping soundly beside Kathleen.

Three hours and twenty minutes passed quickly as they slept deep in the restful sleep that comes from exhaustion and worry. The train whistle startled them all awake as the steam engine made its approach to the Chatham Four Corners Station. The loud whistle and unfamiliar surroundings confused Maeve when she opened her eyes, and she cried out for Kathleen. Sean tried to calm her, but she needed more comfort than her older brother could give her. He looked back behind him, and Kathleen nodded. She moved up to their seat and sent Sean back to sit with Thomas. As the train eased in closer to the station Sean could not hold his curiosity any longer.

"It went well, Da? What happened?" He spoke low, nearly a whisper.

"Tis not the time, Son. I am here, and we are leaving as planned, and there is money enough to pay for it. We'll let that be it for now, yes?"

"Aye," Sean agreed, disappointed but understanding that there would be a better time and place to discuss what had happened at Muldoon's.

Thomas took his watch out of his pocket and turned the face toward the window so the streetlamps at the train station would give it some light. It was nearly one-thirty in the morning, and they still had a short connecting ride from Chatham Four Corners to Albany. When the train came to a full stop, Thomas got up and made certain everyone gathered their belongings. As they headed for the door, he turned and checked again. They were drifters now, wayfarers who carried all their earthly possessions with them and could not afford to leave anything behind. He exited the train and spotted a ticket window not far from the tracks. Thomas made his way to the window while Kathleen and the children, sacks in hand, waited nearby. The air was fresh and clean, no stench hanging heavy about them to fill the lungs with putrid vapors. The night was still and quiet but for the occasional steam escaping from the release valves on the train's engine. It filled Kathleen with a peace she had not known in a very long time, and she felt an unfamiliar spark of hope in her soul. It was a thing she had long forgotten, replaced by complacency and forced contentment, and it felt warm and welcome.

"Is there a train runnin' this late into Albany?" Thomas asked the man at the window.

"There is. It's the last leg of the last run from Manhattan to Albany. You'll need to find lodging once you get there and wait till morning for a transfer, if you're going further, that is," the man said. "How many tickets do you need?"

"Six," Thomas answered.

"Six adults?" the man asked. Thomas prepared to be hoodwinked again.

"No, two adults and four children," Thomas responded slowly, waiting for the ticket man to overcharge him, and once again he would practice humility and pay the price.

300

"It's a quick trip from here to there. It'll be two dollars for each adult and another dollar per child. That comes to eight dollars," the man said, verifying Thomas's suspicions that the man at 32nd Street had taken advantage of him.

Thomas reached into his pocket, pulled out a ten-dollar note, and laid it on the counter. The man pushed six tickets toward Thomas and counted out his change.

"No, you keep the change," Thomas said as he turned to walk away. "Call it a return for honesty."

"But ..." the ticket man protested, shocked at the Irishman's generosity and not understanding the meaning behind Thomas's remark. His protest was lost in the night air as Thomas walked away.

Kathleen and the children stood near the conductor waiting for Thomas to arrive with the tickets. As he walked up to meet them, he could see the lack of sleep on the children's faces, eyes drooping, Maeve leaning into Kathleen. He handed the tickets to the conductor and shuffled his sleepy family onto the train. Once settled, he turned to Kathleen to talk about the time ahead.

"Katie, darlin', tis a short ride to Albany. Maybe thirty minutes at the most. Once we arrive we'll find some lodgin' and get some sleep, though I'll want an early start to St. Louis in the mornin'. I'll find out what time the early train leaves so that we'll be prepared."

"Thank you, Tommy. We're all needin' a bit of sleep not sittin' upright in a chair." She smiled a sleepy smile at Thomas, and he nodded his agreement.

The trip to Albany was indeed a short one. They arrived twenty-five minutes after leaving Chatham Four Corners. Thomas asked the conductor as they left the train what time the morning train would depart for St. Louis. The conductor told him that the St. Louis train would depart at eight o'clock sharp.

"And where might we find decent lodgin' nearby?" Thomas inquired.

"Well, there's the Stanwix Hall Hotel just up the block. Pretty fine establishment ..." the conductor said, drifting off and not wanting to offend the Delaney's, but judging by their clothes they couldn't afford it. "There are a few other moderately priced hotels near there, as well."

"Thanks, then," Thomas said as he walked away to rejoin Kathleen and the children. They stood near the edge of the landing looking off into the nightscape of Albany. It looked to be much nicer than where they had come from, though Kathleen knew that most things looked better under the cover of darkness.

"The mornin' train leaves at eight," Thomas said, "and there are several hotels just a block or so up the street." He decided to bypass the Stanwix in favor of a *more moderately priced establishment*, as the conductor had advised. It wasn't that they couldn't afford the lodging, for Thomas knew they could, but he would not subject his family to more scrutiny, more belittling, more condemnation. Their day would come, he was certain of it, but for now he would find somewhere suitable to lay their heads.

Thomas carried Maeve, and Sean carried his parents' sack. He was surprised by how heavy it was, unaware that it was weighed down with the coins, the pistol, and the ammunition. The weight of the sack piqued his interest but he was too tired to even consider taking a look inside. They walked a block and a half up the street just as the other late-night passengers were doing. The hotels all had their lights on and were apparently used to patrons checking in after midnight. The Stratton Inn looked nice enough without the fussy atmosphere they would have likely found at the Stanwix. Thomas went to the counter and explained that he and his family needed a large room with at least two beds. The clerk assured him they had what he needed, for a price. There was a hint of superiority in the man's attitude but he was not as blatantly rude as others Thomas had encountered. The man gave the price, and Thomas paid it without hesitation.

"You'll have use of the private lavatories, if you choose," the man offered. He pointed down the hall to the right. "They are located down there."

"And our room?" Kathleen asked. The children were nearly asleep on their feet.

"Up those stairs and to the left. Room 204," the man said. Kathleen thanked him while Thomas got the key and gathered up sacks and children and headed for the stairway. Sean and Eamon perked up at the sights around them and the knowledge that they would stay somewhere so fancy, even for a night. They arrived at room 204 and Thomas unlocked the door. Sean had a fleeting memory of entering the boat captain's room, and he tapped his left pocket where he had placed the man's watch before leaving their flat. At some point he would show Da that he too had a working pocket watch, but he would wait until the threat and the danger were far behind them.

"Oh," Kathleen gasped as the door opened revealing a clean white world that she thought must surely resemble heaven. "Tommy, 'tis too fine a place for the likes of us!"

"Nonsense, Katie. Circumstances not of our makin' have held us down, but that's not sayin' we don't deserve somethin' as simple as a clean room and a comfortable bed. Come in, everyone, and take off your shoes."

The children put their sacks by the door and took off their shoes. They looked around the spacious room. Two large beds and one smaller one were placed directly across from the door. Each was covered with a pretty white coverlet and had large fluffy pillows to rest one's head

303

upon. There was a white chest of drawers on the other wall with three large drawers for folks who were staying a while and had clothes enough to fill it. On top of the chest was a pitcher of water and bowl for washing up.

"Children, I know you're tired, but we cannot lay in those beds without cleanin' up a bit," Kathleen said. She poured some water into the porcelain bowl and found soft cotton cloths and a small cake of soap wrapped in white paper nearby. When Kathleen removed the paper from the soap, the beautiful scent of lavender took her back to her childhood home where there was always sprigs of lavender bundled and drying in their cottage. She did not allow herself to surrender to emotion. There might be time for melancholy once her head rested peacefully on one of the soft pillows, but she had children to attend to first. Kathleen turned toward the younger two, helped them out of their clothes, and washed their faces, hands, feet, and arms. She walked them over to the smaller bed, pulled back the bedding, and encouraged Sorley and Maeve to climb in. She kissed them tenderly and watched as they fell asleep almost immediately.

"Sean, Eamon," she said as she turned to the older boys, "I will let you go next. There are clean cloths and a lovely cake of soap there for you to use." The boys stripped down to their underclothes and washed. Kathleen wandered nearer to Thomas. He had taken something out of his pockets and was reaching inside their sack. Kathleen saw the large bundle of banknotes he pulled out and her jaw dropped.

"Shh, Katie, let it be," Thomas whispered. He removed a couple bills to replace what they had spent and placed the bundle back into the sack. He turned to her and smiled. "Are ya gonna see what the labratories are all about?" he asked, mispronouncing the name of the unknown luxury awaiting downstairs.

"I suppose I might," Kathleen replied, kindly ignoring his mispronunciation. She had overheard Mr. Andy Bingham talking to another man about installing a lavatory in his fine house. She heard them talk about a room inside the house where Bingham could use the toilet and could bathe in a tub big enough for a man to fully stretch out his legs. Even as tired as she was, Kathleen had to see it for herself.

"Can ya find your way?" Thomas asked.

"Aye, Tommy, I've got to see it."

"Sure and you go but be wary. We're in a strange city full of strange people," he cautioned. Kathleen nodded.

The older boys finished cleaning up and climbed into one of the two larger beds. The quiet, deep breathing of their siblings in the next bed lulled them to sleep in a matter of minutes. Kathleen had gone in search of the lavatories and Thomas was alone to finally see how much money he had taken from Muldoon's. There was a winged armchair and a small table near the window, the soft glow of the lantern upon it extending a warm invitation. It did little to calm his nerves, however, as the memory of what had transpired at Muldoon's was fresh in his mind, and the uncertainty of what he had stolen left their future in question. He took the bundle of bank notes and the coin pouches to the chair and laid it all on the table. It was immediately obvious that there was a large amount of money piled before him. He began a quick count, rushing in case one of the children awoke or Kathleen returned early from the lavatory. If his hurried calculations were correct he had made off with over two thousand dollars. Thomas put the coins back into the pouches, removed a one-hundred-dollar banknote from the bundle, and tied the string back around the remaining notes. He put the hundred-dollar note in his pocket and leaned back, running his hand through his hair. He had not meant to come away with the small fortune now in his possession. He had only wanted to pay for their trip west, certain he would find work enough to sustain them once they arrived in the Utah Territory.

There had been news of the gold rush at Sutter's Mill in California and talk of gold and silver mining spreading across the western territories. There was nothing to do now except get his family safely to their new home. He wasn't sure where they would end up, but John O'Riley's letter had mentioned a small settlement called Chinatown near Carson City. Thomas had learned that Carson City was a town in the western Utah Territory about ninety miles east of Sutter's Mill, and that the surrounding area was booming. They were headed in the right direction, he was certain of that. He wondered if John O'Riley's stories were true. He could barely fathom abundant work and open spaces to roam. Thomas hoped with all his being that they would finally see a promise of prosperity realized. He rose from the chair and pushed the money down into the bottom of his sack.

Thomas realized Kathleen had been gone a while, and he began to worry. He checked to make sure the children were sleeping soundly before leaving the room and locking the door behind him. He walked downstairs to where the lavatories were located. There was a door marked *Lavatories* and behind it was a short hallway with doors leading to separate rooms in the basement. All the doors were open but one and Thomas rightly assumed Kathleen must be behind it. He opened the door, mentally taking Katie to task for not locking it behind her as he walked quietly down the seven steps into the private lavatory. He saw a large wooden structure with a toilet built into a wooden bench on one side, a tall section in the middle where a person could stand and let water fall on them from the fixture above, and a large porcelain tub on the other side. And there, sound asleep and naked as the day she was born, was Kathleen, immersed to her shoulders in a healing tub of warm water. Thomas smiled. He walked over and sat on the edge of the tub, watching his beautiful Katie sleeping like a baby. He reached down and quietly scooped up a handful of water, bringing it up and letting it run out down her chest and over the swell of her breasts. He was as taken with her beauty in that moment as he was the first time he ever laid eyes on her. Again, he ran the water over her, then reached up and removed a tendril of her auburn hair that had fallen down onto her face. She stirred but remained in the safety of sleep until her senses alerted her to someone nearby. She awakened immediately and sat up, momentarily confused.

"What ... where are we?" she muttered quietly.

"Shh," Thomas quieted her. "You've fallen asleep in this fine labratory."

"Lavatory," she giggled. "I'm sorry, Tommy. I couldn't resist the heavenly invitation of a hot bath, and sleep took me once I laid back in the warm water. I could die now a happy girl."

"Don't be doin' that now, Mo Chuisle," Thomas teased, "we've got a long journey ahead. Here now, out with ya, girl, and let's enjoy that lovely bed. We've got days ahead of sleepin' in a coach and wherever it stops along the way." Kathleen got out and Thomas reached for a nearby towel that was folded on a stand near the tub. He watched her as she dried herself off and got dressed, and he wondered what he had ever done to deserve her. Guilt and failure flooded his mind, and he stood and held her close.

"I'm sorry, Katie," he whispered in her ear.

"For what, my love?"

"For failin' to give ya the life ya deserve," he said, his voice breaking slightly.

"Here now, Thomas Michael Delaney, tis not your fault ya were born Irish. Not your fault ya found only scorn when we arrived in America. And now, here ya are doin' your best to find somethin' better for us. I regret nothin', Tommy." She kissed him hard and cupped his face in her hands. "No matter what we must endure between here and where we're goin', I'm trustin' ya as I always have. I know, like you, that there's somethin' better for us, and I look forward to findin' it with you and all our little Delaneys." She smiled at him, her face radiant, and Thomas had to look away. His guilt caused her beauty to convict him, and he silently prayed he would find a way to be worthy of her love.

CHAPTER NINETEEN

The bed was soft and decadent. *Like sleeping on a puffy white cloud,* Thomas reflected as he slowly, indulgently stirred awake the next morning. He lay there a moment before noticing the light coming through the window. He bolted up in bed, grabbed his pants from the floor, and scrambled for his watch in the pocket of his worn trousers. It was ten minutes past seven, and his heart began to pound. He called out for everyone to wake up and began a rapid gathering of children and belongings. They had fifty minutes to gather everything together and run to the train station. Every Delaney did their part and Thomas, in his panicked state of mind, was thankful for the fortitude of his children. They would do well enough on the journey ahead no matter the difficulties they faced.

They were dressed, packed up, and out the door in ten minutes. Thomas slammed the key down on the counter and thanked the man for a lovely stay. He ran out the front door and caught up with Kathleen and the children who had gone on ahead. They reached the station fifteen minutes later out of breath and relieved they had not missed the train, though none of them would have regretted another night of luxury at The Stratton Inn.

Thomas paid the fare for the long trip from Albany to Chicago to St. Louis. The eleven-hundred-mile trip cost twenty-two dollars each for the adults and eleven dollars each for the children. Thomas handed the ticket man his hundred-dollar banknote, and after another predictable pause heavy with scrutiny and suspicion, the man handed Thomas six tickets and twelve dollars change. Thomas noticed a woman with a vendor's cart next to the station just setting up to sell her wares. There were other vendors in the area, as well, but Thomas thought the woman had a kind look about her and determined to purchase whatever it was she was selling. He looked back over to the boarding area where his family was waiting. He glanced at his watch and found he had six minutes before departure. Time enough, he thought. He approached the woman, and as he got closer to her cart he could smell something wonderful coming from beneath the cloth that was covering her wares.

"What have ya there?" he asked.

"Some fine Cornish pasties like me mother used to make. Big as your hand, they are," the woman said in a thick English accent, "and only five cents apiece!"

"And what have ya filled 'em with?" Thomas asked.

"Mincemeat, sir. Will ya have one?"

"Aye, I'll have six," Thomas answered, "and I need to hurry. My train's leavin' any minute."

The woman looked delighted as she reached under the cloth and brought out six large pasties. She wrapped them quickly in a thin piece of muslin she pulled out from beneath the food tray on her cart, and Thomas handed her one of the dollar coins he had just received from the ticket man. The woman fumbled through a small cloth pouch she had pulled from her apron pocket, looking for change.

"You keep it," Thomas said as he turned and ran to the train where his family stood anxiously waiting.

"I thank ya, sir!" the woman called after him.

Thomas gave the conductor their tickets. The man in the flat blue cap separated the main tickets from the stubs and punched them both with his L-shaped punch. Each conductor along a rail line had their own unique punch in different forms and shapes. This ensured that the conductor could check the passengers' ticket stubs and make sure that everyone on board had paid their fare. It also tracked a longer journey and recorded each stop and transfer along the way. The conductor gave the punched ticket stubs back to Thomas so he could present them at the transfer stations ahead. Thomas placed the ticket stubs in his pocket, and the Delaneys all boarded the train. The Albany to Chicago train was nicer than the one they had traveled in the night before. The seats were more comfortable, and there was more room between them. Kathleen was getting the children settled in when Thomas addressed them.

"Now, children, it'll be a long ride we're on. We're goin' all the way to Chicago, and then changin' trains to get us to St. Louis. It'll be tomorrow, later than it is now, before we arrive there. We'll need to sleep on the train when night comes. Can ya try and do this for your da?"

The children all agreed, happy that they were in a nicer train and were going to see something besides darkness out the windows. Kathleen put Maeve with Sean again, and the other two boys together just as before, with Maeve and Sorley each placed next to the windows. The train whistle blew a long loud blast and the engine rumbled. The children watched out the window as the train started moving along the tracks and the city of Albany passed them by.

"What's that wonderful smell?" Kathleen asked.

"I bought us a special breakfast to start our journey," Thomas said as he untied the knot the woman had made in the cloth.

"Tommy, we brought some bread and apples with us. Ya didn't need to spend the money," Kathleen scolded, though her words were half-hearted as her belly let out a growl. "Oh my! I suppose I'm hungry enough! What do we have in there, Tommy?"

"Mincemeat pasties, still warm!"

The children responded with delight as Thomas handed them out, one by one, and kept the last two for himself and Kathleen. They were delicious, flaky and light, and the mincemeat inside had a hint of sweet spices. The children ate slowly, quietly savoring each bite of the delicious breakfast. When everyone was done, Thomas passed around the cloth the pasties had been wrapped in so that hands and faces could be wiped clean.

The day passed slowly, and the children tired of watching the countryside pass by. Kathleen engaged the family in a game of *If I Could, I Would*, and Thomas told a story about a mine so deep and dark no man could ever reach the bottom until one day the greatest miner of all, Delaney the Magnificent, reached the bottom and discovered the fabled treasure of the king of the leprechauns. The children applauded, and a nearby woman, traveling alone, smiled as she watched and listened to the story unfold. The Delaneys ate bread and apples from their sacks when midday arrived, and the mincemeat pasties were no longer staving off their hunger. Maeve removed her little carved figurines from her sack and began playing quietly with them next to Sean. Her soft sweet voice lulled Sean to sleep, and she noticed, and smiled, and stood to catch her parents' attention so she could show them her big brother sleeping like a baby.

The long day found reprieve in Erie, Pennsylvania. Erie was an enforced stopping place due to an impassable difference in the gauge of the rails coming into the city and the smaller ones going out. It had been six years since the Erie Gauge War had erupted, and the town of Erie had been turned upside down by violence and destruction. The townsfolk were vehemently opposed to laying new tracks between Erie and New York, for it would have allowed a train to pass through their town without having to stop and transfer to a different one that fit the rails. The town depended on the inconvenience. Many an unfortunate train passenger missed the switchover from the wider-gauged train to the narrow-gauged one and were forced to spend a night. This brought in revenue to the town's restaurants, hotels, and vendors. The war had ended in the winter of 1854 and an uneasy peace had been established between the townsfolk and the railroads. Horse-and-buggy operators capitalized on the need to rush from one rail line to the other and began offering rides, for a price, to passengers who did not want to risk missing their connection by trying to bridge the distance on foot. That was Thomas, and though the thought of spending another heavenly night in a soft, clean bed was tempting, he did not want to be delayed. There was no reason to feel a sense of urgency, as far removed from trouble as they now were, but Thomas had a plan and he knew delays would only make it more difficult to press on.

The train came to a halt and the passengers were instructed to gather up their belongings. If they had more than they could carry there would be a railroad stevedore nearby who could load up a passenger's trunks and baggage and take them on to the next train. Many of them, however, worked for the town's business owners and had no intention of getting the passengers to their connecting train before it left the station. The Delaneys gathered their sparse belongings and exited the train, reveling in the fresh air and the ability to walk about. Thomas instructed them to stay there and stay together as he went looking for a buggy for hire.

"Lookin' for a buggy?" came a voice from beside the station.

"Aye, ya for hire?" Thomas asked.

"I am, for a price," the man said, staring at Thomas's worn clothes and thinking he surely could not afford the three dollars he would charge to get them to their connection on time.

"And what price are ya askin'? I've a wife and four little ones comin' with me."

"Three dollars for the ride up the rails, guaranteed to get you there on time," the man answered. Thomas nodded and took a couple steps backward to catch Kathleen's attention. He beckoned for them to come over, and they gathered up their stuff and hurried to where Thomas was waiting. Thomas helped Kathleen and the children get into the buggy and handed the man three silver dollars. He looked impressed and didn't scrutinize Thomas further for having money in his pocket. He instructed Thomas to hurry and jump in. The driver cracked his whip and the horse was off and running before Thomas was comfortably settled. It was a bumpy ride along the dirt road that ran parallel to the tracks, and Thomas thought it was good for them to get an idea of what their coach ride out west would be like. He mentioned it to Kathleen and the children. Kathleen nodded slightly, dreading the trip, and the children laughed. For them it would be another chapter in their continuing adventure, and it would take much more than the threat of a bumpy ride to dampen their spirits.

The man was good on his promise, and the Delaneys arrived at the transfer location on time. Kathleen thanked their driver. Maeve waved and smiled, garnering her usual response of a wide genuine smile. Thomas pulled the ticket stubs from his pocket as they made their way to the train. It was late in the afternoon, and he knew that the night ahead would present a difficult challenge for them. He hoped against hope that they would all be able sleep on the train. The conductor took the ticket stubs, punched them at the bottom, and gave them back to Thomas as he invited them to board. They found the new train to be smaller and less occupied than the one from Albany. Thomas rightly assumed that many travelers would opt to spend a night in Erie, enjoy a good meal and a nice bed to sleep in, and catch the morning train to Chicago. He glanced out the window and could see several vendors outside selling their wares. He realized that there was little food left in their sacks.

"Stay here, I'll be back," he said to Kathleen. He fetched the canteen from his sack and exited the train. The conductor was standing nearby looking at his watch.

"How long before we're leavin'?" Thomas asked him.

"We've got about ten minutes. Just waiting on any stragglers trying to run from the sixes to the fours." Thomas understood the conductor's reference to the gauge of the rails and nodded. He refilled his canteen with water at a nearby pump and rushed over to the vendor carts. He purchased a bag of peanuts, a packet of jerky, a few fresh peaches, and a small slab of hard, crumbly cheese before making his way back to the train with a couple minutes to spare. Thomas balanced all his purchases in his arms as he boarded, eager to get back to his family and share what he had found.

"Goodness," Kathleen reacted to his armload, "what have ya found us now?" The children gathered close by to see what Thomas had purchased. He stood next to Kathleen as she took the items from him one by one. She did a quick inventory so the children would be aware of what their father had purchased, and they were delighted with the foods that were far removed from their usual fare. The train whistle blew, and the train shifted, causing Thomas to sit quicker than he had planned. Sorley laughed at the surprised look on his father's face and everyone followed suit. Once settled, Thomas and Kathleen sorted through his purchases.

"Are we hungry?" Thomas asked, getting the responses he expected. "Sure and there's plenty here for us all." The children each asked for what they wanted, and Kathleen handed it out as the train began running along the rails out of Erie and on its way to Chicago. It would be midnight or later when they arrived at the Chicago station, and unfortunately if anyone was able to sleep during the trip from Erie to Chicago it would be interrupted by another transfer once they arrived. The train had a Chambersburg sleeping car available but Kathleen told Thomas they would probably be more comfortable leaning on one another.

When their bellies were full, and darkness fell across the land, and the view out the windows offered nothing but night, the rhythmic chugging of the train lulled everyone to sleep. Kathleen had removed two quilts from her sack and draped them across the children before returning to her own seat and leaning into Thomas. She was asleep quickly. Thomas stayed awake as long as he could before succumbing, his sack knotted at the top with his arm through the loop. He could not risk losing the money, the gun, or the ammunition, for he might find that he needed all three to complete a safe journey west from St. Louis.

The train chugged along, skirting the shores of Lake Erie and on past the rolling landscape and golden dunes at the southern end of Lake Michigan. It curved along the lake and went north a short distance before arriving at the Chicago station. When the train whistle blew announcing their arrival Thomas awoke with a gasp. It shocked him that he had slept so soundly and his body hurt from being uncomfortably contorted in the seat. Kathleen woke up and they talked brifely about what lay ahead. Their voices and the slowing of the train caused the children to stir, and when the train stopped in the sudden way it does, the Delaneys were awake and ready. They gathered their things once more, exited the train, and waited for instructions from Thomas. He was undecided and gathered them close, standing beneath the light of a streetlamp where they could be seen and see each other.

"Delaneys, we have a choice to make," he said. "We can stay a night here, arise early, and be off to St. Louis in the mornin'. We would arrive late tomorrow afternoon. Or we can finish our train adventure overnight and arrive in St. Louis in the mornin'. It'll take me some time to find a coach service and secure our place with them for the trip west, so we would have the entire day and overnight to sleep and rest up. What do ya think?"

"Tommy, the children need rest. I'm needin' it myself, but it's already far into the night. If we're needin' to be up early it seems pointless to stay here for a few short hours of sleep. If your description of the trip west is true, we're lookin' at a rough end to our journey. Unless anyone thinks different, I say we get this train travel done and have all day tomorrow to rest and sleep and eat and get ourselves ready for what's ahead." Kathleen looked at the tired faces of her family, hoping they would see the logic in the choice she would make if it were up to her. Thomas and the children all agreed. The train ride had been an adventure unlike anything they'd known, but they were tired and had no desire to delay the completion of this leg of their journey. Thomas asked the conductor about their transfer, and he directed them to the waiting train. The man watched the family walk toward the train, their exhaustion obvious, and he rightly assumed they were another poor family heading west with dreams of better things. Having no idea what and where they had come from, he wondered why a father would expect such sacrifice from his children and his wife, and he shook his head. *Better to stay where you are*, he said to himself, *than to pull up roots and go in search of a fanciful dream.*

CHAPTER TWENTY

The conductor at the Chicago station was right about one thing—the Delaneys were exhausted. The children had no trouble falling back asleep and staying asleep through most of the final six-hour segment of their journey. Thomas leaned against the window with Kathleen leaning on him. His sleep was fitful, haunted by visions of Charlie Connor and the fabricated images of the burning bodies left behind at Muldoon's. Kathleen slept little. Thomas's restlessness kept her awake, and her mind was a jumbled mess of thoughts and questions she could not control. She fretted about what might have happened at the gang's headquarters the night they left the city, and she worried over what might become of them whenever they found a place to call home. There was little sound inside the train car except for the deep breathing of the sleeping travelers. Kathleen wished she could clear her mind of the worry and the fear that plagued her, but it was too powerful to overcome.

Beside her, Thomas jerked awake. He let out a soft tortured cry as he did, and Kathleen knew his sleep had been plagued with images he would likely never share with her. Thomas was like that. He would shield and protect his family from any threat to their happiness if it were in his power to do so. He would carry a burden, even one not his own, if it meant someone else did not need to. She reached over and stroked the side of his face with the back of her hand.

"I'm sorry, Mo Chuisle," he whispered, "I did not mean to wake ya." He reached up and put his hand over hers, then brought it down and lightly kissed it. She smiled at him, and in the dim candlelight of the train car he could see her radiance. "Dear God, I hope we're doin' the right thing," he whispered. "I can't bear to put you through another desperate existence."

"The right place to be is with each other, Tommy. We'll make a good enough life wherever it is we land."

"I want better than good enough, Katie. I want for my children to not go hungry, to wear proper clothes, and get a proper education. I want to give you fine things and an easy life."

"Och, and what would I do with an easy life, Thomas Delaney? 'Tis a boring and meaningless existence to sit on one's arse and discuss the grand things of the world with people ya don't even like!" Thomas laughed quietly. So seldom did Kathleen utter a word that even vaguely resembled profanity. It tickled him to hear it on occasion, and for her part, she loved how it always made him laugh. It was the entire reason she did it.

"Katie, darlin', 'tis a favored man I am to have been given such a gift as you, Anamchara." He leaned over and kissed her softly. Sean, from his seat, heard the conversation after awakening to their quiet voices, and he smiled. There was love traveling with them, love leading them away from hate and bigotry and fear and a miserable degrading life. It had to be right. He closed his eyes and listened to the whispers, the soft chugging of the train, and the deep sleep sounds of his siblings. He feared approaching God after the terrible sinful things he had done, but he did so anyway just to send some gratitude heavenward. Their lives could have gone in such a different direction, and though they were not yet settled and safe, there was more hope of that happening than they'd had in a good long time.

The train pulled into the Illinoistown station around ten o'clock the next morning. The sun was up, the sky was blue, and there was a sense of anticipation tangible in the air. The children had slept better than expected, and they were awake and excited to see another new place. Illinoistown, Illinois was situated on the east side of the Mississippi River directly across from St. Louis, and the train station was at the Wiggins Ferry Company docks. The Wiggins Ferry Company transported passengers across the river to St. Louis. They also transported train cars one at a time aboard the ferries located at the docks on either side of the river. The Delaneys waited for the next available passenger ferry. As they waited, they watched a rail car being loaded onto a ferry. Sean was fascinated by the endeavor and at how well people had adapted to progress and the demands of the growing population out west. He looked forward to the ferry ride across the river and once again thought about Mr. Clemens. The gold watch rested heavy in his pocket. The more he thought about life on the water, the more interested he was. As Sean contemplated the adventurous life Mr. Clemens must live, he felt a keen sense of regret for having stolen from him.

A ferry soon returned to the dock, and the foot passengers were boarded. Their train fare included the ferry ride from Illinoistown to St. Louis where they would find a fleet of omnibuses to take them to their destinations.

Some passengers had to hire men with carts to help transport their belongings off the train and onto the ferry, but the Delaneys continued their self-sufficient journey on their own. The steam ferry fired up and pulled away from the dock. Sean hurried over to the edge where he could take in every detail of the crossing. He watched the water lapping against the side of the ferryboat, and the way it curled away from the bow as the ferry made its way toward the other shore. The air felt cooler as they crossed the river, and the clean fresh breeze invigorated him. From a distance, Kathleen watched her son and recalled playing *If I Could, I Would* with the children recently. She remembered how Sean had surprised them with his wish to be a riverboat captain. She could see his exuberant expression and his rapt attention to the boat upon the water, and she hoped that somehow he would see his dreams realized even if it took him away from her.

The crossing was too swift for Sean's liking. The ferry arrived at the St. Louis dock fifteen minutes after it departed. The passengers left the ferry and Thomas led his family to a waiting omnibus that appeared to have plenty of room for them.

"Where to, Mister?" the driver asked.

"Can you recommend a nice hotel?

"The St. James is nice. It's just a few blocks west of here at Broadway and Walnut." Thomas and Sean both thought it odd that they found themselves on Broadway again, but this one was far removed from and likely much nicer than the one they had known back home.

"We'll try it then," Thomas said. The man guided his horse through the tangle of people and omnibuses and dockworkers hurrying to do their jobs. Soon they were two blocks away from the river and into a decent part of town. The omnibus stopped in front of the St. James Hotel, and Thomas liked the look of it. He helped Kathleen and the children out of the omnibus and onto the street. He paid the man and asked if he knew where there might be a reputable coach service for travel to the western territories.

"Well, you can start with Butterfield if you think you can afford it," the man answered.

"Aye, thanks," Thomas replied with no gratitude in his voice. He wondered how far west they would have to travel to leave judgment behind them.

"Come, Delaneys, let's see about a room," he said in a gentler voice. He left his sack with Sean and had them wait for him just inside the door as he approached the desk. Thomas saw the expression on the man's face. He told himself he would endure the condescending attitude so that they could procure a room for the day and overnight. He and his dear ones were far too tired to walk from hotel to hotel trying to find a welcoming desk clerk.

"Can I help you?" the man behind the counter asked. There was no scorn in his voice, though he made a visual inspection of Thomas's clothing and that of his family's waiting across the lobby.

"Aye, we'd like a room till tomorrow mornin' big enough for the six of us," Thomas said. The man's expression changed immediately, his nose wrinkled, and his lip curled slightly. The scorn surfaced, as it always did.

"Irish?"

"No, Scottish," Thomas replied without hesitation. This man was likely no different than any of the other apathetic people he had encountered who couldn't hear the difference between Irish and Scottish accents and didn't care to learn.

"Ah, all right then," the man said, "we do have a room available until noon tomorrow. You'll be gone by then?"

"Yes," Thomas answered, thinking that Scottish immigrants held no more value than the Irish judging by the man's reluctant admission of a room and the rude question about their departure.

"The room is a dollar and a half per person, two dollars if you want a meal."

Thomas nodded and said they'd like supper later that afternoon. The man informed him that the café was to the left of the lobby and served food until ten o'clock at night. Thomas paid the man and received the key to the room on the main floor.

"Your room is near the lavatories which are outfitted with tubs for your convenience," the man said, his meaning clear. Thomas glared at the clerk as he grabbed the key from the counter and turned back to his family.

"What is it, Tommy? Ya look so angry!" Kathleen said with grave concern in her voice. To be denied a room now, as exhausted as they were, would be devastating.

"Tis no better place for the Irish here than where we came from," Thomas responded. "All the more reason not to tarry. Come, children, let's find our room."

Their room was just across the hall from the lavatory doors as the clerk had indicated. The room was much like the one in Albany, though not as spacious. The children took off their shoes and immediately went for the beds. Thomas watched them, their joy over something as simple as a soft mattress and clean bedding strengthened his resolve to provide a life for them where that perceived luxury might become commonplace.

"Attention, Delaneys," Thomas said with a seriousness that quieted everyone. "Here is our plan, and I'll need everyone to cooperate, yes?" They all nodded, waiting for his instructions. "Make use of the beds this mornin' if ya need some more rest. The trip ahead from here will not be as pleasant as the train. It will be dusty and dirty, cramped, and uncomfortable." Thomas saw the happy expressions disappear and he wished he did not have to be the bearer of such unpleasant information.

"Will it be a long time that way, Da?" Eamon asked.

"Aye, Son, I'm afraid so. Tis a good three weeks, from what I hear. There will be nothin' to do but endure it. Once it's over we'll have reached the west, and life will take a turn for the better. I'd like nothin' more than to tell ya the trip will be better than it sounds, but I'm not willin' to give ya false hope. I want ya to be prepared for what's ahead."

"We'll get through it, Da," Sean replied. "We survived the worst of times back in New York, and with the promise of better things ahead I think we'll do just fine." He looked at his siblings and they all nodded their agreement.

"Right, Son. I'm proud of us all. Children, you've been champions so far. A da couldn't ask for better under the circumstances. I'm goin' out to find a coach I can hire to make the journey west. I think we need to rest as much as possible. Enjoy these lovely beds, and yes, though the man at the desk was more than rude about it, let's make use of the baths too. Mam enjoyed a warm bath in Albany. The hot water pours right into the tub all on its own!"

"'Tis the truth, children," Kathleen agreed, "and I agree with your da. We all need a good soak before we head out west."

"After I get back from makin' our travel arrangements, I'll do the same. We'll have a wonderful supper and get ready for a fine sleep." Thomas paused, hesitant. "I'm right sorry for puttin' ya through this difficult time, dear ones, but I promise ya life will be better once we get where we're headed."

Maeve ran over and wrapped her arms around Thomas's legs. He bent over and picked her up, holding her close and loving her more in that moment than he thought possible. She and her mother were the source of his greatest regret. Her beauty, her bright inquisitive mind, and her gentle spirit so like her mam's, deserved much more than Thomas had been able to provide. Years of guilt, failure, and disappointment flooded his heart, and he prayed God would see their dreams fulfilled. He could not bear to watch his precious family endure another season of want. It would surely break him.

Thomas retrieved the large sack that he and Kathleen shared and walked to the table by the window. He waited a few minutes, looking at the activity in the streets outside and hoping his family would busy themselves with something and pay him no attention. It was just a few minutes before they were unpacking their sacks, pulling out the only change of clothes they owned, and discussing the wonder of having a magic tub just across the hall. Thomas smiled at their conversation as he reached in and pulled out the packet of bank notes and the coin pouches. He quietly untied the notes and counted them quickly, surprised at what he still had left for they had spent more in the last two days than they typically spent in a year, maybe even two. Without needing to count the coins he determined they would have more than enough for their fare, provisions along the way, and a portion to get them settled wherever their journey ended. He placed the packet in his pocket and put the coin pouches back in the sack. As he did, he noticed the revolver and the box of ammunition near the bottom. He took the sack and placed it under the biggest bed where he and Kathleen would sleep. The younger children were too preoccupied to notice, though Sean and Kathleen both saw him. Thomas walked over and leaned close to Kathleen's ear.

"Watch the children and do not let them get into that sack," he whispered.

"But what..."

"Just watch them, Katie. I'll be goin' to find a reputable coach service. I'll buy our fares and get all the information we need so that we're prepared as best we can be. You rest up, yes? Sean, you, too. I'll need you both to be strong for the little ones. This will be hard on them," Thomas said, his voice fading as he turned to leave. "Lock the door behind me, Sean." Sean got up off the bed and followed his father to the door.

"Be careful, Da," he said quietly.

"Aye, Son, that I'll be."

Sean locked the door after Thomas left, and Kathleen got the children's attention so that she could coordinate baths and naps and repacking.

"I'm thinkin' you boys should go first. Eamon and Sorley, you will go with your brother across the hall to the lavatories. You two will fit in one tub if they're anywhere near as big as the one back in Albany. Sean can have his own. No tomfoolery, ya hear me, Sorley?" Sorley nodded and grinned. Kathleen turned to Sean. "Keep them in line, Sean. If they're too much for ya, come back and get me." She said in a voice loud enough for Sorley and Eamon to hear. They knew Mam was a force to be reckoned with if she ever got truly angry. It rarely happened, but they had seen it enough to know that they didn't want to invite an encounter with Kathleen's Irish temper.

The boys gathered their clean clothes, such as they were, and Kathleen found a soap cake from on top of the chest of drawers. She gave the younger boys some quick instructions about how to wash up, and though they assured her they knew how she was not convinced of it. It had been a rare occasion that any of them had the opportunity to bathe. She asked Sean if he wanted her to come along to show him how to use the fancy tub, but he told her he could figure it out. Kathleen followed them to the door, instructing and warning all the way, and as they walked out into the hallway Sean instructed his mother to lock the door behind them. She smiled at her young man and nodded, locking the door after her sons had entered the door across the hall.

Kathleen returned to the bed where Maeve sat playing with her wooden figures. She laid down beside her daughter and listened contentedly to her soft, sweet voice. She was asleep almost instantly. Maeve noticed, smiled down at her beautiful mother, and continued to play. She marveled at how soft the bed was beneath her, how clean and fresh everything smelled, and she hoped that one day she would have one just like it.

In one of the vacant lavatories across the hall, the younger Delaney boys stripped down to their underwear. Sean located the stopper for the drain, turned the faucet handles, and felt the warm water falling out of the spigot and into the tub. He looked around as the tub was filling to see what other marvels were included in the lavatory. He noticed a tall, recessed section at the middle of the lavatory unit dividing the tub from the toilet. It looked like a coffin standing on end and he thought it odd until he noticed that there was a water pipe coming in through the top, covered with a larger circular piece of metal. There were holes in the metal, and Sean thought it must be a stand-up bath. He turned off the tub's faucet and told the boys to finish stripping down and get into the water. He placed the cake of soap on the edge of the tub, stripped down himself, and got into the tall section to test his theory. The water came out cold, causing Sean to yell from the shock of it. Eamon and Sorley laughed hysterically as they watched their older brother dancing around naked under the stream of falling water. After a moment or two of icy torture the water warmed, and Sean reached around and retrieved the soap from the edge of the tub. He rubbed it over his body and set it back down, telling his brothers to use it and to hurry and wash up. The stand-up bath was the most wonderful sensation that Sean had ever known, and he felt as if he could stand there forever and let the warm water run over him. He likened it to a good rainstorm, but warmer and more comforting.

After Eamon and Sorley had washed they began to play. They splashed about in the water and were too loud for Sean's comfort. He finished washing and stepped out of the contraption, walking across the room to where he found a stack of towels for patrons to use. He dried off and dressed in his clean clothes, all the while telling the boys to quiet down and finish up. A knock on the door startled him, his heart pounding as he worried it might be the hotel clerk coming to berate them. If they were asked to leave the hotel, Da would be livid. Eamon and Sorley quieted down immediately, and Sean slowly opened the door.

"What the devil is going on in there?" Kathleen was clearly annoyed. The door to their room directly across the hall was open and Sean could see Maeve standing in the doorway looking worried. "I could hear you across the hall in our room with the door closed!"

"Wasn't me you were hearin' but those two!" Sean pointed to the guilty parties still sitting in the tub.

"Finish up and dry off!" Kathleen said to the boys. "Get your clean clothes on and gather up your stuff. I want ya back over in our room in five minutes."

The boys pulled the wooden plug out of the tub and jumped out. There was no time for more silliness. Mam was not happy with them, and they didn't want to further irritate her. In less than five minutes the three boys were dried, dressed, and carrying their dirty clothes back across the hall to their room. Sean knocked quietly on the door and Mam opened it immediately. Eamon and Sorley paraded by her, clean and contrite, and their sudden humility made her laugh.

"Ya look well-scrubbed and ready for church," she said. "Was it quite lovely?"

"Aye, Mam," Eamon said, "what a thing it is to see warm water falling right out of the pipe and into the tub! I wonder, do they have someone on the other end of the pipe heatin' it up on a stove?"

"I'm sure I don't know, Son," Kathleen responded, "but I'm glad for it! Now, 'tis Maeve's turn!"

Maeve jumped down off the bed and grabbed her clothes. Kathleen decided to wash up but not bathe having just done so two days before. She gathered up the boys' dirty clothes to wash as best she could and hoped they would dry before leaving in the morning. She instructed Sean to lock the door and not to open it for anyone unless it was her coming back from the lavatory or Thomas returning from his business.

"You two behave, ya hear me?" She directed her question at Eamon and Sorley, and the tone of her voice let them know it was more command than question.

"Aye, Mam," they agreed.

Kathleen and Maeve walked across the hall and into the same lavatory that the boys had used. Kathleen turned the handle of the faucet to fill the tub, and Maeve watched in delight. Once the tub was full of warm water Kathleen helped Maeve out of her clothes and into the tub. The soap was still sitting on the edge where the boys had left it. Kathleen picked it up, lathered it good, and tipped Maeve back to get her hair wet. She was old enough to lay back by herself but having no experience with bathing she was timid about laying down in the water. Kathleen's hand on the back of her neck gave Maeve the confidence she needed to enjoy the warm water and the calming sensation the bath gave her. Kathleen washed and rinsed her daughter's hair and then helped her wash every little bit of her. Maeve played in the water while Kathleen took one of the damp towels the boys had left and dipped it in the tub. She put a little soap on it and used it to wash her face, her neck, her arms and feet. She turned on the water in the stand-up bath, got the soap, and did her best to lather, rub, and rinse the children's dirty clothes. Kathleen wrung them out and laid them on a nearby chair before turning back to Maeve. She told her daughter to pull the stopper and allowed Maeve to sit a few minutes and watch the bath water recede. It was fascinating and strangely relaxing, and they both watched until Maeve shivered.

Kathleen lifted her daughter from the deep tub and helped her dry off with a soft, dry towel. Her clean dress, just a cotton shift with a small floral print, was getting small. Kathleen noticed a place on the left shoulder where the seam was coming apart and she told herself she would need to sew it up before it tore any further. All the children's clothes were getting too small and were tattered beyond any hope of repair. She hoped Thomas was right in promising a better life ahead. Having clothes that did not draw scornful glances from merciless people would be worth the difficult journey to get there. She finished buttoning the back of Maeve's shift, turned the child around to face her, and kissed the top of her head. Maeve hugged her mam and helped gather up the damp clothes to take back to their room.

They crossed the hall and tapped lightly on the door. Sean opened it and Kathleen was happy to see the boys laying on the bed talking, drowsy from the warm relaxing bath. She determined it would be good for everyone to lay down and rest until Thomas returned. The children all seemed to agree, and Kathleen was thankful for the luxury of the lavatory. A warm bath was a rare and healing thing, a reward for their fortitude thus far, and a catalyst for a midday nap. All five of them were asleep quickly, the soft beds an indulgent invitation to sleep the day away.

***

Outside the hotel, Thomas made his way through the hot and humid city streets looking for a storefront advertising coach services westward. He grew frustrated as he wandered the unfamiliar streets, but he hesitated to speak to anyone. He had grown weary of practicing tolerance and displaying a humility he did not feel. Thomas knew that when he finally found a coach service they would also judge him by his appearance and assume he was in no position to pay the fare to transport his family across the country. There was a real possibility they would overcharge him, and he knew he would have to swallow his pride once again and pay the price they asked. As he continued wandering in search of the information he needed, Thomas spotted an older man sweeping the porch in front of his dry goods store. He had a kindly look about him, and Thomas decided to take the chance that it was so.

"Mornin', Sir," Thomas offered respectfully.

"That it is," the man replied. He took a second look at Thomas but his demeanor did not change. "Can I help you with something?"

"Aye ..." Thomas hesitated a moment deciding to disguise his words and his accent the best he could. "I was looking to hire a coach heading west," he said, without a trace of his Irish accent or so he thought.

"I see," the man said, "that's a popular place to be heading these days. You're a miner, I'd imagine?" Thomas nodded. "It's not an easy journey from here to there, you know."

"Aye ... I know," Thomas responded, hoping that the man wouldn't wonder why he stammered every time he started a sentence. He told himself to say *yes* when the man asked him a question.

"You've no need to disguise your accent, my friend. My wife is Irish, and I have no aversion to your people," the man said with a smile. He saw Thomas relax instantly.

"Sorry to have deceived ya, Sir," Thomas replied. "'Tis a difficult thing for an Irishman to find a friendly face in this country."

"I know it well enough. I've defended my wife on more than one occasion. Now, about the coach," he said, "there are a few options. All depends on what you're looking for. You can pay more and get there faster or pay less and spend months in a cart train."

"Och, I'm not wantin' to put my family through that!"

"Well, if you can get yourself up to Nauvoo I hear tell there are fellas up there who used to drive for the Butterfield Company. Had their fill of the torturous running of the Overland Mail Service. St. Louis to San Francisco in twenty-five days must be a hellish journey. Those fellas purchased their own coaches and have them for hire. They'll take folks who can pay all the way out to the great salty lake in as short a time as two or three weeks, give or take a day or two."

"Nauvoo?" Thomas wasn't sure what the man was talking about.

"Little settlement north of here. Used to be a big Mormon town but they're all heading west too. I hear the coach drivers are running along the Mormon Trail and flying past the poor souls walking the distance pulling their handcarts. They're not highly regarded by the Mormons, but it's a much quicker way to get where you're going," the man said. He wondered how Thomas could pay for the trip but refrained from a rude and undeserved interrogation.

"And how would one get to Nauvoo?" Thomas asked.

"You can hire a local coach for a price or you can book passage on a riverboat. The river trip takes about sixteen or eighteen hours depending on the weather. Don't know which one suits you better, but those are the most common ways from here to there."

"Thank you, kindly," Thomas responded. "I wish you and your wife an easy road."

"And I the same for you and yours."

Thomas shook the man's hand and turned to leave. He paused a moment or two, trying to get his bearings and figure out how to get back to the ferry dock. He glanced over his shoulder at the shopkeeper, about to ask him for some assistance.

"The ferries are that way," the man called out, pointing east. He had sensed an urgency in Thomas and assumed he would head to Nauvoo. Thomas waved and thanked him once again.

The ferry dock was four blocks east and one block south. Thomas found his way easily and asked about the next riverboat north. The clerk at the dock said there would be a running of the *James McDaniel* north to Nauvoo at seven o'clock the next morning. He advised Thomas that they would likely pull into the Nauvoo dock around eleven o'clock at night and that he should be able to secure a hotel upon arrival.

Thomas returned to the hotel anxious to divulge the next chapter of their adventure and was amused to find the entire Delaney family sound asleep when he entered the room. He smiled as he watched them, and he felt a great sense of gratitude that they had escaped danger and arrived in St. Louis bound for the Utah Territory. Thomas stepped back out, locked the door, and wandered across the hall to make use of the fancy baths he had yet to enjoy. He would have a nice soak, return to the room, and quietly lie down beside his sweet Kathleen. He might sleep. He might lay still upon the pillow-soft bed and stare at the pristine white ceiling, regretting that the road ahead would be neither soft nor pristine. He hoped with every fiber of his being that what they were doing would lead them to a life better than any they could have imagined.

CHAPTER TWENTY-ONE

Kathleen awoke to Thomas snoring beside her, his hair slightly damp and smelling of lavender soap. The harsh light of midday had faded, replaced with the golden summer glow of early evening. It filled the room with a warmth that Kathleen felt all the way through to her soul. She wondered how long they had all been sleeping, fretted a moment, and then affirmed to herself that this was their time to be indulgent. Everything would likely change tomorrow. The journey would become more difficult, and though she didn't know exactly what the plan was, she knew it would demand tolerance, sacrifice, tenacity, and cooperation. She would not allow this sliver of time where they did nothing but immerse themselves in luxury to be devalued or cut short by guilt. She wasn't sure if they deserved it, but she knew they appreciated it.

Maeve stirred and whispered to Kathleen that she needed to use the lavatory. Kathleen nodded and they quietly tiptoed across the wooden floor. They walked across the hall, used the lavatory, and returned as quietly as they could. Thomas was sitting up, yawning and stretching his arms when they got back to the room. He smiled when he saw his two beautiful girls enter the room.

"You two look like sunshine come to life," he breathed.

"Shh, you'll wake the boys," Kathleen replied.

"'Tis time. We need to get some food in our bellies and have a family meeting after."

"Is everything all right, Tommy?"

"Aye, Katie. I made some connections today and I've got a good idea how this adventure will go for us from here to the Utah Territory." His tone of voice was serious, and Kathleen knew that this would likely be the last lovely night they enjoyed for a good stretch of time. She nodded to Thomas and began to gently wake the boys.

When everyone was awake, dressed, and ready to find the hotel's café, Thomas realized how hungry he was. He mentioned it and everyone agreed they were more than ready for a hearty meal. The children had never eaten in a restaurant, and it had been many years since Thomas and Kathleen had enjoyed such an indulgence. Kathleen gave the children a quick but stern set of instructions as they walked the short distance to the café. As briefly as she could, she reminded them how to behave, to talk quietly, say please and thank you, keep your eyes to yourselves, and no burping or wiping faces on sleeves. She exhausted her long list and then prayed silently they would remember half of it.

"Is there something I can do for you?" the man at the door asked. His voice clearly expressed his doubt and his distaste.

"We're lookin' for a good meal," Thomas answered, his voice strained but pleasant. He would not embarrass his wife or children by allowing his anger to cause a scene.

The man turned and looked back into the café wishing he could tell them it was full, but the open door could not hide the fact that there were several tables available. He spotted a round table with five chairs near the back corner as far removed from the main seating area as he could find.

"This way," he said as he walked away, not waiting to see if they were ready to follow him. He took a chair from a nearby table and added it to theirs, turned and quickly walked away without another word.

"Pay no mind to that man and others like him," Thomas said to the children. "Some folks feel unsettled around grand Irish folks like us." The younger three children giggled. Sean did not, nor did Kathleen. They felt the scorn. They fought as Thomas did to remain civil and not give a reason for onlookers to feel validated in judging them.

"Here now," Kathleen said as she picked up one of the paper menus from the table and handed it to Sean. "Sean and Eamon, you help Sorley and Maeve, yes? Everyone find something you'd like and let's enjoy a grand meal." She held up a menu and leaned close to Thomas. "What shall we have, Tommy?"

"I see they have Irish stew on the menu. I'm sure theirs is better than any I'll ever have ..." Thomas waited for a reaction and promptly received Kathleen's elbow to his ribcage. He laughed and continued, "but I think I shall have this baked chicken pie instead, and maybe a bowl of mashed potatoes beside it."

"Wise choice, Thomas Delaney," Kathleen scolded. "As for me, spring lamb with mint sauce. This is such a sinful indulgence that I'm feelin' the need to go to confession!"

"'Tis not a sin to dine on good food, Katie, and ya need to get used to havin' your share of it. When we get settled in our new home and I start workin' you'll not go hungry again."

Maeve and Sorley decided on pork and applesauce, Eamon selected roast pigeon, and Sean chose roast beef.

The waiter was reservedly polite, mostly because his job depended on it. After a brief wait he brought the Delaney's food, steaming hot and wafting such savory aromas that they all imagined they had died, gone to heaven, and were dining at God's great table. They were so quiet as they dined that the arrogant host almost forgot they were there. The waiter kept watch from a distance, preferring to give his attention to the finer patrons in the room who might know about the new trend of tipping their server, a practice introduced in America by wealthy travelers returning from Europe. When he noticed the Delaneys' empty plates he returned to take them away and ask about dessert. Everyone agreed they couldn't eat another bite, though Thomas and Kathleen had a request.

"Could ya bring us a cup of tea and a glass of Irish whiskey that we can take back to our room?" Thomas asked.

"We charge extra for any items taken to the patron's room."

"That's fine. Make sure the tea is good and hot, and the whiskey is Irish," he replied with some assertion, losing his resolve to remain civil in the face of constant judgment. The waiter mumbled something as he walked away and returned a few minutes later with the tea and whiskey. He handed Thomas the bill and watched for the horrified reaction that was sure to come.

"Sure and that was a great deal of food for a mighty reasonable price!" Thomas said louder than he meant to. Kathleen couldn't help but laugh as she watched Thomas play the role of the boisterous, self-indulgent patron. She had a fleeting thought that he would be more believable if he had himself an enormous belly, but too many years of living lean had prevented that from ever happening.

"You pay at the counter by the door," the waiter responded, noticeably disappointed. He walked away as the sound of the Delaneys' laughter increased his aversion to the Irish riff raff that had stained their establishment.

Thomas paid the $3.60 he owed the café and they walked back to their room with their whiskey, their tea, and their very full bellies. Once inside, Thomas announced a family meeting. He ordered shoes off and all Delaneys on the beds. He sat down next to Kathleen, Maeve on his other side, and the boys across from them on the other bed.

"First, a word of thanks to all the brave and determined Delaneys for your cooperation and patience as we traveled from New York to St. Louis. You've done well, and haven't we made it a far ways from home?"

"Aye, Da, it feels like we're in another world," Sorley commented.

"In a way we are, Sorley. We're away from danger, dirt, and hopelessness. All I want in this life is for you all to be happy and healthy and never have another day of hunger. And that is why we're headin' to the Utah Territory."

"What is Utah?" asked Maeve.

"'Tis a place out west, a place where there is work for all men, open skies and fresh air, and a chance to live a life we'd never have had in New York." Thomas hoped the younger children could comprehend how dire their situation had been without him having to go into details about the danger that had been bearing down on them.

"Do they like the Irish there?" Eamon asked what they all were wondering.

"I believe they do, Son," Thomas responded. "Our friend John O'Riley is there and is makin' a fine life for himself. I hope to do the same."

"So how do we get from here to there, Da?" Sean asked. He was eager to hear about the journey ahead. He had felt no discouragement in their travels thus far and looked forward to a new home in a new place. The weight of his fear and guilt had eased with every mile they put between themselves and Muldoon's. Sean could not remember when he had felt so carefree, and he welcomed the change.

"I'm sure enough about to tell ya," Thomas replied.

Everyone gave their full attention to Thomas as he laid out the plan as far ahead as he'd been able to arrange it. There were unanswered questions and more than a couple unknowns, but the greatest portion of the trip was taking shape, and it was time to give them the cold hard facts about the next four weeks.

"There are tryin' times ahead for us. The road from here to Carson City in the Utah Territory will be rough, dirty, and difficult. There are fellas north of here who used to make the long Butterfield run deliverin' mail. They tired of the terrible hardships of that life and are now runnin' folks willin' to pay for it along the Mormon Trail."

"And what is that, Tommy? This trail we'll be followin'?" Kathleen asked. "And how do ya know about it?"

"There was a poster at the docks that told all about it, and I spoke with a shopkeeper in town today who also gave me some information. Mormons are religious folks, in case ya weren't aware of it, and they travel in large groups westward to make new settlements for their people. They walk, mostly, which takes nye on a year to get from here to the Great Salt Lake. Their trail runs through Iowa and the Nebraska Territory along the great Platte River. It continues on along the open frontier and into the Utah Territory where the trail ends at Salt Lake City. There will be rivers and mountains to cross. It will be uncomfortable and will feel like a longer journey than it really is."

"A year!" Kathleen was on the verge of uncharacteristic hysteria. She knew she could not bear a life of dirt, danger, and hardship for a year.

"For the walkers, Katie, which is why we're hirin' a man to drive us there in his coach. Mind you, it will still be a good three weeks, maybe more, before we reach the end of that portion of our journey."

"'Tis better than a year and for that I am greatly relieved, but it's still such a long time, Tommy," Kathleen whispered.

"I know, love, but once we're there, we're there, and our new life can begin. We'll finally know somethin' better than what we've had these past many years. We suffered through The Hunger back home in Ireland, and we suffered through our wretched life in New York. Once this short journey is over, so will our sufferin' be," Thomas assured her. He reached over and pushed her auburn hair back from her face, kissing her lightly on the cheek. He turned to look at his children, and he asked them soundly, "Can I count on ya to be strong for your mam? I'll be askin' ya to be brave and to do your best not to complain. What say the Delaneys?" The children all agreed they could do those things in the weeks ahead.

"These men with their carriages, Tommy, are they here in this town?" Kathleen asked, still trying to piece the confusing puzzle together.

"They're up the river a ways. The man in town said we'll need to start by takin' a sixteen-hour trip north aboard a riverboat, give or take dependin' on the weather," Thomas paused and watched Sean's face light up. "Aye, Sean, we'll be aboard ship again and this time for a fair stretch of time. We leave early in the mornin' and should arrive at a place called Nauvoo in the middle of the night. The shopkeeper assured me we could find lodgin' there 'til we locate a carriage man."

"And what awaits us once we finally reach Salt Lake City?" Kathleen asked. It was a lot to take in and nearly too much to think about, but she wanted to know what to expect.

"I imagine another carriage can be hired there to take us the rest of the way. Miners are makin' their way west every day, so there's little chance of bein' stranded where we don't want to be." Thomas hadn't worked out that part of the journey, but he was certain that the way was well-traveled by those with similar dreams. Upon arrival he would find the answers and get his family to Carson City or somewhere near it.

"Now that our bellies are full and our questions have answers, we need to try to get some sleep. It's early in the evenin', I know, but we need to try. We're gonna be up very early and headin' back to the dock to board the *James McDaniel* goin' north up the Mississippi. If ya find ya can't sleep, at least lay quietly and rest."

Everyone settled into bed and did their best to sleep. The younger three children nodded off within half an hour. Kathleen followed shortly behind, though Thomas lay next to her well into the night worried that he might oversleep, worried that the journey ahead would be too much for his family to bear, and worried that the life ahead would offer no better existence than where they had come from. He thought it was unlikely, but the weight of putting his family through weeks of hardship for nothing more than they left behind on Montgomery Street was a prospect that troubled him greatly. Sean also lay awake for hours. His thoughts were focused on the riverboat, and he marveled at feeling like a child much younger than himself for the excitement he could not quell. He thought too about the great sacrifice his family was making, and the greater one ahead, and how it was almost entirely because of his poor choices. A wave of guilt swept over him, and he vowed to be the support they would need, the help Thomas would appreciate, and the comfort and care his siblings would be demanding from two concerned and weary parents. He would stand in their stead, and he would ease some of their burden on the journey west. It was a small thing he could do, and though it would not eradicate the guilt he carried with him, it would appease it until he was able to move past it.

Morning came before Thomas and Sean were ready to greet it, though Sean was eager to start the day and the journey upriver. Thomas and Kathleen set about getting the children ready and their few items packed back into their sacks. Thomas took a few minutes to remove the money stored in the bottom of his sack. He pulled a chair over into the far corner of the room with his back turned to the activity behind him and estimated what they would need for the next twenty-four hours. He took twenty dollars from the stash and put it in his pocket to cover the riverboat fare, and food and lodging in Nauvoo. As he returned the money to the bottom of the sack he saw the gun safely wrapped in his other shirt. He was uncomfortable with the weapon traveling with them, so close to curious little hands, but he knew that the journey to their destination would traverse lands not governed by law enforcement and that the need for protection was great.

The Delaneys left the hotel at a quarter past six. There was an omnibus outside the hotel loading passengers who were heading to the same place as the Delaneys were. It was a quick trip to the docks, and when their fares were purchased they boarded the *James McDaniel* for the trip to Nauvoo. They were shown to a small sleeping cabin where they could lie down on one of the two small beds inside. Thomas did not pay the extra cost for first class for he knew it would only subject his family to more disapproving stares and disparaging remarks. All along this journey he had felt the irony of having all the money they needed to travel in style, and the reality of bypassing those luxuries to protect them from embarrassment and ill-treatment. They would manage just fine taking turns in the small cabin if need be. They were instructed that they were free to wander around, sit and relax in designated passenger areas, and to be out on the deck if they needed fresh air. The dining room, however, was reserved for first class customers. Take-away food could be purchased for a price at the refreshment window near the galley.

For Sean, the riverboat was the best part of their journey so far. He struck up a conversation with a young Irish crewman who worked below deck as an apprentice, and Sean shared his fascination with life on the water. James Keene was able to sneak Sean below for a look at the inner workings of the great ship, and it ignited his spark of curiosity into a flame. He couldn't say how or when, but Sean knew he was destined for this life, and that one day it would be his.

Kathleen napped with Maeve, both crammed onto one of the small beds while Sorley slept on the other. Eamon walked with his father and they talked of new beginnings, of schools and opportunities for education. Eamon shared an interest in writing stories and the desire to further his education. Thomas felt pride in his son's aspirations, and he was convinced Eamon would be the one to leave the life of labor and physical work behind. He promised his son that he would do everything in his power to make it happen.

The *James McDaniel* pulled into the dock at Nauvoo around midnight. The Delaneys hailed a carriage waiting nearby, and Thomas asked about suitable lodging that might still be open and taking patrons in the middle of the night. Nauvoo was a much smaller town than St. Louis, and Thomas assumed that the opportunities for late-night lodging would be limited.

"I can take you to Rufus Abbott's place. He's long gone out to Salt Lake, but his sister Deborah operates a boarding house there. It's a fine place he built only to leave it to her and head west with his fellow believers. She's a spinster and she runs a tight ship, but the place is clean and comfortable. Sound all right to you?"

"Sounds fine, yes. We're just here until we can find us a carriage driver to take us to the same place Mr. Abbott has gone," Thomas replied.

"Joining the exodus, are you?" the man asked. "If you've got the coin I know a man."

"I've got the coin. Where can I meet the man ya speak of?" Thomas asked.

"I'll pick you up outside the Abbott place tomorrow morning at nine and take you to meet him. He returned from Salt Lake City eight or ten days ago and is looking to make one more run before fall arrives. The weather up north here isn't as forgiving as the Oxbow Route down south where they were running the mail for Butterfield."

The man pulled his carriage up in front of the Abbott home and stepped down. He walked to the door and rapped twice. It was five minutes or more before the door was opened by an elderly woman in a nightgown, holding a lantern and looking a bit disgruntled by the late-night interruption.

"Hello, William, what can I do for you?" she asked. The two obviously knew one another, and Thomas assumed William had delivered other boarders to Miss Abbott in the past.

"I've got a family here needs boarding for a day or two, Miss Abbott," the man replied politely.

The woman looked around him at the family of six. Four children looked like more trouble than it would be worth, but she agreed and invited the family inside. They looked to be a ragged bunch, but Miss Abbott tried not to judge others lest she be judged. She showed them upstairs to a spacious room with two large beds and a smaller one against the wall near the door.

"Will this do?" she asked.

"It will do nicely, Miss Abbot," Kathleen said. "I apologize for interruptin' ya so late into the evenin'."

"It's nothing unusual, young lady. The riverboats deliver people to Nauvoo at all hours of the day and night, and those of us who operate hotels and boarding houses are accustomed to the midnight knock on our door. It's a dollar per night for the room and that includes breakfast and supper."

"'Tis fair enough," Thomas replied. "Can I pay you in the mornin'?"

"Of course," Miss Abbott replied. "Now if it's all the same to you, I'll bid you a good night and return to my bed."

Kathleen designated Eamon and Sorley to share a bed, Maeve would sleep with her parents in the other big bed, and Sean could have the smaller bed to himself. They were exhausted, and no one grumbled over Thomas's instructions to get to bed and get some sleep. They fell into the soft beds without hesitation and drifted off into the peaceful slumber that beckoned them, their exhaustion fueled by long days of travel, daily uncertainties, and the feeling of running hard with the devil at their heels. Dreams escaped them all as they surrendered to the deep realm of restorative sleep. The morning would bring new hope, new direction, and the stitching together of Thomas's vision. He was the last to surrender to the sleep he badly needed. As he drifted off, his mind recounted the reasons they had come this far, and he held tightly to the hope that was now rekindled after years of painful disappointment. He yearned for the day when he could dress Kathleen in fine clothes and provide food and a comfortable place to call home. He wanted them to walk about with their chins up, no longer shamed by their appearance and the lowly place where life had cast them. And he hoped with all his aching heart that the dream they sought as they sailed away from Queenstown, County Cork, nine years ago had not been in vain. There was still time for America to prove herself to the Delaneys, to offer them the bountiful opportunity they had heard about, and to give them reason to believe in the hope of prosperity that had brought them to her shores.

Part Two

Western Utah Territory

Early September 1859

CHAPTER TWENTY-TWO

Kathleen sat on the porch of the little two-story brick home in Chinatown with the late summer breeze blowing softly across her face. The warm Washoe Zephyr blew every afternoon like clockwork, but she had learned to welcome it in the heat of the high desert summer. Maeve and Sorley were playing in front of the house and around beside it, and Sean had gone off for a walk. Kathleen no longer feared his leaving. She encouraged him to explore the area now that they were so far removed from crime and danger. The sweet smell of sage wafted by on the wind, and she marveled at how quickly she had adapted to the barren yet beautiful part of the country they now called home.

Kathleen leaned back against the corner post and closed her eyes. In the peace and serenity that now surrounded her, it was easy to allow the memory of their journey west to fade into that place where insignificant and unwelcome memories are stored. Thomas had been right. It had been difficult beyond imagining but also well worth the four-and-a-half weeks of discomfort they had experienced. The trip from Nauvoo, Illinois to Salt Lake had taken twenty-four days. They spent many nights doing their best to sleep in the coach while their driver, Azariah Jessup, traded off the reins with his newly hired partner. They traveled over the rutted dirt roads of the Mormon Trail and through the shallowest parts of rivers and streams, at times traveling much faster than safety would dictate. There had been toll bridges to cross, insufficient food and supplies along much of the journey, and only an occasional stopover where they enjoyed a bed and a meal. They had stopped at places whose names now blurred together in Kathleen's memory—Garden Grove Settlement, Grand Encampment, Fort Kearney, Fort Laramie, Devil's Gate and Fort Bridger. Some folks were more welcoming than others, but the coaches that traversed the Mormon Trail were always looked upon with scorn by those who traveled on foot pulling their handcarts. Thomas reminded Kathleen that scorn was not a new burden for the Delaneys to bear and she did her best to ignore the whispers and disapproving glances.

Azariah Jessup was a talkative fellow who dominated the conversation at every stop. He recounted his travels with the Butterfield Mail Service and the record-setting route they had mastered. He talked of encounters with the native people who lived along the southern trail from St. Louis to San Francisco, and in one particular conversation he revealed some interesting news to the Delaneys. Just a month before the Delaneys had headed west, there was a monumental discovery in the Utah Territory. Prospectors had discovered a mother lode of silver at the base of Mt. Davidson in the Virginia Range close to where the Delaneys were heading. There was speculation that this discovery might be the largest deposit of silver the world had ever seen. Azariah anticipated an impending rush of folks wanting to go west and an endless opportunity to transport them. Times were about to get interesting, and he would be ready to cash in on the rush to riches. He might have to wait until spring due to the harsh winters of the north, but there was always the option to head south and make use of the Oxbow Route during the winter months. He would pay close attention to what other drivers were doing and make a decision soon.

Thomas had hired a local coach in Salt Lake City for the last leg of their journey. They traveled along the newly improved Simpson's Route, due west through a series of mountain passes to their destination just east of Carson City. It had been ten days of grueling coach travel through the passes. As miserable as it seemed, their driver expressed his gratitude for the trailblazing efforts of Captain Howard Egan who had discovered the passes four years earlier. It had cut travel time from Salt Lake to Carson City by two weeks. Kathleen and the children could not imagine another two weeks of suffocating coach travel through the alternating tortures of dry hot deserts and rugged mountains in the mid-August heat. They were all grateful for Captain Egan's contribution to westward travel.

Once in Chinatown, Thomas had not found John O'Riley. The town itself had seemed less a hub of activity than Thomas had expected. In speaking with some of the townsfolk, Thomas discovered that many of the men from town had gone to the tent city up the hill. The discovery of the silver lode Azariah Jessup had told them about had left the little town nearly abandoned. The population now consisted of some out-of-work Chinese laborers, a rancher or two, a few families who were settled in and didn't want to leave, a market, a livery, and a few miners' families like the Delaneys. Thomas had leased a vacant home, fully furnished, from the banker who was overseeing it and had gotten Kathleen and the children settled with everything they would need. Once his family's safety and well-being were secured, Thomas announced that he was going in search of John and in search of profitable work. Much to Kathleen's dismay, Thomas would relocate to the tent city where miners and other laborers were living, caught up in the unprecedented boom and desperately hoping for their share of the riches.

"We will miss you terribly, my love," she had told him. She knew she could never convince him to remain behind with them. He had a dream, a mission to fulfill, and promises to keep, and for that she respected Thomas more than he knew.

"'Tis only for a time, Katie. We've this nice house here for you and the children, I've paid the rent ahead till spring, and I'll be back then to decide what we'll do after that." He had left her with nearly all the money that remained knowing he would need little and would earn more shortly. He promised to try and venture back down to them at Christmastime, but there was no guarantee that he could keep that promise because of the unpredictable weather in the mountains surrounding them.

For now, as Sorley and Maeve engaged in a sword fight with sticks, and Eamon sat reading a new book purchased at the little store in town, Kathleen was overwhelmed with contentment. She knew fall would arrive shortly with winter right behind, and there would be little to do but wait for Thomas to return. It would be a long season with him absent from their table. She would pray daily for his safekeeping and would look forward to spring.

"Mam, what's this word?" Eamon's voice behind her jostled her back to the present. He was reading *The Gorilla Hunters* by R.M. Ballantyne and much of it was advanced for his reading level.

"Let's see," said Kathleen, taking the book and reading the passage aloud. "O, Peterkin, said I, in a tone of remonstrance." She read it in a flowery voice, haughty and so unlike herself that Eamon couldn't help but laugh.

"Remonstrance. Goodness, that is a big one," Kathleen added. "If I am correct, it is akin to a strong displeasure. It might be a good idea to see if we could locate one of Mr. Webster's dictionaries, yes?"

"That would be grand, Mam. I could learn all sorts of new and interesting words and go about sounding like a well-educated jackeen!" Eamon stood up, tucked the book under his arm, and waddled about on the porch muttering incoherently.

Kathleen laughed at Eamon's parading around like a character one might see in the societal circles they had never known. His love of words and his grand imagination might just lead him to a life authoring tales for others to enjoy. She wanted it desperately for her quiet and contemplative son. Kathleen wanted to see all of her children realize their hopes and dreams and to be allowed to passionately pursue whatever brought them joy. She hoped that this fresh start was indeed the opening chapter of their new story. Her heart swelled with gratitude for Thomas's gritty determination and his tireless dedication to his family. He had endured the prejudice, the scorn, the shame, the humiliation, and the hopelessness of the past nine years with little complaint and no surrender. He had stood in the face of unending defeat and weathered it far longer than most men might have. She would be strong enough to carry the burden of parenting their children alone until they could all be together again. It was by far the very least she could do.

The warmth of late summer carried over into fall and Kathleen was both surprised by it and pleased with it.

She and the children enjoyed regular walks from their house to the Carson River. Sean would sit for hours and watch the water flow past. He took to drawing with pencil, sketching the swirling patterns and curves of the water as it meandered over and around the rocks. Kathleen enjoyed the area and the lingering good weather, though her days felt long without Thomas's company. It was only ten miles that separated Chinatown and Virginia City, but it seemed a far greater expanse between them. She was certain Thomas was working seven days a week, and if they gave him a day off it would be a tedious prospect to try and make the trip down the hill and back up again in one day. He was likely exhausted from the difficult and dangerous work in the silver mines, and she worried about him constantly.

Sorley was getting along nicely, and Kathleen noticed that he rarely used his walking stick. He did have a slight limp but not profound enough to be a distraction. He was a happy child and he and Maeve got along well. Maeve would turn six on the eighth of October, and Kathleen knew the celebration would be difficult for Maeve without her father there to share it. Theirs was a close bond, and Maeve was still young enough to need the sense of safety and security that her father gave her.

"Maeve, dear," Kathleen addressed her daughter as she came downstairs for breakfast one late September morning. "You know 'tis nearly October and there'll be a special day comin.'"

"Aye, Mam, I know." Maeve's voice was heavy with sadness.

"Sweet girl, come here," Kathleen said as she held out her arms. Maeve walked into Kathleen's embrace and allowed a few tears to escape the corners of her eyes. "Sure, and I know you're missin' your da as I am too. We need to be strong for him while he works so hard for us, yes? It would cause him worry and grief to know ya had a sorrowful birthday without him."

"I will try to enjoy it," Maeve said quietly. She was silent for a moment but perked up as a plan began to take shape. "Maybe Li can take us in his wagon to a new picnic spot farther down the river. We could make a fine birthday meal and a cake for me!"

Li was an older Chinese man who lived two houses down the road. He often stopped by to see if there was anything Kathleen or the children needed. He had traveled west to California nine years ago with the same hopes and dreams held by thousands of other prospectors. It wasn't long before Li discovered that the anti-immigrant bias was alive and well out west, and that the high taxes imposed on the immigrant miners would make it difficult to find any real success in mining. Like hundreds of other Chinese immigrants in the area, Li was hired to help build canals and flumes for the mining companies. And like them, he had come to Chinatown from Hangtown, California hoping that things would be different, but it was much the same. Now he earned a meager income by transporting goods and people between Carson City and Chinatown with his horse and wagon. Many times, though, he did so as an act of kindness and expected nothing in return. Li had learned English by listening attentively to the overseers and English-speaking prospectors in California who spoke over him. He was but another invisible immigrant worth their weight in labor but holding little value beyond that.

"You know, I am certain we can hire him for the afternoon. We shall invite him to join our picnic to repay a bit of the kindness he has shown us," Kathleen said. "And what would you be wantin' for this birthday meal?"

"I don't know," Maeve replied. "Maybe some bread, and ham, and cheese to slice. We could make sandwiches! Yes, and maybe some vegetable pickles to go along with it? And, of course, a magnificent cake."

"We shall see what we can do. I will visit McGurty's Market and see about the pickles, but no promises on that. Sandwiches and cake, for certain!" Kathleen knew that food depended solely on whatever was transported over from California. At times there was an abundance and other times a scarcity, but they had not gone hungry a day since arriving. Life seemed too good to be true which worried Kathleen, though she would never admit it. *No sense in inviting doom to the doorstep*, her mother would say.

A plan in place, Maeve's spirits brightened, and the sadness over her father's absence subsided. In the days ahead Kathleen would work hard to finish the birthday dress she had been sewing in the evenings after the children were in bed. The dress and the picnic outdoors along the river would be a much finer birthday than any they had celebrated back in New York.

On a windy October morning four days before Maeve's birthday, Kathleen visited McGurty's Market to see if they had some of what Maeve had requested. She was happy to find some pickled beans to go along with their sandwiches. The larder at home had plenty of ingredients for the cake, but Kathleen wanted to make something decadent. She wandered around the little market and discovered one jar of dewberries canned in a thick syrup. *That will do nicely*, she thought. She placed a dozen eggs in the little basket she brought from home and walked up to the counter. Mr. McGurty smiled at the pretty Irish lass who had recently moved to their town.

"Good morning, Mrs. Delaney!" he greeted her. "It's a might windy out there this mornin', is it not?"

"'Tis that, but warm enough," Kathleen replied.

"We should see warm days for a couple more weeks, and then fall will arrive overnight as it always does in these parts. Are you all well?" He knew that Mr. Delaney had gone up the hill to work the mines and left his pretty wife behind. It was a risk leaving her alone with the children, but it would have been a far greater one to take them along with him to the tent city. There was an unruly and unscrupulous lifestyle to be found where men gathered in the name of greed and where that greed became their conscience.

"We are well, and thanks for askin', Mr. McGurty. I'm thinkin' this is all I'm needin' for now," Kathleen offered. She wanted to move the conversation along. Mr. McGurty seemed nice enough, but something about him always made her uneasy.

"Well, then, it looks like a dollar and fifty cents."

"So much!"

"Unfortunately, the price of food has risen with the number of fortune-seekers who've arrived here, though it seems to be leveling off some now," Mr. McGurty said. Kathleen nodded and thanked him. She placed the jar of beans in the basket with the eggs, picked up the jar of dewberries with her other hand, and headed toward the door.

"You need some help getting that home?" His voice took on a slightly menacing tone, and Kathleen told herself not to return to the market without the company of Sean or the other children.

"I've got it, Mr. McGurty, thanks again," she answered as she scurried out the door.

It was a three-minute walk to Li's house, and upon arriving Kathleen saw his wagon and knew she would find him home. She set the berries on the porch near the door and knocked. She could hear footsteps drawing near, and as the door opened she was greeted with Li Qiang's friendly smile.

"Mrs. Delaney, it is good to see you! Can I help you with something?"

"Good morning, Li," Kathleen said. "This Saturday is Maeve's sixth birthday. She would like to find a new place for a picnic, maybe farther down the river than we usually venture. She asked if ya might know a spot, and if ya could take us in your wagon."

"I do, yes, Mrs. Delaney, and it would be my honor to take your family there."

"We can pay ya for your trouble, and we'd like for ya to join us for sandwiches and some cake after." Kathleen smiled her radiant smile and Li Qiang wondered how he or anyone else could deny her anything.

"I do not think it would be wise for me to join your picnic, but I can most certainly drive you there."

Kathleen knew about proprieties and reputations and the biases that existed between races and nationalities. She knew it more than most folks, and for that reason she was determined to include him once they arrived. They made plans for Li to pick them up on Saturday at eleven o'clock, and Kathleen retrieved her berries and headed home. She found Maeve and Sorley leaping from the top step of the porch to see who could jump the furthest. They paid little attention to her as she walked past, and she was glad that Maeve didn't notice the items she was carrying home from the market. She hurried inside and put the berries, the eggs, and the pickled beans in the larder.

"Where's your brother?" Kathleen asked Eamon who was still working on the monumental task of finishing *The Gorilla Hunters*.

"Upstairs," he muttered.

Kathleen smiled at Eamon's unwillingness to be torn away from his story. She went upstairs to check on Sean and to let him know the plan for Saturday. Sean had a way of wandering, no different from his life in New York in that respect, and yet different in so many important ways. Wandering around the area now meant learning about the natural environment, new trees and plants, animals in their native environs rather than caged on a city street or left to wander through mounds of garbage. Kathleen always allowed it. It was good for him, and she thought it beneficial in helping him to recover from the sorry life he had experienced before they left New York. This weekend, though, he would need to be present for Maeve's special day, especially since her father could not be.

Sean did not know that Kathleen had returned from the market and did not expect her to walk in and find him on the bed counting his stash of money. She stopped at stared, a look of confusion and shock on her face.

"Mam, 'tis what I brought with me from my shameful life back home," he offered. "I'm just seein' what's here, and I'm willin' to give it to ya to help out until Da comes home."

"We've plenty enough to get by until then, Son," Kathleen replied. "What's yours is yours, though I don't know what you'd be plannin' on doin' with it."

"I don't know either, Mam. There's part of me that feels bad for spendin' even a penny of it knowin' how it came to me. But then it seems a shame for it to be tucked away and never used, ya know?"

"I see your point, Son, and it'll be for you to decide what ya do with it. For now, we can hide it away somewhere safe. You'll know when to use it and what for." Kathleen hesitated, trying to recall why she had come into Sean's room in the first place. "Ah, I came to tell ya that we'll be havin' a birthday picnic for Maeve on Saturday, and I'll need ya to come along. Li will pick us up at eleven o'clock and will be takin' us to a new spot along the river. It's what your sister asked for."

"Sure and I wouldn't miss it!"

"Maeve asked only for the picnic, sandwiches and a cake. She's missin' her da somethin' terrible," Kathleen's voice faded. Sean knew she was missing Thomas too.

"Hopefully he'll make it home for Christmas, Mam, 'tis only three months off."

"True enough," Kathleen agreed, though she doubted it would happen.

Early October was blessed with the lingering warmth of late summer, and it lent a softness to the slow passing of time. The golden glow of early evening eased the harsh appearance of the surrounding mountains, dry from the summer's heat and barren of vegetation so late in the season. Kathleen finished Maeve's birthday dress, wrapped it neatly in a piece of matching leftover fabric, and tied it with string.

Saturday morning brought excitement to the Delaneys' home. Kathleen sent Maeve and Sorley outdoors, and Sean followed with his sketchpad. He sat on the porch and worked on a drawing of the massive cottonwood tree that stood across the dirt road from their house. Sean had noticed the bare gnarled branches once the leaves had fallen, and he was determined to sketch it. Kathleen busied herself with frosting the cake she had made the night before and decorating the top with circles of dewberries. It was lovely when finished, and she was proud of her handiwork. She set about carving the ham and making six sandwiches with ham and cheese just as Maeve had requested. She wrapped each of them in flour cloth and set them inside a large basket with a lid, along with the jar of pickled beans and a knife to cut the cake.

Li's wagon stopped in front of the house at precisely eleven o'clock. The children greeted him warmly and helped their mother carry the birthday picnic items to the wagon. A quilt to sit on, the food basket, Maeve's gift, and Sean's sketch pad were all placed in the back of the wagon, and the children climbed in. Kathleen asked Li to wait a moment so she could get one last item from the kitchen. When she returned from the house, she was holding the magnificent cake with fluffy white frosting and rows of purple-black dewberries around the edge. Maeve's eyes widened, her face glowing with delight.

"Mam! 'Tis the most beautiful cake ever!" she called out. Kathleen smiled as she handed the cake to Li. She climbed up onto the bench seat next to Li and placed the cake in her lap. And they were off, traveling through the tiny town past McGurty's Market, down a narrow dirt road that followed alongside the Carson River. The mood was celebratory, and Kathleen felt a happiness that had been difficult to find these past weeks without Thomas.

About thirty minutes outside of town Li drew his cart to a stop near a lush grassy area next to the river. The riverbank was low and sloping allowing for easy access to the water. It was perfect. The children jumped from the cart leaving the picnic supplies behind. Kathleen laughed at their enthusiasm, and Li helped her put the quilt down and place the picnic items upon it. She sat down and watched her children play. They removed their shoes and stockings and played at the river's edge. Sean retrieved his sketchpad after noticing a large tree branch sticking up out of the water and appreciating the way the river caressed it as it flowed past. The younger three children engaged in a grand adventure that saw them all drenched before their hunger got the best of them. They left the water and sought the warm sunshine that flooded down onto their mother's quilt, and the boys gathered near the picnic basket. Maeve's eyes were fixed on the cake.

"Child, you'll wait till you've eaten proper food before havin' a piece of that birthday cake," Kathleen softly admonished. Maeve groaned quietly but was hungry enough to refrain from grumbling. She was eager to enjoy the ham and cheese sandwich, unwrapping it and taking a big bite as soon as Kathleen handed it to her, and she was delighted to see the jar of pickled beans. Mam had given her all she had asked for, and Maeve thought to herself that except for her father's absence the day could not have been any better.

"Li, I made one for you too," Kathleen offered. Li was standing a few feet away from their quilt, and Kathleen held the sandwich out to him.

"Oh, no, I cannot," he replied. "I thank you, Mrs. Delaney."

"Of course ya can, Li, come and join us," Kathleen insisted. The children chimed in and invited their friend to sit and eat with them. Li continued to hesitate until Maeve looked up at him and smiled.

"Please, Mr. Li?" Against his better judgment he relented. Everyone shared the pickled beans and ate every bite of the ham sandwiches. Eamon related the adventures of *The Gorilla Hunters* to everyone's rapt attention. The afternoon sun was directly above them, and Kathleen feared the cake's frosting might melt. She reached inside the basket and removed the knife, carefully wrapped in a towel, and pulled the cake closer to her.

"Can I possibly convince anyone to have a piece of this lonely cake? 'Tis sittin' here so patiently waitin' for someone's birthday celebration to begin." The children all raised their hands and Li smiled at their excitement. Kathleen cut generous pieces and placed them onto the squares of fabric the sandwiches had been wrapped in, handing one to everyone. She watched as everyone enjoyed the sweet messy confection. She thought that maybe she should have brought forks with her but knew they could wash their hands and faces in the river when they were done. Her mind wandered to another birthday celebration just three months ago on their last day in New York, and the fear of imminent danger that had caused them to flee. It seemed like eons ago. Kathleen felt the warm afternoon breeze moving softly through her hair and noticed how it caused the leaves of the nearby aspen trees, now yellow and gold, to quiver. She closed her eyes and let the peaceful sound of the rustling leaves calm her.

"Chinaman got no place eating with a white woman! Get your sorry ass off that quilt!" A vile angry voice jarred Kathleen from her serenity into a world she thought they had left behind forever. Hatred. Bigotry. Anger and violence. It could not be happening here. A large lumbering body charged across the quilt, one foot smashing the remaining cake, the other landing squarely against the side of Li's head. Two more men followed.

"No!" Kathleen screamed. "Stop it! Leave him alone!" She struggled to focus on what was happening as the violent encounter unfolded. Maeve was crying, the boys were yelling at the men, and Li was huddled in a ball on the ground as boots assaulted him from three different directions. Kathleen drew her gaze upward and recognized two of the men from town. They came and went between Carson City and Chinatown, and she knew them to be lumberjacks who worked in the forests up around Lake Bigler. The intruders continued to kick Li, hurling all sorts of hateful insults at him, and telling him to stay with his own kind. In a flash, Kathleen saw Sean's hand grab the knife from the quilt and lunge at one of the men.

"Sean, no!" she screamed.

Blood streamed from the large gash Sean inflicted on the arm of one of the lumberjacks. Sorley and Eamon were crying now too as all three of the younger children huddled close to their mother. The other lumberjack turned toward Sean who was still holding the knife tightly in his grip.

"You leave him alone!" Kathleen screamed at the man approaching Sean, standing to confront him herself. He turned toward her with an evil grin and she immediately saw her error in judgment. She was utterly defenseless against him. The man closed the distance between them, and Sean turned to run at him. A gunshot ripped through the river valley stopping everyone in their tracks.

"Leave her be! Let's go!" a man yelled from a nearby wagon. The lumberjack stared at Kathleen with dark intent, her fear making him even more dangerous. "NOW!" came the voice from the wagon. The three men wandered away leaving Li motionless on the ground, surrounded by the injured lumberjack's blood and more than a little of his own. Kathleen and Sean rushed to him, rolling him over carefully as he moaned in pain. Kathleen was thankful that he was conscious for she had no way to get him into his wagon if he could not walk for himself.

"Sean, get the towel I had wrapped around the knife and soak it in the river," Kathleen instructed. She turned her head for a moment while Sean headed to the river, and she saw the men climbing back into their wagon. She watched the driver turn the team around, and her fear turned to horror as she recognized the driver as Mr. McGurty. She was as sure as she could be that it was the store owner, and an immediate mental battle began to rage. She was unwilling to accept that he could have been involved in anything so ugly and so evil, but she could not deny what her eyes had seen.

"Mam!" Sean called out a second time, holding the towel out to his mother. Kathleen redirected herself to the task at hand and applied the cool wet towel to Li's injuries. His lip was split and bleeding, one eye was nearly swollen shut and was already starting to turn black and purple. He had multiple bruises and abrasions on his face and arms, and Kathleen guessed it would be the same beneath his clothing.

"Children," she called out with more composure than she felt. "Gather everything together and put it in the wagon. Get in and wait for Sean and I." She turned to Sean who stood helplessly by. "I'll be needin' ya to help me get Li to the wagon, and I'll need ya to drive us back, yes?" Sean nodded. He had watched the drivers of the omnibus back in New York, and he had a sense of what he needed to do, but he was still uneasy with the responsibility.

"I'll try, Mam, but I'm not entirely sure what to do," he said.

"I'm guessin' the horse will find its way back. It'll be fine, Son," she reassured him. *Please, God, let it be fine*, she prayed silently.

Sean and Kathleen helped Li to his feet. They each lifted one of his arms and placed it around their shoulders so they could support him as they slowly made their way to the wagon. When they got to the back of the wagon Sean placed Li's right foot into the metal stirrup used to step up and in. Li gave a mighty effort to grab hold of the side rail as Kathleen and Sean pushed him up from behind. Kathleen had a fleeting thought of the impropriety of where she placed her hands, but she reminded herself that the man's pain was far worse than any embarrassment she might suffer. Li climbed in slowly and laid down immediately. Maeve grabbed the quilt and placed it over Li for the ride home. Kathleen did not miss her daughter's selfless act of kindness even now as her birthday celebration lay in shambles like the beautiful dewberry cake, crushed and ruined.

Kathleen climbed up beside Sean, her hands shaking and tears flowing from her eyes unashamedly. This tragedy was her fault. Li's pain and suffering were because of her failure to put Li's best interest at the forefront of the day's celebration. She should have conceded to his polite declinations when she asked him to join their picnic rather than insisting he do so. And Maeve. Dear, sweet Maeve. Her sixth birthday would always be remembered as the day she saw hatred manifest itself right in front of her eyes. No frivolities accompanied them on the somber trip back to Li's house. Innocence had been shattered and broken that day, for even in the heart of the degradation of New York City Kathleen had shielded and protected her youngest three. And now, here, they had witnessed bigotry at its worst.

As the wagon passed McGurty's Kathleen could not bear to look, fearing she would see Mr. McGurty sneering as they went by. Sean pulled the wagon up in front of Li's house, and he and Kathleen got down and went around to the back. They helped Li get out and down to the ground. Li's brother, older and quite frail, came shuffling out the front door when he saw them helping Li toward the house. He did not speak English so Kathleen could only offer meaningless apologies. She was both sorrowful and ashamed. The three of them got Li into the house and settled onto his bed. His brother dismissed them with a wave of his hand, his concern obvious in his expression.

The Delaney household was quiet that night. Kathleen apologized to Maeve countless times for the unraveling of her special day. She apologized to the boys for them having to witness such cruelty and hatred, especially here in their new home where peace and safety were to be the promised reward for their difficult journey west. She apologized to Sean for his having to carry the burden of manhood in defending Li and fending off the attacker. Her heart cried out in regret, sorrow, and remorse for Li. He did not deserve the painful cruelty inflicted upon him today. She had let her guard down. She had trusted the hope that things were different here, and she had allowed herself to forget the ugly and inexplicable side of humanity that hated others for no reason save the color of their skin or the country where they were born.

Kathleen spent more time than usual at the children's bedsides that night. She asked Sorley and Eamon how they felt about what happened and gave them the opportunity to talk about it. Sorley was concerned for Li, and Eamon hoped Sean was okay after having to attack the lumberjack with the knife. Kathleen's heart swelled with pride at the compassion her boys displayed. They talked and they prayed for Li's injuries to heal quickly. When Kathleen entered Sean's bedroom, he was lying in bed staring at the ceiling. He reassured his mother that he had no regrets about defending Li with the knife, and Kathleen touted his bravery and how strong he was. His only concern was their new life, their new beginning, and the hatred that apparently existed everywhere. Kathleen brushed the dark hair off his forehead and he let her. She told him that somehow, despite the madness of world, things would get better. She promised him their lives would find more peace than battle, more joy than darkness. Kathleen wasn't sure how, though she did not voice it to him. She was fiercely determined to see it happen. For the sake of her family, for Li and everyone like him who suffered unwarranted cruelty, for all people, she pleaded with God quietly in the tortured shadows of her mind that it would be so.

When Kathleen entered Maeve's room, she found her sitting on the edge of her bed. Her heart broke for the monumental disappointment her daughter must be feeling.

"Maeve, dear, I'm so very sorry," she began.

"Aye, Mam, I know. 'Tis not your fault that those terrible men ruined our day and hurt poor Li. I'm not so very disappointed, just worried about our friend. Will he be all right, do ya think? Will those men find him and do this again?"

"Och, I wish I knew, dear girl. We shall say our prayers and ask the Holy Father to keep watch over him, yes?"

Maeve nodded and they prayed. After a very sincere amen from Maeve she stood to pull back the blankets on her bed. Kathleen noticed how small the nightgown looked and realized how much Maeve had grown in the past few months. It was then that she remembered the dress, the beautiful blue dress with petite pink roses printed on it.

"Maeve, did ya find your birthday gift when we picked up and left the picnic?"

"I don't recall, Mam, but I don't think so. I'm sorry, Mam ... so sorry." Her voice broke on the last apology, and Kathleen pulled her close. She stroked Maeve's auburn hair, so much like her own, and whispered reassurances to her as she cried. "Would ya like to sleep with me tonight?" she asked.

"Yes, please," Maeve sobbed. "I'm feelin' afraid tonight and wishin' Da were here with us."

"Me too, Maeve," Kathleen whispered. She picked up her daughter and carried her to her bedroom. They snuggled in close together and Kathleen hummed a tune softly beside her daughter until Maeve's slow rhythmic breathing signaled her surrender to the healing power of sleep. Kathleen was not far after.

CHAPTER TWENTY-THREE

The evenings were getting colder, and Thomas missed the warmth of Kathleen's body next to his. His nights were often filled with restless sleep and haunted dreams, his mind assaulted by images of burning bodies. Their screaming would awaken him from the nightmare of what he had done. He was conflicted day and night by the great sin he had committed and the blood on his hands. He hated the tormentor inside who never relented, who carved away at his self-worth, who cast guilt upon his shameful actions, and who lurked in the shadows of his memory constantly. In his own admission of guilt, however, there was a vindication that allowed for the smallest semblance of reprieve. Sow Madden and Beeny Cohen had committed unspeakable acts, and though Thomas had not witnessed them he knew it to be true. Their fate should not have rested in Thomas's hands for he was not judge or jury, and he knew that doling out judgment and condemnation would bring those very things down upon himself when he stood before the Creator. Yet he had to believe they deserved their fate. It was the best he could do to the quiet the battle within.

A sharp November wind blew through the canvas tent with little regard for the protection it should have offered the men inside. Thomas knew he should get up and get a cup of John's stout coffee and some beans before heading to work, but the warmth of his bedding kept him there longer than he intended. The promise of miners' shacks, nearly finished and available for the winter months, was all that kept him going.

"Tommy!" John's voice bellowed just outside the tent. "Get yer arse out here or we'll be late. I'm in no mood to listen to Carrington wailin' about how much we're costin' the company!"

Thomas crawled out of bed, pulled on his trousers, and put on his heavy wool coat. He stepped into his boots and walked out into the cold wind. John handed him a cup of coffee and a bowl of beans before kicking some dirt onto their campfire to extinguish the flame. Thomas ate hungrily and choked down John's terrible coffee. Even though Thomas knew his money was accumulating nicely, he wasn't sure how long he wanted to work in the mines. He would stay through the winter no matter the hardship and reassess his options in the spring. He worried every day about Kathleen and the children. Thomas knew he had left them with enough money to provide for their needs, but were they safe? Were they well? Were they lost there alone without him?

"Let's go, Delaney, the wagon's here," John called out. Thomas dumped the last of his coffee on the ground, threw the cup inside their tent, and ran to the wagon for the quick trip to the open pit where they had been extracting ore for weeks. The men used shovels and picks to dig ore from the ground. Tunnels were created to enable the miners to go deeper in the lode, but often the unstable rock and earth gave way and collapsed causing potentially deadly cave-ins. Thomas had seen the earth swallow more than one man since arriving in the Utah Territory, and he was ever watchful as he labored in the pit.

"Ya seem a bit melancholy, Tommy," John said as they worked side by side.

"Och, I'm missin' my Katie and the children somethin' fierce," Thomas admitted.

"I'm sorry for your heavy heart, brother. I think minin' is a lonely man's work. Lonely because he has no one, or lonely because he does." Thomas nodded. Indeed, it was. His current mood had begun when he missed Maeve's birthday, but he was hopeful and doubtful, all at the same time, that he might be home for Christmas.

The only banker in the rapidly growing community of Virginia City arrived in town once a week on payday, traveling up the hill from the bank in Carson City. Sheldon Lamberth had a makeshift shack where he carried out transactions for miners like Thomas who weren't interested in squandering their earnings away on liquor, cards, and women. Lamberth was holding Thomas's earnings, and Thomas had every intention of seeing how much he had saved before Christmas arrived. He would love nothing more than to return to Chinatown and spend a couple days with his family. To arrive with gifts in hand would make it all the merrier. The weather would be his master, either granting or denying his desire to travel down the hill. Late November was already cold and windy, and December would likely bring snow and even colder temperatures.

A commotion on the other side of the pit drew Thomas's attention away from his musing. As he turned toward the source of the noise, he could see men running with their shovels all heading to the same location.

"Cave-in!" John called out as he ran. Time was deadly, and the importance of alerting the other miners to the cave-in was of the utmost importance. Buried men would not live long beneath tons of rock and soil. Thomas ran, praying, grateful it had not been him and ashamed for thinking it.

The men worked for nearly two hours searching for the three poor souls believed to have been in the tunnel when it gave way. It was to no avail. The somber air surrounding the site was made heavier by an overseer's comment that there were greater losses to worry over than a couple of micks. Thomas bristled at the prejudice that still existed even twenty-four hundred miles from New York. He felt it. The Chinese workers who were hired to earn a meager income building trenches and mining structures felt it. The Native Americans who were enslaved, abused, and annihilated by white men encroaching on their lands felt it. The Jewish community, though smaller, felt it too. Thomas wondered at the hate that existed in the hearts of so many men. It seemed there was no escaping it.

There was a shutdown that followed the cave-in as the superintendent surveyed the situation and decided how and where to proceed. Thomas walked away from the pit hoping to find some solace on the rugged hillside nearby. The stiff wind carried just a hint of sage upon it, and the always-blue sky was streaked with wisps of sheer clouds. Thomas noticed four men standing near their wagon at the west side of the pit, looking down at the tent community below. They were unfamiliar to him, and as he wandered closer he could hear them discussing the construction of a proper town, of homes and saloons and churches and a general store or two. The men spoke of getting supplies by wagon train up the mountain from Carson City after those supplies were transported to Carson from the other side of the Sierra Nevada. They voiced a concern about the imminent need for those supplies and for enough men to be employed in the massive construction project.

"The difficulty we'll face," said a burly man with a checkered waistcoat and black jacket, "is drawing men away from the promise of bountiful wages in the mines."

"You're right, Butler, able-bodied men come west for gold and silver, not brick and lumber," another of the men agreed.

"Right, indeed," said the third man in the group. He shuffled his feet and kicked some dry soil in frustration. "Listen, men, there's money to be made here for all of us and many others—miners, builders, masons, painters, barkeepers, schoolteachers, and preachers. I'm thinking the preachers will be the busiest of the lot trying to save the souls of the harlots and hooligans!" The men all laughed but agreed with the assessment.

"You're correct, Will," said the man called Butler, "and I think if we keep in mind the business principle that an attractive wage will attract a workforce, we'll find men to help build this town."

Thomas argued with himself over the desire to interrupt a conversation he should not have been privy to, and to find out more about their venture. Seeming too eager could make him look like a fool, but passing by an opportunity like this just to protect his already-bruised ego would be a grave mistake, and he knew it. He cleared his throat and approached the men.

"Beggin' your pardon, gentlemen," he began. "I'm apologizin' for standin' too close and hearin' your dilemma, but this minin' life is not for a man with a lovely wife and four wee ones at home. I did my share of hammerin' nails in my younger years and would be beholdin' to ya if I could do so again. The name's Thomas Delaney." Thomas extended his hand and the men were congenial and polite much to Thomas's relief.

"Well, Mr. Delaney, it seems our serendipitous meeting here today might benefit us all. We're finalizing the legalities of our construction company and hope to be raising the rafters, so to speak, just after Christmas. Are you willing to work through the winter when the weather permits?" the man named Will asked him. He appeared to be in charge, and Thomas sensed a soundness to his character.

"Aye, I'll work whenever ya need it, sir," Thomas responded.

"William J. Piedmont," Will said, "but my friends call me Will." He shook Thomas's hand again and the other men introduced themselves. Bert Butler, Jacob Hemmel and John Parmalee, along with William Pierpont, comprised the newly formed VC Builders, Incorporated.

"Thomas," Will interjected, "can you be ready to start work on the 28th of December? We're signing our articles of incorporation in Salt Lake City on December 10th. After that, we will make arrangements for a large wagon train to begin transporting lumber and supplies from the port at San Francisco to Carson City and then up here to Virginia City. We have a man here name of Cadwallader Wynne, a Welshman, who we've taken on as a building supervisor. He lives in the little cabin just past the tent city." Will smiled and continued, "He's a character, but he comes well recommended for his carpentry skills. Had a hand in the boom at Hangtown a few years back."

"I'll be ready," Thomas answered. "Shall I be reportin' to him on the 28th, then?"

"Yes," Will answered. "We'll be putting him in charge of recruiting builders, masons, and the like, and we'll be hoping he finds enough strong men to get this town built! We will let him know that we've hired you so that he's expecting you after Christmas. Happy to have you aboard, Delaney!"

Thomas did not return to the mine. The land speculators got back in their wagon and offered Thomas a ride down to the tent city if that was where he was headed. It was exactly where he was headed, down to the tents and away from the mines. They arrived at the muddy, makeshift town and let Thomas off before heading back down to Carson City. He thanked them again as their wagon pulled away. He gathered up his meager belongings from the tent he shared with John O'Riley and tucked them into his sack. Thomas looked around the area and found a piece of torn canvas on the ground. He took a small piece of wood from their firepit, blackened from the morning's fire, and wrote *Gone Home* on the canvas. He laid the note on John's blanket and put a rock on top to hold it down, knowing that the ever-present afternoon wind would rip through the tent and take the note with it unless it was secured.

Thomas turned and left the tent without looking back. There were no regrets save a hint of guilt for leaving his friend there without him. He hoped John would be safe and well, and he determined to give him an explanation to his sudden disappearance when he returned after Christmas. Thomas started the long trek on foot down the hillside to Chinatown. There were always wagons coming and going and he was certain he could catch a ride with one of them. He walked for three hours or more before two wagons, empty and returning to Carson City for mining supplies, passed by him slowly. Before he could ask they offered. He jumped into the back of the nearest one and propped himself up in the corner behind the driver.

"Where ya headed, stranger?" the driver asked.

"Chinatown, if you're headed that way."

The driver nodded and assured Thomas that he could take him there before turning toward Carson City. The ride was bumpy and dusty, and the wind continued to blow, but Thomas felt impervious to it all. He lowered his chin, closed his eyes, and drifted off to sleep.

Disjointed fragments of his life peppered his dreams, carrying with them an array of emotions. He relived the joy of seeing Sean come into the world in their tiny cottage in County Cork. He felt the pain of losing so many to the Great Hunger and the misery aboard the ship headed for the shining beacon of hope across the ocean. Anger at the ill-treatment he and Kathleen had received upon arriving in America resurfaced and caused him to mutter as he slept, the driver wondering what memories haunted the man behind him. Thomas's mind drifted back to Ireland, to running across the vast green rolling hills with his brother Michael, taken later by the Hunger, and then back again to New York's dirty streets, their own hunger, and the trials of living in abject poverty. Without warning the dream thrust him into a burning room where he stood untouched by the raging inferno all around him, screams of burning men assaulting his ears, so real and so filled with pain that he awoke in a violent start.

"No!" he yelled as he awoke, sitting up straight, disoriented and confused. It took him a moment to realize where he was.

"You okay back there?" the driver called out.

"Aye, sorry, bad dreams," Thomas replied, embarrassed at his outburst.

"We're coming to the last curve in the road before we reach Chinatown. I'll let you off just outside of town and continue on to Carson, if that's okay with you," the driver said. "They're wanting lumber up at the mine by morning.

They'll be working on a way to shore up those tunnels so they don't cave in on any more of you fellas."

Thomas responded to the man, confirming the need for such safety measures. He offered a quiet whisper of gratitude to God that he had met the land developers and now had a better future ahead of him. The driver stopped just around the last bend, and Thomas gathered up his things and thanked him for the ride. The wagon turned toward Carson City, and Thomas turned toward home. It felt good to think about a place called home that was not overrun with starving immigrants and the plethora of rats that ate better than they did. He looked forward to living, for a time, with his family in a home they would only have dreamed about had they stayed in New York and tried to survive the ravages of poverty. He revisited his brush with Providence today. It was surely divine intervention that had given him a way out of the mines. He could still provide for Kathleen and the children but would be doing something he enjoyed without the daily risk to life and limb that the mines presented. If he were correct, and he was certain that he was, Kathleen would be as happy about his new opportunity as he was.

As the dirt road led him into the little town Thomas whistled a tune. He barely noticed the brisk wind rushing past him. His stomach wrenched in the familiar response to hunger, and yet his only thought was getting to see his beautiful Katie and the faces of his children. Everything else faded into insignificance. Thomas passed by five houses, each looking quite similar to the one before it, probably built by the same builder like so many towns when they're first established. Like Virginia City would be by his own hand. He thought about being part of the founding of a town, of watching his handiwork create a community with homes, stores, churches, and schools. He felt a rush of optimism at the thought of having a regular job where he might be treated with a measure of respect. Thomas never minded working and providing for his family. It was the demoralizing encounters with prejudiced hiring men on the docks of New York, and working in the mines and wondering if each day would be his last, that caused him to be weary of the burden of gainful employment. This new opportunity might be his earthly reward, and Thomas dared to let himself hope that it was.

The sixth house on the dirt road through town was the current home of the Delaney family. Thomas's heart tumbled in his chest as he spotted Eamon sitting in a chair on the porch, bundled up in a quilt with his face in a book. He had likely sought the quiet surroundings of a day too cold to draw the other children outdoors. Thomas was whistling the Delaney favorite, *Reilly's Daughter*, and he watched as Eamon slowly lowered his book and peered out over the top of it refusing to believe what his heart hoped for.

"Da!" he called out, his voice breaking. "Da's home!" He threw his book aside and ran down the steps to the street in front of the house. Thomas dropped his things and swept Eamon up in a tight embrace. He watched the door of the house fly open and the other children running toward him. Maeve leaped up into her father's arms and held so tightly around his neck that Thomas found it difficult to breathe, but he refused to loosen her grip. Sorley's arms were around Thomas's waist, and as Sean approached Thomas took one arm from Maeve and pulled Sean close. Overwhelmed with love for his children, there was no way for Thomas to prevent himself from weeping. Through the blurred distance he could see the shape of Kathleen standing on the porch, hand over her mouth.

"Here, children, let me go see your Mam and give her a proper greeting!" The children laughed, for they knew Thomas meant to shower his wife with kisses. They ran back to the porch, Thomas following behind them. Sorley took his mother's hand and led her down the steps toward Thomas. She ran the last few steps and threw herself against Thomas with such force that they tumbled over onto the ground. The children laughed and soon the entire Delaney clan was piled on top of one another. When they stood and noticed the condition of their clothes covered in dirt and tiny sticks and brown leaves the laughter returned.

"Tommy, I've missed you so!" Kathleen said, her voice shaking with emotion.

"As I have you, Mo Chuisle, Mo Chroí," he said, kissing her again.

"But why are ya here? Have they let ya go? Are ya hurt?" Kathleen stepped back and inspected Thomas from head to toe. Everything looked intact though quite filthy.

"I'm a fine specimen, am I not?" Thomas paraded around the yard in exaggerated vanity. The children laughed, overwhelmed with joy that their father was back with them.

"You're covered in dirt from head to toe! We'll make use of the hip bath in the back room. I'll start the water heatin' on the stove, and we'll have ya cleaned up soon enough!"

They all went back into the house, arms and hands interlocking. Kathleen put two large pots of water on the woodstove in the kitchen, and Thomas related his story as the children gathered around. He told them of the long arduous hours in the pit mine, the dangers, the cave-ins, and the prejudice that still existed against the Irish, the Chinese, and the native people who were nothing more than slaves forced to work for the mining companies. He told of the cave-in just that morning, of losing three more good men to the ravenous belly of the earth, and of the sadness that caused him to walk away from the mines to clear his head. When Thomas told them about his chance encounter with the men from the building company and how they had offered him steady employment and a way out of the mines their faces lit up.

"Oh, Tommy, 'tis a miracle! I've been so worried about ya day and night, and now to know you'll not have to return to the mines is what I've been prayin' for. What will ya be doin'?"

"I'll be helpin' build the town, Katie. Homes, saloons, stores, churches, a jail, whatever it is they're needin'! I start directly after Christmas," he finished with a smile.

"You'll be home for Christmas!" Kathleen nearly shouted. The children celebrated and Thomas laughed at their enthusiasm.

"Ya missed your ol' da that much, did ya?"

"Aye, Da," Maeve replied, her voice breaking and tears running down her cheeks.

"Aw, Stóirín, come here," Thomas said. He lifted her up and held her close, touched by her tender heart. He wiped tears from his own eyes and continued. "We shall have a fine few weeks together before I head back up the mountain, yes?" Maeve nodded and Kathleen agreed. "If things go well," Thomas added, "I hope to build us a home of our own in Virginia City where we can be together every day."

"Is it a fit place for a family, Tommy?" Kathleen asked. She knew of the rough nature of mining settlements and the unsavory characters who frequented them.

"Not now, Katie, no, 'tis not," he answered. "But when we get the town built, when we have proper churches and shops and homes and a jail to house the hooligans, we'll have a fit place for a family to live. Can ya bear with me while I help make that happen, my love?"

"Aye, Thomas Michael Delaney, I can bear with ya through all things," she answered.

CHAPTER TWENTY-FOUR

"This has me worried, Katie," Thomas said after hearing about the incident with Li and the men from town. "I will not tell ya to end your friendship with Li, for that would be behavin' no different than those who did this. I'm only concerned that your friendship with him might cause you or the children to be harmed. However, I cannot see a way around leavin' ya here while I go back up the mountain to work."

Kathleen had been forced to tell Thomas about the incident one Sunday afternoon in early December. Maeve had asked if they could take some of their leftover Mary Washington Cake to Li. Kathleen stiffened at the mention of Li's name and fretted over the subsequent conversation between Maeve and her father. She would never have asked Maeve to lie about it, but she had hoped the conversation would not come up. Now, after hearing about the terrifying attack from his young daughter's point of view, Thomas had one more thing to worry over. And as worried as he was, he was honest enough with himself to recognize that it was anger that was his immediate and strongest emotion. Having to accept that there was no escape from hatred was a difficult reality, and it was something he had done reluctantly, but knowing that these men had carried out that hatred directly in front of his innocent children, endangering them in the scuffle, made his Irish blood boil. He kept a calm façade as he continued his conversation with Kathleen, but in his mind he knew that resolution would come, and it would be fueled by his anger and his fierce love for his family.

"Tommy, I have looked in on Li and have taken soup and bread to him more than once since the attack. No one has bothered us over it," she reassured him.

"Sure and that's fine but how will I know you're safe? And Li, who's to watch over him as well? I need to think on this."

"I'm sorry to worry ya so," Kathleen apologized. "Li has been a good friend and always stops by to see if we need anything. I am heartbroken over his pain." Her voice broke on her last words as her guilt returned. Thomas loved her intensely in that moment for her compassion and for her unconditional acceptance of others who, to many people, existed only to serve and to be subservient. He stood from the chair at the kitchen table and held her close. Why was it that so many people seemed incapable of compassion and kindness? Why couldn't people support and encourage one another instead of tearing them down? That kind of love and acceptance came naturally to people like Kathleen. Perhaps, he thought, compassion is most often found in those who have suffered at the hands of their oppressor. They seemed to possess a better understanding of mercy and grace. It *must be so*, he thought to himself.

Thomas decided to visit Li and also to pay a warning visit to McGurty. He kept these plans from Kathleen, but he could not return to Virginia City after Christmas until he addressed the issue. For now, he would treasure every moment at home with her and with the children. He listened intently to Eamon recounting the exciting adventures he had read about in *The Gorilla Hunters*. He spent time with Sean, impressed by his sketches and supportive of his fascination with the river. Sean spoke of his dream to become a riverboat pilot and was encouraged by his father's positive input. He would have expected something quite the opposite.

Sorley and Maeve recounted their adventures along the river, omitting the sad events on Maeve's birthday, and all the things they had discovered since moving to Chinatown. They laughed as they told their father about the quail who scurry across their path rather than using the wings God had given them, and they shared their excitement at having seen a small herd of wild horses on the foothills just outside of town. They spoke of their ongoing contest to see who could be the first to snatch a lizard from a rock, and of being frustrated by the lightning-quick speed of the little fence lizards. Li had told them that the lizards would sleep until the weather warmed, and the children were disappointed that they would have to wait until spring to begin their pursuits again. The giant cottonwood tree across the street had become the source of much of their playtime, and Thomas suggested he could easily attach a swing to the large low branch he had noticed.

Each day he gave his full attention to every conversation. They were treasured and stored away for the days ahead when the memories would be all he had. He hoped that these joyous times would push aside the guilt and pain that would once again torment his sleep after he returned to Virginia City. He had not had a nightmare since being back with his family, but loneliness and worry would likely cause them to resurface.

As Christmas neared, Kathleen busied herself with baking and secret projects that kept her sequestered in her bedroom much more than usual. Thomas took the opportunity to attend to his own business on one of those days. He put on his coat, kissed Kathleen's cheek, and told her he was going for a walk to clear his head and plan for the days ahead. That he was now just two weeks away from leaving again was never discussed, for none of them wanted to ruin the perfect days with sadness. The children were busy with Christmas activities of their own. Thomas had found a small pine tree near the river and had cut it down and returned home with the Delaney's first Christmas tree. The children were fascinated with the concept of a tree inside the house and had set to work making little decorations from things they found around the house, and from treasures they had collected outdoors as they wandered in search of ideas.

Thomas knew which house was Li's—the children had pointed it out to him—and he arrived shortly, rapping on the door. He could hear shuffling inside and was immediately sorry he had knocked as firmly as he had. The poor man had to be living in constant fear. The door opened an inch or two and a face peered through to see who was standing on the other side.

"Good mornin', I'm sorry to be botherin' ya. Are you Li?" Thomas asked.

The door closed and a moment later another man appeared. He opened the door fully and Thomas could see a small scar on his face near his upper lip.

"I am Li," the man said. "My brother does not speak English. I am sorry he did not answer you."

"'Tis fine, and sure enough I didn't mean to frighten him," Thomas responded.

"You are Mr. Delaney?"

"Aye, that's me," Thomas smiled, knowing that nothing went unnoticed in a town as small as theirs. "I'm here to see how you're gettin' along, and if there's anything ya need."

"We are fine, thank you," Li replied.

"I'm also here to thank ya for bein' a good neighbor and a good friend to my wife and children while I've been away. I want to apologize for what happened to ya. Our family has been on the receivin' end of hate and its sorry behavior, and there's nothin' to say except that it's wrong. Your friendship with my family should never be the source of sufferin' or abuse, and I want ya to know that if there's anything I can do to remedy that situation I will."

Li nodded. He appreciated the kindness of Mr. Delaney. He had spent little time with Kathleen or the children since the day of the picnic and had rushed Kathleen from his threshold when she delivered her soup and bread so that no one would see. He had taken to driving his wagon to Carson City for groceries and other supplies rather than enter McGurty's Market and risk ill-treatment and the potential for more physical violence.

"It is kind of you, Mr. Delaney, but to change the world you must first change the hearts of men. There is little I can do but keep to myself and stay away from trouble."

"Have ya been workin' since that day?"

"I have not," Li said.

"Would ya be willin' to take supplies from Carson City up the mountain to Virginia City after Christmas?" Thomas asked.

"I am willing, yes, but do not know if the mining company would hire me. They refused me before."

"I'm goin' to work for a buildin' company, and they will need supplies taken up the mountain regularly. I can inquire about it and let ya know if they would like to hire ya, if that would be all right." Li nodded, taken aback by the man's sincerity. Thomas bid him farewell and walked further into town to McGurty's Market. His anger was surfacing as he reflected on Li's meek and gentle demeanor, and the black hearts of those who would inflict such pain and suffering on him due solely to the color of his skin. When he arrived at the door of the market he was hot under the collar.

"Good morning," McGurty called out in a friendly voice.

"I'm not so sure of it," Thomas shot back at the man.

"Oh, and why is that?" the store owner asked, on edge now.

"Do ya know my name?"

"No, sorry, I'm afraid I don't." McGurty felt a sense of panic rising though he wasn't sure why.

"Thomas Delaney." Thomas watched McGurty's expression change, his color fading. "Aye, Kathleen's husband. Father of her children. Friend to Li. I am *that* Thomas Delaney."

"Listen, Delaney," McGurty started weakly.

"No, you listen. You hear my words, and ya don't forget 'em. I know what your hooligans did to Li. I know what men like you do because ya hate without reason." McGurty tried to explain, to interrupt Thomas's accusations and cast blame on the men he had recruited to carry out his plan. Thomas stopped him with a cold, hard stare and a raised hand, his voice low and threatening. "You leave Li alone. You leave my wife alone. You show them both respect if they walk into your store, do ya understand me? If any harm comes to anyone in my family, or Li and his family, death's dark angel will be at your door. Do ya hear me?"

"I hear you, but I don't appreciate you coming into my store and threatening me with violence. You have no right. You have no proof except the testimony of a Chinaman, and they can't testify in court so your accusations are meaningless." McGurty's argument momentarily empowered him, and he stood a little taller.

Thomas took two more steps toward the counter. He placed his hands down on the smooth wooden surface and leaned in toward McGurty just inches from his face. The storekeeper took half a step back, his resolve crumbling.

"The angel of death, McGurty. Swift justice. It'll come at ya so fast you'll be cold before ya see it. I'll ask ya one more time; do ya understand what I'm sayin'?" McGurty nodded. He didn't like the look on the face of the Irishman, and he swallowed hard.

"Now here's another thing," Thomas continued as he backed away from McGurty's ashen face. "I'll be part of a buildin' project about to begin up the mountain. There will be supplies delivered to Carson City, and wagon trains will be transportin' it all up there. The storekeepers in Carson stand to make a fair amount of money once this project begins. I can encourage, or then again discourage, the company and its drivers to include your market on their run. It would be a word from me and all the shopkeepers in Carson will profit nicely while your days are spent sellin' eggs and butter to the ladies of Chinatown. Does that threat get your attention?"

"Are you trying to blackmail me?"

"Oh, no, McGurty, I'm threatenin' you. And I will surely follow through on both of my threats if I get wind of anything I don't like. Are we clear?"

"You'll hear of no more trouble from me, but I can't control what others do," McGurty argued.

"Sure and I'm thinkin' ya can. And you'd better. One bad report, McGurty, just one and all of this," Thomas waved his arms around him, "is gone."

He turned and left, stomping across the porch and out into the street, the dry dust clouding up around his footsteps. His heart was pounding wildly, his hands shaking. Anger was an ugly beast and one he could not always tame, but McGurty deserved a good dose of it, and Thomas was certain McGurty took his threats seriously. He would be wise to do so.

After Christmas, when the building project began in Virginia City Thomas would talk to Cadwallader Wynne about directing some of the company's business to McGurty's. He would make good on allowing McGurty to profit along with the Carson City vendors as long as McGurty made good on his word to refrain from any more unsavory behavior. Thomas knew that in keeping his word, and the peace, and following through with his inclusion of McGurty's Market on the wagon train run, he would also ensure Kathleen's safety.

Thomas breathed deep as he walked, letting the cold December air clear the negativity and anger. He would not take it back into his home. He stopped in the street in front of his house and looked at the giant cottonwood. The large horizontal branch would be perfect for a swing. He imagined Maeve swinging in the springtime breeze, smiling her radiant smile as the warm sun kissed new freckles onto her cheeks. He leaned his head back and gazed heavenward, repentant once again for the evil things he had done. He stared at the great expanse of sky with a sense of humility before asking God to protect his family. Life was coming into its own. *Beauty from ashes*, he thought to himself. Prosperity from oppression. Darkness into light. Thomas could hear his sweet mother's voice always reminding him to hope for better things, encouraging him to push on.

"*Remember, Tommy,*" she would say, "*'tis a fool who curses the darkness and praises the light, for ya won't see one without the other.*"

"I'll remember, Mam," he whispered now.

***

The week of Christmas arrived and the Delaney house was busy with more of it than ever before. Kathleen baked something nearly every day. She shared with Li and his brother, and with the quiet lady next door who lived alone and rarely ventured out. Kathleen loved that she could share with others. She would always remember Mrs. Callahan's kindness in making sure they had bread when there was no other food to eat. She was also careful to put aside much of her baked treats for their Christmas Eve and Christmas Day celebrations. Anything left would go with Thomas to Virginia City when he went back up the mountain to work.

As talk of their celebration became a daily occurrence, Thomas remembered his wish to return home for Christmas with gifts in hand. He had been planning on making a trip to Carson City to speak with Sheldon Lamberth about his account, and it would give him the perfect opportunity to see what he could find for Kathleen and the children.

Carson City was established and renamed a year before the Delaneys moved to the Utah Territory. Mr. Abraham Curry had purchased the large ranch and trading post at Eagle Station, a well-used stop along the Overland Stagecoach Route. He had the area surveyed and platted and renamed it Carson City after the river that flowed past it, which was so named after Kit Carson by explorer John Fremont. In the year between its founding and the Delaney's arrival, Carson City had grown substantially. With the discovery of Henry Comstock's silver lode, the town became a hub of transportation in the supply chain that ran from San Francisco to Virginia City. In the winter of 1859, it was a proper town with shops and markets, churches and blacksmiths and stables, a bank and a jail, and other services that growth and progress bring along with them.

"Katie, I've arranged to borrow Li's horse and wagon tomorrow mornin' to go to Carson City. I need to speak with Mr. Lamberth about the money he's been depositin' in his bank for me," Thomas said.

"Och, if I weren't so busy I'd love to ride along, though the journey might be fearfully cold. Will ya be warm enough, dear? I'll send a quilt with ya to place over your lap."

Thomas knew better than to brush off Kathleen's doting on him, though he would not drive the wagon to Carson City with a blanket on his lap like a feeble old man. He nodded and thanked her, smiling at her sweet face and the love he always saw dancing in her green eyes. Leaving after Christmas would be even harder now that he had enjoyed some time with all of them, but if his dream of building his own house came to fruition they might be together again by springtime.

Wednesday morning was cold but calm. The sky was a wintery shade of blue, and Thomas's breath made little clouds around him as he hitched up Li's horse to the wagon. It took him longer than it should have, but he hadn't made use of a horse and wagon since he lived in Ireland. He promised to be back before dark and thanked Li again for his generosity. The road was rutted and bumpy from overuse, and Thomas did his best to steer the wagon around the worst of it. Two hours later he arrived in Carson City. He was thankful that their streets, though still hardpan dirt and uneven in places, were much easier to maneuver. He was thankful too that the streets were not filled with garbage, animal carcasses and violence like the ones they had known in New York. He moved the wagon slowly down the main street looking for Lamberth's bank. As he did, he spotted the original trading post, a dry goods store, two markets, and a bakery selling San Francisco's sourdough bread that had gained immense popularity during the California gold rush ten years earlier. Thomas made a mental note to come back to this area of town as soon as his business with Lamberth was finished.

Near the end of the town proper, Thomas saw a small building with a sign hanging above the doorway reading *Sheldon Lamberth, Banker*. He stopped the wagon in front of the bank and tied the horse's reins to the post. Inside, the bank was quiet and appeared empty. Thomas noticed that the place was immaculate, tidy as a spinster's house, and exactly what he would have imagined knowing Sheldon Lamberth's fastidious demeanor. He cleared his throat and waited. Lamberth appeared shortly carrying a cup of hot tea, his round glasses resting down low on the tip of his nose.

"Mr. Delaney! What brings you here?"

"Mornin', Mr. Lamberth. I'm wonderin' how much money I've got here in your bank, if ya don't mind," Thomas said politely.

"Indeed, Mr. Delaney, let me get the ledger."

The banker retrieved a large leather-bound book from a shelf filled with many volumes that looked just like the one in his hand. He laid it on the counter and opened it to the place where a red ribbon extended above the top edge of ledger's many pages. His fingers ran over the familiar rows and columns, each week's transactions entered meticulously. He never tired of seeing the orderly grid on the pale yellow pages, and he took great pride in keeping it just so.

"Here we are. Thomas Delaney. Seems as though your last deposit was a few weeks ago, but until then you were quite diligent about being a good steward of your money. Admirable in these times when men work so hard only to waste their wages on vice and frivolity." There was a hint of disapproval in Lamberth's tone of voice and Thomas understood it. He had often marveled at the brief span of time a miner's wages remained in their pocket as many of them spent their money as quickly as they made it.

"It looks like your current balance is $342.50. Impressive, Mr. Delaney. Are you looking to make a withdrawal today?" Sheldon hoped not for he appreciated men like Delaney who saw value in being frugal.

"Only a small one, Mr. Lamberth. Christmas, ya know," Thomas smiled, evoking one from the banker who seldom did.

"I do know," he replied. "Mrs. Lamberth has her eyes on a rose-patterned teapot over at the trading post. How much will you need today?"

"I'm thinkin' thirty dollars should cover it," Thomas said.

"So much?"

"I've a wife and four children, Mr. Lamberth, and I'm needin' a new coat and a sturdy pair of shoes for my new job."

"No longer in the mines? What will you be doing?"

"Workin' for a buildin' company. They have a grand plan in the works to build a proper town at Virginia City. Homes, saloons, churches, and I'd venture to say even a bank, Mr. Lamberth." Thomas smiled, knowing Lamberth was worried about losing even one customer. He appreciated the reliable care Lamberth had given his earnings and was happy to give him some encouraging news.

"Well then, I look forward to seeing this grand plan unfolding, and I might even think about a second location once this town is born." The banker excused himself and returned to the back room where he had been when Thomas entered the bank. He carefully turned the rotary combination lock on the large safe, stopping precisely at each number, and once the final number was lined up with the red arrow Lamberth opened the heavy door that secured the cash inside. He counted out thirty dollars, closed the door, and brought the money out to Thomas.

"Thank you kindly, Mr. Lamberth," Thomas said.

"It's a pleasure doing business with you, Delaney. Can I look forward to your continued business once your new job commences?"

"Aye, ya can indeed," Thomas assured him. He bid the banker a good day and returned to the wagon. He circled it around and went back to the businesses he had passed on the way in. Shopping was an unfamiliar luxury for Thomas, and he was hesitant to begin. He hitched the horse and watched the folks of Carson City coming and going, purchases being made behind dusty windows, and people enjoying the season. Thomas ventured forth and was soon caught up in the festive mood. He imagined it to be much like a game, a challenge of sorts, with the goal to be laden with parcels wrapped in brightly colored paper and tied with string, perfectly suited to those who would receive them. Time passed more quickly than he had imagined, and as he was finishing up his final purchase at the trading post, he spotted a small brass wind chime. Thomas ran his fingers lightly across the slender brass tubes and was drawn to the sound of it. He imagined it to be a sound Li would appreciate, an item similar to one he might have owned in China before coming to the unforgiving culture of the western United States. He asked the clerk how much it would cost him for the shoes and coat he had already placed on the counter, and the chimes. He checked to see how much money remained in his pocket and was thankful that he could complete his purchase and have a few coins left.

The ride home was much colder. The afternoon wind, like clockwork, stirred and began to blow. Thomas hunched down and, caring not who might see him, wrapped Kathleen's quilt tightly around him. His mind wandered as the wagon bounced over rocks and battled the ruts in the hardened earth. He thought about how difficult their journey had been, how uncertain their basic survival had been, and how the promise of life itself had walked a precarious line for much of their existence in New York. Thomas hoped he had done a good job of persevering. He tried always to be positive and hopeful for Kathleen and the children. Misfortune was a relentless predator and had never seemed far from their threshold, but Thomas had always battled hard to preserve hope. He had tried to encourage and reassure. He tried not to curse the darkness, and he hoped that his mother looked down upon him with favor.

CHAPTER TWENTY-FIVE

Christmas week flew past Thomas like a winged creature sailing by on a brisk wind, pushing him ever closer to the end of his time at home. The days were bittersweet as he looked forward to the end of the week and the first ever Delaney Christmas celebration. In the past, an extra slice of bread or a small dessert might have added something special to their holiday, but an honest Christmas and all its joyous celebration had never visited their flat on Montgomery Street. He was excited about the joy they would share and his newfound ability to give gifts to those he loved so dearly. He couldn't wait to see the children's excitement as they opened the unexpected gifts and took part in the Christmas morning revelry so common to so many, save the poor who needed it worse but rarely saw a gift come their way. For all the festivity and anticipation, Thomas also battled a great sadness as the time neared for him to return to Virginia City. He refused to dwell on the parting and focused instead on every moment they had together.

Kathleen and the children had been gathering sprigs of sage, small pine branches, and pinecones during the week. The Irish tradition of decorating the house with holly would be replaced with what was available nearby. On the morning of Christmas Eve, the entire family worked together to clean and tidy up in preparation for the festivities. By midday the holiday was in full swing, and the Delaneys were creating new traditions. The children gathered around the table to help Kathleen make wreaths from the pine and sage, adding dried fruit and some ribbon. They made one for their own door and one for Li and his brother. The house smelled of good things from the earth—sage and spices, pine, the essence of fruit simmering in a pot on the stove, and a freshness carried in from the outdoors whenever anyone went in or out. It was worlds apart from their previous existence. It smelled like health and home, safety, and life lived the way it should be.

"'Tis time for us to take a wreath to Li and his brother and to wish them a very merry Christmas," Kathleen said. She hoped everyone would want to participate and was overjoyed to see Sean and Thomas both getting ready for the short walk to Li's house. As they were leaving Kathleen saw Thomas tuck a small parcel wrapped in brown paper inside his jacket.

"What have ya there, Tommy?" she asked.

"'Tis for you to find out," he replied with a smile. He herded the family out the front door, noticing the wreath Kathleen and the children had made for their own door hanging on the other side of it. The persistent afternoon wind had not yet begun, and the dry cold air of the high desert was tolerable as they walked. They arrived at Li's house and Maeve knocked on his door. Their friend opened the door with a smile, having seen them through the window as they gathered on his porch.

"Hello, Delaney family!"

"Merry Christmas, Mr. Li," Maeve greeted him. He smiled and placed his hand softly upon her head. "Merry Christmas to you all," he replied.

"The children and I made this wreath for you to hang on your door here," Kathleen pointed to the outside of the door, knowing this was likely an unfamiliar tradition for Li and his brother. He nodded and took the wreath Kathleen held out to him.

"It is very beautiful! Thank you, children, I will hang it there today. Would you all like to come in?" His voice was soft, timid, and still apprehensive about the friendship he cherished.

"Tis a busy day for us, Li, and we have much yet to do, but thank you, dear friend," Kathleen answered. Li nodded and smiled. There was a hint of relief detectable in Li's response, and the Delaneys understood it completely. There would be no ill feelings between them, for they all knew the uncertainties of living in the dark fringes of society, unaccepted and unsafe to move about in the same way that others did.

"Of course, and thank you again!"

"Li, I have somethin' I would like to give ya," Thomas said before Li closed his door. He removed the small parcel from his jacket and handed it to Li. Li set the wreath down on a chair just inside his door and took the parcel slowly from Thomas. The children were immediately interested, for no one had mentioned giving anything but the wreath to Li. Li was noticeably appreciative of Thomas's kindness.

"Mr. Delaney, I should not accept this from you," he politely responded.

"Sure and you should, Li, for you've been a good and generous friend to us. Open it if ya want," Thomas encouraged.

Li stood for a moment looking down at the parcel. Receiving a gift from someone like Thomas Delaney was unprecedented, and it nearly overwhelmed him. He slowly pulled the string to loosen the bow, and as he peeled the paper away from the contents his face was clouded with strong emotions. He was filled with a melancholy for simpler times in the country of his birth, gratitude and disbelief for the fearless friendship given to him by the Delaneys, and a warming of his soul over something so meaningful and familiar to him. His family home in China had similar chimes hanging outside their door, and as he held it up and moved it slowly back and forth the sound of it stirred his emotions. His eyes welled up and his tears spilled over unashamedly.

"How do I thank you for this?"

"Your friendship is enough, Li" Kathleen answered. She was touched by Thomas's kindness in remembering Li with such a thoughtful gift.

Maeve lunged forward and wrapped her arms around Li. Thomas and Kathleen smiled at their daughter's unbridled love for someone that society had labeled unworthy. Kathleen wiped the tears from her own eyes, and everyone exchanged a final Christmas greeting. The walk home was quiet, but their hearts were filled with a sense of celebration.

Preparations began immediately for a light meal and a generous amount of Kathleen's baked goods. There was tea with milk and an extra spoonful of sugar for the children, and a small glass of whiskey for Thomas. He was pleasantly surprised that there was some of the golden *uisce beatha* left on the top shelf in the pantry.

"I'm more than thankful to see a bit of the water of life tucked away and waitin' for my return!" Thomas commented as he lifted the glass to his lips. The sweet strong liquid cast him back to Cork and the days when life was simple and beautiful. He dared to hope that maybe they had found the same kind of life here.

"Aye, and did ya think I'd be swillin' your whiskey while ya were workin' your poor fingers to the bone?"

Thomas couldn't help but laugh aloud at the vision of Kathleen drowning her loneliness in a bottle of Ireland's finest. That day would never come.

Kathleen giggled and shook her head. She busied herself clearing the table and cleaning up while Thomas and Eamon worked together to tell a tale, previously unheard and woven together as they took turns adding to it. It ended with a loud cheer from Sorley and Maeve.

"All right then, there is more to do, and I'll be needin' all your help," Kathleen called out. "If we're to be celebratin' holy Christmas the way our fathers did, we'll need to be settin' three places at this table."

"But we've finished our meal, Mam," Maeve reminded Kathleen. "I can't eat another bite!"

"We'll be settin' a table for the Holy Family in case they come by in the night, Maeve," Thomas said. He recalled the same tradition in his own home and the excitement he had felt as he helped his mother set three places at their table.

Sorley and Maeve helped Kathleen set the table. A fresh-baked loaf of raisin and caraway bread was sliced and arranged on a plate in case Mary, Joseph, or Baby Jesus were hungry, and a candle was lit in the center of the table to light their meal. Thomas advised the family that they must leave the front door unlocked, and that it was time to light the candles.

"Which candles, Da?" asked Sorley.

"'Tis tradition in Ireland, Son, to light a candle in every window so that the Holy Family can find their way. Nearly every family in Ireland has a child named Mary, and she's the one to light the candles or choose someone else to do it for her. For those without a Mary, tis the youngest child who shall have the honors. Maeve," he said as he turned to face her, "you shall be our Mary, yes?"

"Yes!" Maeve responded, excited to be given such an important role in their Christmas tradition.

The boys gathered candles from the pantry and fastened them onto the nail in the center of the tin disks that served as candleholders. Thomas lit one, and the entire family walked through the house placing candles on the windowsills. Thomas handed Maeve his lit candle at each window so that she could light the others, and she did so with a somber and respectful countenance. Kathleen smiled behind her, amused by how seriously she fulfilled her new responsibility. When all the windows were aglow with candlelight, Thomas led the family outside to see how beautiful it looked.

"Oh, Da, the Baby Jesus and his family will surely stop here!" Maeve responded.

"If they do they'll feast on caraway bread and butter, and if they don't stop they'll notice our warm lights and find their way, now won't they?"

"Aye, they will."

The night wore on and the candles burned down halfway. As bedtime approached Kathleen reminded the children that the good Saint Nicholas might also see fit to stop by their house that night but only if children were asleep in their beds. The possibility of a visit from Saint Nicholas was new to the children, and the excitement of that possibility threw them all into a frenzy of bedclothes and evening prayers. Even Sean was caught up in the anticipation, and Thomas's heart soared with gratitude for the grace given to them, and for God seeing fit to save his son from a life that would have destroyed him. He was childlike again, laughing and eager to see how this new tradition would play out.

"Now to sleep with ya and no stirrin' in your beds. I'd be sadly disappointed if Nicholas passed by our home without stoppin' because a misbehavin' Delaney was sleepin' with one eye open!" Thomas gently warned. He blew out the candles in the children's rooms, assuring them that the ones in the front of the house would stay lit long enough for the Holy Family and St. Nicholas to see them. With the children settled and having promised they would stay in bed with eyes closed, Kathleen set about gathering up the gifts she had been working on. She put them under the little tree and smiled. Five gifts under the tree looked like a king's ransom.

There was a vast chasm of difference from last Christmas to this one. Kathleen clearly remembered how Mrs. Zimmer had sent a small parcel of vegetables home with Thomas as he passed by empty-handed on his way home from the docks. Kathleen had cooked them in a pot of water all day until they were soft, and she had borrowed Mrs. Levy's hand mixer to blend it together. Maeve loved turning the crank and was delighted at how the mixer gave the soup a creamy texture. It had seemed like a genuinely lovely dinner at the time, but tomorrow's Christmas dinner would be decadent by comparison. Everything here in their new home felt luxurious. They slept each night in warm soft beds, sheltered and safe, well-fed and sated, and filled with hope. Kathleen turned to face Thomas. He was sitting on the couch watching her, his heart filled to overflowing with peace and gratitude.

"Oh, Tommy, forgive my ever doubtin' ya. Life is rich, and I am filled with a fear that things are better than we deserve, and that the fates will toss us back on our heels before long."

"Katie, come here," he whispered. She walked over and sat beside him. He pulled her into his lap and stroked her soft cheek. "Don't fear the unknown, and don't be believin' that we don't deserve these things in the same way that other folks do. We've been through our darkness and now we're bein' blessed by the light, yes? 'Tis as my mam said, and I always believed her words even when there was no light to be seen."

"I love you, Thomas Michael Delaney." Kathleen kissed his lips and placed her hands on his cheeks. "I am blessed beyond measure, darkness or light, just to be with ya and called your own."

"And I, you, Kathleen Mary Delaney." He held her close, unable to fend off the sadness of knowing he would have to leave in a couple of days, and knowing his heart would break every time he thought of her. They sat together holding close the half of their heart that would soon be absent. When the candle in the front window flickered, low and nearly out, Kathleen got up and went about the house putting out the candles for safety's sake. She placed a damp towel over the bread on the table to keep it moist so that they could have some in the morning.

"It's time for bed, Tommy. Are ya comin'?"

"Aye, I'll be there shortly," he said with a smile. She watched him for a moment, wondering at his mischievous grin, but surrendering to her body's desire for the soft warm bed and the sleep she badly needed.

When Kathleen was nestled beneath the covers of their bed, Thomas retrieved his parcels from the storage bench in the back room and placed them under the tree. He found incredible joy in seeing the gifts there, waiting for morning and for the joy they would give his beautiful children. He marveled at the way life moves a person from valleys to mountaintops, and yes, from darkness to light.

Thomas wandered to their bedroom and nestled in close to Kathleen, falling asleep with his arm around her.

Morning intruded into the quiet of night with an excited squeal. Maeve had wandered downstairs first and was overjoyed to see that Saint Nicholas had indeed stopped by their house in the night. Kathleen giggled, sat up, and grabbed her shawl from the chair in the corner. She hurried out to the tree and put her hand to her mouth in feigned disbelief, though the presence of unknown packages gave rise to her own excitement.

"My heavens! What are all those packages under our tree?"

"Mam, the saint came by in the night," Sorley called out excitedly. Thomas wandered out from the bedroom, yawning and pretending not to notice the packages. He scratched his belly, faked another yawn, and rubbed his eyes as he made his way to the table.

"Och, I'm hungry for some of your caraway bread, Katie! I'll get us a good fire goin' and we can gather round the table for a bite," he said as he bent down to stir up the ashes and get a new fire started.

"Da, look!" Maeve shouted, pointing at the tree.

"Aye, hold on there a minute, wee lass," he said in the most uninterested voice he could muster.

Maeve started jumping up and down, and Thomas could hear her behind him. He fought hard to keep from laughing as he put more wood into the stove and watched the coals ignite the fire. He closed the stove door and headed to the table to remove the towel from the uneaten bread.

"Oh, dear, now wouldn't ya know it? No one saw our candles, and no one at all bothered to stop by the Delaney house last night! What a poor misfortunate family we are!"

"Da, look *here!*" Maeve shouted again. He could hold out no longer, and he turned and gave a performance that had Kathleen in stitches, hands slapped against his cheeks, running in circles and squealing like a child.

"He came, he came! The saint came by and brought me some gifts!" The children were all laughing at his ridiculous behavior. Thomas could even hear Sean laughing aloud, and he ramped up his antics. He waved his hands in the air and ran to the tree, bending down to peer beneath it. "Aye, I'm sure these are all for me, for I've worked my poor weary fingers bare to the bone these past months. Greatly have I suffered, sleepin' in a cold tent with nothin' but John O'Riley's nasty snorin' to soothe me to sleep, and besides that I am, as you know, the prettiest of all the Delaneys." He paraded around the living room in such a manner that Kathleen laughed until her stomach hurt.

"Da, stop, and let's see what all of this is!" Eamon's serious nature was growing impatient as the excitement grew too much for him. He was smiling, but the anticipation was getting the best of him. He gave Thomas a wide-eyed pleading look. "Please?"

"Aye," Thomas agreed, falling down onto the couch, breathless and laughing at himself. "I'm sorry to say they're probably not all for me."

Kathleen was determined to make each moment of their first Christmas morning celebration as special and memorable as it could be. She cautioned the children about the rudeness of not giving each person their own time, and that an orderly unwrapping, one person at a time, would be the way they would handle this exciting event. Kathleen's contributions were new shirts for the boys, including Thomas, and a pretty blue dress for Maeve to replace the one left behind on the day of her birthday picnic. The gifts that Thomas had purchased were marked only with the names of the recipients, leaving the identity of the giver a mystery. The addition of those packages beneath the tree gave credence to the story of Saint Nicholas visiting in the night. Thomas had selected the gifts carefully with each person in mind. For Maeve there was a proper doll with a cloth dress, shoes, and a hat, and for Sorley, a brightly painted wooden train with a steam engine, three cars and a caboose with wheels that turned. Eamon received three new books and a blank journal with five pencils for writing his own stories, and for Sean, a new sketch pad with pencils, a blank book to record his stories, hopes, dreams and observations, and a copy of *The Pirate* by Sir Walter Scott. Kathleen's gift was a new sewing box with dried lavender sewn into the cloth lining. It was filled with thread and needles, pins and scissors, ribbon and buttons. It was delightfully fragrant, and she was overjoyed with the thoughtful present from Thomas.

"Nicholas is as generous a saint as ever walked the earth, don't ya think?" Thomas asked. Everyone agreed.

"Here now, I'm wonderin' if he didn't drop a small parcel in our tree as he put the gifts below it. I see somethin' there, right in the middle by the wee seed-and-pebble house Eamon made. See it there, Sean?" Sean got up and peered into the tree, not seeing what his father was talking about. He looked again and saw a small package wrapped in pink paper, tied with white string, with the name Katie written upon it.

"'Tis a gift for Mam," Sean said, smiling at his father's ploy. He walked over and handed it to his mother, encouraging her to open it.

"I've gotten my gift and surely don't need two!"

"Open it, Grá Mo Chroí," Thomas said, his voice tender.

Kathleen opened the gift. As she folded back the paper, she found a beautiful tortoiseshell comb adorned with mother-of-pearl and silver filigree. She put her hand over her mouth, taken aback by the lovely adornment. Never had she owned anything so exquisite. She pulled her auburn hair up on one side and placed the comb into her wavy locks. Thomas noticed how the shimmery surface of the mother-of-pearl seemed to glow against the burnished color of her long wavy hair.

"'Tis beautiful, Mam!" Maeve exclaimed. The boys all agreed, and Kathleen put her hand up to it.

"Tommy, you shouldn't have," she started.

"Sure and I did not! The good Nicholas saw fit to leave a little somethin' extra for the most beautiful woman he'd ever laid eyes upon. I can't say as I blame him!"

Kathleen gave Thomas a long and lingering kiss that sent the children into fits of disgust. She laughed and told them all to be quiet. The morning was peaceful, relaxing, warm, and perfect. They enjoyed the caraway bread and butter, tea with milk and sugar, followed later in the day with a fine meal of spiced beef cooked in a large pot with potatoes, carrots and onion, and a healthy serving of creamy mashed potatoes. Everyone ate until they were ready to burst and waited hours before enjoying a slice of Kathleen's delectable apple pie. The day wore on and the Delaney home was filled with the goodness that had long escaped them. It felt right as Thomas watched his children. Eamon and Sean were both reading, Sorley was rolling his train through the house, and Maeve was engaged in a fanciful adventure with her new doll, now named Mary and destined to be next year's candle lighter.

Kathleen's voice, sweet and soft, was humming as she tidied up. How favored their lives had been, Thomas thought, to have ended up here, so far removed from the demeaning life they had lived in the stench and filth of New York. Why had Providence intervened, allowing them to escape starvation, abject poverty, and criminal vengeance to find this life, this fulfillment of a dream that seemed unobtainable? It wasn't that they deserved it more than any of the poor souls still left there, trapped in a life of hopelessness and despair. *'Tis just our time*, Thomas thought to himself. Their darkness had lifted, and the light had replaced it just as it does each morning. Each new day. They had not garnered all the treasures of the earth, but it felt very near to that. Maeve put down her doll and wandered to the couch where her father was sitting, quietly securing the memory of this moment safe inside, safe to recall when he was away and missing them. She sat down next to her father, and he pulled her close to him.

"Da," she whispered.

"Aye, Maeve?"

"Will this last forever?"

"Will what last forever, Stóirín?"

"This goodness," she replied.

"Goodness will last as long as our love does, yes?"

"Aye, Da. Forever."

Epilogue

Hannibal, Missouri

June 1861

Samuel Clemens paced the porch from one end to the other. It was a bitter pill to swallow having lost his job after all of his hard work and experience, but river traffic had come to a halt when the war between the states broke out. He had enjoyed his time on the Mississippi, the lazy meandering of the river passing by the lush greenery on either side, and the interactions with interesting folks who boarded his steamboat for new places. He would sorely miss it and was skeptical about the adventure ahead of him.

Clemens' brother Orion had suggested Samuel accompany him to the new Nevada Territory. Orion was headed there on an appointment by President Lincoln to serve as the Secretary of the Territory under Territorial Governor James Nye. Orion spoke of gold and silver, of men getting rich, and of the west being the land of unlimited opportunity for those who had an eye for it. Samuel had agreed to give it a try. He thought about getting himself some basic equipment and panning for gold, though he was not partial to getting his hands dirty.

He paced some more as the morning sun rose higher in the Missouri sky. Samuel had arranged for a local coach driver to pick him up at precisely eight o'clock so he could catch the nine o'clock running of the Hannibal and Saint Joseph Railroad. Once in Saint Joseph, he would meet up with Orion and they would board a stagecoach bound for Nevada by way of the Overland Stage Route. It was said to be a rough ride and he supposed it would be. It might be worth writing about one day.

Samuel picked up his satchel and descended the two steps to the yard. A glance in both directions showed no sign of the coach driver. He set his satchel down and placed his hand on the watch pocket of his vest as years of habit would dictate. He cursed under his breath as he realized he was instinctively reaching for the gold pocket watch pilfered from his hotel room several years ago. He was certain he would never get used to the empty space where his grandfather's watch belonged. He had, of course, replaced it with a meaningless timekeeping trinket from the local mercantile, but he kept that one in his pants pocket. His vest pocket was reserved for his grandfather's watch, irreplaceable and painfully missed.

A cloud of dust approaching told Samuel the coach was moving quickly and that it would arrive in time to get him to the train station. His westward adventure was about to begin. Perhaps Orion's accounting of the bounteous supplies of gold and silver was correct. Once he arrived and garnered some of that bounty, perhaps Samuel would have a shiny gold replica made of his grandfather's watch, for he could recall every etch and line from memory. Perhaps the Nevada Territory would be a place of new beginnings. He gave a slight nod of his head as he boarded the coach. It was time.

Sandra Frost grew up in Western Washington but migrated to Nevada in 1997. She has traveled the western United States extensively with her husband and has also visited Ireland and Scotland. She hopes to continue her exploration of the beautiful Southwest with her daughter and granddaughter.

When she's not writing, Sandra is a case manager for a local nonprofit. Her passions include photography, travel, reading, and being Nana to the best granddaughter in the entire universe.

Made in United States
Troutdale, OR
11/10/2023

14455682R00257